RANDOM WALK

A NOVEL FOR A NEW AGE

Lawrence Block

TOR

A TOM DOHERTY ASSOCIATES BOOK
NEW YORK

RANDOM WALK

Copyright © 1988 by Lawrence Block

Cover painting © M. Morales 1988

A TOR BOOK

Published by Tom Doherty Associates, Inc.
49 West 24 Street
New York, NY 10010

Library of Congress Cataloging-in-Publication Data

Block, Lawrence.
    Random walk / Lawrence Block.
        p.   cm.
    "A Tom Doherty Associates book."
    ISBN 0-312-93092-5 : $18.95
    I. Title
PS3552.L63R36 1988
813'.54—dc19   88-19716
                                                        CIP

First edition: October 1988
    0   9   8   7   6   5   4   3   2   1

_F_

Author's Note

This book is about a walk, and it seems appropriate to acknowledge a debt of gratitude to some of the people who have provided valuable assistance along the way. I owe much to Thomas Mullane, Marilyn White, and Martin O'Farrell, three among many who taught me to follow the path a step at a time; to Sondra Ray, Fredric Lehrman, Leonard Orr, and Bob and Mallie Mandel, indispensable teachers; to Peter Russell, for *The Global Brain,* and Raphael, for *The Starseed Transmissions;* to Durchback Akuete, for his gift of spiritual empowerment; to Lloyd Youngblood and Danny Slomoff, for their example as powerful healers; to Mary Elizabeth Weber and Joan Pancoe, for timely guidance and channeled wisdom; and to Babaji.

I am grateful, too, to William Smart and everyone at the Virginia Center for the Creative Arts, where the actual writing of this book took place.

Finally, I owe more than I can ever say to my most wonderful wife Lynne, to whom *Random Walk* is dedicated. It could never have come into being but for her incomparable generosity of spirit and her selfless unconditional love.

ONE

He was heating water for a second cup of coffee when the phone rang. He crossed the room, answered it.

"Guthrie, it's Kit. I didn't wake you?"

"No, the sun beat you to it."

"Are you sure? Your voice—"

"You're my first caller. It hasn't been used." He coughed, cleared his throat. "There," he said. "That better?"

"I wasn't criticizing, I just . . ." Her voice trailed off. He waited. "Guthrie? I'm not interrupting anything?"

"No," he said. "You didn't wake me and you're not interrupting anything. Hold on, will you?" The kettle was whistling. He measured coffee into the filter, poured water through the grounds, carried the cup back with him and lit a cigarette. Through smoke he said, "Making coffee. *Now* you're not interrupting anything. What's up?"

"You got anything on this afternoon?"

"Not really."

"Because I was thinking maybe you'd drive me up to Eugene."

1

"Sure, I could do that. I guess the car'll make it."

"What's the matter with your car?"

"Nothing in particular. I just—"

"Because we can take my car."

"We can?"

"Jesus," she said, "I don't care whose car we take, we can fucking *rent* a car if you want."

"Kit? What's the matter?"

"Oh, shit," she said. He waited, drew on his cigarette, took a tentative sip of his coffee. Brilliant invention, the coffee filter. You could make one cup of coffee at a time, and it was as easy as instant and better than what came out of a drip pot or a percolator. And, when you weren't making coffee, a very tiny person could use the filter to catch very tiny butterflies.

She said, "I don't need a ride, I need company. I've got an appointment at two o'clock."

"What for?"

"An abortion."

"Oh."

"So I sort of thought—"

"You want to figure an hour and a half to drive there," he said, "plus traffic and time to park."

"It's a clinic," she said. "They have parking."

"So let's say I'll pick you up about noon. It's ten-thirty now. That give you enough time?"

"Or I'll pick you up," she said.

"No, I'll drive," he said. "Twelve o'clock, okay?"

She was waiting in front of her apartment building. He watched as she strode to the car, a slender darkhaired woman in Frye boots and straight-leg jeans and an Oregon State sweatshirt. "It doesn't show yet," she said. "It's only nine or ten weeks, for Christ's sake."

"Huh?"

"You were staring."

"Not at your stomach. At your tits."

"Hah."

"At your sweatshirt, actually. You didn't go to State."

"No, of course not. But I figured since I'm getting the abortion in Eugene, let the people there feel morally superior to a Statie. If I was getting the abortion in Corvallis I'd wear a U of O shirt."

"I see."

"If I had a Reed shirt I'd wear that. *Everybody* likes to feel morally superior to the Greedy Reedies."

He lit a cigarette. She rolled down her window and said, "Actually, it's Marvin's shirt."

"That asshole."

"Funny, he always speaks well of you."

"I'll bet he does. Is it—"

"His kid? Jesus, no. I haven't even seen him in six months. Is he even in town? I think I heard he went back to Berkeley."

"I'm not the person to ask."

"Well, neither am I." She fell silent. They were on the Interstate, heading north toward Eugene, when she said, "The thing is, I don't know whose it is."

"You're not talking about the sweatshirt."

"The kid. There's three people who might be up for Father of the Year honors. The funny thing is I've been a very proper lady lately."

"I can't remember the last time you came by Paddy Mac's."

"No, I've been staying out of the bars. And I'm all alone when I lower my lamp. I haven't been seeing anybody since Marvin the Asshole, and we broke up in the fall, and it's June already. Today's what, the second?"

3

"I guess."

"I don't know how you thought he could have been the father."

"Well, people have been known to get back together for a quickie even after they've broken up."

"Yeah," she said, and her face softened into a smile. "Yeah, we did that, didn't we?"

"Once or twice."

"Want to pull over at the next rest area? Nothing safer than a pregnant lady. That's a joke, incidentally."

"I sort of thought it might be."

"Because I feel about as sexy as a burn victim."

"That's a pretty image."

"Yeah, I thought you'd like it."

They fell silent. Traffic was light and he kept the speed just over sixty miles an hour. The car, a Buick Century, had been originally equipped with a cruise-control device, but it had been broken when he bought it and he had never bothered to get it fixed. The car had been four years old when he got it and that had been four years ago; when the new models came out in the fall, the Buick would be nine years old. It looked its age, too. Cars rusted quickly in western Oregon, and the Buick, never garaged and rarely washed, was going fast. It ran reasonably well, always started and never stalled out, but there were noises under the hood that might well be cause for anxiety if you knew what you were listening to.

Around Exit 154 she said, "I have to tell you, Guthrie. I hate this."

"You want me to turn the car around?"

"No, of course not."

"Because you don't have to go through with it."

"Yes I do. If I broke the appointment today I'd make another one tomorrow. I'm not gonna have the kid."

"Well, that's up to you."

She nodded. "It's not as though I've never done this before."

"Oh?"

"Once at college. Once about—what, five years ago? Something like that."

"Not when you and I—"

"No, earlier. Months earlier, maybe a year earlier. I wouldn't have aborted a child of yours without telling you."

"Jesus."

"What?"

"I wonder if anybody ever did."

"Did what? Abort a kid of yours? Didn't it ever happen that you know of?"

He shook his head.

"You mean this is your first time?" She laid a hand on his. "Don't worry," she said. "I'll be gentle."

"Funny."

"The irrepressible Kit Winston, cracking jokes even as she goes under the knife. Or under the vacuum cleaner, as the case may be. You could have fathered a child that somebody aborted. I mean, sleeping around, one-nighters. Look at me, there were three guys I slept with during the period of a couple weeks when it must have happened. And they'll never know. What could I tell them? 'I just had an abortion and you've got one shot in three of being the father'? So if you slept with somebody who slept with other people too—"

"I get the picture."

"Or if she had the baby, as far as that goes. There could be all these little Guthrie Wagners scattered around, and they wouldn't know it and neither would you."

"Hey, cut it out, huh?"

"I'm sorry. Did I touch a nerve?"

" 'I'll be gentle,' " he said. "Some gentle."

Halfway between Cottage Grove and Eugene she said, "You figure it's a sin?"

"Abortion?"

"No, jaywalking. You weren't brought up Catholic, were you?"

"Baptist, but then my mother had an argument with somebody and we started going to the Methodist church."

"I suppose there's a difference."

"No end of differences."

"I always figured goyim was goyim. How are the Baptists and Methodists on abortion?"

"I suppose they're against it, but it was inconceivable that the question would arise, because screwing was sinful enough in the first place. What are you smiling at?"

" 'Inconceivable.' "

"Oh."

"I don't think Jews believe it's a sin. Oh, the orthodox ones do, but not Jews like my parents."

"What kind of Jews are your parents?"

"Practical Jews."

He frowned. "Is Winston a Jewish name? I thought it was English. Winston-Salem, Winston cigarettes."

"Weinstein, darling."

"Oh."

"You didn't know that? My grandfather changed it. His brother stayed Weinstein, but his brother's sons changed to Winston, too. And for my sixteenth birthday I got this cute little shiksa nose to match my name."

"That's not your nose?"

"It is *now*. Dr. Perlmutter's finest work, and I should have asked him to sign it, don't you think?"

"What was your old nose like?"

"You know, there really wasn't anything wrong with it. It had character, that's all. Not quite as much character as Streisand's, but character all the same."

"Why did you have it—"

"Done," she supplied. "Why did I have it done? Beverly fucking Hills, man. And sixteen years old, and my nose was one more thing about myself not to like. Maybe it was a rite of passage, you know, circumcision for girls. How do I know why I did it? It seemed like a good idea at the time."

"Jesus, the things I've said that about."

"How about you? That your original nose, kid?"

"My original shiksa nose."

"Your original sheggitz nose, you mean. Speaking of names, how'd you get named Guthrie? They name you after Woody?"

"You asked me this before."

"I did?"

"Years ago."

"Ms. Memory. So tell me again. They named you after Woody?"

He shook his head. "Arlo."

"Come *on.*"

"What's the matter?"

"How old are you? Thirty-six?"

"Thirty-seven."

"And when did *Alice's Restaurant* come out? Twenty years ago?"

"My parents were always on the cutting edge."

"Anyway, imagine naming a kid after Arlo Guthrie."

"What's wrong with Arlo Guthrie?"

"Nothing, you lunatic. Did they name you after Woody or didn't they?"

"I don't think they ever heard of Woody Guthrie, and if they had they wouldn't have named a dog after him.

7

Guthrie was a family name, my mother's mother's maiden name. I told you all this."

"You told some other girl."

"I told several other girls, but I definitely told you."

"It does have a faintly familiar ring," she admitted. "If it's a family name, maybe you're *related* to Woody."

"Maybe."

"That'd make you related to Arlo, too."

"I guess it would, wouldn't it."

"I think take the next exit. Not this one but the next one."

"All right."

"Guthrie? Honey?" Her hand again, cool on his. "Thanks for doing this. Really."

The clinic was a compact white clapboard building with parking space in front for a dozen cars. The waiting room was done in Grand Rapids Early American—maple furniture, an oval braided rug. He sat with Kit for twenty minutes. Then her name was called and she followed a nurse through a door.

Another woman, much younger than Kit, sat across from him turning the pages of *Runner's World.* The magazines all seemed to be either running magazines or business publications like *Forbes* and *Business Week.* They probably indicated the interests of the doctor or doctors who ran the place, he decided, rather than that of the clientele. No *Parents' Magazine,* no *Modern Bride,* no *Jack and Jill*—

I'm not the father, he wanted to tell the woman across from him. *I'm just a friend, just a shoulder to lean on.*

Jesus.

You couldn't smoke in there. One sign told him so, while another thanked him for not smoking. The carrot and the stick, he thought. The good cop and the bad cop.

Outside, he lit a cigarette. There were seven cars in the parking area, he noted, and all of the others looked better than his. Maybe it was time to start feeding the savings account so he'd be able to trade before the end of the year. Of course he could trade now, as far as that went; he had a few dollars in the bank, and the Buick would serve as the down payment if he didn't go after something fancy. He made good steady money behind the bar at Paddy McGuire's. His rent was cheap, he owned the Buick free and clear.

No alimony to pay. Thirteen years since he married Aileen, almost eleven since the divorce, and she hadn't sought alimony. He hadn't the slightest idea if she'd remarried, or where she was living.

No child support. No children—unless Kit's fantasy was true and one of his one-nighters had borne fruit.

Not that there had been so many one-nighters. But every once in a while some lady thought it was a good idea to go home with the bartender, and over the years all those ladies added up.

But at least the kids you didn't know about didn't cost you anything. Well, check that—there might be a karmic debt, that was always a possibility, but even if there was it didn't amount to much in dollars and cents. Bastards or no bastards, he could certainly handle a car payment.

Except that he didn't want to buy a new car. Or another used one.

Nor did he much want to hang onto this one, with its fenders rusting out and its springs starting to sag and its paint checking and God knew what going on under the hood.

He leaned against the car now, a tall lean man with a thick growth of shaggy nut-brown hair. He wore a red plaid flannel shirt and a pair of Lee jeans with the cuffs folded up. His belt had a large brass buckle with *Coors* in flowing script, a promotional gift from the salesman. He had a pair of waffle-soled Nikes on his feet, good running shoes, but he'd never run in them. He'd gone through a couple pairs of shoes since the last time he did any running.

A year and a half, maybe two years of running in his late twenties. Then almost a year when he went to the Y religiously three times a week and worked out with free weights. Flirtations, brief ones, with Tai Chi and aikido. Yoga. Transcendental Meditation. Silva Mind Control and est.

A life drawing class. A Berlitz home study course in French. Subliminal tapes—*Improved Self-Image, Stop Smoking, Stop Procrastination.*

The year with the weights had left him broader in the shoulders and stronger in the chest, and he suspected the other disciplines had had a few good lasting effects of their own, although it was hard to see what he'd gained from the *Stop Smoking* tape, or how his performance in that area might have improved his self-image.

And an uncertain self-image it seemed these days. He had worn a beard until recently, its color a little ruddier than the hair on his head, but it had started to show a little gray, and he supposed that had probably had something to do with the decision to shave it off. He still wasn't used to his face without the beard; he would catch sight of himself in the back bar mirror at work and be surprised by the face that looked back at him. It seemed to him that he looked younger without the beard, that was what everyone told him, and yet his face now showed signs of age that the beard had concealed.

Lincolnesque was how a girl had described him, years ago. He supposed by that she had meant interestingly ugly, but he didn't know that it really suited him; his face seemed to him neither that interesting nor that ugly, and certainly not that presidential. Still, he wasn't sure but that her comment might not have prompted him to grow his first beard, back in college.

He could always grow it back now. And shave it off again if he didn't like it. And then regrow it and buy a new car, and sell the car if he didn't like *that*, and—

You could take a walk, a voice in his head said.

Clear as a bell, clear as a fucking bell, as if some little man crawled up inside his head and spoke to him. Great, he thought. Just like all those people who get messages from the CIA beamed in through the fillings in their teeth. Voices. Just what he needed.

He finished his cigarette and went back into the waiting room.

Twenty minutes later the need for a cigarette drove him outside again. By now it was raining, a light drizzle that was just enough to make him get in the car. He lit the cigarette, and, as he breathed out smoke, fatigue washed over him in a wave. He put the cigarette in the ashtray and closed his eyes for a moment.

He woke abruptly with the sensation of having dreamed vividly but no recollection of the dream, no sense at all of what it might have been. His cigarette was gone, burned to ash in the dashboard ashtray. He looked at his watch. It was a few minutes past four, but he didn't know how long he'd been out because he had no idea when he'd gotten into the car.

He went back to the clinic to wait for Kit.

"Piece of cake," she said.

"Rough, huh?"

"No," she said. "No irony intended. It was really nothing. I've had worse times in the dentist's chair."

"I've had the worst times of my life in the dentist's chair."

"Well, this was nothing. Really."

11

"Great."

"I guess."

"What's the matter?"

"Well, this doesn't make any sense, but I sort of feel it ought to be more unpleasant."

"They ought to hurt you."

"And lecture you and tell you you're bad. Yeah. I don't really mean that, but yeah, sort of. I figure I killed something today. I committed a sin."

"Cut it out."

"I'm not beating myself up, I'm stating an opinion. I think it's a sin. I don't think it's a crime, I don't think it shouldn't be legal, I'm not sorry I did it, but I think it's a sin, I think it's fucking *wrong.*"

"So you're a bad girl."

"I'm not a bad girl. But that doesn't mean I'm gonna sit around and feel terrific about this."

"Okay."

It was raining again. It had stopped, and now it had started again. She said, "It was a girl."

"The uh—"

"The growth I had removed. I wish they didn't tell you. It makes the whole thing a lot more personal."

"That's terrible. They just tell you?"

"No, you have to ask."

"Oh."

"Even then he didn't want to tell me. I insisted."

"Oh."

"I always have to know. The first one was a girl, the second was a boy, and now this one. Girl boy girl."

"Keep it up, Kit."

"This is called cauterizing the wound, man. Otherwise it'll fester later on."

"It doesn't sound like such a piece of cake to me."

She sighed. "Physically it was nothing. Emotionally it

was nothing at the time, but I seem to be having trouble passing the afterbirth. I'll be okay."

"I know."

"Fucking diaphragms," she said savagely. "You feel about as spontaneous as a commencement address, and you're all gummed up with glop so that a person would have to be crazy to go down on you, and then the fucking thing doesn't even do what it's supposed to. Some women wear diaphragms for years and never have a problem. Maybe they don't fuck. Maybe that's their secret."

"Didn't you have an IUD?"

"You bet I did. I got it after the second abortion because I didn't want to go through all that again. I had it for five or six years, however long it was."

"Did you have problems with it?"

"Never."

"Then—"

"Then I started hearing all this crap on the news about women dying because of IUDs, or giving birth to otters, or whatever was happening to them, and I went to my doctor and had him remove it and got fitted for a diaphragm, and the rest is fucking history." She closed her eyes. "Besides," she said quietly, "I was thinking about getting pregnant."

"You were what?"

"I wasn't going to mention this," she said. "I'm thirty-two, I'll be thirty-three in September."

"Ah, the old biological clock."

"Tick fucking tock. And I got to thinking. I'm nowhere near getting married. There wasn't even anybody I wanted to have an affair with. I was with Marvin, and I didn't even like him enough to have an affair with him, but I did because there was nobody else around I liked better. And when we broke up I knew I didn't want to get married, and you don't really have to get married to have a kid. So I had the IUD removed."

"And got pregnant on purpose?"

"No! Of course not."

"Well—"

"I had the IUD removed partly because I was scared, I already explained that, and also so that if I did decide to get pregnant, I could just do it, I wouldn't have to make a doctor's appointment first. 'Hi, you're neat, let's have a baby together, excuse me, I gotta call my gynecologist.' So this way I had the option of leaving the diaphragm out, but I never made that decision and I never did leave the diaphragm out, and I got pregnant anyway without intending to. Unless you're gonna get into unconscious motivations, in which case please stop the car and let me out now, because I don't want to have to listen to that."

"Jesus, Kit."

"Well, you know what I mean. 'You must have wanted to be pregnant or you wouldn't *be* pregnant. You must have wanted to get a splinter under your thumbnail or you wouldn't *have* a splinter under your thumbnail.' "

"You must have wanted a hair up your ass," he said, "or you wouldn't have—"

"A hair up my ass," she finished. "Well, who in her right mind wouldn't want one? Anyway, before I could explore the possibility of getting intentionally pregnant, I got unintentionally pregnant."

"Got it."

She sighed. "And of course I thought about keeping the kid." She looked at him. "But that seemed like such an ass-backwards way of doing it, you know? I mean it's not fucking parthenogenesis, who the father is is important, you know? Even if you raise him yourself half his cells come from somebody else, and that makes a difference, doesn't it?"

"I suppose so."

"One of the guys I slept with was an Indian. American

14

Indian. Now I don't think I'm a racist, or at least not that much of one, and I don't think I'd object to having a child whose father was an Indian, but the idea of not knowing. What do you do, wait and see if the kid can track game in order to figure out who his father was?"

A little later she said, "This is crazy."

"Let's hear it."

"You'll think it's crazy."

"Okay."

"I'll tell you anyway. What would you think about the idea of having a child?"

"You and me?"

"Ain't nobody else here, boss."

"Jesus, Kit."

"I'd take care of it. The financial part and all that, and you could be as much or as little of a father as you wanted. I know it's crazy. Please remember that I said in front it was crazy."

"Just this afternoon—"

"I got rid of a kid, I know, and now I'm talking about getting pregnant again. I don't mean tonight, all right? I don't mean right away. I just mean it's something to think about, okay? Because you're healthy and decent-looking and smart and you've got good genes. There isn't any insanity in your family, is there?"

"I'm the only one."

"And you've got a sense of humor, and that's important, because who would want to have a humorless kid? And you're, fuck, you're *nice,* Guthrie. And I think if you're gonna have a kid, the father ought to be *nice.* You know?"

His shift at Paddy Mac's was supposed to start at six, but he'd called and told Harry he might be late. It was close to eight by the time he got there. He took over behind the stick, and after a few minutes he had his rhythm and he was into it.

He'd stopped at Kit's for a cup of coffee and between that and the day's events he was pretty wired, so he had himself a couple ounces of scotch to take the edge off, then nursed two bottles of St. Pauli Girl all the way to closing time. The crowd was enough to keep you busy but not enough to drive you crazy, the drunks didn't cause any trouble, and all in all it was the right kind of night to come down from the day's craziness with.

After he closed up he poured himself an Irish Mist and sipped at it while he swept up and cleared the register for Harry's shift the next day. He drove home, took a hot shower, and went to bed.

He slept late the next morning, made himself a cup of coffee, then went out for a big breakfast at the Greek place on the next block. When he got home the phone was ringing, but it quit before he could answer it. A little later it rang again and it was Kit—she felt fine, he'd been wonderful, and she was sorry she'd been so crazy.

"You'd think you would want a woman friend along for something like that," she said, "but I couldn't think of a woman in this town I wanted for company yesterday. You know, there are certain occasions when only an ex-lover will do."

"I know."

"Assuming it's an ex-lover you're on good terms with. As opposed to, say, Marvin the Asshole."

"Funny, he always speaks well of you."

"He never even spoke well of me when we were an item. Anyway, thanks, huh?"

"Forget it."

"And what I was babbling about toward the end there, that proposal I made for our biochemical collaboration, just forget I said anything, okay?"

"It's forgotten, Kit."

"Good," she said. "But, uh, give it some thought, Guthrie."

"Forget about it but give it some thought."

"Oh, *you* know what I mean."

He spent the afternoon at home watching a baseball game. NBC had the Mariners playing the Yankees, and he watched it without paying too much attention. He got to the bar in time to start his shift at six. The crowd was typical for a Saturday night, a little too raucous and a little too loud, but that was part of the deal, it came with the territory. In the quiet bars with light crowds you couldn't make any money.

You could take a walk.

He didn't hear that voice again, he'd only heard it the once, but he remembered it and he found himself thinking about it. At first it seemed to be saying that he could step out of his life, that he could walk away from it and everything and everybody in it. But he'd done that, for God's sake, walked out of one job and into another, out of one apartment and into another, out of one town and into another. Paddy McGuire's was as good as any place he was likely to work, and tending bar was as good an occupation as he was likely to find for himself. It wasn't what he'd had in mind when he went to college, but it was hard to remember what he might have had in mind, and he suspected none of them had been things he'd wanted, just things he'd thought he was supposed to want.

Roseburg wasn't heaven, but neither was it hell. He had lived in Eugene and he could move back there. He'd never lived in Portland but he liked Portland and he could go there. But he couldn't think of any reason to do that. He had lived, years ago, in California, and he had been born and raised in Ohio, but there was no reason to believe that his life would improve if he returned to either of those places.

There was no real reason even to believe it would be different. It was like the car. He could get a new car, or a newer old car, but he wouldn't garage it or run it through a car wash regularly, and he'd forget to get the oil changed, and before too long he'd re-create the car he already had.

Around eleven-thirty a girl at the end of the bar started finding excuses to chat with him, and an hour before closing she yawned theatrically and said she guessed she'd better be heading on home. She was looking for him to suggest she hang around until he closed the place, but he decided not to get the hint. "Well, I guess I'd better go," she said finally, annoyed. Her hips rolled as she walked, perhaps to show him what he was missing.

He went home alone and went to bed sober. Lying there, waiting for sleep to come, he felt on the verge of something.

If there were dreams, he didn't remember them. But when he woke the idea was simply there. He knew what he was going to do.

He gave it a day. He did a load of wash at the laundromat, found an old backpack on a high shelf in the closet. There was a state map in the Buick's glove compartment. It had been there when he bought the car. He spread it out on his kitchen table and sat staring at it, then folded it and tucked it into the zippered compartment on the front of the backpack.

Not a very large backpack. He'd originally picked it up to use as a book bag at college, and he'd hardly used it since. Surprising he still owned it.

Sunday was his night off. He stayed home and watched *Sixty Minutes* and *Murder, She Wrote* and an early Woody Allen movie on cable. He felt keyed up and thought he wouldn't be able to get to sleep, but he fell asleep early and woke up early, and awoke knowing that he hadn't changed his mind, that he was really going to do it.

He went to his bank, drew all but ten dollars from his savings account, left enough in the checking account to cover the checks that hadn't cleared yet. At a surplus store on Front Street he bought a nylon money belt and looked at hiking boots. He tried on a couple pairs but they were stiff and uncomfortable compared to his running shoes and he figured they'd take forever to break in.

Besides, he wasn't going to be climbing mountains or slogging through swamps. He went to the sporting goods store down the block and picked up a new pair of Nikes and let it go at that.

He packed socks and underwear and T-shirts and an extra flannel shirt and a sweatshirt, then returned to the surplus store for a light nylon windbreaker, presumably waterproof, and a cotton hat. He saw a canteen, an aluminum flask in a khaki canvas wrapper and sling, and thought it was probably a good idea. He looked at other camping gear, but it all seemed complicated, and a pain in the ass to carry.

He went over to Cactus Jack's for a bowl of chili and a beer, then drove to Paddy McGuire's and got there around one-thirty. He told Harry he was leaving, that he wouldn't be coming in that night.

"That's a lot of notice," Harry said. "That's really great, man."

"Something came up."

"Yeah, right. We straight financially? You paid yourself from the till Sa'day night, right?"

He nodded. "I was thinking," he said. "You want to buy my car?"

"Your car?"

"You know. The Buick."

"Don't you need it, man?"

"Not really."

"Where are you going?"

"Heading east."

"Uh-huh, and you don't want to say more than that. You in any kind of trouble, Guthrie? Stupid question, if you are you don't want to say, but are you, you know, short? You want to borrow a couple of bucks?"

"I just want to sell the car," he said. "I'd take it to a dealer but I really don't want the hassle. Whatever I got for it I'd worry I got screwed."

"What do you want for it?"

"I don't know. Whatever it's worth."

"You know the book on it?"

"It's eight years old, I don't think the book goes that far back."

"Well, let's look at it." Outside, Harry walked around the car, started the engine and listened to it. He opened the hood, listened some more, slammed it shut. "I don't really know what I'm looking at. How's it run?"

"Drive it around the block."

"Just tell me how it runs."

"I think it runs okay. I had some transmission work done on it about six months ago. The tires aren't bad. The spare's bald but the rest are decent."

"You got a lot of rust."

"No kidding."

"What do you want for it?"

"I don't know. Five hundred bucks?"

"I don't honestly know if that's high or low. Be different if I needed it, but I really don't. Shit. Three hundred?"

"All right."

"No, that's probably screwing you. Three hundred dollars, a bicycle's three hundred dollars these days. More than that, even. Split the difference, four hundred. How's that?"

"Better than three."

All in all, he had twenty-three hundred dollars and change. He stashed an even two thousand in the money belt and centered it in the small of his back, adjusting the straps around his waist. He added an extra pair of jeans to his pack. There wasn't room for much else, and he couldn't think what he was forgetting.

Cigarettes. He had an open pack and two others, all amounting to perhaps a day's supply. He went around the corner for a carton.

What else? He tried to think if there was anyone he had to call and decided there wasn't. Roseburg was a small town; everybody at Paddy Mac's would know tonight, and everybody else in town would know in a day or two.

The apartment? The rent was paid through the end of the month. By then, well, either he'd be back dealing with things or it would be somebody else's problem. Because you could just walk away from things. They couldn't make you come back for your clothes and books and records.

By three-thirty he was out of there. The pack rode easily on his back. The old Nikes—the new ones were packed —felt as comfortable as ever on his feet. The sun, obscured by clouds most of the day, was shining.

At the edge of town he stopped at a gas station to use the men's room and fill his canteen. By four he was heading east on Route 138.

TWO

The duplex was just off Evans Avenue near the University of Denver. The upper and lower flats were identical, each running to around twelve hundred square feet, with three bedrooms and one and a half baths. The lower flat, where the owner and his family lived, had been better maintained than the upstairs rental unit, but when was it ever otherwise? The tenants, a young couple named Minnick, hadn't abused the property too badly. They were graduate students with an infant son, and they'd made the third bedroom into a study, its walls given over entirely to bookshelves and bulletin boards, its floor space pretty much filled by a pair of desks improvised out of filing cabinets and plywood. They stood awkwardly like any tenants during a prospective buyer's inspection, worried that they might have to move, afraid they might be blamed by buyer and seller alike for the condition of the property.

The husband was lean and gawky, with knobby wrists and a prominent Adam's apple and a haircut that suggested his wife had taken up barbering as an economy, and a false economy at that. The wife was short, with a round face and round glasses that magnified her light brown eyes.

A faded blue blouse was buttoned tight across her plump chest. Mark wondered if she was nursing the kid.

She wasn't actually pretty, but there was something about her that stirred him.

Downstairs, he accepted a cup of instant coffee from the owner, a Mr. Bedrosian, and busied himself writing numbers on his yellow pad. He made Bedrosian wait awhile after he'd figured out what he was going to offer.

Then he said, "Well, it's a nice piece of property, Mr. Bedrosian. I like what you've done with it."

"It's a sound house," Bedrosian said. He'd said that before, more than once.

"But I'll tell you," Mark said, "I can't quite see the numbers you came up with. Now if I'm going to create a positive cash flow for myself here, you'd have to show me some flexibility on the selling price *and* the financing."

"I see," Bedrosian said. In Mark's experience, that was something people said when they didn't.

"I'd like to buy her," he went on. "And I think you genuinely want to sell—"

"No question about that."

"—and if you're a motivated seller, I think we can probably cut a deal that'll work for both of us. As far as I'm concerned, the only good deal is one that's good for all concerned. If you don't win, I don't win either."

He actually believed this, and he was convinced this had more than a little to do with his success in real estate. At forty-two, he owned one- and two-family houses in four states, and his net worth was somewhere between four and five million dollars. He had accomplished all of this in, well, not quite eight years.

And he'd started with next to nothing. Eight years ago he'd been working for his wife's father, selling hardware and pots and pans in a small store at a second-rate

23

shopping mall in Topeka. Then he read one of those books, getting rich in real estate with no money down, and it was as if the book had been written with him and him alone in mind, as if the author had called him up and was telling him all of this over the phone. Everything was clear and simple; everything made perfect sense.

He did exactly what the book told him to do. Ten days after he read it he made his first offer for a house. It was turned down, but in the course of the following week he made a dozen more offers, and three of them were accepted. By the end of the first month he owned eight houses and was generating a positive cash flow from every one of them.

John Randall Spears, the man who wrote the book, traveled around the country teaching seminars and selling a set of audio tapes, and after he'd been in real estate for two years Mark attended one of the seminars. He got a few tips that made it worth his time, but most of what the man had to say was already spelled out in his book. Mark had read dozens of other books in the meantime, and had learned something from all of them, but you didn't really need anything beyond that first book. If you read it and understood it and did exactly what it said, you would get rich.

"I give this seminar four times a week," John Randall Spears had told them. "We've got two hundred men and women in the room tonight, and that's about average. Last year twenty thousand people took this seminar. Now how many of them do you figure are getting rich?"

Maybe half, Mark figured. Or maybe that was high. Say a third, to be conservative.

"One in fifty," Spears said. "One in fifty! That means four people in this room tonight are going to get rich and the rest of you are just getting another day older. And do you know what's going to keep the rest of you stuck right where you are?" He pounded his fist into his palm. "Sitting on your butts! I'll make a few predictions right now based on some of our data. Of the two hundred of you, sixty of you won't even study the classified ads for more than a day or two. Maybe fifty of you'll actually go and look at some properties. Fifteen or twenty of you'll go so far as to make a written offer to purchase. Six or eight of you'll keep on making offers until one of 'em's accepted. And about four—that's two percent—that's one in fifty, just like I said—will keep on making offers and buying more property and those are the ones who'll wind up rich. Now the rest of you"—and he shook his finger at them—"you can't say you're not getting your money's worth out of what we've been doing here tonight. Because it's entirely up to you whether you're in that two percent winner's circle. And, if you don't get off your butt, if you don't choose to go for it, you'll still have gotten one thing out of it. For the rest of your life you can never really pretend you didn't have a chance. You've got that chance. You'll always have that chance, and every day you can take it or not take it."

Mark Adlon had found the talk inspiring, but then he hadn't really needed further inspiration at that stage. And, however inspiring the talk may have been, the fact remained that it would only inspire one person in fifty to go the whole nine yards. (Although, he noticed, it did indeed inspire a substantially higher percentage than that to shell out $398 for the set of tapes.)

It was getting dark by the time he left the duplex. He was staying downtown at the Radisson. He found a parking space in the garage for the Lincoln and took the elevator up to the VIP floor. You paid a couple more dollars for a room there and for that they gave you a concierge on the floor, and a breakfast buffet and a complimentary newspaper outside your door in the morning, and drinks and hors

25

d'oeuvres in the evening. It wasn't all that big a deal, but it was deductible, and it made sense to treat yourself well. The more you established yourself in your own mind as successful, the more other people cooperated in your increasing success. And, when you felt good about yourself, you had better judgment and your instincts were sharper and you made better decisions.

In the room he fixed himself a light scotch and water, drank half of it, shucked out of his suit and stood under a hot shower. He put on a sport shirt and slacks, finished his drink, and put through a call to his wife in Overland Park. (The house in Topeka had been rented out after they'd moved to suburban Kansas City; then, a year or so ago, the right buyer had come along and he'd sold it.)

He said, "Well, girl, we now own a third house in Denver. Or we will in a couple of days. The owner's a nice old guy who wants to live in Florida. His sister has a place in Kissimmee and he wants something just like that, with orange trees in the backyard."

He was on the phone for ten minutes. He told her about his day and heard about hers. He had a son in the eleventh grade and a daughter just two weeks away from junior high graduation, he had a big house with landscaped grounds and a forty-foot pool, he had property management firms to collect the rents and contend with the tenants, and all he had to do was keep on keeping on and he'd get a little richer every day, and have a little more fun.

Over dinner, a plate of fettucini Alfredo and a big bowl of salad at a downtown restaurant full of wood and polished brass and hanging plants, he found himself thinking of Bedrosian's tenant. Well, *his* tenant now, or in a couple of days when the sale went through.

The wife, the little pouter pigeon, with her round body

and her round face and her round eyeglasses. And the round breasts, straining the front of her shirt. He found himself looking appraisingly at a couple of the waitresses and other women in the restaurant.

He ordered a cup of coffee, and while he waited for the girl to bring it he sat with his eyes closed and breathed slowly and deeply through his nose, holding the breath for a few seconds between the inhale and the exhale. He let himself tune in to his own inner rhythms and he recognized what he found there.

He drank his coffee, added a tip to the check and paid with a credit card. Outside, he walked a few blocks on the pedestrian mall where the restaurant was located. He went back to his hotel, got the Lincoln out of the garage, and drove around. Several times he saw women at bus stops and offered them rides, but they all turned him down. Only one even bothered to speak; from the others he got a stiff-lipped stare and a quick shake of the head.

In Littleton, south of the city, he stopped at a 7-Eleven. The clerk was a very tall youth with a dirty apron. Mark bought a pack of gum and left, flipping the gum into an empty oil drum on his way back to his car. He passed up two more convenience stores because there were too many cars parked out in front. The next one was another 7-Eleven and there was only one other customer, a fat woman buying ice cream. Her entertainment for the night, he thought. Then, as she was paying at the register, two young men came in for beer and cigarettes.

He stood to one side at the magazine counter, feigning interest in a copy of *Car & Driver.* Every few seconds he would look over the top of the magazine at the girl behind the counter. She was taller than little Mrs. Minnick and her hair was a lighter brown. Her figure looked good, from what he could see of it. And, while she looked nothing like the woman he had seen at Bedrosian's house, there was some quality about her, something that might have been vulnerability, that reminded him of the other woman.

She would do. That was the thing: she would do.

He waited there at the magazine counter, a forty-two-year-old millionaire an inch or so shy of medium height, with wavy blow-dried brown hair that was just starting to go gray at the temples. He'd put on weight in his eight years in the real estate game; he was tons more active than he'd been in the past, but all the running around gave him a hell of an appetite and it was easier to eat what he wanted than struggle with it. His face had filled out and he was getting a little jowly, but the up side of the extra weight was that it didn't hurt you in business. A plump man looked prosperous, and at the same time trustworthy. You wouldn't want to be out-and-out fat, but a few extra pounds was all to the good.

The two young men paid for their Marlboros and Bud and left. He heard their engine start, turned to check the lot outside. There was only his Lincoln, parked off to the side, and a Honda Civic that must have belonged to the girl.

His heart was racing, racing. He walked to the rear of the store, pausing at the display of auto care products to pick up a quart can of motor oil. He stationed himself in front of a glass-fronted food locker full of frozen burritos and pizzas. He called out, "Miss? Could you come here a minute?"

"What's the matter?"

"I need your help with something."

She was not quite his height. Young—maybe twenty-six, twenty-eight. He could smell her perfume and her sweat.

"What is it?"

Her name was Cindi. It said so on her little plastic name badge.

"Back there. Do you see where I'm pointing?"

"Where?"

She looked, frowning, leaning forward, and he swung the can of motor oil in a vicious arc, connecting solidly with the back of her head. She fell without a sound, and as she dropped one leg swung out behind her and dislodged a couple packages of Beer Nuts from a display.

He thought, *Now, quickly, before anyone comes in.* But he wanted her awake, he wanted her knowing what was happening. He caught her up under the arms and half carried, half dragged her into the back, where two doors set in a wall of unfinished concrete block opened into restrooms. In the men's room, he propped her up against the sink. He stood between her legs and put his hands on her body, filling his senses with her.

She was still out, and for a moment he was afraid she was dead. But he could see a pulse working in the hollow of her throat.

He tore a couple of paper towels from the dispenser, wadded them up and crammed them into her mouth. He said, "Cindi?" When she failed to respond he ran water in the sink and splashed a little on her face. He said, "Cindi? Open your eyes, Cindi. Open them."

She stirred. Her eyes fluttered, then opened. Brown eyes, not too well focused yet. Perspiration beading her upper lip.

He leaned his lower body against her. He settled a hand on either side of her throat. Her eyes were bringing his image into focus and he saw the fear coming into them now, the terror, and he said, "You look at me, Cindi, you look at me, darling," and he held her eyes with his and ground his hips into hers as he choked the life out of her.

He wiped the faucets, the sink, the doorknob. With a paper towel around his hand he pressed the button to lock the door behind him, and he kept the towel over his hand as he pushed the door shut. He used it again to wipe off the can of motor oil, which he returned to its proper place on the way out of the store.

Two customers were waiting at the register, another was heating something in the microwave, and one of them asked Mark if he knew where the clerk was.

"In back," he said. "She'll be out in a minute."

Back at the Radisson, the concierge greeted him by name as he got off the elevator. Well, that was part of what you paid extra for, that sort of personal touch.

He showered again and put on a robe. He sat at the desk for half an hour, going over his schedule for the next day, checking through the real estate listings. He caught the eleven o'clock news and the first few minutes of the *Tonight* show, turning it off at the end of Carson's monologue.

In bed, he went over the day's events as if they were on videotape. He pushed the mental fast-forward button during the dull spots, then moved to slow-motion from the point where he walked into the 7-Eleven. He did a freeze-frame on her face at the end, the knowledge and raw fear coming into her eyes, then the light going out of them.

He clung to that image and slid off to sleep with it.

THREE

Sara Duskin dozed off in the taxi. She wasn't tired, really, but she had things on her mind and her thoughts just wound inward and inward, curling on themselves until they had led her far away from consciousness. When the taxi stopped in front of her house she awoke instantly, and her eyes were open by the time the driver turned to tell her they had arrived.

She turned her head to look at the meter, turned her head again to look down at her purse. She paid him, tipped him, and walked up the driveway to the door.

She heard Thom dribbling a basketball, then looked and saw him arcing a shot at the basket mounted on the garage. She was fitting her key in the lock when he caught sight of her and ran to her.

"I thought you were home," he said accusingly. "I saw the car and I thought you were home."

"Didn't I tell you I was going to the doctor?"

"Yeah, but I thought you came back 'cause the car was in the garage. And then the door was locked, and I rang and rang and you didn't open it."

"Wasn't the key on the hook? In the garage?"

"Yeah, but I thought you were home, see, so why would I bother with the key? And then I figured you were asleep, so I got the key and went in, and you *weren't* home, and it was spooky."

"Were you scared?"

"I didn't say I was scared, just that it was spooky."

He followed her into the house, and while she heated water for tea he poured himself a glass of milk and helped himself to a handful of Oreos.

"I won't spoil my dinner," he said.

"I don't care if you do."

"You don't? What'd you get from the doctor, drugs?"

"You guessed it, sport. A little coke, a little smack—"

"What's smack?"

"Heroin. Gosh, don't they teach you anything in that school of yours?"

"I could *buy* heroin, Mom. You want me to buy some without leaving the school building?"

"In Fort Wayne?"

"Right here in beautiful downtown Fort Wayne. You want me to buy some what-did-you-call-it? Smack?"

"Don't do me any favors. The doctor gives me a good price."

"I'll bet." He looked down at his glass of milk. "How come you didn't take the car?"

"I got a ride."

"I thought you took a cab."

"I did. That's what I got a ride in."

"How come?"

"Oh, I thought I might be tired, and it might be easier to let somebody else drive."

"Is that the truth, Mom?"

He had such an earnest gaze, and he was such a fine-looking boy. Thirteen years old, tall for his age, and blond,

32

and with such clean-cut chiseled features. It was such a joy to see him; it was so good to be able to see him—

"Mom?"

"It's the truth," she said, "but it's not the whole truth."

"What's the whole truth?"

"I don't think I can drive anymore, Thom."

"What did the doctor say?"

"He didn't say anything good."

"What do you mean?"

She took the teabag from the cup, set it in the saucer. She reached for his glass of milk and added a little to her tea.

"There's crumbs in it," he said. "From the cookies, I dunked them and there's crumbs."

"So?"

"So now you've got cookie crumbs in your tea."

"So?"

"So nothing. What did the doctor say?"

"He says I definitely don't have glaucoma."

"Isn't that good?"

"Not in this case, because they can arrest glaucoma. There are drops they give you, and if you take them regularly your vision doesn't get any worse."

"He gave you drops last week."

"Right."

"Even though he didn't think it was glaucoma."

"Right. Because the eyeball pressure wasn't elevated, but he thought the drops might arrest the symptoms just as if the pressure were elevated as in true glaucoma."

"But it didn't?"

"No, it didn't."

"What does that mean exactly? Your eyes are worse than they were last week?"

"That's right."

"And you knew that already because that's why you took the cab instead of driving."

33

"Uh-huh."

"Mom?"

"What?"

Are you gonna go blind, Mom? She could hear his question as clearly as if he had spoken it aloud. But he was not yet ready to speak it. Instead he said, "What can you see, exactly? I mean, how bad is it?"

She thought for a moment. "You see that roll of paper towels?"

"Sure I see it. Why? Can't you see it?"

"Of course I can see it, dummy. Didn't I just point it out to you?"

"Huh?"

"Bring me the roll of paper towels, sport. Thanks. Now what we want here is the cardboard tube, so let's take all the paper towels off. If we fold them—that's right—we'll be able to use them again. Sweetie, you look utterly mystified."

"Well, you've got to admit you're acting pretty weird, Mom. First a cab, then unrolling the paper towels. Didn't I do something like this with toilet paper when I was a little kid?"

"You can't possibly remember that."

"I remember you talking about it. Did I get in trouble?"

"No, but you got laughed at. Okay, we now have a cardboard tube. Now, voilà! We tear it in half and we have *two* cardboard tubes."

"And if we put them together we have a whole one again. And if—"

"Hold 'em to your eyes, Thommy. Like binoculars, but right up against your eyes."

"Like this?"

"Like that. Pointing straight out, that's right. Now you see what I see."

"Oh, wow," he said. "That's as much as you can see?"

34

"Gimme. No, as a matter of fact I can do a little better than this." She shortened both tubes until they were about four inches long. "Here," she said. "Now try it."

"You can't see very much."

"No."

"Just straight ahead? So if a car was coming from the side—"

"That's why I took a taxi."

"Wow," he said. He was still holding the cardboard tubes to his eyes, looking experimentally around the room. He said, "Was it this bad last week, Mom?"

"No. He said there's been further deterioration and vision loss since last week."

And he hadn't had to say that; she'd already known. Her field of vision was shrinking, and it sometimes seemed to her that she could feel it drawing in. He'd tested her: *Now keep your eyes straight forward, Mrs. Duskin. Now I want you to watch the red dot. Without moving your eyes, just be aware of the red dot. Tell me when it disappears.*

The red dot (and the yellow dot, and the blue dot) had disappeared sooner this week than last. Each time it passed from her field of vision she said "There" or "Now" or "Oooops," and the ophthalmologist made a pencil mark on the sheet of graph paper. When he had finished, he connected the dots to form a pair of irregular circles. While she studied them, he handed her without comment her test from the preceding week. The circles then had been larger.

"What's going to happen, Mom?"

"He doesn't really know," she said. "Since he doesn't know exactly what's wrong with me, he can't tell exactly what will happen next. My condition could just spontaneously arrest itself; the deterioration could stop of its own accord. Or it could clear up completely."

"Or?"

Softly she said, "I think I'm going blind, Thommy."

35

"You think so, huh?"

"I'm pretty sure of it."

"Do you know—"

"How much time I've got? Not too long, I don't think. He wants me to see a specialist."

"You better go right away."

She shook her head. "I'm not going."

"Why not?"

"Because it won't do any good."

She thought he'd argue with her, or ask her how she could be so sure, but instead he said, "Mom? Are you scared?"

"This tea's good," she said. "I'm probably spoiled now, I'll want cookie crumbs in it all the time."

"Are you scared, Mom?"

"No," she said. "No, I'm not. Funny, isn't it?"

She did some counseling at Indiana-Fort Wayne, and if one of her clients had said the same thing she would have labeled it denial. How could you fail to run the gamut of negative emotions at the prospect of blindness? One of her senses, perhaps the chief one, was being taken away from her. Her world was shrinking and turning dark around her. How could she react other than with fear and rage?

Yet, from the beginning, it had not felt like deprivation. It had felt like a gift. From the onset, when she started catching flashes of white light out of the corners of her eyes toward the end of the day, and then when her field of vision began to have an occasional halo around it, from those first symptoms she had sensed that more was being given to her than was being taken away.

She was not being singled out for punishment. Rather, she was being chosen for something. For something *important.*

Charming, her professional self commented. Instead of paranoia, she was opting for grandiosity.

Except she didn't feel grandiose. If anything, she felt curiously humble.

She was forty-one years old, the widowed mother of a thirteen-year-old boy. She stood five-four in flat shoes and weighed 105 pounds. Except for her pregnancy, her weight had not varied by more than a pound or two since college. It stayed the same, irrespective of her diet. The great majority of the female students she counseled, and not a few of the males as well, had some sort of problematic relationship with weight and food. Many struggled with their weight, and some had serious eating disorders, anorexia and bulimia. Half the world was hungry, she sometimes thought, and the other half was either starving itself or alternately gorging and vomiting.

She had a heart-shaped face, a strong straight nose, a small mouth. Her forehead was broad, with a sharply defined widow's peak. Ten years ago, weeks after a drunk driver had crossed the centerline on State Road 37, she had found herself wanting to change her hair style and combing tentative bangs down onto her forehead. Almost immediately she'd realized what she was doing, trying to deny her widowhood by covering her widow's peak.

The hair had been dark brown then. Now it was a soft gray and she wore it as she'd been wearing it for twenty years, falling evenly to within an inch of her shoulders. Her eyes were also gray, a surprising shade a full tone deeper than her hair. They were no less imposing to look upon now that they had begun to lose their function.

Since he'd already spoiled his dinner with Oreos, she didn't bother cooking. They had a pizza delivered and ate it in front of the television set. Neither of them watched; he was doing his homework, and she had her eyes closed and let her gaze turn inward.

He said, "Mom? This is gonna sound dumb."

"I'm glad you warned me."

"Well, here goes. Uh. Is there something you don't want to see?"

"Oh, God."

"Well, I just thought—"

"I thought the cobbler's kids were supposed to go barefoot. But what about the psychologist's kids?"

"Psychobabble, huh? I'm sorry."

"Don't apologize, Thom." She opened her eyes, surprised for an instant by the smallness of her field of vision. Her mind's eye still had a wide screen, and it was as if she saw less now when she opened her eyes.

She said, "I asked myself the same thing. On a metaphysical level everything that happens to us is the result of a choice we make. Even your father, on some level or other he elected to be in that accident—"

"I still don't get that. I mean, he was driving along minding his own business, right? And some drunk came sailing at him from out of nowhere, and it's his fault?"

"I didn't say it was his fault."

"You said he chose it. He called up somebody and had an accident delivered."

"Why do you think he just happened to be there?"

"Because he was coming home, wasn't he? He was on his way home."

"So it was just bad luck, huh?"

"I guess."

"Coincidence."

"Right."

"Well, you can believe in luck and coincidence, sport, or you can believe that they don't put pepperoni on your pizza unless you order it that way."

"So Dad had this desire to get killed in a car wreck and—"

"Well, to die."

"And it went into some computer up in the sky, and they dispatched a drunk driver to do the job."

"Well, something put them in the same place at the same time."

He was silent for a moment. Then he said, "Why did Dad want to die?"

"I don't know."

"You blame him for dying, huh?"

"Not anymore."

"You used to?"

"Oh, God, yes. How could he do that to me? To us? Leaving us all alone like that, the son of a bitch. Survivors are usually angry with loved ones who die, unless they're too occupied with feeling guilty for having survived. Or unless they just stuff the feelings and aren't aware of them."

"I can't remember how I felt. It was a long time ago."

"I know."

"Sometimes I think I can remember, but it's like unrolling the toilet paper. I remember that it happened, but I don't really *remember*. Are you going to have the last piece of pizza?"

"Take it."

"Are you sure? I already had three."

"Take it."

"Thanks. Can I ask you something? If Dad chose to be in a car wreck, aren't you choosing to uh—"

"Go blind."

"It's hard to say the word."

"It'll get easier. Yes, of course I'm choosing it, but I don't think it's because there's something I don't want to see. I think there's something I *do* want to see."

"I don't get it."

She closed her eyes. "I think," she said, "that I'm going to be able to see far more with my eyes closed than I was ever able to see with them open. Thom, ever since I started to have trouble with my eyes, I've been getting glimpses of things."

"What kind of things?"

"It's hard to explain. At first it would happen at night when I went to bed."

"Like dreams?"

"No, not like dreams, because it would happen while I was awake. I would close my eyes and I would start to get pictures. Almost like watching a movie, except that when I tried to focus in on an image I would lose it."

"I get things sometimes. Like if I stare at a light and then close my eyes, and you get these colors, and they sort of change color and finally fade away."

"This is a little different."

"What kind of things do you see?"

"All kinds. Scenery. People's faces. Sometimes they'll be having a conversation."

"Do you hear what they're saying?"

"I *know* what they're saying. Some of the time, anyway. It's very flickery, it's like a film that keeps cutting from one image to another. Or sometimes it's just one picture that flashes on the screen, and it's there for a while and then it vanishes and nothing else comes on."

"They turn the lights on and the show's over."

"Something like that. A lot of the time I see people walking down a highway."

"Where are they going?"

"I don't know yet," she said. "I'm *starting* to know."

"Yeah?"

"I'll tell you what I think's happening. I think that as I lose my eyesight, this other kind of sight is expanding. It

40

doesn't just happen late at night now. It can happen any time I close my eyes. It doesn't always, but it seems to be happening more and more." She heaved a sigh. "I think it's a gift, Thom."

"A gift."

"I think so."

"And you chose it."

"It was offered to me, and I chose to receive it."

"You picked out your own present. Mom? What do you figure it is that you see? The future?"

"I don't know. Maybe."

"Like having a crystal ball in your head. Hey, can you see how I'm going to do on my science final?"

"When is it?"

"I think a week from Wednesday."

"Well, that's easy, then," she said.

"Are you serious? You really know how I'm going to do on a test I haven't even taken yet?"

"Uh-huh."

"Well?"

"You're not going to take the test, champ."

"I'm not?"

"Nope."

"Why? Am I gonna be sick? Am I gonna *choose* to have a cold that day?"

She shook her head. "You're going to choose to be elsewhere."

"What do you mean?"

"I mean I think we'll be out of here by then, Thommy."

"Out of here?"

"Gone. Out of Fort Wayne."

"We're moving?"

"'Fraid so."

"Where are we going?"

"I don't know yet."

"Do you know when?"

"Soon. Before your science final."

"We're just gonna pick up and go? Just like that? Are we going to take the car? We can't take the car, you can't drive. What are we—"

She held up a hand. "Stop. No more questions. I don't have any more answers just now. Okay?"

"But—"

" 'More will be revealed.' Okay?"

At breakfast the next morning she said, "I want you to stay home from school today, sport. I'm going to need you to help me."

"Gee, it's the week before finals. Oh. I won't be taking finals, will I? Or is it just the science exam I'm gonna miss?"

"You won't be taking any of your finals. In fact, it's possible you won't be going back to school at all this year."

"Really?"

"Breaks your heart, doesn't it?" She took a bite of toast, a sip of tea. "At nine-fifteen I want to call the office and tell Rysbeck I'm not coming in. I hope they can issue a check right away. I've got sick leave and vacation time coming."

"Are you quitting your job?"

"That's right. Then we're going to have to do something about the car. It's not paid off, but I think it's worth more than we owe on it. I'll call Angert Motors and find out what I can do."

"You're selling the car?"

"Well, I can't see to drive it, Thom, and you can't drive for three more years yet, so I don't see what good it is to us. I suppose we could knock the windows out and use it as a huge outdoor planter, but aside from that—"

"Mom."

"What?"

"I'm a little worried."

"Thank you."

"For what?"

"For admitting it."

"The thing is, I'm scared."

"Okay."

"I mean, don't you think this is a little crazy? I mean, you're going *blind,* like, and I don't know how we'll even be able to *do* anything if you can't see. I mean, how'll we get places if you can't drive? How will you work, how will we have any money, how will you even fix dinner, I mean—"

"Take a breath."

"It just seems so *crazy!* Like you want me to leave school now and miss finals. Two more weeks and school's over, it's vacation, so why can't we wait until then? Doesn't that make more sense?"

"I'm sure it does."

"I mean, what's the rush? I mean, why do we have to rush to pack up and go somewheres when you don't even know where we're going? If you really want to know, I think you're acting crazy. That's what I think."

"I know it is, Thommy."

"Mom, I didn't mean it."

"Sure you did. It's okay."

"No, I—"

"You meant every word of it, sweetie, and there's nothing wrong with that."

He rushed to her and his embrace was fierce. He said, "I don't want us to go anywhere. I don't want you to be blind. I don't want any of this. It's not *fair.*"

"I know."

"I mean it. It's not fair. It sucks."

"I know."

"I hate this. What's so funny?"

"Oh, I was just thinking. The other day, when I tried to

43

imagine telling you that I was going blind? I had this image of you jumping up and down and shouting, 'Oh, goodie, we'll be getting a dog!'"

"You're terrible."

"I know."

" 'The good news is we're getting a dog. The bad news is it's a seeing-eye dog.' "

"Some joke, huh?"

"You're really terrible."

"I know," she said, stroking the blond hair, kneading the nape of the neck. "I'll tell you what. Fix your terrible mother a cup of tea—"

"With or without cookie crumbs?"

"Without. And I'll try to explain why everything's so crazy and why it all has to happen so fast."

"Okay."

"I don't know where to start. *Okay*. These pictures I've been seeing, these visions."

"People walking on a highway."

"That's one of the themes, yes. It's not just a batch of visually interesting images."

"What do you mean?"

"What I mean is that it's all part of something very big and very important. There's a reason why I'm losing my eyesight and getting this other sight in its place. I'm being given an important part to play in something very big that's happening."

"What is it?"

She closed her eyes. "Things are happening very rapidly," she said. "Everything is getting ready to change. I don't understand it, but maybe I don't have to understand it. I don't understand electricity but when I turn the switch the light goes on."

"Unless the bulb's out."

"All of a sudden," she said, "things that used to be

44

important don't matter anymore. My work doesn't matter. Your finals don't matter; your whole education doesn't matter. The car doesn't matter. Whether or not I go blind doesn't matter. Do you hear what I'm saying, Thommy? None of that stuff matters."

"What does?"

"Going forward. Letting go of everything that's not necessary. Thommy, I close my eyes and I see things, but I don't see all of it. I know we have to leave here within the next couple of days. I want to make arrangements about this house and money and everything before then, but if I can't handle any of it we'll just walk away from it, because the important thing is to go. We'll know more when we have to know more. You know what it's like? It's like driving at night. You can only see as far as the headlights reach, but you can go all the way across the country that way."

"Not if we sell the car. Not if you can't see to drive."

"Oh, shit," she said. "I'm not doing a good job of explaining this."

"That's okay," he said. "I sort of get it."

Explaining to Thom, she spoke with powerful assurance. Alone, she was less supremely confident. There were doubts, there were fears. But there was always enough certainty to overcome them.

She felt guided.

She sat down with a vice president at her bank and arranged to pay the mortgage payments and taxes out of a line of credit secured by a second mortgage. Angert Motors sent a man out to look at her car, and she wound up getting twelve hundred dollars for her equity in it. Hal Rysbeck cut through a maze of red tape at the school and got her a check for most of what she had coming; the rest would go to her bank and be credited to her account. And a very nice

45

woman at Klopfer & Klopfer Realty listed her house for rent and agreed to have a moving firm pack and store her personal articles.

It all went so smoothly that she took it for confirmation that she was acting appropriately. The universe was endorsing her action by cooperating at every turn. But if there had been any snags she would simply have let go of whatever was stuck. She was willing to leave the car in the driveway for someone to repossess, willing to let the mortgage go unpaid until the bank foreclosed or the city sold the house for back taxes. None of that really mattered because something else, something new, something still incomprehensible, mattered so very much more.

She had had her last appointment with the ophthalmologist on Monday. That Thursday, she and Thom took a taxi to the Greyhound Terminal downtown, where a very helpful black man worked out their route for them and sold them their tickets. They would go from Fort Wayne to Chicago, where they would change to an express bus that went through Davenport and Omaha and Cheyenne en route to Salt Lake City. There they would change to another bus that slanted northwest through Idaho, stopping at Boise en route to Portland.

"Now that's Portland, Oregon," the man said, grinning. "You absolutely sure you want Portland, Oregon, and not Portland, Maine?"

"As sure as I am of anything," she said.

FOUR

Oregon 138 extends east from Roseburg, terminating when it runs into US 97 at Diamond Lake Junction. The distance between the two points is about eighty miles as the crow flies, but the road meanders, following rivers and creeks and finding its way through the Cascade Range, and that adds another fifteen miles.

Guthrie Wagner covered fourteen miles the first day. Some years back, when he'd been running, he'd reached the point where he was doing seven-minute miles in short races. His regular training pace was slower, between nine and ten minutes a mile, which translated into a little better than six miles an hour. He wasn't sure what a comfortable walking pace would turn out to be, and he found out it was somewhere between three and four miles an hour. Even with a pack on his back, and without having done anything to condition himself, he seemed able to sustain that pace without effort for hours at a time.

He didn't know this the first day because he couldn't tell how fast he was going or how much ground he was covering. It was around four by the time he got out on the two-lane blacktop, and it was getting dark by the time he found a place to stay, a little mom-and-pop motel in Glide. But his map told him he'd covered fourteen miles, and it was ten minutes of nine when he thought to look at his watch, so he felt he could figure on managing a three-mile-an-hour pace without difficulty. Of course the going would get tougher when he started to get into the mountains, but he'd be in better shape by then.

Twenty miles a day, say. Three hours in the morning, three hours in the afternoon.

He showered off the road dust, then ran a hot tub and soaked some of the soreness out of his feet and legs. He ached a little, but in a satisfying way. He dried off and sat in a chair with his feet up, studying his map. There was a television set in the room but he didn't think to turn it on.

Six miles to Idleyld Park, eighteen to Steamboat, sixteen to Toketee Falls. Then nineteen to Diamond Lake and twenty-two to Diamond Lake Junction. At that point he'd have to decide whether to go north or south on 97, but for the next four days or so all he had to do was keep on walking west.

It might not always be convenient to stop in the towns, and they wouldn't all necessarily have motels, as far as that went. They were small towns, pinpoint dots on the map, little more than wide places in a narrow road.

Early June was a little cold for sleeping out. Especially when you got into the high ground of the Cascades. Especially when you didn't have a tent or a sleeping bag, or even a blanket.

He stopped for lunch the next day in Idleyld Park. He ate a hamburger, drank a cup of coffee, smoked a cigarette, and headed on toward Steamboat. The road hugged the northern bank of the North Fork of the Umpqua River, and about ten miles out of Idleyld it entered the Umpqua National Forest.

The road was rolling and winding, with a noticeable overall upgrade. Running, he used to hate hills; walking, they were less of a hassle, but he could feel them.

Dense stands of mixed evergreens lined both sides of the road. When there was a gap in the trees, or when he reached the top of a rise and could see for some distance, he looked out over rich green forest and saw mountains still crowned with snow. At first he was taking note of each beautiful scene, clicking off mental snapshots, but after an hour or so he stopped noticing the beauty and instead let himself become one with it.

There was very little traffic on the road. He walked on the left, facing oncoming cars, and he stepped off onto the shoulder when a vehicle approached. Around the middle of the afternoon, without any conscious intent, he realized he was giving a wave to passing cars. Most of them waved back. Some of them honked.

He stayed that night at the Modoc Motel in Steamboat. The third day he woke to birdsong outside his window and got an early start. Even with the grade slowing him down he was in Toketee Falls by early afternoon. He had a thick bowl of soup and a couple of sandwiches at a lunch counter run by two women, sisters. They were members of the Worldwide Church of God and their restaurant was closed Saturdays and Sundays. You could smoke, there were ashtrays on the counter and at the three tables, but two hand-lettered signs warned against the use of profanity on the premises.

He lit a cigarette and tried to imagine Kit's reaction to the signs. It would be verbal, he decided, and no doubt eloquent, and it would probably get the two of them thrown out of the place.

There was a motel on the western edge of Toketee Falls, and a court of tourist cabins farther on, but he didn't really

49

feel like stopping this early. He had the sisters pack him up a couple of sandwiches and a piece of pound cake, and he bought a candy bar and two packages of salted nuts at the Arco station.

He walked for another couple of hours, taking it slowly now, giving way to the upgrade instead of fighting it, reducing his pace and resting whenever he felt the need. While it was still light he left the road and walked fifty yards or so into the forest. He found a spot where the trees were a little farther apart—you couldn't really call it a clearing—and he cleared the pine needles from a circle ten feet across. In the center of the circle he arranged pine needles and a few scraps of paper for tinder, then gathered twigs and heavier branches from the forest floor. He brought back several armloads of wood, more than he figured to need, because it would be difficult to replenish the supply in the dark.

The fire caught quickly and burned well. He sat cross-legged in front of it, feeding wood to it, getting half-hypnotized gazing into the flames.

All along his route that day he had passed areas specifically set aside for public camping. For a couple of dollars you got a place to pitch your tent, a barbecue pit with firewood cut and stacked for you, and access to running water and indoor plumbing. Pitching camp on his own like this was probably against regulations, and he was certain he risked a stiff fine with his fire.

He was unworried. He knew he wasn't going to set the woods on fire, and no one would be able to see flames or smoke from the road.

He ate the food he'd brought, putting aside half a sandwich and a Clark Bar for breakfast. He would have liked coffee, but the spring water in his canteen was no hardship. He tended his fire and breathed fresh air tinged with wood smoke while the sky darkened and the birds quieted down around him.

For perhaps two hours he did nothing but feed branches to the fire and listen to the night sounds of the forest. His mind was still. He barely thought. When his eyelids started to droop he wrapped a spare shirt around his extra pair of jeans for a pillow and stretched out alongside the fire.

When he awoke the sky was light and his fire was cold ashes. He packed up, stomped the ashes to make sure there wasn't an ember still alive, shouldered his pack and made his way back to the road.

There were several motels in Diamond Lake and he stayed at one called the Fair Harbor Inn. There was a coin-operated washer and dryer alongside the Coke and ice machines, and after he'd taken a long hot shower he got change at the desk and did a load of wash. He sat in a redwood lounge chair beside the pool while each machine in turn went through its cycle.

When he'd put his laundry away he returned to the office and asked the round-shouldered owner where he could get a decent meal. "You don't have a car," the man said.

"No."

"Well, the Blue Bonnet's real good if you like plain cooking, but it's about half a mile down the road."

"I think I can manage that."

"If you like chili," the man said, "I'd have to say you can't go wrong there."

The chili wasn't bad. It was a little mild for his taste, but the girl brought him a bottle of Tabasco and that gave it a little more authority. He drank a beer with it and had a second beer for dessert, and it was while he was drinking the second beer that he realized he hadn't had a cigarette since morning. He'd reached the top of a rise around nine-thirty and had taken a few minutes to check out the view, referring to his map to determine what mountains he was looking at. Mount Bailey, Mount Thielsen, Black Rock Mountain, Pig Iron Mountain—there were great names and imposing mountains, but he wasn't confident he was matching them up correctly. Nor did he suppose it mattered much.

And, looking at the mountains, he'd lit the first cigarette of the day. And it had thus far been the *last* cigarette of the day, and that was strange.

In fact, he'd hardly been smoking at all since he left Roseburg. He'd started out with a carton in his backpack and three loose packs, one of them about half gone when he set out. This was his fourth day on the road, and he hadn't touched the carton, and he had an unopened pack in his jacket and another pack in his shirt pocket with, let's see, three cigarettes left in it. Which meant he'd smoked something like a pack and a half in the past four days, and he normally smoked close to twice that much in a day. Two to three packs a day, that's what he'd been smoking for nearly twenty years.

That he should reduce his cigarette consumption so dramatically was remarkable. When he was running he had several times tried to quit, and he'd managed to cut down some, but at the best of times he never got much under a pack a day. But what was astonishing was that he'd cut down without even knowing it. Except cut down didn't really say it. Why, he'd virtually stopped altogether.

He took a cigarette and held it between his thumb and forefinger. It felt funny in his hand. He put it in his mouth, took it out, put it back, shrugged, and lit it. He took a puff, inhaled, blew out the smoke and watched it rise to the ceiling.

It tasted all right, but he didn't seem to want to finish it.

He started to force himself to take another puff, then changed his mind and stubbed it out in the ashtray.

Back at the Fair Harbor Inn the owner emerged from the office as Guthrie was heading up the graveled drive. He said, "Well, did you have that chili?"

"I did, and it was real good."

"They do all right by you," the man said. "You want to stop by for a minute? I just made some coffee, if you could do with a cup."

The motel office had a pair of wooden armchairs with vinyl cushions flanking a console television. A drama about a Los Angeles law firm was playing, the sound pitched almost inaudibly low. Guthrie took his coffee black; the owner, whose name was McLemore, stirred in a powdered creamer and two sugars. His wife was in Grants Pass, he said, spending a few days visiting her mother.

"She has Alzheimer's," he said. "By God, that's an awful way to end up. Here's a woman who never did any harm her whole life and she finished up like that. You read about that man, I think he was down in Florida, his wife had Alzheimer's and he shot her?"

"Didn't he go to jail?"

"Isn't that terrible? You got the scum of the earth walking around free and that man has to go to jail. I'll tell you, if my wife got like that, I'd put her down. What kind of man wouldn't do for his wife what he'd do for a dog? And I'll tell you something else, I don't believe people around here would convict you. I don't know what kind of people live in Florida, but we're not like that here."

The coffee wasn't bad. It could have been stronger, but it wasn't bad.

"Now you're doing some hiking," McLemore said. "I'll tell you, it's not every day someone comes in here on foot. Where'd you walk from?"

"Roseburg."

"Roseburg! Why, that's got to be seventy-five miles."

"Just about."

"How long you been walking?"

"Today was the fourth day."

"Four days. So you're making pretty close to twenty miles a day. Where you headed? Crater Lake, I guess?"

"I don't think so."

"No? You ought to see it if you never have, as close as you are to it now."

"I was there a couple of years ago. I think I'll pass this time around."

"And just head on back to Roseburg? Least you'll be going downhill on the way back."

"No, I think I'll keep going for a while."

"Headed where?"

"East, I think."

"East!"

"I think so."

"How far you gonna go? You thinking to cross the whole country?"

"I might."

"Your shoes holding up?"

"So far."

"How 'bout your feet?"

"They're all right."

"By God," McLemore said. "Twenty miles a day, well, yes, you just about could find places to stay, couldn't you? Where'd you put up last night in Toketee? His cabins aren't worth a damn, and the motel's not a whole lot better."

"Well," he said, "actually, last night I camped out. I got a few miles past Toketee and just walked off the road into the woods and spent the night there."

"You probably weren't a lot worse off than in one of

those cabins, from what I hear about 'em." McLemore frowned in thought. "None of my business, but I could have sworn you weren't carrying but a little knapsack when you checked in."

"That's right."

"I wouldn't have thought you could fit a sleeping bag in there."

"I don't have one. I slept in my clothes."

"In your clothes. You mean what you're wearing now?"

"Well, a different shirt and my other jeans. And I put on an extra pair of socks."

"And that little windbreaker, I guess."

"Yes."

"And that's all?" McLemore stared at him. "Weren't you cold?"

"A little, but it wasn't bad. I had a fire."

"A fire."

"A campfire, I let it burn down when I went to sleep. I suppose it was against the law, but—"

"Forget the law. You slept out in the open last night in your clothes. No tent, no sleeping bag, no blanket. Mister, are you telling me a story?"

"What do you mean?"

"Maybe you parked down the road. Maybe you *drove* here from Roseburg."

"Why would I do that?"

"Don't ask me. Maybe you're one of those psychological liars, or maybe you don't want anybody seeing your car. Or maybe you just want to see if you can make a fool out of a person."

"I don't know what you're talking about."

"You know what the temperature got down to last night, mister? The low forties, and it wouldn't have been any warmer closer to Toketee. You sleep without cover on a night like that and you'd wake up chilled to the bone, providing you woke up at all. A man'd freeze to death, likely as not, sleeping out like you said you did."

Guthrie looked at him.

"You expect me to believe you, mister?"

He stood up. "You can believe whatever you want," he said. "It doesn't make a whole lot of difference to me. Thanks for the coffee." He walked to the door, opened it. "It didn't *seem* all that cold," he said.

South of Diamond Lake the road forked, with 138 swinging to the right and heading east along the northern border of Crater Lake National Park. There was a little more traffic on this part of the road, and it would be heavier in July and August, when the tourists came.

The Fair Harbor Inn gave you complimentary coffee and doughnuts in the morning, but he hadn't wanted to deal with McLemore at that hour, so he'd stopped for breakfast on his way out of town. He stopped again at an Amoco station for a Coke around eleven and realized he hadn't had a cigarette since the one he'd taken a puff of after dinner the previous night.

He thought about that, and about having slept out on a cold night without having much felt the cold. Maybe the two phenomena went together, maybe nicotine withdrawal generated heat.

Did he want a cigarette now?

No, he decided. He didn't. He seemed to have lost the habit, as if he had walked out from under it just as he'd walked out from under all the encumbrances of his life. His apartment, his job, his car, his friends, his books, his records, his furniture, most of his clothes, he'd walked away from them all, sloughing them off like a snake shedding its skin.

The image, he decided, was an apt one. He was walking

away from all the parts of himself that he had outgrown. Somehow, evidently, he had outgrown the need for tobacco, because God knew he'd never had the intention of quitting. He hadn't quit. Quitting had simply happened to him.

And the night in the woods?

Maybe McLemore had been wrong about the temperature. Maybe it had indeed been warmer closer to Toketee Falls. Maybe the trees, besides breaking the wind, had served to hold in the heat from the campfire.

One of these nights he'd have to try it again, and see what happened.

But not that night. Diamond Lake Junction wasn't much more than a crossroads, but there were a couple of motels positioned to catch tourists en route to Crater Lake. He stayed in one that got WTBS on cable, and he watched the Braves shut out the Dodgers in L.A. During commercials he kept looking at the map, and in the morning he looked at it again. He could go north on US 97 toward Bend, or he could go south to Klamath Falls. He looked at the map, and he tried to calculate the best route to, well, to wherever he was going.

His mind kept juggling possibilities. Klamath Falls was closer, but from Bend he could proceed more directly east. Then too, the first dot on the map south of Diamond Lake Junction was forty miles away, while if he headed north there were towns spaced at fairly frequent intervals. On the other hand, he'd probably find places to stay whether or not there were dots on the map, and he could always sleep in the woods again and find out if he froze to death this time. On the other hand—

North.

Not a voice in his head this time, but something close to it. Counsel from some source within or without him. *Go north,* it gave him to understand. *Don't work things out, don't try to think your way through it. Just listen, and you'll always know where to go.*

He hadn't shaved since leaving Roseburg, which seemed to indicate that he was growing his beard back. Now, after the better part of a week, there was enough there to trim up a little. He didn't like the way it felt on his neck, and he didn't like the way the whiskers grew almost to his eyes.

He lathered his neck and shaved it, and he shaved around his cheekbones, and then he said the hell with it and shaved the rest of it, too.

He seemed to have given up *deciding* things, he realized. It looked as though the only way for him to find out what he was going to do was to wait and see what he did.

Earlier he'd had remarkably good weather. It had rained some since he left Roseburg, but never while he was out in it. It rained evenings while he was inside, and the other day he'd waited out a brief downpour in a service station, but he'd managed the trick of getting across the Cascades without once getting caught in the rain. Rain was still a possibility on this side of the mountains—he was a long ways yet from the state's eastern desert—but it was less likely, and it wasn't something he had to worry about this particular day.

Because the weather was perfect, with the sun bright and warm in a startlingly blue sky, and only a few puffs of cloud high overhead. He walked along, keeping a fairly brisk pace with no effort, the pack riding easily on his shoulders.

Two hours out of Diamond Lake Junction, and perhaps that many miles past a clutch of houses and stores called Beaver Marsh, he heard a horn sound on the other side of the road. He turned to see a dark blue Datsun pickup, the window rolled down on the driver's side and a man's face looking at him. The man was motioning for him to come over.

There was no traffic in either direction. He crossed the road, and the fellow said, "Hey, hop in. Toss your gear in the back and come on around."

"Thanks," he said, "but I'm walking."

"Well, I can see that, hoss. If you was driving, I wouldn't have stopped for you."

"I appreciate it," he said. "But I don't really want a ride."

"Something wrong with my truck?"

"Not that I can see. I'm just out for a walk, that's all."

The fellow scratched his head. He looked to be in his late twenties, with a lot of strawberry blond hair and an inch-wide strip of beard the same color running down along the edge of the jawline. His upper lip was shaved clean, as were his cheeks and neck. He was thick in the chest and big in the arms, and he had a tattoo on his left forearm showing a spider in its web. He was wearing an Olympia Beer gimme cap and a red T-shirt with nothing written on it.

He said, "Just out for a walk."

"That's right."

"I always figure why walk when you can ride, but you can suit yourself, I guess. Where you headed?"

"East."

The fellow grinned, showing crooked teeth. "Well, shit," he said. "Where you're goin's north."

"I know. I'm going north as far as Bend, and then—"

"You're walking to *Bend?*"

"That's right."

"You're kidding. That must be eighty fucking miles!"

"More like seventy, I think."

"Seventy miles. You're planning on walking seventy miles?"

"Not all today."

"Not all today. Well, shit, I just hope not. Where'd you come from?"

"Diamond Lake Junction."

"Just down the road? You live there?"

"No, I stayed there last night. I live in Roseburg."

"You mean to say you walked all the way from Roseburg? You know what you did, hoss? You walked across a fucking mountain range." He snorted. "I never heard of anybody doing that before. And I sure as shit never heard of anybody walking to Bend."

"Well—"

"How far you planning to go today?"

"That depends. Maybe all the way to Crescent, maybe just to where the cutoff to Eugene is."

"That's 58, runs to Eugene. Hop in and I'll run you to Crescent. Not that there's anything in Crescent. Hell, I'll run you clear to Bend, save you three or four days if you want. That's where I'm headed."

"Thanks, but—"

The fellow squinted, focusing pale blue eyes at Guthrie. "You got a real thing about walking," he said. "Don't you?"

"I guess I do."

"Say it was raining. You'd take a ride then, wouldn't you?"

"I don't know," he said honestly. "I don't think so, but I can't really say for sure."

"Might depend how hard it was coming down."

"It might."

"Well, hell, I won't keep you. You got a lot of ground to cover. I got to go to Bend, take care of my business, then turn the truck around and go back home to Klamath. Maybe I'll see you again on the way back."

"Give a honk if you do."

60

"Well, I'll do that."

"And thanks for the offer. It was decent of you."

He waited while some cars passed, then crossed to the other side of the road. The fellow in the truck pulled off the shoulder onto the road, honked twice, and headed off to the north.

FIVE

Walking to Bend, Jody Ledbetter thought. Walked across from Roseburg, and now he was walking to Bend. You met all kinds and sooner or later you heard every damn thing, but whoever heard of anybody walking from Roseburg to Bend?

And he'd said he was going east. Going to Bend first, and then going east.

East where? East to the Idaho line, say? Or east to Chicago?

Nice enough sort of a dude. Course there was a minute there when he'd thought the guy was turning him down because either Jody or the truck wasn't good enough for him, but fortunately that little misunderstanding hadn't blown up into anything. No, he was an okay-seeming guy, and you didn't get the feeling he was crazy. A lot of the people you ran into these days tended to be on the weird side, and it wouldn't make any difference if they told you they were walking to Chicago or flying to Paris. But this dude looked okay and sounded okay. The only thing crazy about him was what he was doing.

And how crazy was that? The dude was going to Bend, and then from Bend he was going someplace else. Jody, on the other hand, was also going to Bend, and from there he was going right back where he started from.

And it wasn't as though there was anything that sensational to get back to in Klamath Falls. Lumber was bad and farming was worse, which didn't leave a whole lot, so he wasn't exactly living in the middle of the land of opportunity. What he was living in the middle of was a trailer, and a hell of a messy one at that, messier ever since Carlene had gone back to her mother, but not all that neat before she left, as far as that went. Seventy miles was a long way to walk just to get to Bend, but two hundred and seventy miles was a long way to drive, and that's what the round trip amounted to, and when he was done he'd be back in Klamath Falls.

Well, shit.

There was a Circle K up ahead and he braked and downshifted and pulled in. He had plenty of gas but he was dry even if the truck wasn't. He went back to the cooler and started to pull a couple of cans of Coors loose from the plastic webbing, then changed his mind and grabbed the whole six-pack.

The kid at the counter said, "I think we got Olympia."

"Say what?"

"Olympia. I think we got some in the cooler. You're wearing an Olympia cap."

"Well, shit," Jody said. "I got a John Deere cap home. If I was wearing that would you try an' sell me a tractor?"

He got back in the truck, started it up, and headed back south in the direction he'd come from.

He saw the walker a long way down the road. He waited a minute to make sure it was him, then gave a honk. The dude waved, but Jody didn't think he recognized him or the truck. Which stood to reason, because he wouldn't be expecting to see Jody so soon; a Lear jet couldn't have made it to Bend and back that quickly.

He braked to a stop alongside of the dude and leaned across to roll down the window on the passenger side.

"It's a pretty warm day out and that sun's startin' to cook some," he said, "and I was thinking you might could use a beer about now." He handed a can of Coors through the window. "You do drink the stuff, don't you?"

"I sure do, and this is the right day for it." He cracked the can, and Jody broke one open for himself, and they raised the cans aloft and drank. "Ah, that's good," he said. "I thought you said you were going to Bend."

"I did."

"What did you do, fly?"

"Didn't go yet. Decided I'd rather buy you a beer than clutter up the back of the truck with machine parts."

"That what you were going to Bend for?"

"More or less. This farmer outside of Klamath's looking to save on energy by generating his own electricity with a windmill. Well, I guess it makes sense, you get all that damn wind and you might as well use it. Me an' my brother are doing the work for him, and there's a gear assembly we need, and the closest one we can run down is in Bend." He threw the door open, climbed down with his beer in tow. "Exciting way to spend a Saturday, huh?"

"Working with windmills sounds interesting."

"Does it? I guess."

"This stuff goes down easy. You know, I can't believe you drove back here just to bring me a beer."

"That right? I got to tell you, hoss, I can't believe it myself. I can't even believe I stopped to give you a ride first shot out of the box. I don't hardly never stop for people I don't know, and I sure don't stop if they aren't even hitching, and I definitely don't when they're all to hell and gone on the other side of the road. Anybody walks facing oncoming traffic, he's not looking for a ride, he's out for a walk, right?"

"Generally, yeah."

"So why'd I stop? Crazy, I guess. Though not a whole lot crazier than a man who sets out to walk to Chicago."

"Who said anything about Chicago?"

"Nobody, I don't guess. Where are you headed? After Bend, I mean."

"I don't know yet."

"You said east."

"That's as much as I know."

"Guess you take it as it comes."

"Pretty much, yeah."

"You mind a personal question? Are you by any chance Jewish?"

"No. Why?"

"I didn't really think so. I was thinking today's Saturday, and I know there's some Jewish people won't ride in a car on their Sabbath. But if that was it you'd say that, you wouldn't come up with a whole story about walking from Roseburg to Bend."

"Not hardly."

"Of course not, but it was going through my mind so I thought I'd ask. The Jewish people I know, they all ride on Saturdays anyway."

"Same with the ones I know."

"Here, have another beer. Hey, go ahead, I got six and I'm not about to drink five myself. And they'd just get warm in the truck."

"Well, one more, then. Thanks."

"My name's Jody."

"Guthrie Wagner."

"Pleased to meet you, Guthrie."

"My pleasure. Say, do you smoke, by any chance?"

Jody's eyes narrowed. "Just how do you mean that?"

"Oh, no, I just meant cigarettes. See, I got a carton of cigarettes in my pack and they're no good to me."

"Why the hell not?"

"Well, it looks as though I don't smoke anymore."

"'Looks as though'? What, did your doctor make you quit or something?"

"It just happened." Guthrie shrugged. "I don't know how to explain it. I started out on this walk Monday, and I think it was the day before yesterday I noticed I wasn't smoking anymore."

"You just quit."

"I guess."

"Without trying to."

"Seems that way."

"What kind of cigarettes?"

"Camels."

"Camel filters or the real ornery kind?"

"Short and unfiltered."

"Shee. You know, my brother smokes them sometimes. He smokes the filters, but now and then he wants something lowdown and nasty." He chuckled. "Myself, I never got the habit. Tried it a couple of times and never liked it. Same thing with chewing. Only bad habits I ever tried that I didn't like, come to think of it." He underlined the remark with a long drink of beer, then added a belch for punctuation. "Excuse me, but that did feel good. I might could take them for my brother, if you got no use for 'em."

"My pleasure. I'm glad to lighten the load."

And so now he was driving north again with a full carton and an unopened pack of unfiltered Camels on the seat next to him. Was that why he'd stopped to offer Guthrie a ride, and why he'd gone back with the six-pack? Just so he could trade two beers for a carton and an extra pack of cigarettes?

All part of God's wondrous plan, he thought, and praise the Lord and pass the plate, hallelujah and amen.

When he reached the Circle K again he slowed for a moment, then stomped savagely on the gas pedal. A mile or so further down the road he braked to a stop, let a car pass him, and swung the pickup around so that he was facing south again. He drove back to the Circle K, made a left turn into their lot and parked.

He didn't have a sack, or any clothes but what he was wearing. His shoes were ankle-high work boots with heavy lug soles, well broken in and comfortable enough, but he didn't know how good they'd be for long-distance walking. Guthrie had running shoes, he'd noticed, and maybe that was what he ought to have.

Well, if he got as far as Bend, he could get some there. Odds were he'd quit before he got that far, stick out his thumb and hitch back to Klamath. Or hang in as far as Bend and get a ride back from there. But if he got to Bend and felt like keeping on with it, he could buy whatever he needed. A sack, some clothes to put in it, other shoes if it turned out he needed them.

Of course, all this was assuming Guthrie was willing for him to come along. A man sets out to walk across the country all by himself, it stands to reason he wants to *be* all by himself. The dude had been friendly enough, but it was no particular strain to be friendly when you knew you were going to be shut of a person in another five minutes.

So there was no point calling until Guthrie showed up.

There were two beers left. He cracked one of them and sat in the truck watching the road, sipping the beer slowly, nursing it along. When Guthrie finally came into view he trotted across the road to intercept him.

"Me again," he said. "I got one beer left if you think you can handle it."

"I'm afraid two's my limit for now."

"Yeah, well, I'm having trouble finishing my third, far as that goes. I see you're wearing your hat."

"The sun's pretty warm."

"That one of those hats you can wet on a real hot day?"

"Supposed to be. It hasn't been hot enough yet for me to find out."

"Well, you stay with it, it likely will be. Say, Guthrie?" He looked away as he spoke. "I was wonderin' if you could stand some company for a spell."

"What do you mean?"

"Well, see, I was thinking about walking along with you."

"To Bend?"

"Well, I don't know as I'd stick it that far. I was never one to walk if I could ride or stand if I could sit. Or sit if I could lay down, far as that goes. But I got to tell you, I been tryin' to drive away from you and not havin' too much success with it. You got any objection to me taggin' along? If either of us don't like it, well, all they got to do is say so and we can go our separate ways."

Guthrie didn't say anything at first. Well, shit, Jody thought. He's trying to figure out how to say no and be polite about it.

But he said, "Yeah, I'd like that, Jody."

"You mean it?"

"But don't you have to buy a gearbox in Bend? And what are you going to do about your truck?"

"Sort of a gear assembly. What am I gonna do about the truck? If I got enough change I'm gonna make a phone call." He rooted in his pocket, came up with a handful of silver. "Won't take a minute," he said, and crossed the road to the Circle K. There was a pay phone just to the left of the doorway.

He made his call and when his sister-in-law answered he said, "Patty, let me talk to Linc, if you please." He waited, leaning a shoulder against the brick wall. When his brother picked up he said, "Bud, there's a Circle K on 97 about midway between Beaver Marsh and Chemult. You know where I'm talking about?"

"What did she do, the carburetor flood out on you again?"

"No, she's running fine," he said. "Bud, what I'm gonna do, I'm leaving the truck right here at the Circle K. Just listen to me, will you? I got something I got to do, I'll be gone for a while. And hey, I didn't get up to Bend so I didn't pick up that gear assembly and shit." He held the receiver at arm's length and closed his eyes, shutting out his brother's words.

Then he said, "Look, Bud, I'm telling you where the truck's at. You got keys so I'll just lock it and leave my keys in the ashtray. Oh, speaking of that, there's some cigarettes for you. Camels, a carton and an odd pack. And I'm hanging onto the money for the windmill parts, so that's whatever it is, three hundred fifty dollars I owe you."

He rolled his eyes skyward and listened to his brother's response.

"Well, Bud," he said, "all I can say is that's how it is. You know where the truck is, and you can pick it up or not, and what it comes down to, I guess, is fuck you. Nothing personal and all, but fuck you, hoss."

He hung up and walked over to the truck. Guthrie had crossed the road to stand in the Datsun's shade. "One thing," Jody said, "is if a person wants to pick up and go away, they can't stop you."

"Damn straight."

He dropped his keys in the ashtray and closed it, left the unopened beer on the seat with the cigarettes, chucked the open beer into the brush at the edge of the parking lot. He rolled up the windows, locked the doors, ran a hand through his mop of bright hair and replaced his cap.

"Hard to believe that's all there is to it," he said. "I feel like I used to feel in high school, right before a football game. All pumped up. You ready to go?"

"Whenever you are."

"Then let's do it. But look, you're the expert, you know what I mean? You're the one walked over the mountains. Tell me if there's something I'm doing wrong, because I don't know a whole hell of a lot about walking."

"It's pretty simple," Guthrie told him. "The main thing is you have to remember to alternate feet."

"Left right left right."

"That's the idea."

"Well, I'll concentrate on it," Jody said. "By an' by, I might could get the hang of it."

SIX

In Chicago, the bus terminal in the Loop had coin-access cubicles in the restrooms where you could take a sponge bath, freshen up, and change your clothes. When Sara emerged from the ladies' room Thom was waiting for her. Downstairs, she sat with their suitcases while he picked out a couple of paperback science fiction novels. He had already read fifty pages of one when it was time to board their bus for Salt Lake City.

They sat together four seats in back of the driver. She'd given Thom the window seat. Across the aisle, a very thin man with a sallow complexion was dosing himself with cough medicine. He had the whole seat to himself. Directly in front of him, a middle-aged couple sat holding hands. Thom looked out the window until the bus had left city traffic for the Stevenson Expressway. Then he returned to his book.

Sara sat with her eyes closed most of the time. She slept some, but it was difficult to tell where consciousness left off and sleep began. Her sleep was light and dream-ridden, her conscious periods hazy and dreamlike. Movies revealed themselves to her mind's eye. Snatches of speech sounded

71

in her mind. Sometimes it was of a piece with what she was seeing, sometimes not.

South and west of Joliet the bus left Route 55 for Interstate 80, the road it would stay with clear through to Salt Lake City—and, after she and Thom left it, all the way on to San Francisco. They crossed into Iowa at Davenport, and Thom nudged her awake as they moved onto the bridge across the Mississippi. She looked out the window. Her field of vision was too narrow to show her much, but when she sat back and closed her eyes she saw the entire river, from its headwaters at Lake Itasca to its delta at New Orleans. She could see, in one panoramic view, the whole great river through all its history—paddle-wheelers, Indians in war canoes, Huck and Jim on a raft, mills and factories spilling chemicals into the water, jet contrails overhead. People battling the rising waters, stacking sand-bags to stop a flood. Railroad bridges, bridges for cars. Ox-drawn prairie schooners crossing on ferries. Eyes closed, her field of vision was so great that it could encompass all the river's time and space without any shrinkage or loss of detail, and it was all in flux, all in motion, all evolving not before but behind her eyes—

"I wish you could see this," he said.

"Oh, Thommy," she said, and clutched his arm. "Oh, if you could see what I see—" He wanted to know what she meant and she told him about it, described what she saw and heard and sensed and felt and knew of the river.

He was in awe. "You see all that? How does it all fit at once?"

She took his book from him, pointed at the page he was reading. "How big a picture would you need to hold everything on this page?"

"A pretty big one," he allowed, but he still couldn't comprehend how she saw what she saw, and she didn't know how to get it across to him.

"But it's wonderful," she said. "I never knew what a river was."

"You didn't?"

"Well, what's a river, Thom?"

"Water going someplace, I guess. In a straight line, except sometimes they're not straight, they meander. Bigger than a creek or a stream, and moving fast enough so there's a current, and I think it has to be fresh water—"

"That's a definition," she said. "That's how you look at a body of water and decide whether or not it's a river, by whether or not it fits certain standards. But what's the river?"

"What you just said. A body of water that fits certain what-you-said. Standards."

"What part is the river? The water?"

"I guess."

"But it's only in the river for a while. It flows in from some other stream and flows out into the Gulf of Mexico. There's always new water coming in and old water flowing out. So what's the river? The land on either side is the bank of the river, the mud underneath is the bottom of the river, but what's the river?"

"I don't know."

"I think the river's a certain time and space," she said, "and sooner or later every drop of water in the world gets to take its turn being a part of it. And then they go somewhere else. This drop goes to the Gulf, and this drop evaporates, and somebody drinks this drop—"

"And this little drop goes to market, and this little drop stays home—"

"A little of the world's energy is gathered up into a river," she said, "and the water makes sure it's never empty."

* * *

73

Iowa City and Des Moines. Rolling hills in eastern Iowa, then the plains in the west. The highway was straight as a die west of Des Moines, and almost perfectly flat. They crossed the Missouri into Nebraska and stopped at the terminal in Omaha. They had covered almost five hundred miles since leaving Chicago ten hours ago.

They had half an hour to eat before they had to reboard the bus. There was a restaurant in the bus terminal but it didn't feel right energetically, and when she closed her eyes she saw slivers of broken glass. The people in the booths and at the counter had the air of the hunt about them, as if they were all at once predators and victims.

She took Thom's arm and led him back into the terminal and across the lobby to the Farnam Avenue entrance. On the sidewalk, she turned without hesitation to the right and walked half a block, where they found a brightly-lit cafeteria between two stores that had closed for the weekend.

The place was clean, the prices reasonable, and the food decent. An old man with wispy white hair smiled shyly from an adjacent table, then went back to his newspaper crossword puzzle. On the sound system, an orchestra was playing "Moonlight in Vermont."

He went back for a second glass of milk. She sipped her tea. He said, "Mom, you knew this place'd be here, didn't you?"

"I knew something would be here."

"Did you like see a picture of it?"

"Not exactly. Let me try to remember." She closed her eyes. "I sort of saw us sitting at a table."

"You saw us?"

"I saw the idea of us," she said. "And I walked to where that would be, and here we are."

"This is pretty weird, Mom."

"No kidding."

74

"Were those Indians in the bus station? Over by the lockers?"

"They certainly looked like Indians."

"Is this the West?"

"Well, I think so. We're west of the Mississippi. We just crossed the Missouri. Of course you don't have to be this far west to see Indians. There are Indians all over the country."

"Indians. Can I have a horse?"

"A seeing-eye horse."

He started to giggle and was quickly convulsed with laughter. "Oh, you're bad," he said. "You're really bad."

They were back in their same seats when the bus pulled out of Omaha. The thin man with the cough syrup had gone, and in his place sat a light-skinned black woman wearing a scarf. The middle-aged handholders were gone, too, and a young soldier in uniform sprawled over both the seats they had occupied.

They crossed the Platte, skirted Lincoln, crossed the Platte again at Grand Island, hugged its northern bank for a hundred miles and crossed it a third time, following the south fork and then Lodgepole Creek into southern Wyoming. They had another meal break in Cheyenne, let off passengers, took on passengers, and rolled on west through Laramie and Rock Springs.

It was dark as they rode through Wyoming. But she could see. They reached the foothills of the Rockies as they neared Laramie, and she saw the mountains and felt the magnetic power of them. She saw bighorn sheep, sure-footed on the sheer slopes, the rutting males clashing head-on in ritual combat, saw mountain goats white and silent, gazing motionless over the valleys. She saw the mountains forming, willing their way upward out of the earth's convexity, stretching like plant growth toward the sun. She saw mountain men, fur-clad hunters and trappers as solitary as bears or badgers. She saw prospectors, she saw hard-rock miners from Wales and Cornwall. She saw the buffalo dying, carcasses rotting in the sun, and she saw the land sliced by rail lines and cordoned off with fences. She saw Stone Age people who'd lived in the mountains and left not a trace of their presence, and she saw Indian wars, and she saw ranch houses with big dish TV antennas and solar-powered generators.

Thom slept at her side. He woke up once outside of Rock Springs and walked up the aisle to the lavatory, then returned smelling faintly of liquid soap and slipped back effortlessly into sleep. She dozed off herself, and when she opened her eyes he was already awake and they were coming into Salt Lake City.

They had almost four hours before their bus left for Portland. They checked their bags and had breakfast, then followed signs to Temple Square, where they joined a group for a guided tour of Mormon headquarters. You couldn't enter the temple unless you were a paid-up tithing Mormon, but there was a great deal else to see, and just by standing in front of the temple she could sense the spiritual balance within it.

After the tour he said, "Mom, your eyes are getting worse, aren't they?"

"How can you tell?"

"I don't know, I just can. They are, aren't they?"

"The tunnel's narrowing. And there's a little less light at the end of it."

"But you're not afraid?"

"Oh, a little bit, Thommy. The idea of not having my eyes to see with is scary. I have to keep reminding myself that I'm getting more vision than I'm giving up."

"Why can't you have both?"

"Some people probably can. But in my case I evidently have to let go of one in order to open up to the other."

"And the way you can see now is better?"

"It's better for me. At least it is right now."

"That was great the way we found that place in Omaha. Can you see where we're going to have lunch?"

"We just had breakfast."

"Well, aren't we going to eat before our bus leaves?"

"I suppose so."

"Well—"

"How does Chinese sound?"

"Is that what you see when you close your eyes?"

"Nope. It just occurred to me we haven't had any in a while."

"You know where there's a Chinese restaurant?"

"No, but somebody else probably does. Sometimes you let your inner vision guide you, sport, and other times you ask a cop for directions."

On the bus he said, "What happens when we get to Portland?"

"I think we get a room for the night. We could probably both stand a night's sleep in a real bed. And I know we could use a bath, and we're not likely to smell all that sweeter twelve hours from now."

"Is that when we get into Portland?"

"He said fourteen hours. I forget where we stop. Boise, but there was someplace else."

"I wasn't paying attention. Mom? Besides a hotel room, what else do we do in Portland?"

"Get on another bus."

"We're not staying in Portland?"

"Just long enough to sleep and shower. And eat—God knows I wouldn't dream of making you miss a meal."

"Those spareribs were good."

"I'm glad you approved."

"So was the lo mein. Do you suppose the Chinese people at the restaurant were Mormons?"

"I haven't the faintest idea."

"Aha, something you don't know. *Are* there any Chinese Mormons?"

"Didn't they say so on the tour? There must be, they send missionaries everywhere. Why?"

"I just wondered. Where do we go from Portland?"

"I don't know."

"You don't *know*?"

"Not yet," she said. "But I will."

In downtown Portland they shared a fifteen-dollar room at the Jack London Hotel on South Alder. The bathroom was down the hall. They took turns soaking in the huge footed tub, then got into their beds. He fell asleep right away. She lay awake for a while listening to the man next door, whose cough sounded serious, and possibly tubercular.

After breakfast they stopped at a Salvation Army store, where Thom noticed a used paperback of *Martin Eden* on a table outside. He wanted to buy it because they'd just stayed at the Jack London. "It's good we didn't stay at the James Joyce," she said. "You're a little young for *Finnegans Wake*."

At the bus station she asked the clerk for two tickets to Bent. "There is such a place, isn't there? Or it could be Ben."

"There's Bend."

"Yes, Bend," she said. "Of course, Bend. Is there bus service there?"

"Or there's North Bend," the woman said helpfully.

"Are they close to each other?"

"You'd think they would be, but they're in different

directions altogether. Bend is south and east of here and North Bend is on the coast next to Coos Bay, if you know where that is."

She didn't, but it didn't matter. She closed her eyes for a moment, then opened them. "Is there bus service to Bend?"

"There is, but we don't go there. Trailways does, though. You know where their station is?"

She didn't, but the woman gave her directions and it wasn't far. Their timing was perfect; there was a bus leaving for Salem and Bend in forty-five minutes.

The ride to Salem took less than an hour on the Interstate. There half the passengers got off and a handful got on, and they headed south and east on Route 22. The road wound and climbed its way through the mountains, and the bus stopped at every little town it came to, and it took all day to get to Bend.

When they arrived her inner vision was perfect. She knew just where to go, and without hesitation she led Thom through the little bus station to the street, where a man with a visored cap was sitting on the fender of a rusted-out Ford and reading a newspaper. He asked if she needed a taxi and when she nodded he took their suitcases and put them in the trunk.

She asked if there was a motel called the Pine Haven. There was, he told her—just south of town on 97. The Pine Haven turned out to be a U-shaped one-story structure of twenty-seven units. It had modest rates, a small pool, cable TV, a 7-Eleven next door and a Wendy's across the road. It also had a vacancy, and they took it.

"This is neat," he said. "They even got HBO. I wonder what's on."

"Something wonderful, I'm sure."

"Hope so. That pool looks pretty good. Did I bring a swimming suit?"

79

"Wear a pair of shorts."

"Underwear?"

"No, regular shorts. I know I packed your blue shorts, and they're polysomething, they'll dry overnight."

"Won't it look weird?"

"Do you really care?"

He thought it over. "Not a humungous amount," he decided, and threw himself down on a chair. "We're here, huh? This is it?"

"We're here and this is it."

"We weren't supposed to go to North Bend instead?"

"No."

" 'This is the place.' Isn't that what Brigham Young said when he saw Salt Lake City?"

"His very words."

"When was that they told us?"

"I forget. Eighteen-something."

"No, I mean when was it we were there. Yesterday? No. Wait a minute. We were in Portland last night, yeah, yesterday morning we were in Salt Lake City. 'This is the place.' And he wasn't even going blind."

"Well, different strokes for different folks."

"Different visions for different decisions. Hey! Did you hear that?"

"Not bad."

" 'Different visions for different decisions.' I like that."

"Your cleverness is matched only by your modesty, sport."

"Thanks," he said. He puffed his cheeks, blew out air, slapped his palms together and then against his thighs to simulate hoofbeats. "Now what?"

"Take a swim, if you feel like it."

"Yeah, but what I mean is now that we're here, now what?"

"They're very close."

"Who are?"

"Our friends."

"We've got friends coming?"

"Uh-huh."

"Who are they?"

"Two men. One is taller, with dark hair. The shorter one has a beard."

"And they're coming here? Do they know us?"

"Not yet."

"Okay."

She looked at him. His image dimmed for a moment before her eyes, then sharpened. She said, "Thom, I got the name of the town. I missed it by a letter, but I got it. And I knew about the motel."

"And the cafeteria in where was it, Omaha. You're doing great, Mom."

"You don't think I'm crazy?"

"No, of course not."

"Okay. I don't think so either, but sometimes I'm not as sure as I am the rest of the time. What's happening is there are two men coming to Bend. They're on their way now, and they should get here soon. I don't know exactly when. Maybe tomorrow, maybe not for another day or two."

"How will we know when they're here?"

"We'll know."

"Okay. You mean *you*'ll know, and you'll tell me."

"Right."

"Meanwhile I'm going swimming. They won't think I'm a jerk if they see me swimming in regular shorts?"

"They'll think you're a man who makes his own rules. Thommy? I should have thought to pack your bathing suit. We'll get one for you tomorrow or the next day."

* * *

The following day she sat out by the pool gazing down the highway. He spent part of the time swimming, part of it reading and watching television. At mealtimes she sent him over to Wendy's and he brought back food for the two of them.

Her eyesight was almost gone. It seemed to her as though she saw demonstrably less every time she opened her eyes, and that what little sight she had left was something she was holding onto by a thread. On the one hand she had to hold onto it, and at the same time she had to let go, it would be such a relief to let go.

With her eyes closed she kept seeing them, walking up the road, one with his hands plunged into his pockets, one talking, gesturing broadly with his hands.

Oh, she saw so *much*.

She waited, but they didn't come that day. The next morning she woke up knowing they'd be there soon, and she sent Thom across to Wendy's and waited for him in a chair beside the pool. They ate breakfast there, and then he went in to watch a Clint Eastwood movie on HBO.

After lunch she had him sit out at the pool with her. "They'll be coming very soon," she said. "I want you to watch the road for me. They'll be walking on this side of the highway, and they'll be coming from the right."

"Two men."

"The taller one is wearing a knapsack."

"What about the shorter one?"

"He isn't carrying anything."

"Well, he's got the beard. I guess that's enough."

"Just watch for them, will you?"

"Is it okay if I read at the same time? I'll look up every few minutes."

They sat together, and then she must have dozed off, and something stirred within her just as he touched her arm and said, "Mom?"

She opened her eyes. For a moment she saw nothing, nothing at all, and she thought that the last of her eyesight had gone, but then it came back, just the narrowest beam of sight, and she looked as if down a very long tunnel and saw two men at its very end.

"Go to them," she told him. "Tell them your mother wants to see them."

"Just tell them that?"

"Go."

She stood up. It was a tricky business walking; she had to look down to see her feet, then had to raise her eyes to see what was ahead of her. It was easier, really, to close her eyes and trust her feet to find their footing.

She walked down the blacktop driveway to where the three of them waited. And yes, the tall man had a pack on his back, and yes, the shorter man had a beard, but there was more red in the yellow than she had seen in her mind's eye.

And there was such a rich aura around them, and such a good energy coming from them.

"We've been waiting for you," she said. They looked at her, not sure what she meant, and she said, "I'm Sara Duskin. This is my son, his name is Thom."

They introduced themselves. Guthrie Wagner and Jody Ledbetter.

"I'm so pleased to meet you," she said, and held out a hand to each of them. They took her hands, and a current ran through the three of them, so strong that she almost gasped. And they could feel it, too, and she looked at each of them, looked at them in turn because her field of vision could not encompass both of them at once.

83

"Oh, yes, yes," she said, holding tight with her hands and letting go deep inside herself, letting the last of her eyesight slip away forever.

And then she saw:

Saw Guthrie learning to ride a two-wheeler, biting his lip in concentration, his father steadying the frame of the bike with one hand and running along beside him, saying Yes, you're doing it, you've got it now, don't quit, yes—

Saw Jody in the womb, impatient to be born, a breech presentation trying to thrust himself ass-first into the world, and the obstetrician trying to reposition him, big hands working to shift him, and she picked up the thought of No no no, damn you, no, let me do it my way—

Saw Guthrie at Boy Scout camp, his khaki shorts down around his knees, and an older boy playing with his penis, and Guthrie wanting him to stop, but not knowing how to make him stop—

Saw Jody fighting with his older brother, and losing, and brooding over it, and coming back the next day and blind-siding his brother with an axe handle, and getting punished for it, getting the strap from their father and locked for hours in a musty attic room to think about it—

Saw Guthrie on his wedding day, standing up stiff and scared in a suit, wondering who this stranger was beside him, and then the divorce, and wondering where it had all come from, and where it had all gone—

Saw Jody in a tattoo parlor in Seattle, just out of high school, drunk, proud, excited, scared to be scared, watching the spider in its web taking form upon his arm—

Saw Guthrie at his father's funeral, dry-eyed—

Saw Jody at his mother's grave—

Oh, she saw their whole *lives*! She saw into them, she saw all the joy and all the pain and all the grief, all the rich human beauty. "Oh," she said, her gray sightless eyes open now, her face radiant. "Oh," she said, her heart wide open now, warmth flooding her chest, tears streaming from her eyes. "Oh, my friends," she said, tightening her grip on their hands, transported by waves of her love for them, of their love for her, of all the love that was suddenly so abundant in the universe.

"Oh, my friends," she said. "My *friends!*"

SEVEN

When he got off the phone Mark Adlon went to the bar in the sun room and poured two fingers of Dewar's Ancestor into a highball glass. He took it and a matching empty glass into the kitchen, where he filled both glasses with ice cubes from the automatic ice dispenser built into the refrigerator door. He topped up the scotch with spring water and filled the other glass with lemonade, then carried them both out onto the patio where his wife was reading the latest issue of *People* magazine.

"Oh, thank you, dear," she said.

"It's plain lemonade, but if you want a little vodka in it—"

"No, I'd rather have plain."

"That's what I thought."

He took a seat alongside her, set down his drink on the glass-topped coffee table, and looked out across the expanse of lawn.

"The days are really getting long," he said.

She nodded. "Just two weeks to Midsummer Eve."

"I never understood that," he said. "If it's the first day of summer, why call it Midsummer Eve? Midsummer Eve ought to come in the middle of summer, shouldn't it?"

"You would think so, wouldn't you?"

Marilee Adlon was three years older than her husband, although they had decided, around the time they moved from Topeka to Overland Park, to reduce her official age by five years. People made certain assumptions about a couple when the wife was older, they had agreed, and simply by revising her age they could avoid these assumptions.

Certainly she had no trouble passing for the forty years she admitted to. In high heels she was almost exactly the same height as her husband. Her face was a long oval, her eyes somewhere between brown and green. Her hair, a rich brown with red highlights, was shorter than she usually wore it; she'd been to the beauty parlor during the past week, and had had a styling and a permanent.

She touched her hair now, patting it with the fingertips of both hands. "I think I'm getting used to this," she said. "Do you like it?"

"It looks fine."

"What about the color?"

"What about it? Isn't it the same?"

"Good, that means the difference isn't all that noticeable. Adrian wanted to lighten it by what he called a quarter of a shade, whatever that means. It looks *much* lighter to me, but if it doesn't to you—"

"I'm not the most observant man in the world, but *I* didn't notice any change. I don't see it now, not even after you've called it to my attention."

"Well, I'm glad to hear that. I don't mind having it lighter so long as nobody notices. Now isn't that ridiculous, what I just said? But you know what I mean."

"Sure."

She picked up her glass and took a long sip of lemonade,

making a sound of appreciation. "That *is* good," she said. "I'm glad you didn't put vodka in it, it wouldn't taste as good." She put the glass down. "I'd probably be completely gray by now," she said.

"You think so?"

"Oh, I do. When I've been a while between touch-ups, and I get a look at the roots, all I see is gray. I'll tell you, I'm glad I never let it get started."

Her hair had started to show some gray in her early thirties, and she had immediately responded by coloring it. Since then, her hair color had gradually grown lighter than its original shade—this was not the first time that Adrian or one of his predecessors had worked his subtle magic —and, while her hair never appeared lighter from one month to the next, you had only to look at an old photograph to see how much lighter it had indeed become.

"I wonder what it would look like gray."

"You could let it grow out."

She shook her head. "No thank you. You wouldn't like it, Mark."

"I'd like it just fine however you wore it."

"That's very loyal, but you wouldn't like the look, believe me. For one thing, I'd look ten years older. Instantly, immediately."

"That would still leave you looking a couple of years younger than the calendar says you are."

"Aren't you a sweetheart," she said, putting her hand on his. "Or is there something you want?"

He laughed. "No, but there's something I hate to have to tell you. I'm going to miss Jennifer's graduation."

"Oh, that's a shame. Have you told her yet?"

"I thought I'd wait and tell her tomorrow. I wasn't absolutely certain until I spoke to Koenig just now."

"Well, you couldn't tell her now. She's out with Carole

Keller and the Parkhill girl." She sighed. "You know, I almost should have had that vodka. I'm a little jittery tonight."

"Oh?"

"Just a lot of nervous energy. I feel fidgety, that's why I can't keep my hands off my hair."

"I thought you were just getting used to it."

"Yes, but I also can't seem to keep my hands still."

"Is that right," he said. "You say Jennifer's out for the evening?"

"Well, I don't think she'll be too late. School tomorrow, of course."

"And Luke's out, his car's gone."

"I think he said something about the baseball game."

"Yes, that's right, he told me he was going to watch the Royals. Well, *I* know why you're so fidgety."

"Oh, really?"

"Yes, really. And Dr. Adlon knows just the treatment you need."

"Oh, my," she said. "So early in the evening?"

"We're all alone."

"So we are. Of course the phone could ring."

"Not if I took it off the hook."

"What a clever man you are," she said.

Upstairs they undressed quickly and in silence. She left the drapes undrawn—there were woods behind the house, and no one could see into any of the bedroom windows. She got into bed and he joined her, taking her in his arms. For a long moment he held her, feeling the length of her body against his.

Then she lay on her back and closed her eyes. His hand touched her cheek and swept slowly down over her body, cupping the roundness of her breast, brushing the flat plain of her stomach and the slight convexity of her abdomen. When his fingers reached her pubic mound she opened her thighs, and he moved to crouch between them.

He touched her, first with his breath alone, then with his mouth. This was what she liked, and as always he found himself wholly in synch with her inner rhythms, automatically varying the pace and intensity of his lovemaking, speeding up, slowing down, speeding up again, teasing a little, holding her off, and then, finally, taking her all the way.

Her climax was powerful, a long rolling wave of passion to which she utterly gave herself over, swinging her head from side to side, crying out, sobbing, her whole body bucking and twitching beneath him. It was men who were always seeking sex, he thought, but it was women who got so much more out of it, their comings a whole artillery barrage in contrast to the single staccato bark of a male orgasm. He continued his ministrations, coaxing the last little spasm of fulfillment out of her, then moved at last to lie down beside her with her taste dark and rich in his mouth and her scent filling the whole room.

"God," she said.

"See? I knew what you needed."

"You always do." Then, "Are you all right?"

"I'm fine."

He had gotten an erection shortly after he had placed his mouth upon her. This happened some of the time, but not always, and it did not seem to be in any way related to the pleasure either of them took in the act. He had remained erect throughout, and was so now, but he felt under no obligation to do anything about it. He lay there until it had softened and shrank. By then she was asleep. He covered her with the sheet, got dressed, and went downstairs.

* * *

For some years now their lovemaking had always taken this form. It was the only way that gave her real pleasure, and she had once admitted that she had usually feigned her orgasms during coitus, something he had half known all along. His oral attentions to her, usually a prelude, now became their sole practice.

He sometimes wondered how she thought he found fulfillment. Perhaps she assumed he climaxed while performing upon her, either spontaneously or with manual assistance. Perhaps she suspected he masturbated afterward, or used prostitutes. Perhaps she didn't think about it. Whatever her thoughts, she kept them to herself.

She certainly wouldn't have wanted to know the truth. That his orgasms were very infrequent, and, in recent years, never accompanied by seminal ejaculation. And that he had not had intercourse in eight years.

Not since the first time he killed a woman.

It had not eluded Mark that there might be something noteworthy in the fact that his first act of murder had taken place within two months of his first real estate deal. He was reasonably self-analytical, and he thought he knew why the one development in his life had precipitated the other. It was not, to be sure, that purchasing that first duplex north of Gage Park had somehow corrupted him, that it had instilled a desire not previously present. On the contrary, the hunger to kill women, to find release and fulfillment in their death, seemed to him to have been part of his sexual makeup all his life.

His earliest fantasies, before he'd had the wit to accompany them with masturbation, had involved the torture and death of helpless female partners. When he did discover masturbation, violent and murderous fantasies always played a part; when he tried to perform the act without the fantasies, out of moral revulsion for them, either he was not able to climax at all or his orgasm was weak and unsatisfying.

He had never considered acting on his fantasies. As far as he was concerned, they were a perversion forever confined to his inner life, taking place exclusively in the theater of his mind. No one would ever know the truth about his sexual impulses, and whatever secret shame he suffered would be their only consequence.

He had had fears at one point that he might crave to act them out. While he was not a virgin when he married Marilee, his experience was minimal; oral sex from prostitutes, a brief clothes-pushed-aside coupling with a girl he'd dated a few times, both of them drunk the night it happened. On none of those occasions had he had any urge to injure his partner, and when he met and fell in love with Marilee he found such urges inconceivable. He loved her, he revered her, and the thought of her suffering any injury whatsoever, let alone at his hands, was unendurable.

Making love to Marilee, he found himself using his fantasies almost from the beginning. They were not invariably present, but without them he sometimes had difficulty performing.

But fantasy was fantasy and reality was reality. In his mind, horrible scenarios were acted out; in his bed, he and Marilee expressed their perfect love for one another. It was at the very least ironic that his mind and body should be following two such wholly different scripts, that his children were conceived in love to the cerebral accompaniment of burnings and dismemberings, stabbings and garrotings. But he loved them none the less for it, and they brought him no less joy.

He worried about his fantasies less as time passed. Once in a while he would try to do without them, but they always returned, and he grew increasingly to take them for granted. They were mental Muzak, sometimes barely noticed on a conscious level, but the business ran less efficiently in their absence.

Of course it was his success with real estate that enabled him to turn fantasy into fact. Not that he woke up one morning and told himself, Hey, I just bought a house, I think I'll go kill a girl. But his real estate dealings empowered him, transformed him from a man floating through life, working for his father-in-law, barely scraping by, to a confident enterprising self-starter in charge of his own destiny.

He felt alive, he felt successful, he felt strong. But he also felt increasingly restless, and several nights he had left the house while Marilee and the kids were asleep, getting in the car and driving for hours over country roads around Topeka.

Then one night, itching with restlessness, he found himself driving into Kansas City. Downtown, somewhere around Central Avenue, he'd come upon a flock of black streetwalkers in wigs and hot pants, strutting on the pavement and working the cars that cruised the street.

Several times in recent years he'd gone with prostitutes, paying twenty dollars to sit in his car parked on a dark street while a girl's head bobbed in his lap.

He drove past them, circled the block, drove more slowly this time.

The girl he chose was tall, with long legs and full breasts and an implausible red wig. Skimpy royal blue hot pants were snug on her taut butt, and the tails of her clinging sky-blue blouse were tied in front to create a bare midriff. Her skin was very dark, her nail polish the color of dried blood, and her name, she told him, was Bambi.

And her price?

"Twenty dollars," she said, and sized him up. "Unless you be wanting to spend some money, and then we can go to my room and take our time."

Her room was the end unit at a hot-sheets motel. She evidently rented it by the night, because there was no charade of going to the office to register. She already had the key, and they went straight to her room.

She set a price of a hundred dollars, and he didn't bargain. It struck him that he had bought property that same week for no cash down, took title to a sixty-thousand-dollar house without parting with a dime of real money, and here he was shelling out a hundred dollars to rent a girl's flesh for—what, an hour?

She performed orally, then spread herself on the bed for him and smiled in invitation. He started to mount her and his erection softened. She grabbed and pumped with her hand, impatient, and hurt him, and he slapped her hand away. She looked at him, a measure of irritation showing on her face, and that triggered his rage, an oceanic rage that welled up out of nowhere and turned the world red.

He slapped her, his open hand catching her full force across the face. Her head snapped back. She clawed at him. He caught her wrist with one hand, bending it back, and he doubled his other hand into a fist and buried it in the pit of her stomach.

She opened her mouth to scream. He punched her in the face, hammered at her face with his fists. His cock was rock-hard, a bar of steel.

When he stopped she was unconscious, her nose broken, her mouth bleeding, her face horribly bruised. An orgasm had erupted out of him, as unexpected and unstoppable as his rage, and rivers of semen pooled on her middle.

He stood up, but he had to sit down again. He was

shaking so bad he couldn't stand, scared as he'd never been scared in his life.

For all of that, he had never before felt so utterly alive.

But what was he going to do about the girl?

She probably ought to go to the hospital. He couldn't take her there, but could he just leave her here? Suppose she'd memorized his license plate number. Even if she hadn't, she could certainly recognize him again. Of course he didn't come to Kansas City that often, and rarely at night.

Had he told her he was from Topeka? Had he, God help him, told her his name?

"I'm Bambi."

"My name's Mark."

But no last name, and there'd been no card to sign at the desk, no desk at all, no likelihood that he'd been seen or his plate number noted. All she knew was that his name was Mark and he was from Topeka and he drove a Chevy Nova—this was long before the days of the Lincoln. And she might get somebody to come looking for him, because, Christ, he'd really done a job on her, he could have killed her—

Be a lot simpler if he had, he realized. Safer, easier all around. No loose ends.

You could still do it.

His mind didn't know what to make of the thought. His body, however, responded instantly and unequivocally, his penis springing fully erect, painful in its urgency. Just moments ago he had shuddered in the most powerful climax of his life, and now he was gripped by desire greater than anything in his experience.

She had removed her sky-blue blouse. He got it from the chair where she'd hung it, felt its silky texture in his hands.

95

He got on top of her, spread her legs, thrust into her inert flesh. A low moan bubbled up through her puffy lips.

He wrapped the blouse around her throat, took an end in each hand, and drew his hands apart.

She died. He came, and felt reborn.

After the ecstasy, the horror.

First, though, the urgent need to get away, and to escape safely. He had no idea what he might have touched, but he used a towel to wipe his prints from every likely surface. The five twenty-dollar bills he'd given her were in her purse, and while he didn't think currency would hold fingerprints well, neither could he think of a compelling reason to leave them behind. He doubted that he'd left many fingerprints; the motel room was soiled and squalid, and his natural inclination had been to avoid unnecessary contact with anything in it.

He fled. He forced himself to observe the speed limit returning to Topeka, not wanting anything that might establish his presence in Kansas City that night. Back home, he drank two ounces of whiskey straight from the bottle, scrubbed himself in the shower. First thing in the morning he took the Nova through a car wash. She had been in the car, and when the boys scrubbed and vacuumed the interior, they might remove some traces of her presence.

There was a three-paragraph story the following day in the Kansas City *Star*, and no follow-up to it over the next several weeks. When a month had passed without incident he allowed himself to believe that he had gotten away with it.

It was, after all, hardly the crime of the century. A black streetwalker, beaten to death in a sordid motel room. What clues did the police have to work with? No license number, no eyewitness description of the killer, no fingerprints. He'd left his seed on her belly and in her loins, and he'd very likely left pubic hairs entwined with her own, but so, he suspected, had other of her clients. The police could tell a lot about you from that sort of physical evidence, and once they had reason to suspect you they could either clear you or tighten the ring of circumstantial evidence with blood and semen and hair, but in the absence of other clues they would have no reason to beat a path to your door.

He had killed. For no reason more rational than rage he had battered a young woman senseless. With no motive more justifiable than blood lust he had strangled her. The thought sickened him even as the memory continued, God help him, to thrill him.

Well, it would never happen again.

But of course it did.

Again and again and again. In eight years, he had killed an astonishing total of fifty-three women. Every now and then the urge would come on him, triggered by a scent or a smile or a pout or the swell of a breast or the curve of a hip. His blood would race with the need for satisfaction, and there was only one way that kind of satisfaction could be achieved.

Sometimes he fought the urge, stifling it for a greater or lesser period of time. Sometimes he gave in to it as soon as he conveniently could. He was always prudent, always kept risks to a minimum, but as soon as an appropriate victim provided herself, he took her.

He was clever about it, and he took a certain pride in his cleverness. Early on he realized that the best way to avoid detection was to keep the authorities from suspecting that his various homicides were all the work of a single killer. He read about other serial killers, and they all seemed to be wedded to some variable that stamped all their killings as having been done by the same hand. They used the same murder method, or they picked the same type of victim, or they left the same kind of diorama at the murder scene.

He purposely did things differently each time from the last. Now a knife, now a scarf, now his bare hands. An icepick, a hammer, a length of clothesline. One time the girl would be nude, another time she'd be fully clothed, and on the next occasion she might be tied up. He had a lifetime of delicious fantasies to draw upon and an imagination more than equal to the task of supplying new fantasies. Of his fifty-three episodes, no two had been quite the same.

No cute crap, though. No blood smears on the walls, no lipstick marks on the dead woman's forehead. He was not playing a game with the police. The thrill was not in tempting fate, in almost getting caught. The thrill—and God knew it was thrill enough—the thrill was in the doing.

Mrs. Minnick, whose round plumpness had inspired him in Denver, had never been at risk. He had been careful from the beginning never to select a woman whom he knew personally, or one who could be connected with him in any conceivable way. The simple act of murder was the only tie between him and his victims.

That was his rule, but he had broken it once. One afternoon he'd been showing a house in Kansas City. The prospective tenant was a divorced woman, new in town; her children were in school and she was looking at houses and apartments, and oh, she was just too delicious to resist, with thin wrists and ankles and lank blond hair and librarian's glasses and rabbity front teeth, not traditionally pretty but wonderfully desirable.

He asked her enough questions to determine that no one knew where she was. And it was still impossibly risky, because anyone in the neighborhood might have noticed her car parked in the driveway, but he weighed the risks and decided she was worth it. God, she was nice!

He picked up a heavy glass ashtray and knocked her unconscious with a series of blows to the back of the head. He used a cord from one of the floor lamps to tie her hands and feet, and gagged her with her own pantyhose. He hurried down to his own car and fetched a large screwdriver from the trunk. She was conscious by the time he got back, flopping around on the carpet like a beached fish.

He talked to her for a while, and he felt her tits through her clothes and reached up under her skirt to fondle her. Then, when he just couldn't stand it another minute, he thrust the blade of the screwdriver up one of her nostrils and into her brain.

Afterward, in the quietest part of the night, he carried her out of the house and loaded her into the trunk of her car. He drove to Crown Center and left the car at a municipal parking ramp. He took a cab back to his rental house and drove his own car home. He threw the screwdriver down a storm sewer, and he tossed the pantyhose and the lamp cord into a trash can. A day later he vacuumed the carpet where she'd flopped about and put a new cord on the lamp.

Now, while Marilee slept, he made himself a cup of tea with milk and sugar and took it to his den. He put the TV on but devoted most of his attention to the newspaper, giving the real estate listings and the financial pages a thorough review.

His daughter came home around ten-thirty. He heard her and called to her, and she came in and sat with him for a few minutes before going upstairs. After she'd kissed him and left he remembered he hadn't said anything to her about missing her graduation.

Well, he'd tell her the next day. Or leave it for Marilee to handle. Anyway, he didn't think Jennifer would be all that torn up about it. She'd get a good present, and that ought to take some of the sting out of his absence.

He put the paper aside and thought, by no means for the first time, of the clashing inconsistency of his life. He loved his wife and daughter, was indeed devoted to them, and at the very same time he was passionately addicted to the sport of killing women for pleasure. For that was what he did; he hunted them down and killed them with the same delight that some other men killed deer—not for the chase or for the venison, but for the unutterable joy of killing.

The women he preyed on were other men's wives, other men's daughters. How would he feel if someone else used Jennifer as he had used Cindi in Denver? How would he feel if some other man gazed greedily into Marilee's eyes while she died?

He forced the thoughts aside. They had come before, they would come again. He forced them aside.

And thought instead about some of the things he had done over the past eight years and some of the women he had done them to. He gave himself up to his memories and let himself be stirred by them.

A shame he hadn't had more time in Denver. She was nice, Cindi, and he would have liked taking his time with her. And yet there was something especially exciting about the speed of it. Just a couple of minutes and she was gone, almost before she knew what was happening to her.

He got up, paced back and forth across the oriental carpet. Jesus, he'd done Cindi just a week ago and he was ready to go again. Usually it was a month or more before he felt this agitated, but he felt like going out right this minute.

He wouldn't, of course. But neither would he wait a month. There was no real need to space his killings, so long as he didn't do anything to attract attention. It was not as though there was an annual bag limit for hunters. Women were not an endangered species. They were all over the place; the country was teeming with them.

The summer stretched out before him, warmly inviting. There was no reason he couldn't make himself a gift of the next three months. His business dealings would largely run themselves. At the same time, the prospect of business would justify extended absences; all he had to do was announce that he had a big deal taking shape, and he could be out of town for the whole summer without ruffling anyone's feathers. He need only call home a few times a week, and drop in once or twice to take care of business locally, and he could have the whole summer to himself.

And it was still two weeks until Midsummer Eve. His count stood at fifty-three now. By the first day of autumn, how great a string might he have?

Seventy? Eighty? A hundred?

He remembered John Randall Spears thundering at them during the real estate seminar. "If your properties yield up a positive cash flow, there is nothing in the world to prevent you from acquiring more of them. If you can own one house you can own a hundred houses, you can own a *thousand* houses. There is no limit to the amount of wealth you can create. There is no limit to the amount of property you can own!"

No limit.

EIGHT

There was a unit vacant at the Pine Haven, over near the southern tip of the U, and Guthrie and Jody took it for the night. Jody sprawled on his bed, eating Wendy's french fries and sipping a cold one from the 7-Eleven. The CNN announcer was telling of an earthquake in Guatemala, a drought-induced famine in Africa, a terrorist bombing in the north of Ireland. When they cut to a correspondent for a report on acid rain, Guthrie asked him if he minded if he turned it off.

"Hell, go right ahead," he said. "Who wants to listen to all that shit?" He yawned, scratched himself. "Get me some clothes tomorrow. Nothing like taking a good shower and putting on shorts you been wearing three days straight. Or is it four?" He yawned again. "Pick up some clothes and a sack to haul 'em in. These boots worked out better than I was afraid they might, but I'll get me some soft shoes, too, so I can change if I want. And I got to tell you, hoss, these socks are ripe."

"You didn't have to tell me."

"Already got the word, huh? Sorry about that. Sara and Thom'll need knapsacks, too, instead of those suitcases they brought. I'd think we'll be able to find whatever we need here in Bend."

"I would think so."

"Canteens for everybody, too. A little ways east of here it starts getting dry, and it might be pushing it to have two people sharing a canteen like you and I been doing. Guthrie? How you feel about all this, hoss?"

"About all what?"

"Everybody invitin' theirselves to your party."

He thought about it. At length he said, "She's special. Sara."

"Yeah. Guthrie, she don't *appear* blind. When she looks at you—"

"I know."

"The boy's all right, too. Thom. Thom with an H—he's right particular about that H."

"A blind woman and a boy."

"Just what you needed, right? You figure they'll slow us down much?"

"Well, I don't see them picking up the pace and pushing the two of us past our normal limits."

"I don't know."

"Oh?"

"Just a feeling I get. Like bein' around that woman might push anybody past their normal limits."

For that matter, Guthrie thought, it was hard to know what one's normal limits were. He had begun to suspect, when he first realized he had unwittingly quit smoking, that some of the ordinary rules of life had been somehow suspended. He'd tried to tell himself that walking out of his life had lessened the stress he was under, and this in turn had reduced his need for tobacco. But it had never been stress that made him smoke; he'd smoked because he was addicted to nicotine, and the greatest stress imaginable had always been that of trying to go without a cigarette when he wanted one.

Then he'd had another hint when McLemore had just about called him a liar for saying he'd slept out without a tent or a sleeping bag. He not only had survived, but he'd done so without being especially conscious of the cold, as if his spirit had set up some sort of energy force field that protected him as effectively as any construction of down and canvas.

He and Jody had slept out their second night together, in a stand of mixed hardwoods and conifers north of La Pine. They'd had a small fire and cooked hot dogs that they'd bought in La Pine, and they'd slept in their clothes on either side of the dying fire, and neither of them had been bothered by the cold. The fire, which had burned down low by the time they went to sleep, could hardly have provided much warmth. The only explanation he could come up with was a force field.

"I know such things can happen," he'd told Jody. "I know a couple of people who've done fire walks, where you walk twenty feet across a bed of burning coals in your bare feet."

"And you don't get burned?"

"Not a blister. The leader has you chanting and half hypnotized into some kind of altered state, and your mind creates an energy field that keeps the heat from reaching you."

"It's not just that you don't feel it 'cause you're hypnotized?"

"No, because your clothes don't burn either, and how would you hypnotize a pair of pants?"

"You actually know people who did this?"

"Several of them. There's one fellow who goes all over leading fire walks, he's from California—"

"Where else?"

"—and I think he's led something like thirty thousand people over the coals. But he has this whole ritual he has everybody go through, and we just had a force field settle over us without any effort on our part."

"If that's what it was."

"If that's what it was," he agreed. "But I can't think what else it might have been."

"Well, maybe we're just hot stuff, hoss. Ever think of that?"

Hot stuff indeed. Guthrie, a heavy smoker leading a sedentary life, had managed twenty miles a day across the Cascades without any ill effects, and each day's ordeal seemed to be leaving him stronger than the day before. Jody, younger and stronger but clearly overweight and out of shape, had matched his pace without straining; at least as remarkable, he'd hiked seventy miles in the same pair of socks without raising a blister. (A stench, perhaps, but not a blister.)

Could a boy and a blind woman keep up with them?

The question, he decided, was academic. In the first place, their pace was however slow or fast they decided to go; it wasn't as though they had a train to catch. And, whether Sara and Thom could keep up or not, the four of them were going to stay together. From the moment she'd clasped his hand he'd known that much.

In the morning they ate a light breakfast and did their shopping. By eleven o'clock they were out of Bend, heading east on US 20. The first town on the map was Millican, some twenty-six miles south and east of Bend. Guthrie thought that might be further than Sara and Thom could be expected to go their first day, especially since they were getting a late start. And they were out of the national forest now, and he wasn't sure of the etiquette involved in pitching camp on private land. He'd heard it wasn't too good an idea to wander far from the roadside. There was always the chance you'd stumble on somebody's marijuana plantation. The growers, whether or not they owned the land where their harvest was maturing, were capable of a murderous response to intruders.

But they'd sleep somewhere, he was sure of that. Meanwhile it was another perfect day, the sun in view much of the time, with clouds scudding across its face just enough to keep the heat down.

Would whatever was protecting them keep them from being badly sunburned? Could a force field keep out ultraviolet rays? That was another question he couldn't answer, and it was tough to play a game when you had no clear understanding of the rules.

Without conscious agreement, they took turns walking with Sara. She would walk on the left, her right hand in her companion's. There was no hesitation in her step, and her partner did not have to warn her of approaching cars. She seemed to be well enough aware of her immediate environment even without seeing it.

Walking with Jody, she said, "I hope I'm not slowing you down."

"You're doing fine, ma'am."

"You can call me Sara, Jody."

"Hell, I know that, but it's rare enough I get the impulse to act respectful. At first I thought I had to tell you about every piece of gravel on the ground in front of you, but you know just where to put your foot, don't you?"

"Do you look down all the time when you walk, Jody?"

"No, 'course not, but I'll drop my eyes now an' then so I don't step off a curb or into a ditch. It's sort of like you get the same message without dropping your eyes."

"I think that may be what happens." She smiled. "This

is all new to me, you know. I still had some sight until yesterday afternoon."

They stepped onto the shoulder at the approach of a truck not unlike the Datsun he'd left at the Circle K. Jody gave a wave and the old boy at the wheel raised his index finger in acknowledgment.

"Hope my brother got the truck all right," he said. "You haven't got the kind of second sight to check on a blue Datsun pickup parked a few miles north of Beaver Marsh, have you? I just locked her up and walked away from her."

"That was very brave of you, Jody."

"You think so, ma'am? I don't know as I'd put it in the same class with getting in the ring with a bull."

"A bullfighter knows what to expect. You were walking into the pure unknown."

"The road to Bend's a far cry from the dark side of the moon. I could about drive it in my sleep. I see your point all the same, not knowing what I was getting myself into. Thing is, I knew what I was getting out of, and it didn't take a whole lot of courage to walk away from that."

"Perhaps not."

"What did I have? Working for my brother, plus whatever pickup jobs came along, hauling trash to the dump for somebody or putting up somebody's storm windows in the fall and taking 'em down in the spring. Living alone in a trailer that don't look a whole lot like a model home. I'm married."

"Yes."

"She walked out on me. Went home to her mother."

"Yes."

"Easy to tell things to a person who can't look you in the eye. I slapped her around some, Carlene. I don't know as it's what you'd call wife-beating, but I did slap her some. You knew that, didn't you, ma'am?"

107

"Not exactly."

"What's that mean? 'Not exactly.' You can see things about people, can't you, ma'am?"

"Certain things. I can see"—she searched for the words —"I can see the picture of a person's life."

"You mean like a movie?"

"No," she said. "More like a huge oil painting, so large and with so much detail that you can't take it all in at once, but you're seeing it all at once."

"That's hard to imagine."

"I know."

He thought about it. "Well," he said, "somewhere in that picture, whether you can see it or not, there's me giving Carlene a crack in the mouth. I'm not real proud of that."

"No, you're not."

"I never did it that I hadn't had a few beers, but I don't guess that's any excuse. My father drank beer and whiskey every day of his life and he never laid a hand on my mother."

"He ever lay a hand on you, Jody?"

"Ha! Wasn't usually a hand. The strap, more than likely. But I don't know as I ever got it that I didn't deserve it."

"Did Carlene deserve it?"

"A woman never deserves to have a man hit her."

"Does a child deserve to get hit with a strap?"

"Well, see, I was a pretty bad kid. I did things I shouldn't oughta have done."

"Oh?"

He felt something shift deep within his center. "I didn't deserve it," he said, his voice like a bell. "He thought he had to hit me but he was wrong. I didn't need to get hit with no strap."

"Can you forgive him, Jody?"

"Oh, shit. Oh, oh, shit."

"Can you forgive yourself for hitting Carlene?"

He hiked his T-shirt out of the waistband of his jeans, used the bottom of it to wipe tears from his eyes. He said, "You know something? She *wanted* me to hit her. I never knew that until this minute. That's how we picked each other. She picked me to slap her around and I picked her to have someone to slap. How come I never knew that before?"

"Can you forgive her, Jody? And can you forgive yourself?"

"Look at me, I'm crying. I'm ashamed of myself, carrying on like this."

"Never be ashamed to cry, Jody." She put her arms around him. "Can you forgive yourself and everybody else? Can you forgive your father for hitting you and Carlene for wanting to be hit? Can you forgive your mother? Can you forgive the obstetrician for not letting you be born the way you wanted? Can you forgive everybody who ever tried to push you around?"

"Do I have to, ma'am?"

"What do you think?"

"Tell me."

"No, you tell me, Jody."

His head was on her shoulder, his big chest heaving with sobs. "Oh, God," he said. "I forgive . . . I forgive everybody. Oh, Jesus. Oh, dear Jesus."

"It's all right, Jody," she said. "You're all right now. Everything's all right."

Later he said, "I don't know what-all happened back there."

"You let go of some stuff."

"Is that what I did? I must of been carryin' it a fair spell."

"All your life, Jody. How do you feel now?"

"Like a house with the doors and windows open. I don't know. I guess I feel good."

"You can trust the feeling."

"I guess. Ma'am, did you say you were a psychologist?"

"A sort of a psychologist. I had a master's in social work, I did counseling."

"What you did just now, is this the sort of thing you used to do?"

"I didn't do anything just now, Jody. You did it all."

"Well, I sure never did it before, ma'am, and here I spend an hour holding your hand and damn if I don't fall apart. Did you used to have this happen in your work?"

She waited a moment before replying. Then she said, "I used to *try* to have this happen in my work. But it hardly ever did."

He nodded. He said, "This whole thing that's happening. The four of us walking. It's special, isn't it?"

"Yes," she said. "It's special."

Shortly after sunset Guthrie suggested they look for a place to bed down for the night. He wasn't sure of the distance, but he estimated that they were at least two hours west of Millican, with no guarantee that there would be motel rooms available there. "Besides," he said, "it'll be dark before we get there, and I know Sara doesn't like to walk in the dark."

"You're right," she agreed. "I'm afraid of the dark."

They found the perfect spot a quarter of a mile down the road in the middle of a small grove of trees. Someone had camped there before, or at least picnicked; there was the residue of a fire in the center of a clearing, with a small supply of firewood and tinder stacked alongside. Guthrie got a fire started and they sat around it and ate the food they'd bought at a store a few miles back. They sang songs, and then Thom suggested that somebody tell a ghost story. Guthrie told one about a dead boy who came back to life, improvising towards the end because he couldn't remember the original ending. Thom wanted more, but nobody knew any more.

So Sara told the story of how she'd met her husband, not liking him at first and not thinking he was really interested in her anyway. Jody told about his trip to Seattle right after high school graduation, and how he'd got the tattoo; he carefully left out the whorehouse visit that had been a highlight of the trip, but did mention how the three of them, staggering drunk across Pioneer Square, had come upon a pair of lovers on a blanket on the grass, and that one of their party—"And it wasn't me, I swear to God it wasn't me"—had unzipped his pants and baptized the passionate pair with urine.

And Thom told about the summer he'd spent a year ago at northern Michigan, and how one of the campers in the next cabin had drowned on a canoe trip. Thom hadn't gone on the trip, his cabin had another activity scheduled, and that morning he'd said, to the boy who would later drown, *"Have a good time on the river, asshole."* "So then he drowned," he said, "and the last word I said to him was asshole."

If it was cold that night, no one felt it. In the morning they straightened up the campsite and gathered wood and kindling to replace what they had burned. They were on the road early, and had pancakes and sausage for breakfast in Millican.

After breakfast, Guthrie walked with Sara. Thom and Jody were just a few paces ahead of them at first, but gradually the gap widened.

Guthrie said, "I'm glad we slept out last night."

"We found a perfect spot."

"I'd be glad even if we hadn't. It did something for us as a group."

"Bonded us."

"I suppose that's the word. Evidently we're supposed to go through this together, whatever it is. So it'd probably be better if we got close with one another."

"I agree," she said. "And we don't have much time."

"What do you mean? You just got here, lady. You can't be planning to leave us already."

"No, hardly that. But it won't be just the four of us for too much longer."

"Oh?"

"You sound apprehensive, Guthrie."

"Well, I didn't plan on a mob scene."

"What did you plan on?"

"I didn't plan, period. I decided to go for a walk."

"You didn't just head on down to the corner store for a Coke and the evening paper."

"No, I knew what I was doing. At least I knew I was walking away from my life and into—"

"Into what?"

"Into something different. I *still* don't know what I'm walking into, so I certainly didn't know then. You know how the idea came to me? I was waiting for a lady to finish having an abortion. It wasn't my kid." He frowned. "I don't know why it's important to include that last bit of data."

"It'll come to you."

"Gee, I'd never guess you were a psychologist in real life, Sara."

"Touché."

"One thing I did know was that I didn't want company. I was going to do this by myself. I never seriously considered asking anybody to keep me company. It was something to do all by myself."

"And then Jody showed up."

"And by then I was ready for company. I wasn't so sure it was a good idea when he invited himself along, but I figured we could try it out for a day or two and see how it worked. And it worked fine, we hit it off great and his company turned out to be just what I needed."

"And then Thom and I turned up."

"And then you two turned up, and who could argue with that? A beautiful blind lady with gray flannel eyes and the power to cloud men's minds so she cannot see them."

"That was The Shadow, and I think you got it wrong."

"I wouldn't be a bit surprised. It was pretty obvious that the two of you were sent. I mean, when people are waiting for you on the outskirts of the metropolis of Bend, they must have a hotline to the center of the universe. Correct me if I'm wrong, but I don't think there was even a bright star over the Pine Haven Motel."

"There was a whole sky full of them."

"I'll bet. No, it never even occurred to me to wonder whether I wanted the two of you along. You were supposed to be there, no question." He shrugged. "But I'm not sure I want this to turn into a major group effort."

"I'm not so sure you have any choice."

"Really?"

"Really." She released his hand for a moment, smoothed her forehead with her fingertips. "Thom and I weren't sent here all the way from what Jody would call Fort Fucking Wayne in order to play four-handed group therapy. And you didn't walk over the mountains for that, either. A whole lot of people are going to be joining us."

"What am I, the Pied Piper?"

"Something like that. Not for rats and not for children. A sort of Pied Piper for pilgrims."

"Pilgrims are supposed to be heading somewhere."

"But do they necessarily know where?"

"I don't know. Maybe not. How many people, Sara?"

"I don't know."

"A dozen? A hundred? A thousand?"

"I don't know. A *lot* of people, Guthrie. I don't know how many."

"An army. What are we going to do, hold hands across the country? You remember that circus, with all the press coverage and TV cameras, and when they were all done they raised something like a buck ninety-eight for the homeless of the world?"

"I remember."

"Is *that* what this is about? Is it some kind of fucking telethon? Who's gonna be waiting at the next stop sign, Jerry Lewis?"

"Guthrie?"

"What?"

"Guthrie, why not just take it as it comes?"

"I know," he said. "I know."

There was a motel in Brothers, but it was still early when they reached it and they didn't feel like breaking for the night. They kept going.

Late in the afternoon Sara heard an engine running off to the left and asked what it was. She was walking with Thom, and he told her it was a man on a tractor.

She called to the others. They closed the gap, and she suggested they ask the man on the tractor if they could spend the night on his land.

Jody went over to talk to the farmer. He was a man about fifty, tall and stout, with big jughandle ears and a bulldog jaw. He wore overalls and a striped blue and white cap that looked like mattress ticking, and he had a little trouble grasping what they wanted. Were they going to put up tents? Would they be building a fire? And where were they headed, anyway? The only city of any size was Burns, and that was eighty-some miles down the road.

Once he got it all straight, he had no objection to helping them out. They could sleep in his barn, he said, as long as he had their word that they'd go out of the barn and stand well away from it if they wanted to smoke.

"It ain't enough to be careful," he said. "People are always saying they'll smoke in the barn but be careful about it, and next thing you know the barn's burned down, because the only way to be careful about smoking in a barn is not to do it."

Jody explained that none of their party smoked. The farmer was glad to hear it, but not entirely convinced.

The barn was a massive structure with a hayloft and half a dozen box stalls and milking stanchions for twenty cows. The farmer—his name was Oscar Powers—explained that he kept a small dairy herd, in addition to fattening beef cattle. He also had some acreage in sugar beets and alfalfa.

He showed them where they could sleep and told them to break up a couple bales of hay for their bedding. He was back fifteen minutes later with his arms full of blankets. "My wife said you'd need these," he said. They thanked him, and ten minutes later he was back again. "My wife said you're probably hungry, and we've got plenty. She said for you to come on up to the house soon as you're settled, so's you can wash up before we sit down."

They ate beef and roasted potatoes and three different vegetables from the kitchen garden. There was a pitcher of fresh milk on the table and big graniteware mugs of coffee served with the meal and replenished throughout. Lindy Powers was a little dumpling of a woman, a soap opera fan and a member of a quilters' club. She called her husband Ockie and never allowed his plate to be empty.

Two Powers sons were with them at the table; a third

115

boy, older, lived with his wife in Corvallis. "He went to school there," Powers explained, "and now he has an office job working with computers. I can't hold it against any boy who doesn't want to farm these days. I wouldn't have any other life for myself, but I have to say I wouldn't wish it on a dog."

There was pie for dessert, topped with thick cream. Afterward they had hot showers before trooping back to the barn, and in the morning Mrs. Powers sent her youngest boy to the barn with a basket of hot breads and a pot of coffee. The same boy returned as they were getting ready to leave, his father at his side.

"John here has it in mind that he'd like to walk a ways with you," he said. "If you've no objection."

The boy was nineteen, tall and loose-limbed, with dark home-barbered hair and a tentative expression. He had hardly said a word at dinner.

"I don't mind him going," Oscar Powers said. "He's a help to me but his brother and I can manage. And there's nothing here for him. Half a year at State was all the college he wanted, and he's not crazy enough to be a farmer. His mother's putting clothes in a sack for him, if you don't mind him going with you."

Guthrie said, "You want to come with us, John?" The boy nodded, smiling, and Guthrie told him he'd be welcome.

Powers said, "He's been talking about enlisting in the service. I can't say I understand what you folks are up to, but I'd sooner trust him to you than to the generals."

A few miles down the road they stopped at a gas station to top up their canteens and buy snack-packs of cheese and crackers. The attendant, a cheerful young man with freckles and a missing incisor, knew John and asked him what he was up to. When he learned the group was walking east to the Idaho line he thought that was the greatest thing he'd ever heard.

"I never done anything like that," he said. "I never done anything, really."

"Come on along," Jody suggested.

"Aw, now," he said. "Somebody's got to run this place. Everybody can't just do what they want."

"Why's that?"

He shrugged and shook his head, still smiling, the tip of his tongue showing where the tooth was missing.

Two miles further a weathered shack called itself the Split Rail Restaurant. A woman in her early thirties ran the place and lived in two rooms behind the restaurant. She was tall and thin, wore her blond hair in a braid, and wore jeans and boots and a man's shirt. She didn't say much, just listened to their conversation as they had their coffee, but when it was time to pay they couldn't find her. She appeared after a couple of minutes wearing a hat and carrying a canvas shoulder bag.

"I don't have a backpack," she said. "I figure this'll do until I get something better. But I haven't got a canteen either, and there's some dry country between here and the Rockies." John said that he hadn't a canteen either, that he was carrying his water in a plastic bottle with a screw cap. "Now I should have thought of that myself," she said. She got a half-liter container of Coke from the icebox, cracked the cap, spilled out its contents, filled it from the tap, capped it and tucked it into her bag. "I should have asked did anybody want some of that Coke," she said. "I wasn't thinking."

She wouldn't take money for the coffee. She rang "No Sale" on the cash register, stuffed the bills into a pocket of her jeans, and left the change where it was. She switched off the fire under the coffee, threw a couple of other switches, and turned the sign in the window from "Open" to "Closed." She started to lock the front door, then turned away from it. "Anyone wants to move in," she said, "they're welcome to it. It's just the best place in the world if you want to put in twelve hours a day to clear a dollar an hour." After they'd walked together for a few hundred yards, she said, "My name's Martha Detweiller. You folks want to tell me your names?"

Within the hour a four-wheel-drive AMC Eagle pulled up on the other side of the road. The rear doors opened and a man and woman got out, both of them wearing backpacks. The man had freckles and a chunky grin, and one of his front teeth was missing.

"I thought about it," he said, "and I couldn't think why everybody couldn't do what they wanted, and just 'cause somebody has to pump Mr. Ballard's gas doesn't mean it has to be me. I had to close up and I had to call Ballard and let him know I was taking off, and then I had to go home and explain to Ellie what was goin' on. This here is Ellie, an' she still don't know what's goin' on, but she's up for it whatever it is. And I'm Marlon but everybody calls me Bud, and that there's Richard and it's too early to tell yet what everybody's gonna call him."

And it was then that Guthrie noticed that Ellie's backpack was not a knapsack but a sling, and that there was a baby riding in it. Ellie was a slender woman with long brown hair and luminous skin. She looked slightly glassy-eyed, and Guthrie didn't blame her.

He found Sara and took her by the hand. "You didn't mention that somebody was going to show up with a baby," he said. "I suppose you didn't want to spoil the surprise."

"I'm as surprised as you are."

"Oh yeah? The Prophet Disarmed. I hate to be a spoil-sport, but—"

"But is it safe to have a baby along on a trip like this?"

"That's my question, yeah."

"Can I see him?"

"You just about have to take a number and wait. Little Richard's very popular right now."

Sara extended both her index fingers and the baby gripped the tip of each and made fists about them. Pure heart energy flowed forth from the infant; the only reading she could get was serenity and love and joy. When Richard released her fingers she took Ellie's hand and was not surprised to pick up the same vibrations, the identical sweet innocence.

"It's safe to have a baby along," she told Guthrie.

"Safe for us or safe for him?"

"Both."

"How the hell are they going to feed him? Babies drink milk, don't they?"

"What a fount of information you are, Guthrie."

"I am smiling benignly at you, Sara. I just wanted you to know that."

"I'm sure you are."

"The point is they drink milk and they have it fairly frequently, don't they?"

"Every four hours, when they're very young."

"And they have to get their diapers changed."

"Very good, Guthrie."

"Well, you can carry diapers, but what about milk? You bump a canteen of milk on your hip for a couple of hours and you wind up with cottage cheese."

"Guthrie, don't tell me you thought they were strictly decorative."

"What?"

"Breasts."

"Oh, Jesus," he said.

"I know. What'll they think of next?"

* * *

119

They spent the night in an unplowed field. There was no one around of whom to ask permission, and no one sensed they'd be at risk. Bud and Ellie had brought a zip-up sleeping sack for Richard. Everyone else slept uncovered, and even without a fire everyone was warm enough.

"I think we can forget about motels from here on in," Guthrie told Jody. "There's eight of us now, nine counting Richard. Four rooms minimum, and you can't count on finding that many vacancies. And we went from four to nine in a day. God only knows how many of us there'll be a week from now."

"Motels cost, too. Not everybody's got money."

"I know. Last night was great, having supper with the Powerses and sleeping in the barn. And it's good we did it last night, because there's too many of us to do it again. It's a good thing we can sleep out safely because we don't have a whole lot of other choices."

"You sound like it bothers you some, hoss."

"Maybe I just have trouble adjusting to new realities. What are we going to do if it rains?"

"Grab a bar of soap and take a shower."

"That's another thing. How are we going to take showers if we never get motel rooms?"

"They've got showers at public campgrounds, and we can pay a fee and use them even if we don't stay at the site. And there's no law says we have to all stay in a bunch every damn minute, you know. Some of us could stay at a motel or in somebody's barn and some more could find a place on down the road. We stay flexible, we'll know what to do when we have to do it."

"You're right."

"Besides," Jody said, "we got good people today. John's got something stuck in his throat, but soon as he spits it out he'll have a lot to say. He's got two older brothers, and he grew up thinking nothing he had to say was important.

120

He'll get over that. And Martha's purely a no-bullshit type, she cuts right through the crap. She's been madder'n hell at somebody, and when she quits sittin' on it she may carry on enough to make the hills shake some, but you just wait an' see what she's like afterward."

"Sara tell you all this stuff?"

"No."

"Where'd you get it, then?"

"I don't know." Jody tugged at his beard. "Just come to me, I guess. Now Bud an' Ellie, they're real neat, and ol' Richard's just loving the whole trip. He looks out at the mountains like they belong to him."

"I just hope they don't slow us down too much."

"They won't. I noticed something. The first day somebody walks with us they're a little slow, or their feet bother them, or whatever it is. But once they get caught up in the flow, why, the others just carry them. It's like we pass energy back and forth, and the more it gets passed around the more there is of it. I tell you, hoss, I feel stronger the more of us there are."

"How do you mean stronger?"

"Every way there is. Stronger in the body and stronger in my mind and spirit. Don't you feel it?"

He thought for a moment. "I guess I do feel it," he admitted. "I just don't trust it."

"Sara'd say that's just your mind."

"Right, don't pay any attention to your thoughts, they're just coming out of your mind."

"You can trust it, Guthrie. It's real."

"I suppose."

"You all right? You look a little ragged around the edges."

"Just a headache. One of the women probably has an aspirin."

"A headache? Stand up a minute."

121

"What for?"

"Stand up," Jody said, and got to his feet himself. He steadied himself, took several deep breaths, gave his hands a shake and held them down at his sides. Guthrie asked him what the hell he was doing.

"Letting my hands tingle," he said. "Don't talk, just let me do this." He kept his hands at his sides for another twenty seconds, then placed them on either side of Guthrie's head. He held them in that position for half a minute, let them drop, and heaved a sigh.

"There," he said.

"What was that all about?"

"First tell me how's your headache."

"It's gone. How'd you do that?"

"Beats the hell out of me, hoss. You saw what I did. I just let the power flow down into my hands, and then I sent it into the part that hurts."

"When did you learn how to do that?"

"I don't know. An hour ago? Martha had a cramp in her shoulder and I was massaging it and not getting anywhere, and suddenly it came to me to try getting energy in my hands and putting the energy on her. So I did, and it worked." He shrugged. "Guess it works on headaches, too."

"It's amazing," Guthrie said. "The headache's really gone. Uh, thanks."

"All part of the service. Just pay the nurse on the way out." He laughed. "Don't get too carried away, hoss. It's not like curing cancer or casting out devils, and I didn't heal nothing that an aspirin wouldn't have got rid of. But I'll tell you, it sure is a nice feeling to be able to take away a person's pain."

NINE

There were twelve of them by the time they reached Burns.

Gary was a hand at the Kay-Bar-Seven Ranch. Two of the other hands had seen the group pass on the road and cut across the range in their 4-by-4 to check the party out; later that day they sat around laughing about the fools who were trying to walk across the country, and Gary rode out the next morning, found them and fell into step. He was tall and thin, narrow in the hips, his brown hair cropped short and his cheeks pitted with old acne scars. He smoked Marlboros—he could have modeled for their advertising —and he looked wary when Jody told him how Guthrie had spontaneously given up the habit crossing the Cascades.

"You have to quit smoking to stay in this group?"

Sara assured him otherwise. "You may quit," she said, "and you may not. Nobody gets anything from this walk that he didn't come here to get."

"Well, that's good," he said. He sounded at once relieved and a little disappointed.

"The thing is," Jody added, "the only way you'll know what you came for is when you see what you get."

Les and Georgia were waiting for them. Their car, a Cadillac Seville, was parked at the side of the road headed toward Burns. The left rear tire was flat.

Les was standing in the road leaning against the car. He was a big man, about six-three and weighing close to two hundred fifty pounds. He was in his mid-fifties and he was wearing white Levi's, a western shirt with pearl buttons and a lot of silver braid, a string tie with a turquoise slide, and a pearl-gray ten-gallon hat.

Some of the walkers, the ones in front, called out to him. He scowled across the road at them.

John Powers said, "We'll get that tire changed for you, sir."

"I already jacked her up and changed her," he said. "That's the goddamned spare on there. The goddamned spare is flat, it came from the goddamned dealer's that way, and if I ever get this goddamned car back to Pendleton he is goddamned likely to hear about it."

He was from Pendleton, where he had extensive holdings in timber and ranchland. He had gone down to Reno to celebrate a successful business transaction. He stayed at Harrah's, saw some shows, ate some good food, drank a lot of first-rate Tennessee whiskey, smoked some cigars that were supposed to have been smuggled in from Cuba, but he frankly didn't believe it, did reasonably well at the crap table and substantially less well at blackjack, and, somewhere along the way, met up with Georgia, whom he was now bringing back to Pendleton as the fourth Mrs. Lester Pratt Burdine.

He had driven to Reno on US 395, which runs through Pendleton to Reno and all the way south to San Bernardino. He was returning to Pendleton the same way, with his new bride on the front seat beside him. There is a twenty-seven-mile stretch from Burns west to Riley where 395 and 20 run together, and it was there that the Seville's left rear tire had gone flat, and the spare had revealed itself to be in the same state. It had, however, not done so until he had changed tires and lowered the car from the jack.

"And ever since then," he said, "I've been standing here waiting to see a goddamned state trooper so he can send someone out with a new tire. Drive five miles over the speed limit and you'll see more goddamned troopers than you can shake a stick at, but get a flat smack in the middle of a goddamned federal highway, make that *two* god-damned federal highways, and you could about die waiting for one to turn up."

He'd thought of walking to a service station but he didn't know which way to walk. He couldn't remember passing a station since Riley, and that was a good eight or ten miles back. There was a bitty town called Hines a couple miles before you got to Burns, but that was still at least fifteen miles away, and he couldn't remember for sure if there was a station closer than that.

They told him they were walking on toward Burns anyhow, and they would see that he got help. There might well be a garage in the next few miles; failing that, there would surely be some place with a phone. They could call the Triple-A and make sure that someone came to his assistance.

"I'd walk along with you," he said, "except I don't want to leave Georgia here. And I don't know that I can walk that far myself."

"Couldn't you flag a car?"

"Now that is the whole goddamned thing," he said. "There was no end of cars while I was changing that tire. There were even people who stopped without being asked, wanted to know if I needed help. Well, it doesn't take

125

more'n one man to change a tire, so I said thanks all the same and sent them on their way. And from the moment I got the jack down and saw the spare was flatter than Floyd's feet, I never saw another single goddamned car. Not in either direction, not a single car."

He wound up walking toward Burns with them, and Georgia came along rather than stay in the car. She was a honey blonde of thirty who managed to look older by trying to look younger. She had a baby-doll face, but carried so much tension in her facial muscles that she looked as though she was made of pink velvet on a steel frame. She wore a cowgirl outfit, smart and expensive, but had the wit to get a pair of flat shoes from her luggage to replace the high-heeled Tony Lama boots.

There was a roadside telephone a mile and a half down the road. Les made his call, and they took a break from their walk and waited with him and Georgia until the truck arrived from the garage in Burns. Les and Georgia shook hands all around and got into the truck to ride back to the Cadillac. The others watched the truck until it was out of sight, then got underway again.

John said he hadn't thought they'd go back to the car. "I figured they'd stick with us," he said.

"And just leave that Caddy there?"

"What's he care about a car? He can buy another one if he wants. And he seemed real intrigued with everything we were saying. So did she, even more than he did. I thought she'd want to stay with us, and then he'd decide to stay, too."

Somebody said he could buy another wife as easily as he could buy another car. Jody said he was just as glad they'd gone their separate ways. "They're not exactly the type for this hike of ours," he told Guthrie.

"Oh? What type is that?"

"You know what I mean. She's not a whole lot more than

a tough little hooker, and how he got to be so tall is by standing on his money. I don't figure they'd be a whole lot of fun to be around."

"That's not who they are. That's just the package they're wrapped in."

"Maybe."

"Remember the fellow in the Datsun pickup?"

"Fellow in a Datsun? No, when was that?"

"Oh, about ten days ago on Route 95. He wanted to give me a ride when I wasn't even looking for one."

"Oh, that guy," Jody said. "Oh, come on, hoss. I wasn't all that bad."

"Never said you were."

"But I do get your drift."

"I thought you would."

To Sara, Guthrie confided a certain amount of surprise that the Burdines had turned back. "There's always a fair amount of traffic on this road," he said. "At least there is since 395 came in. It's not a parade, but you see a car every few minutes. But the traffic shut down the minute they needed help, and it didn't start to flow again until they'd joined up with us."

"And you don't think that could be coincidental?"

"No more than you do. Anyway, coincidence is just God's way of remaining anonymous. No, they were supposed to meet up with us. And while I agree with Jody that they're an unlikely pair of pilgrims, at least on the surface of it, I thought they'd get caught up in the flow of whatever it is that's happening." He hesitated. "I thought we were irresistible, I guess. That once you walked a mile or so with us you were hooked."

For a moment he thought she wasn't going to respond. Then, her hand light in his, she said, "The path is not for everyone, Guthrie."

"No, I don't suppose it is."

127

"And that's very sad, because there are people who ought to be here and they never will. But I think it's partly true, what you suggested. Once you start on the path, I don't think you can really stop. You can slow down, you can get sidetracked, you can drag your feet, but I don't think you can turn your back on it completely. I'm not absolutely positive about this, but I don't think you can."

Les and Georgia Burdine couldn't. A few miles down the road the tow truck caught up with them, the Caddy's back end winched up and the big car rolling on its front wheels. The truck stopped, the door opened, and Les and Georgia stepped down. Les said something to the driver, and the truck pulled away, towing the Caddy in its wake.

"You're not going to believe this," Les announced. "The fool brought the wrong size tire. I told him what size tire to bring and he brought one that won't fit on the goddamned automobile. Can you believe that?"

"Easily," Martha told him.

"You can? I have to tell you I couldn't. So he's hauling the car back to his garage in Burns, where he's got a whole pile of tires the right size, and he's going to see if he can't put one of them on for me."

"How come you didn't ride there with him?"

"Well, there's not a great deal to do in Burns. There's an Indian reservation, and there's a whole lot of places selling supplies to ranchers, but if you've been to Burns once you wouldn't call life a failure if it never brought you back there again."

"And we liked you folks," Georgia put in, "and we thought we'd walk with you a little while, and then when we get to Burns our car'll be ready and we can go."

"We might not even get all the way to Burns tonight," Martha said. "I think Guthrie was saying something about stopping within the next hour. Gary knows whose land this is, and he says there'd be no objection to our camping out on it, so that's probably what we'll do."

"Well, we'd probably wind up staying in Burns otherwise," Les said, "and the Best Western's as good as they got there, and it's no great shakes from what I hear. I can't remember the last time I slept out under the stars. You think you can manage with the ground for a mattress, little lady?"

Georgia muttered something. "I've had worse" is what it sounded like to Martha.

"Then tomorrow we'll go on to Burns with the rest of you," he went on, "and I guess you'll stay on 20 going east, while we collect the car and drive north to Pendleton."

Jody went around offering five to one that they'd stay with the group after Burns. He couldn't find anyone who would bet with him.

A couple of things happened that night.

First of all, Martha blew up at Guthrie. He said something innocuous that she took the wrong way, and she had a fit. She told him that he had no right to control her, that no one had elected him God, that she'd been putting up with his crap all her life and she didn't want to take it anymore. She kept working herself up, and ultimately she began hyperventilating. Jody and Sara got her to lie down and made her keep breathing until her body was vibrating with energy. Then, abruptly, she got up on her knees, laid her head back and roared. Loud wordless cries came one after another from her mouth, rending the night air. She howled for five full minutes, and then her voice cracked in the middle of a howl and she rolled onto her side and curled up in a ball and began to weep quietly. Jody covered one of her hands with his, and Sara laid a hand on her shoulder. After a little while the weeping stopped and she appeared to be asleep.

129

Not long after that, Richard was formally introduced to his grandfather. This was a neat trick, because the man had died before Richard was born.

What happened is this: Ellie had walked off twenty yards or so in order to nurse Richard without being obvious about it. Just as she was switching the baby from the right to the left breast, she was undeniably aware of her father's presence. She had been his only child, and Richard was thus his only grandchild, and her father, dying with cancer, had fought to hang onto life until the completion of her pregnancy. He had lasted longer than his doctors thought he would, but still took his last breath a month and three days before Richard was born.

Now, suddenly, he was here in the high desert of western Oregon. She could feel him there with her, she thought she ought to be able to look around and see him. She felt his mind lock onto hers, and she got that he longed to know his grandson.

She looked down at the baby sucking lustily at her breast. Aloud she said, "Richard, I want you to meet your grandfather. His name is Andrew McLeod. Daddy, this is your grandson, his name is Richard Andrew Wilkes. Isn't he beautiful, Daddy?"

And then Richard's mouth opened to release her nipple. He turned his head. His eyes held hers but only momentarily, and then they swung around to lock on something Ellie couldn't see. The baby smiled hugely, and gurgled with pleasure; whatever he saw, it was clearly something that he liked.

For a long moment they stayed like that, the two of them or the three of them. Then Richard sighed and rolled over to seek her breast again, and Ellie felt something relax and let go and leave them.

"Oh, Richard," she said.

130

When he finished nursing she carried him back to the group. Before she could ask, Georgia Burdine offered to hold him for her, and Richard accepted the transfer without a murmur. Ellie found Bud and told him what had just happened to her, and in the course of telling him she started to cry, and he held her while she wept. Then the two of them walked slowly off into the night.

Richard never once cried in his mother's absence but lay in Georgia's arms beaming up at her like a tiny Buddha. Whenever his eyes met with hers she wanted to weep. She couldn't even see his eyes clearly in the gathering darkness, but she could feel it when he was looking at her; some current passed from his eyes to hers, and she felt old things welling up in her chest. She didn't cry, but each time it happened something hard softened, something that was tight became a little looser.

She had been holding the child for ten minutes when Les sat down next to her. Neither of them spoke. After perhaps ten minutes more Ellie appeared to reclaim her baby, and he went to her with a little whoop of delight.

"He loves you," Les told Georgia, "but he wants his mama."

"Just so his mama wants him. They were gone a long time; I was starting to wonder if I was gonna get to keep him. Where do you suppose they went?"

"A young couple on a moonlit night? Use your imagination, honey."

"You think so? I hope they were careful or they'll wind up with Irish twins. You know what that is? That's babies less than a year apart."

"Is it supposed to be bad luck?"

She looked at him. "If you've got a second baby before the first one's a year old," she said, "you've already *had* bad luck."

131

"Oh. Of course you and I wouldn't have to worry about that. I mean, if we were to go off the way Bud and Ellie did—"

"Are you serious? You mean just go lie down in the grass?"

"You lived in cities all your life, didn't you, Georgie girl? About time you learned some country ways."

She got to her feet. "If you can even *think* about it," she said, "after all that driving, and jacking up the car and changing a tire, and then all that walking—"

"Did I do all that today? That's the trouble with getting old, your memory goes and you start to forget things."

"If you can still be in the mood," she said, "I guess I can at least call and see if you're bluffing."

He put an arm around her and led her off toward where Bud and Ellie had wandered earlier. The moon was three-quarters full, the night still and silent. He said, "Bluffing. You think this here is a poker game? Well, you just shove all your chips in the pot, little lady, and I'll show you what I've got in my hand."

It was well before noon the next morning when they reached Burns. They made plans to meet in front of the post office at one-thirty; that would give them plenty of time to buy what they needed and eat a meal before they reassembled and headed out of town.

They went their separate ways. Gary picked up a pair of soft shoes to spell his boots. Bud and Ellie replenished their supply of Pampers. John wrote a postcard to his parents. Les went to the garage to see if the car was ready. Guthrie picked up a Portland paper and read stories about a world conference on population control, a massacre of Indians by government troops in Brazil, a confrontation of warships in the eastern Mediterranean, and a man in

Yakima who had killed his wife and four children with a shotgun before hanging himself with his belt.

When they regrouped at one-thirty, the Burdines showed up with backpacks and canteens, and Les had managed to equip himself with a stout bamboo walking stick. The car was ready, and he'd made arrangements to have it delivered to his home in Pendleton. Everyone was relieved that Les and Georgia were staying with the group, and some of them were gracious enough to pretend to be surprised.

There were five new people who joined the group in front of the post office:

Lissa was a waitress at the restaurant where Martha and Jody had had lunch. She was twenty-four, and she told them that she had had a fantasy for the past three years that a rich handsome man would come into her restaurant and take her away with him. "But the closest I ever get is a cowboy with a mattress in the back of his pickup," she said, "and as far as he wants to take me is half a mile up a dirt road. Only person's going to get me out of here is me."

Sue Anne was working at Wembley's when Lissa came in to buy a backpack and a canteen. She was a few years older than Lissa and about twelve pounds heavier than she wanted to be, a divorced woman with a son nine and a daughter almost eight. "I don't believe this," she said. "All of a sudden everybody wants a backpack. And canteens! I sold three already today and I can't remember the last time I sold one. There are these people in town—"

Lissa said she knew, that she was going with them.

"You're not," Sue Anne said. "Just like that? You mean it? You tell Grace she's gonna be short a waitress?"

Lissa nodded.

"She holler at you?"

"Started to. Then she said she wished she could go with me, and she would if she didn't have her ma to look after."

133

She hooked a finger under a thin gold chain around her neck, raised it to show a pale blue crystal. "She gave me this," she said.

"Grace gave you that? It's pretty. What is it?"

"I think she said aquamarine."

"It's real pretty." She reached out, drew in her breath sharply when her fingers touched the cool surface of the crystal. A look passed over her face, and she said, "This here's the last backpack but one, so you can have it, but there's only the one canteen and I'm keeping it for myself. You know where I bet they might have canteens? Western Auto. I'll walk over there with you if you want to go see."

"You're coming too? What about your kids?"

"Well, what about them? They're visiting their daddy and that bitch in Spokane. I talked to them on the phone Sunday and all I heard was how they got a heated pool, they got a golden retriever, they got a rear-projection TV with a dish antenna. They like it so damn much, they can just stay there for a while."

Jordan was Thom's age, thirteen, but not as tall. He was the son of a black father and a Flathead Indian mother. The two boys had got to talking in front of a shelf of science fiction paperbacks at Goody's Trading Post, where they discovered that they liked a lot of the same authors. They got Cokes from a machine and stood around drinking them, and Thom told Jordan he was from Indiana, and that he'd never even seen an Indian until he crossed the Mississippi River.

"You got black people back where you are?" Jordan wanted to know.

"Oh, sure. The school I used to go to, I think about a third of the kids were black."

"No shit? Because it's the other way around here. We got

Indians up the ass, but it's being half nigger that makes me exotic."

Jordan never said anything about joining the walk. He didn't pack any clothes or bring along anything other than what he was wearing. But he stuck close to Thom, joined Thom and Sara and John for lunch, and, when they all met in front of the post office, he was there with them, acting as if it were a foregone conclusion that he was a member of the party.

Douglas was a friend of Gary's, a transplanted Californian who worked at Western Auto and had a shop at his house where he produced handmade hunting knives as a sideline. The knives sold readily at knife and gun shows for upwards of two hundred dollars, but each one represented a minimum of fifty hours work and a substantial investment in high-grade steel and fancy woods or ivories for the grips, so there was little profit in the trade.

Douglas was ready to go as soon as he learned what Gary was up to. The woman he lived with, also a former San Diegan, thought it was the craziest thing she'd ever heard of. When she learned that the group included a blind woman and a nursing infant, she declared that she'd heard everything.

"The only thing is you're all headed in the wrong direction," she said. "Aren't lemmings supposed to throw themselves into the sea?"

Douglas told her he was going. She said to be sure and have a good time, and send her a postcard now and then. "Why don't you just meet the people?" he suggested. "You know Gary's all right."

"I always used to think he was one of your more normal friends."

"So give it a try. Meet the people, maybe walk out with

135

them this afternoon. If you don't feel good about it you can always turn around and come back."

"Great, I can walk all the way back alone."

"You can hitch. Besides, if you don't like it the chances are I won't like it either, and we can hitch back together. Just join in for a few miles, Bev."

"This has a familiar ring," she said. "It's like a couple of years ago when you swore you were only going to put the tip in."

"If you don't like it—"

"That's the trouble, Douglas. I wind up liking it."

Douglas was a sort of half-assed survivalist, and Gary had a hard time talking him out of bringing along a ton of camping gear. He was sure they'd be more comfortable with a tent and sleeping bags, and he wanted to bring a mess kit and a compass and water purification tablets and a hatchet and fishhooks and line and God knew what else. "These people are into traveling real light," Gary told him. "If it weighs a lot or if it won't fit in a small pack, leave it behind."

"But you can't sleep uncovered in the mountains," Douglas insisted. "You'll freeze."

"They've been doing it all along."

"Well, I'm certainly taking the first aid kit. It doesn't make sense to go anywhere without gauze and tape and antiseptic and aspirin."

"Don't really need aspirin," Gary said, grinning. "We got an old boy from Klamath Falls who puts his hands around your head and cures your headache."

"How is he with menstrual cramps?" Bev wanted to know. Gary said it hadn't come up, but he was sure Jody would be willing to try. "Well, why not?" she said. "It won't be the craziest thing I did all day. But he better watch where he puts his hands."

* * *

136

They left Burns in a compact group. As they put a little distance between themselves and the city, they tended to spread out along the highway in twos and threes. Here and there someone walked alone, but usually not for long.

Guthrie asked Sara if she'd had a chance to get a reading on Jordan.

"I just picked up a lot of self-hatred," she said. "Nobody wants him and he doesn't belong anywhere."

"Yeah, I got that much and I'm not even blind. I was a little concerned about him just joining up with us. As far as I can tell he didn't say a word to anyone back in Burns. He just walked on out of town. So I asked him if his people wouldn't come after us to get him back. You read about these cults spiriting children away from their parents; I sure don't want to turn into something like that."

"What did he say?"

"He said he didn't think the people of Burns were going to get up a posse to bring back a half-nigger Indian. He said his mother was in the state hospital and his father was doing time for manslaughter, and the aunt he lived with would do a victory dance if she ever noticed he was gone. I'm glad he's with us, the poor little son of a bitch. I don't think he could have had too good a life in Burns."

"Or too long a one, either."

"He'll be good company for your boy, too."

"He'll be good company for all of us."

"Uh-huh." They walked a little ways in silence, and then he said, "People have so goddam much to walk away from. Every time I find myself wondering what we're walking toward, I tell myself that's beside the point. Sara, I read a newspaper back in Burns and there wasn't a single good thing in it. The baseball scores were the closest thing to good news, and even there somebody had to lose for everybody who won. I don't usually get bothered by the fact that major league baseball is a zero-sum universe, but

137

that puts it ahead of the rest of the world, where one person can lose without somebody else winning."

"I suppose I'll miss being able to read a paper," she said. "But so far I haven't."

"There was a man in Washington State who killed his wife and kids with a shotgun and then hanged himself with his belt. All that went through my mind reading the story was wondering why he'd used the shotgun on the rest of them and then used a different method on himself. I asked Jody."

"I'll bet he had an answer."

"He had several suggestions. Maybe the guy ran out of shells. Maybe he was sickened by the mess a shotgun makes. Maybe the gun barrel was longer than his arm, and it didn't occur to him that he could work the trigger with his toe."

"Maybe he knew you could get an erection by hanging yourself."

"You can?"

"So I understand. There are accidental suicides all the time, people trying to half hang themselves for sexual pleasure who go a little farther than they intended."

"This really happens?"

"Oh, the literature's full of it. It happens quite frequently."

He shook his head. "I suppose all knowledge is valuable," he said, "but I'd have a hard time saying how my life is richer for knowing that."

Three hours out of Burns, a Ford Taurus passed them at high speed, heading west. A few minutes later the same car returned in the eastbound lane, braking hard and fishtailing to a stop, then pulling onto the shoulder across the road from the main body of walkers.

The driver got out of the car, slammed the door, and

stalked across the road. He was a man in his mid-thirties, average in height and build. He was wearing a three-piece navy pinstripe suit, a yellow tie with black pin dots, and a pair of black scotch-grain wingtip shoes. He had taken his car keys with him, and he strode along with them clutched in one hand.

A couple of people tried speaking to him. He didn't reply, or give any clear indication that he had heard them. There was a wild look in his eyes; they seemed to be focused off in the middle distance somewhere. He walked at a good pace, his arms swinging madly at his sides, his back ramrod-straight.

After he had gone perhaps half a mile he became aware of the car keys. He looked at them as if unable to guess what they were or where they'd come from. Then he reared back and hurled them into the field to his left.

Another half mile down the road he shrugged out of his suit jacket, compressed it into a ball, and flung it into the field. His vest was the next to go, after another quarter mile. Then his necktie. Then his wristwatch.

Not too surprisingly, he had attracted a great deal of attention. No one was quite prepared to interfere, but everybody was waiting to see what he would litter the landscape with next.

But instead he walked for the next half hour without discarding anything. Gradually his arm movements became less exaggerated and his face lost its look of manic concentration. He had been staring straight ahead; now he occasionally looked to the left or right. Twice he yawned.

Then he said, "My name's Jerry. Christ, I'm hungry, I don't mind telling you. Anybody know where you can get a sandwich around here?"

"You win," Bev told Douglas. "The hell with it, I don't care, I'll be a lemming too. You win."

TEN

Hitchhikers were so easy. It seemed to Mark that they were virtually asking to be killed, and he wondered if there wasn't something fundamentally suicidal about a girl who stood alone by the side of the road, actively seeking rides from passing strangers.

He'd been driving on I-70, heading toward St. Louis, and at Columbia he'd left the Interstate and drove north on 63. The main campus of the University of Missouri was in Columbia, and there were always students on roads in the area, thumb out, looking for a ride.

Today was no exception. It was right around the end of the term and the highway was full of young people in jeans, most of them with suitcases or duffel bags in tow. There were more boys than girls on the road, and what girls he saw were accompanied, either by other girls or by boys. He slowed once at the sight of two girls. He had never done two at once outside of fantasy, and his pulse quickened at the thought, but he knew the risk was far too great. One of them would stand a very good chance of getting away, and if that happened he would be in trouble.

Still, he braked the car almost to a stop just to let himself get a good look at them. They were both blondes, both clad in jeans and sneakers and school sweatshirts, both round-faced and pug-nosed and plump. And both gave him the finger when, just as they rose to approach the Lincoln, he bore down on the gas pedal and sped away.

He smiled at their reflection in the rearview mirror. He wondered if they were sisters and decided they probably were. He had slowed down to look at them in the expectation that it would fuel his fantasy, and indeed it did. He saw himself with the two of them, making one watch while he did the other, letting her know just what was coming, and then finishing her off.

Oh, nice.

He kept driving, slowing down again at the sight of a woman alone, speeding up angrily when a second glance revealed a slim boy with long hair.

A couple miles farther he found her.

She was perfect. Jeans, UM sweatshirt, Birkenstock sandals on dirty feet. Long dark brown hair in a ponytail secured by a rubber band. An oval face. Pale blue eyes, a short straight nose, pale thin lips, even teeth. Unplucked eyebrows, unpolished nails. No makeup, no lipstick.

Narrow waist, slim hips, nice little ass. Hard to tell about the breasts because the sweatshirt was baggy.

Time would tell.

She had to struggle to get the duffel bag into the backseat. Then she climbed in front, propping her large handbag on her lap, reaching over to fasten her seat belt across her body. She said, "Are you going as far as Kirksville? I live in Edina, that's down the road from Kirksville."

"Well, I can run you all the way to Kirksville."

"Oh, that's great," she said. "This is a great car, too. This a Lincoln?" He said it was. "I guess they're nicer than

141

Cadillacs, aren't they?" He said it was probably a toss-up. "I'm getting a car in the fall. They didn't want me to have one my first year, like it'd be too distracting? Like if I had a car I wouldn't go to my classes, but if I didn't have a car I'd have to study out of boredom? But, you know, that's how parents think, isn't it?"

She chatted and he made conversation, not really paying any mind to the words she spoke. She was just right and he was going to do her and the excitement was absolutely wonderful. On the one hand he wanted to drive forever, putting off the act indefinitely, prolonging the tantalizing feeling that gripped him now. And, at the same time, he wanted to stop the car that instant, to kill her *oh God yes* before another moment went by.

He waited, and a third impulse came. He had the thought of letting her go, of driving her all the way to Kirksville, even turning there and taking her straight to her home in Edina, and of never touching her, never doing her the slightest injury. She would hop out of the car and drag her duffel bag up the driveway to her house, never knowing how close she had come to death.

He had that urge some of the time. Every now and then he acted on it. Every now and then he would open his hand and release the helpless bird that fluttered within, watching benevolently as she flew away. He entertained the thought, then dismissed it. No, not this one. This bird would not be doing any more flying.

A mile down the road, he braked smoothly and turned onto a gravel road heading east.

"Where are we going?"

"There's construction up ahead," he told her.

"I didn't see a sign."

"I don't think there was one. I came down this way this morning and everything was all snarled up. We'll cut over to the next road going north and miss all that traffic."

Her eyes were wary. She thought it was going to be okay, she still felt pretty safe, but it had at least occurred to her that it might not be, and it was giving her something to think about.

He slowed, turned left onto a narrower road.

She said, "Are you sure this is a road? It's just a dirt road, I think it's just a farm road—"

"It goes through."

She was fumbling in her purse, and some instinct warned him. He slammed the brake pedal to the floor. She was propelled forward against her seat belt. He held the wheel with his left hand and swung his right, backhanding her full force across the mouth. She cried out.

He took the bag from her lap. Just below the top layer of articles he found a canister of Chemical Mace. She cringed when he displayed it.

"I wasn't going to do anything," she said. "I swear I wasn't."

He looked at her.

"I just got scared and I wanted to hold it," she said. "I got frightened, I . . . please don't hurt me."

"Be quiet."

"I'll do anything you want. Just don't hurt me."

"Be quiet. And sit still."

It was, as she had guessed, just a farm road. It would probably be safe for the next few minutes. But it would be safer still off the road, and he had her cowed now, she wouldn't try anything. Off the road, screened from sight by shrubbery, there would be no need to hurry.

He got the car where he wanted it and cut the ignition. She was calmer now, and a little more sure of herself. "I'll do anything you want," she said. "Honest, anything. Just so you don't hurt me."

He nodded. "What's your name?"

"Bethany."

143

"How old are you?"

"Nineteen."

"Take off your clothes, Bethany."

"Here? Or should I get out of the car first?"

"Stay in the car. You'll have to unhook your seat belt first, though."

"Oh, right."

She kicked off the sandals, opened her jeans and raised her hips up off the leather seat to squirm out of them. He took them from her, tossed them into the backseat. She took off the sweatshirt next, and then the T-shirt under it. No bra, and her tits were bigger than he would have guessed, milky white and very nice.

"Very nice," he said aloud.

She colored, and hesitated, and he said, "Yes, Bethany, the panties too," and she took those off and he flipped them into the back.

He had been wearing a suit jacket. He got out of it and tossed it in back with the clothes she'd removed. He filled his hands with her flesh. She was, he noticed, not terribly clean about her person. She had a discernible body odor, along with the very palpable smell of her fear.

He made her lie down on the front seat, and he laid his body on top of hers, pressing her down onto the seat. He could feel the heat of her loins through his trousers, he could feel her tits through his shirt, and he took her face in his hands and looked at her sweet young face.

"Just don't hurt me," she said.

"Oh, Bethany," he said. "Oh, you poor darling, it's no fun if I don't hurt you."

He watched her face as she took in what he'd said, and it was lovely, just lovely, and he didn't want to put her through any more and couldn't stand any more himself. So he placed the heel of his right hand under her chin, his fingertips just grazing her lip, and he cupped her forehead with his left hand, and he pushed up on her chin and back on her forehead and snapped her neck.

#57.

The first woman he killed, the black prostitute in the downtown motel, had been dispatched in a manner that was unplanned, impulsive, and extremely hazardous. He had left traces of his presence that a police laboratory could have found. And, although the pleasure had been unprecedented in his experience, it had been managed in such a manner as to make the aftermath uncomfortable and awkward.

Since then he had learned how to keep risk to a minimum while maximizing his pleasures; he was, indeed, conditioned to think in those terms, since they were essentially identical to one's goals in real estate investment.

Almost from the beginning he had stopped having intercourse with his partners. It was a pleasant sensation, certainly, to have one's sexual organ within a slippery envelope of flesh at the critical moment, but physical sensation of that sort played such a minor role in the excitement of the act as to render it almost irrelevant. And it was virtually impossible to achieve physical intimacy of that sort without leaving traces—pubic hair, semen, each capable of yielding no end of information to a trained forensic pathologist. On top of that, the act left traces upon oneself, and there was always the chance of catching a disease. While there was undeniable poetic justice in the notion of a woman infecting her killer with something at the least loathsome and at the worst life-threatening, he had no desire to afford one of his victims an opportunity for that sort of revenge.

So he tried keeping his clothing on, and the pleasure was no less intense for it. His orgasm came not as a result of

Lawrence Block

friction between his penis and another object but as the pure inevitable response to his mental excitement. He usually pressed against a woman when he killed her, but he didn't have to in order to reach full release.

But that, too, had a messy aftermath. He'd have to wash his underwear or throw it out, and sometimes his trousers had to make a trip to the dry cleaner. It took a while to hit on the solution, in part because he wasn't looking for one at first; for the first year or more, each killing was followed by a vow that he would never kill again, and so there seemed little reason to seek a better way to manage it.

He tried putting on a condom first. That worked, certainly, but there was something ridiculous about it, and he hated it. And then, on one occasion when impulse and circumstance provided him with the opportunity to kill a very pretty waitress in the parking lot of a Mexican restaurant in Houston (lying on the asphalt between two parked cars, crushing her windpipe with a tire iron), he had used all the strength available to him to hold back his orgasm.

It was enormously frustrating, but the act was thrilling all the same, and he'd simply hurried back to his motel room to stretch naked on his bed, reliving the episode in his mind while he relieved himself manually. He masturbated again the following morning, but this time he held back his ejaculation to defer his pleasure, and in so doing he made an astonishing discovery: it was possible to have an orgasm without ejaculating.

Since then he had learned that he was not the first person to find this out. A whole school of yoga practiced the retention of semen in sexual activity, and it seemed to be a part of various Chinese disciplines as well. Something was released—some kind of energy, something that demanded to be released—but the ejaculation was held back and the semen retained. At first when you did this you wound up with an ache in the pit of your stomach and a feeling of uncomfortable fullness in your loins, but as you became proficient at it and used to it the sensation was diminished, and what ache you did feel was not unpleasant.

And you weren't scattering your seed that way. Instead your system reabsorbed it, and retained its energy. You were stronger, and you could repeat the sex act almost immediately, and each further repetition, instead of draining you, simply energized you more.

He trained himself, practicing constantly through self-stimulation until he had mastered the new technique. Something he read suggested he could increase his muscular control by an exercise which involved cutting off the flow of urine in midstream. He did this, and developed whatever muscle was involved, but it was mental exercise that played the greater role. You had to build a filter into the mind so that it held back the passage of seed but allowed the spill of orgasmic release. He had some failures along the way, but he had more successes, and eventually he retained his semen as a matter of course, without much conscious effort at all.

Once he was able to do this regularly when he killed women, any thoughts he had about stopping the killings came to a permanent end. Evidently there was something in the passage of seed that engendered depression and remorse, because he felt neither once he ceased to ejaculate. He was still careful not to kill too often, he still sought to minimize risk, and he still had to take pains from time to time to keep his conscience at bay. But he knew he was not going to give all this up, and he didn't even delude himself that he wanted to.

He left Bethany on the ground, screened from the farm road by a clump of brush. He piled her clothes beside her and weighted them down with her duffel bag. He went

147

through the articles at the top of her handbag, wiping off anything he could have touched that might hold a print. He kept the canister of Mace.

On the way back to Columbia, he stopped for another hitchhiker, another college girl, this one returning for the summer session. She was an open-faced blonde and she reminded him a little of the sisters who'd given him the finger as he drove away from them. She was more solidly built, though, with a sort of bovine cast to her features.

She was silent in the seat beside him, and he didn't attempt to make conversation with her. He let himself savor the memory of Bethany and enjoyed a few brief fantasies of repeating the act with this blond girl, whose name he did not know. He could drive her up the same farm road, he could leave her dead behind the same clump of brush.

Instead, he drove her all the way into Columbia and dropped her off at her dormitory, then found his way back to I-70 and continued toward St. Louis.

If he'd found her before he found Bethany, he would have done her without a moment's hesitation. Or, if she'd been irresistibly attractive, he might not have let the episode with Bethany keep him from having her, too. But she just wasn't that appealing, and he wasn't that ravenous.

In St. Louis he checked into a motel out toward the airport, unpacked and took a shower. He called a couple of realtors and made appointments for the next several days. He spoke to a man at the firm he used to manage his rental properties in the area, and handled some business over the phone. He relaxed awhile in front of the television set, then put on a tie and jacket and drove downtown for a big meal at Tony's. He drank a half bottle of wine with his veal and had coffee and a brandy in the lounge. After dinner he walked for a couple of blocks to clear his head before collecting his car from the attendant and driving back to the motel.

In the morning he saw one of the realtors he had called, and then dropped in on his property management people just because he was in the neighborhood. He had a light lunch with the man he'd talked to on the telephone the previous afternoon, learned more than he cared to know about a local political scandal, and didn't discuss business at all.

In the afternoon he went to a supermarket and pushed a cart up one aisle and down the next. He took something off a shelf every now and then and put it in the cart, but he wasn't really shopping. He was looking at women. It was a wonderful place to observe them because they were remarkably unselfconscious, totally absorbed in the business of shopping and unaware that anyone might be looking at them. There were several very nice women in the supermarket, and he walked the aisles in a constant state of physical excitement.

When he'd spent as much time there as he wanted he abandoned his cart in the dairy section, picked up a couple of items he needed—a tube of toothpaste, a pack of six disposable razors, a box of Nutter Butter cookies—and hand-carried them to the checkout counter. The girl on the register (Sandy, according to her name tag) had a sunny smile and a pretty face. Her fingertips grazed his palm when she gave him his change.

"Have a nice day," she said.

He had dinner at a Pizza Hut not far from his motel. His waitress was darling, and so were two or three of the other waitresses, and several of the customers. Afterward he sat in his car for half an hour with the motor off and the lights out, waiting to see if anyone interesting came out alone, but no one did and he tired of the game. He went back to the motel and called Marilee. Both kids were home, and he talked to them, talked some more to Marilee, had another shower and went to sleep.

The following morning he saw another of the realtors he'd spoken to the first day. He wound up going around with her to look at a couple of properties. Her name was Janet, and he had always found her quite attractive, but he knew her professionally and had never allowed himself to entertain fantasies about her. By now he knew her too well; even if there were no risk, he wouldn't have been interested.

Nor was he much interested in either of the properties she took him to inspect. That was all right, he liked to look at property, you always learned something that way. She drove him back to her office and he picked up the Lincoln.

He drove around. The streets were full of women; the city was full of women. At a stop light, the car next to his was a Dodge convertible with the top down; the driver had a tight sweater and a pouty, sullen mouth. Country music blared on her radio. He let her pull ahead when the light turned and followed her for a dozen blocks until she sailed through an amber light that was red when he reached it. He didn't want to run the light, and by the time it changed she was gone.

He headed back toward the motel, but stayed on Lindbergh Boulevard past Florissant and parked at the Jamestown Mall. All of the stores were full of women and a remarkable proportion of them looked good to him. It was crowded everywhere, you couldn't even think about doing anything.

A salesgirl in a gift shop asked if she could help him. "Just looking," he said.

In the Waldenbooks store, he browsed the shelves and

studied the other customers. One book caught his eye, a paperback, and he carried it up front to the register.

The cashier was a woman about his age with a receding chin and a barbed Ozarks twang. She rang the sale and said, *"Men Who Hate Women.* Well, I met a few of those and I sure hope you're not one of them."

"Not me," he said. "I love women."

He left the mall and drove into Florissant, cruising up one suburban street and down the next. He stopped on a block of brick-fronted ranch houses set on quarter-acre plots. Each house had a young tree planted on the strip of grass between the sidewalk and the street, and most of the trees still had their trunks wrapped with tape. A large proportion of the cars parked in the driveways were either station wagons or hatchbacks.

He parked his car at the curb, got a clipboard from the trunk, and put a couple of pens into his shirt pocket. He crossed the street and walked up to the door of the first house he came to. He rang the bell.

The woman who answered it was middle-aged. She wore a patterned housedress and was smoking a cigarette.

He said, "Water company. Did you report a drop in pressure?" She said she hadn't. "Sorry to bother you," he said, and turned away from her.

There was no one home at the house next door. The woman at the third house was pregnant, and carrying a whining infant. He asked her the same question, and she too denied having reported problems with the water pressure, and he thanked her and left. The woman in the fourth house was pretty—light brown hair, dark brown eyes. He said, "Water company. We've been having problems with the water pressure in your area. Have you had any difficulty?"

"No," she said. "It seems okay." She turned from him,

151

called back into the house. "Adam, you stop your fussing. I'll just be a minute."

He thanked her and left. At the house after hers, he waited a long time before the door was answered. The woman was in her late twenties, and the minute Mark saw her he was glad her neighbor had had a child in the other room. Otherwise he'd have missed out on this one, and she was much too good to miss. She was just a little thing, barely over five feet tall, with a lovely figure and deep dark blue eyes. Oh, wonderful, just wonderful.

"Water company," he said. "We've been having some problems in your area. Have you had any difficulties with the pressure?"

She thought about it. "Uh, no," she said. "Not really."

"How about the appearance and flavor of the water?"

"I don't know," she said. "The coffee was all right this morning. I don't know as I drank any water, not just plain by itself."

"I see," he said. "Is it all right if I come in? I'm not interrupting anything?"

She shook her head. "I was just watching TV is all."

"You're not busy with the kids then?"

She shook her head. "Still in school."

Wonderful. He drew the door shut after him. "Now if I could just check the water in the kitchen taps first," he said. "Which way's the kitchen, if you don't mind?"

She led the way. She was wearing khaki slacks and he watched her rear as she walked. He caught up with her at the threshold to the kitchen, clapped a hand over her mouth and wrapped her in a choke hold, her throat caught in the crook of his arm. She struggled, but she was just a little thing and he was much too strong for her. Her struggles ceased and she slumped unconscious, limp in his grasp.

152

He undressed her there in the kitchen. He used a paper towel to protect his hand and went through drawers until one yielded an electrical extension cord. He cut it in half and used one piece to tie her ankles together and the other to bind her wrists behind her back. He stripped to the waist and picked her up in his arms and carried her through the house until he found the bathroom.

He set her down on the tile floor, stopped the bathtub drain and ran a lukewarm tub of water. The tub was still running when she groaned and opened her eyes.

She looked at him. Her mouth opened but she didn't make a sound. It didn't too much matter if she did; the window was closed, and he had drawn the bathroom door shut. No one could hear any sound she could make.

When the tub was as deep as he wanted it he shut off the water and turned to her. "Now I'm just going to give you a nice bath," he said. "That's all." And he picked her up in his arms—she had luxuriously soft skin, she was wonderful to touch—and placed her on her back in the tub.

He used his hands and ran the soap over her teacup breasts, down over her belly, lathered her pubic hair. He put the soap back in the dish and sluiced water over her to rinse her. Her eyes were wide, rolling in terror, but she still hadn't uttered a sound since regaining consciousness.

"You're so sweet," he said, bending to kiss her on the lips. He took hold of the hair at the back of her neck and drew her head down under the water, pinning her down with his other hand on her breast. She tried to struggle, and he could feel her heart hammering. He looked down at her face, just an inch or so below the water surface. Her huge eyes stared at him. She held her breath until she couldn't hold it anymore, and bubbles issued from her nose and mouth. He pressed down on her chest and her lungs emptied, spewing forth more bubbles. He took his hand away and her lungs filled with water. Her eyes still stared up at him from under the water, but the life was gone from them now.

#58.

When he was breathing normally again himself he unfastened the electrical cord from her wrists and ankles, dried off both pieces, put them in his pocket. He used a washcloth to remove his prints from the edge of the tub, and he dropped the soap into the water; if it held any of his prints, they would soon melt away.

He got his shirt from the kitchen and put it on. He picked up all of her clothing and left it folded on a chair in the master bedroom. By the time he left the house, clipboard in hand, he had erased every trace of his presence in it. With any luck at all, she'd go in the record books as a victim of accidental drowning.

He walked back to his car and drove away. For a few minutes he was lost in the suburban maze of Florissant, but then he got his bearings and found his way to the motel. He parked, but before getting out of the car he took the two lengths of electrical cord from his pockets.

They triggered a sense memory—the girl rolled onto her side while he drew her wrists together behind her back —and he followed the memory all the way to the end, with the blue eyes staring up at him from underwater, the lips parted, the life gone from her, his now, part of him. His body thrilled with an electric sensation not much reduced from the orgasm that had transported him as he drowned the darling little bitch.

Without thinking much about it, he fashioned a loop at either end of the piece of cord he was holding. The loops were large enough to admit his hands, and the length of cord between the loops was about eighteen inches. He flexed his fingers and felt the muscles working in his forearms.

Why not?

He started up the car, drove out of the motel lot and took the beltway around to Webster Groves, a suburb not unlike Florissant but southwest of the city. He drove around until he found a neighborhood substantially identical to the one where he'd left the girl floating in her bathtub, and he parked the car at the curb and walked up to the first house he came to, clipboard in hand, and the woman who opened the door was a willowy brunette in her mid-thirties, and he just could not wait to kill her.

He said, "Electric company. I'm afraid we've got a problem. Could you show me where your fuse box is?"

It was in the basement, but he never did see it. He let her get to the bottom of the cellar stairs, and there he clubbed her on the nape of her neck with his closed fist. The blow drove her to her knees, and before she could recover he had his own knee planted in the small of her back for leverage. He dropped the wire around her throat, and an instant later she was dead.

Oh, heaven!

#59.

ELEVEN

When Phil Donahue said he would be right back after this message, Mame Odegaard flicked off the set with the remote control device and carried her coffee cup into the kitchen. This was not the simple process it had once been. Mame was sixty-seven. Five years ago, which would have been some three years after her husband's death, she had begun to be bothered by arthritis. The condition had progressed, and it was now quite severe.

She could walk, but not without the aid of an aluminum walker. She could tend for herself, but everything took longer than it used to, and was more trouble, and often involved pain. Even doing nothing involved pain—pain in her fingers, pain in her toes and ankles, pain in her knees, pain in her hips. She took Tylenol every four hours and it was easier on her stomach than aspirin, but no matter what the doctors said she would swear it wasn't as effective as the aspirin, it didn't get past as much of the pain. But then perhaps aspirin wouldn't be as effective now as she remembered it, because her condition had worsened since she switched to Tylenol.

Her son wanted her to move in with him and his wife,

but he worked for the government and they lived in Maryland, just outside of Washington. They had a very nice house but it was their house, not her house, and this was his second wife, he and Ruth had been divorced for some years now, and she had been real close to Ruth and just couldn't warm up to the second wife, Stephanie. They got along all right, but a visit was a far cry from living under the same roof, and she didn't want it.

And she didn't want to live in a city, either. Nor did she like the idea of a retirement village in Arizona, which he kept proposing to her. There would be people around, he told her, people her own age, and she'd have activities, and the harsh winters of western Oregon would be a thing of the past. And, most important, things would be easier for her. She wouldn't have to do so much for herself, and the heat would help her arthritis, and life would be, well, easier. Easier and better.

And it probably would, she had to agree, but it wasn't what she wanted. She'd lived at this house beside the road for forty years, moving into it just three years after she and Karl were married. She'd birthed both her children in that house, and she'd buried her daughter from it, and her husband, too.

She could walk out her back door and be steps from the Malheur River. She could see Cottonwood Mountain from her back door, or she could stand on her front step and look at Sourdough Mountain. She had been looking at her mountains for forty years and she wasn't in any big hurry to give them up.

She rinsed her cup in the sink and walked to her front door now, and out onto the step. She looked first at the mountain, as if to confirm that it was still where she'd seen it last, and then at her mailbox at the foot of the drive. The flag was down, which was supposed to indicate that the mailman had come. When she collected her mail she put the flag up, even if she didn't have any letters to be picked up. Then he would put the flag down when there was mail for her, and that way she would not have to walk the hundred yards to the road for nothing. It was a long walk, and she didn't like to make it for no reason at all.

She walked down to the road, positioning the aluminum frame, taking a step, gathering herself, moving the frame, taking a step, covering the hundred yards one small step at a time.

The box was empty. Actually this was not that surprising. Sometimes she forgot to put the flag up. For years she had only done so when she was leaving a letter, and old habits were hard to change. It was early, too, it wasn't eleven, Donahue was still on. She almost always watched the whole of the Donahue show, and even then the mail usually didn't arrive for another hour, so why had she even looked to see if the flag was up or down, let alone walked all the way out here?

Now she didn't know for sure that she'd left the flag down, and she didn't know for sure that the postman hadn't come, since there were days when he came extra early, just as there were days when he came quite late. So either he hadn't come or he hadn't had any letters for her, there was no way to tell, and it didn't much matter, since either way she'd made the trip for nothing.

Of course it didn't hurt her to walk. Well, that wasn't the right way to put it. It pained her some, but it was supposed to do her good in the long run. The arthritis was worse if she didn't exercise than if she did, which was another argument against moving to some retirement home where people would do things for her that she now had to do for herself.

Now that she was here, she might as well wait for the mail. Save making the trip again later on.

A car passed. The driver honked and she waved. She

leaned her weight on the aluminum frame and enjoyed the warmth of the sun on her arms. Crazy to stand out here—it might be hours before the mail came, and since when did she center her whole day around the mail delivery? All she ever got in the mail were bills and seed catalogues and invitations to subscribe to magazines or contribute to politicians or buy a set of porcelain commemorative thimbles from the Franklin Mint. Her son never wrote. If he had something to say he picked up the telephone.

What was she doing out here? Why had she walked out here in the first place, why had she turned off Donahue ahead of time?

Something made her stand there patiently. And then she saw the first of them coming down the road from the west. She may have sensed them before they came into view, but then they came into sight around the bend, a whole troop of hikers strung out along the road.

You rarely saw hikers on the road, and never so many of them. She felt excitement at the sight of them, and wondered why. They had come out of nowhere, from the west. They would disappear into nowhere, in the east. Why should their brief presence mean anything to her? If she wanted to be stirred by something, let her be stirred by Sourdough Mountain. It wouldn't walk off and leave her, it had been there when she was born and it would still be there when she died.

But when the first of them reached her she said, "Well now, just look at you, and aren't there a wonderful number of you? My house is open and the kitchen's down the hall on the left. My well's deep and the water runs cold and clear. And there's a bathroom off the kitchen if any of you would care to use it." She said all this in one breath. Now she took another breath and said, "My name's Mame Odegaard. You'll excuse me if I just stay here. I'd show you

159

to the house but you might perish of thirst before I got all the way there." She beamed at them. "It's nice to see you. I hope you're not in too much of a hurry, because I'm glad of the company. I don't get much of it here, being sort of out of the way for most people."

They stayed with her for almost an hour. They filled their canteens, they used the bathroom, they harvested a few handfuls of berries from the patch she told them about down by the river bank. While they were there the mail did finally come, and of course there was nothing in it worth looking at, just some bills and circulars and a letter wanting to know why she wasn't renewing her subscription to *Country Crafts Magazine.* If they really wanted to know, she thought, she could send them a picture of her hands.

When they couldn't think of another excuse to stay, and she had run out of things to offer them, they each took her hand and thanked her and wished her good-bye. She felt no sadness at the prospect of parting, but she did feel wistful. The craziest thing she'd ever heard of, a slew of fools walking across the country, but if she were younger she'd be going with them and she knew it. Younger? It wasn't her age that was holding her back, sixty-seven wasn't old, not nowadays. It was the damnable arthritis. How could you walk across the country when you couldn't walk to the mailbox?

But something made her say, "Now do you know what I wish? I wish I could walk just a little ways down the road with you. So that no matter how far you went on without me, I'd still be going with you in spirit."

"Then that's what you'll do, Mame."

"Oh, I'd slow you down. I can't do that."

"You'll walk with me," one of them said. His name was Les, she remembered, and he was the biggest of the lot, with a fancy western shirt and an imposing bamboo walking stick. "It don't matter how slow we go, ma'am. The rest of these folks can go on ahead and I'll catch up with 'em later. I've been holding down my pace to stay with them all morning, and if they get out in front a mile or two it'll give me a chance to stretch my legs."

Two of the younger men suggested they could interlock their arms to make a chair and carry her that way. Sara, the blind woman with the beautiful gray eyes, said no, that Mame should walk with Les. But how would she get back when she had gone as far as she wanted to go?

"I'll walk her back," he said, "or I'll carry her back if she's had enough walking. You people aren't gonna get that far out in front of me. You'll stop for lunch, or to look at a mountain, or to dig in the dirt for arrowheads. Mame and I could walk for an hour and I'd still catch up with you by the time you're ready to make camp for the night."

"But do you want to do that?" she demanded. "Don't you want to stay with your friends?"

"Oh, these folks aren't my friends," he told her. "They just want me for my money."

And so they walked together. Her pace was shamefully slow but he didn't seem to mind in the least. He walked with a rolling gait, so that he seemed to be moving all the time even though he was keeping pace with her. At first it pained her to see the rest of them drawing away from her, but before long they vanished around a bend in the road, and once they were out of sight she was less aware of the widening gap between them. Now she and Les were no longer at the rear and falling ever farther behind; instead, they were off on their own, and keeping up with each other just perfectly.

He spoke some about his business career, and about his marriages. "One was worse than the next," he said, "and after the last time I swear I never thought I'd do it again,

161

and if I hadn't been drinking Jack Daniel's on top of French champagne I wouldn't have, and surely wouldn't have picked Georgia to marry. But do you want to know something? I think it might last awhile."

She talked about her marriage, and her husband's death. She told how he'd ignored warning signals and broken doctor appointments. "They might have saved him if he went to them on time," she said, "but he was scared of what they'd find, and so he went and died for fear he might be dying. Damn the man anyway, making me a widow with his damnable cowardice."

Les said something, but she didn't even hear him. She was too shocked by her own words and the tone of her own voice. Why, she'd never said anything like that before. She'd never even *thought* anything like that before.

Or spoke of anyone, least of all Karl, in that tone of voice.

She talked about her daughter, her second-born child, born with a defective valve in her heart, sickly all her life, always a near-invalid, and dead, God rest her, at seventeen.

"And all those years until then," she said, "she stayed alive but she wasn't alive. She couldn't really live, do you know what I mean, Les? She couldn't run. She couldn't climb a full flight of stairs. She caught cold all the time, she got weary in the summer's heat. And I wanted to shout, 'Go ahead! If you're not going to live then go ahead and die!' But of course she didn't die. And then she did die, and I buried her."

Was that true? Had she ever wanted Mary Frances to die? No, it couldn't be true, it was just the excitement of the day, making all manner of unseemly things come popping out of her mouth.

And Les said, "Mame, you don't have to push yourself. Just walk at a nice easy pace."

"I'll take that as a joke, Les."

"No, I'm serious," he said. "You're walking much faster than you did when we first set out."

"Well, if I am I didn't realize it," she said. "I'm certainly not straining. *I* thought I was going the same snail's pace as always. Plant the walker, take a step, shift your weight, move the walker. *You're right.* I *am* going faster."

"I told you."

"I guess my joints are warming up a little," she said. "All this activity, and out in the sun and all."

"Karl was just trying to protect me," she said. "He thought I couldn't manage without him. He should have known better than that, but he didn't. He needed the idea that I needed him. He had to think I wasn't enough without him, because he thought *he* wasn't enough unless he was needed by somebody." She sighed. "He was a sweet man. He didn't dare believe he had cancer. He tried to fight it by closing his eyes to it, and then it was too late."

And, a little later, "Why did Alan have to move to Washington? What was so wonderful about him that he deserved a better life than his mother and father had? What made him too good for his home, too good for his family? Why, he even came to discover he was too good for his wife, and so he had to leave Ruth and marry the new one, Stephanie."

And, after that, "I couldn't bear knowing I would lose Mary Frances someday. I loved her so much I couldn't stand the idea. And so I wanted her to hurry up and die and get it over with, but I was afraid to want that, so I cut off the feeling, and by doing that I held back some of the love, because I was afraid to love her as much as I did."

And, finally, "Les, do you want to know what the real story is about me? I just always wanted to hold onto everything. I couldn't bear to let go of a thing. I was always

163

afraid people would leave me and I'd be the less for it. Why, these past years, staying on in that house. Les, I was trying to hold onto those mountains."

"They're fine mountains, Mame."

"Well, they're fine without me, and I'll be fine without them. I swear I'm all of a sudden seeing things faster than I can fit words to the tune of them. Les, do you need that stick?"

"Pardon?"

"That bamboo cane, that stick of yours. Do you need it to walk?"

"Oh, hell, no," he said. "I thought I might when I bought it, but I mostly picked it up because it struck me as a handsome piece of workmanship. There's not a great deal you'd admire to purchase in Bend. Why?"

"Could you take this metal frame away from me, and just let me try your stick for a little while?"

"You think you'll be all right with it?"

"I think I'll be fine with it. I *know* I'll be fine with it."

It was just the most remarkable thing.

She never seemed to be hurrying, because as the arthritis withdrew she went on putting the same amount of effort into her walking, and it kept producing greater results. Her body straightened, her stride lengthened, her step quickened, and she simply could not believe what was happening to her.

Except that she could believe it, she had to be able to believe it, or else how in the world could it happen? Because there were moments when she fastened on that thought—*I can't believe this*—and then she would feel something seize up inside of her, something curled within her bones, and she would begin to give back a little of what she had gained. Somehow she knew that she couldn't have this unless she was prepared to believe it, and so she willed that belief into her bones and breathed deeply to fuel herself and kept those feet moving.

"Mame, if we go much further, it's going to be a long walk back."

"Les, do you really think I'm going back?"

"I don't guess you are, not to stay. But isn't there anything you need to get from the house?"

"Like some cash money and something to wear? There is, but there's nothing I want enough to go back for it. Les, I don't even want to look back. I might turn into a pillar of salt. I remember Mary Frances heard that story in Sunday school and thought it was a pillow of salt."

"You'll wish you had any kind of a pillow tonight, Mame. We just bed down on bare ground."

"Walk twenty miles and a body could probably sleep standing up. Les, you can throw that thing away, that walker. Or just leave it by the side of the road. Some old crippled lady might come along and have a use for it."

There was a long curving uphill stretch to the road, and at the top of the rise you could see a long ways. "There they are," she said, pointing. "They must have stopped to take in the view."

"Slowpokes," he said.

"We'll catch 'em."

When someone at the rear of the procession turned and caught sight of the two of them, word passed the length of the column and all of them came back to wait for the pair to catch up. When Mame reached them, walking like a girl, there was a long moment of awed silence. Then, tentatively, someone began to clap. And then everyone was applauding, and it rolled and echoed in the hills like thunder.

TWELVE

The morning after Mame joined them, Guthrie bought an Idaho map at a gas station outside of Vale, and before nightfall they had crossed the Snake into Idaho and made camp outside of Payette. The group had continued to grow—two college students had joined in as they marched through Ontario, Oregon, and a loose-limbed farmhand with a half pint of Mad Dog 20–20 in each of his hip pockets had fallen into step with them shortly after they crossed the state line. Guthrie didn't have their names straight yet, let alone know what they were about.

He squatted by the fire, studying the new map, and when it burned lower he went off a ways and went on studying it by flashlight. The map was a puzzle, and when he made the mistake of trying to puzzle it out he wound up feeling like a lab rat in an unsolvable maze. The state was all mountains. Except for the Interstate, which did not lend itself to their sort of travel, all of the roads moved in a devious fashion, tracing circuitous paths through the Rockies. He found one promising route, more direct than most, that proceeded east along the Salmon River. But the line on the map suggested that it might be only a rudimentary road, perhaps no more than a foot trail, and when he checked the table of symbols he found out it wasn't a path at all, it was part of the line of demarcation between the Mountain and Pacific time zones.

Talk about walking a thin line, he thought. Every false step would cost you an hour.

He gave up analyzing, and then the route seemed to jump out at him from the map. He found Sara sitting up beside the dying fire and led her off to one side.

"I think I've got our route," he said. "I don't know, though. There's a stretch of 21 through the Sawtooth Range that's marked 'Closed in Winter.'"

"It's still June, Guthrie."

"I know that. Still, the roads they close in the winter may not open all that wide in the summer. It looks as though we're in for a lot of steep climbing and bad roads and places with more bears than people. Does our celestial protection plan have a clause about bears?"

"I didn't read the fine print."

"What I'm getting at is we've got a woman with a kid strapped on her back and another who's only thirty-odd hours out of an aluminum walker. Are they going to be able to make it?"

"Guthrie, I think Mame can cover any stretch of ground you or I can."

"I think the same thing, only I feel like an idiot for thinking it. I've been wanting to talk to you about this all day. What the hell happened?"

"With Mame? She had a healing."

"That sounds as though she scratched her knee on a thornbush and it mended without leaving a scar. That's not what Mame had. She had a complete recovery from crippling arthritis."

"Isn't it more or less the same thing?"

167

"The way an ice cube's the same thing as the chunk that sank the *Titanic*. What happened to Mame was a miracle."

"I agree."

"So—"

"Every healing's a miracle, Guthrie. Say you scratch yourself on a thorn. The skin is broken, the flesh is torn, and although you don't even give it a moment's thought the blood coagulates and the cells reach out to one another and they grow back together. You don't think that's miraculous?"

"It may be hard to understand, and it may make you want to congratulate God on designing a good system, but it's ordinary, isn't it? It's the way things work."

"Just an everyday miracle," she said. "You know, you can cut a piece of paper with a scissors, then patch it with Scotch tape, and you can leave it like that for a year and not have the paper grow back together again."

"Sara—"

"I remember when my brother broke the leg off one of the dining room chairs by rocking on it, and my father glued that chair and put a couple of screws into it. But when Eddie broke his own leg skiing they didn't use glue or screws, they just put it in a cast and it grew back together. Why do you suppose skin and bone mend themselves and wood and paper don't?"

"I get the point. Life is a fucking miracle. But what happened to Mame wasn't an everyday miracle. It was unusual, it was impossible, it was harder than your average run-of-the-mill miracle."

She was shaking her head. "There's no order of difficulty in miracles. They're all impossible. You can't divide them into major and minor miracles. This wasn't the first miracle we've witnessed on this pilgrimage. Look how many of us have had healings of the spirit. Look what's happened to Jody, to John, to Martha. Even for those of us

168

who haven't had a lot of tears and high drama, look how our spirits have been healed. We're all becoming the people we really were all along. The deposits in the joints of our spirits are melting and washing away like Mame's arthritis, and we can move and laugh and sing again."

"You're saying it's the same thing?"

"Of course it's the same thing. But Mame's not the first person with a healing on the physical level. Look at you, for God's sake."

"Me?"

"You spent twenty years addicted to nicotine. You think that's not a physical condition? Nicotine's more addictive than heroin. If you run animal experiments, habituating them to a drug and then giving them free choice between the drug and water, you can determine what percentage get addicted. You get different percentages with different drugs, and there's some variance with species. With nicotine the addiction rate is at or near 100 percent irrespective of species. *And you quit.* Don't you think that's a miracle?"

"Lots of people quit smoking."

"Without trying? Without even intending to? And with no withdrawal symptoms and no craving?"

"Okay, it's a miracle."

"You had an even more obviously physical healing, didn't you? Didn't Jody take away your headache?"

"Oh, right. With his hands. He's been doing that for a lot of people."

"He takes away pain with his hands." She smiled softly. "Jody grew up thinking he caused people pain. What better gift could he get than the ability to take their pain away?"

His head whirled, and he thought he'd probably need Jody's services again soon. He said, "To get back to Mame—"

"She cured herself of arthritis, Guthrie. That's all. All cures are the same. They happen when you decide on a

169

cure and manifest it on a physical level. Sometimes you go to a doctor and he gives you something that triggers it. Sometimes you go to a church. Sometimes you go to someone like Jody, who gives you a transfer of energy that starts the process in motion. Then your body remembers what it's supposed to do, and the bone knits or new skin forms or calcium deposits dissolve. That's what a healing is, that's what a miracle is. The wonder isn't that they happen. The wonder is that they only happen some of the time."

"Her healing was so fast, Sara."

"I know. We usually don't let ourselves mend that quickly because we know it's not possible. But Mame was in a hurry. If she spent a month healing herself we'd be in Idaho before she was ready to walk."

"I hope we'll be out of Idaho by then. We'll be in Montana."

"The point is we'd be out of reach. Mame needed to heal fast, so she didn't listen to the part of her mind that knew you couldn't walk out from under that bad a case of arthritis in a couple of miles. She healed her spirit by undoing all the knots that she'd tied in it over the years, she let go of everything she'd been holding onto too tightly, and every step she took helped make her whole again." She considered for a moment. "The first step set it all in motion. But she had to stay with it, she had to walk through the parts that hurt more than the arthritis."

"Could she have done it without us?"

She spread her hands. "I don't know how to answer that. People cure themselves all the time without walking across the country to do it. Sometimes it's a cold, sometimes it's a shaving nick, sometimes it's a terminal illness. People choose their diseases and sometimes they choose to heal them. So Mame *could* have healed herself. She didn't even have to walk to do it, with us or without us. But she probably wouldn't have been able to make the choice to do it. There's something magical about this walk of ours, Guthrie."

"I know that."

"It lets people make choices they never could make before. Martha's sinuses are clear for the first time in years. And Gary's not smoking. He doesn't know whether or not to be happy about it, he liked smoking, but when he lights a cigarette he takes one drag and puts it out."

"I remember what that was like."

"Sue Anne cured herself of cancer. Most people would probably call that a miracle."

"When was that? I didn't know she had it."

"Neither did she. She didn't know she had it and she doesn't know it's gone, and I'm not sure whether I ought to tell her or not. She knows on some level, she had to know or she couldn't have made it happen, but she doesn't have any conscious knowledge and maybe she doesn't need any."

"How do you know she had it?"

"I picked it up when I first held her hand. I could see it, a mass in her right breast, and it felt—I don't know, *hot,* sort of."

"To the touch?"

"No, I only touched her hand. I felt heat from the lump in my mind when I scanned her. And then I made a point of taking her hand later that day to see if I got the same reading, and I did. There were some similar hot spots in her uterus, and I believe breast cancer frequently metastasizes there."

"Jesus. And you didn't say anything?"

"I wasn't sure what to do, Guthrie. I'm a blind headshrinker, not a board-certified radiologist. I'm willing to trust my diagnostic skills, but why should anybody else be? If I sent her to a doctor and I turned out to be right,

171

then he would remove her breast and her uterus and that might be enough to save her, or the same factors that led her to create the cancer in the first place might bring about a recurrence. In any event, she'd be in a hospital somewhere." She smiled. "I thought it might be more efficacious to keep my mouth shut and wait for a miracle. But I decided to scan her every day so that I could monitor the condition."

" 'Trust everybody but cut the cards.' And when you scanned her—"

"The cancerous mass was reduced in both sites. That was yesterday morning. By last night the uterus was clear and the lump in the breast was smaller and there was no heat coming from it. And this morning it was completely gone."

"Jesus."

"Well, I suppose he may have had something to do with it. Depending on your belief system."

"What happened, Sara? I don't mean metaphysically. Where did the cancer *go?*"

"To cancer heaven, I suppose. Who knows what happens in spontaneous remissions? The cancer cells died. Maybe they killed themselves, maybe the other cells ganged up on them and ate them. The body does this sort of thing all the time, there are all these little SWAT teams cruising around the bloodstream on search-and-destroy missions."

" 'The Walk That Cures Cancer.' It sounds like something from the *Enquirer.*"

"I know it does. You know what they say, just because it's in the *Enquirer* doesn't mean it's necessarily a lie."

"I know, some of that shit actually happens."

"My gums are getting better. My dentist says I've had significant bone loss, he's been after me to have periodontal surgery for the past year and a half. My gums bleed easily and some of the teeth are a little loose in their sockets. But make that past tense. My gums don't bleed anymore, and my teeth are no longer loose, and I wouldn't be surprised if I'm regenerating some of that bone. That's supposed to be impossible, but so what? 'The difficult we do at once; the impossible takes a little longer.'"

"Except when it doesn't."

"Except when it doesn't. 'The Walk That Cures Periodontal Disease' wouldn't sell as many tabloids, but if it means I get to keep my teeth, I'm not complaining."

"No, I don't blame you."

They fell silent. The moon was a pale sliver, and every possible star glinted overhead. The sky tonight seemed to Guthrie to have depth. Usually it looked two-dimensional to him, like the painted interior ceiling of a great dome, but now the stars appeared strewn at random across an infinity of space.

An owl called in the distance. The sound died, leaving the silence more pronounced. Guthrie said, "Is that what we're walking for, Sara? Healing?"

"That certainly seems to be a part of it."

"Sometimes it feels like an encounter group and other times like a visit to a faith healer."

"It has elements of both, but the intensity is greater here, I think. And so are the results. And when something really dramatic happens, like Mame's walk, it gives everybody a sense of the possibilities. I don't know what the limits are. Maybe there aren't any."

"Why are some of us getting healed while others aren't? Douglas has a bum hip, he's had it since he was in high school, and I haven't noticed any improvement since he got here. Mame walked away from her arthritis just like that, and his limp's no better than when he joined us."

"Maybe he's not ready to give it up. Or maybe it's not

173

the healing he came for. Yes, we're here to be healed. But that's not the only reason we're here."

"What else is there?"

"I don't know yet. I get flashes of it but I can't see enough to guess the shape of it."

He had another question, but he had to force himself to ask it. "Sara? What about your eyes?"

"What about them?"

"Has there been any healing?"

"Of my vision?" She patted his hand. "I'm not going to be getting my eyesight back, love. It's gone."

"What does that mean? That it would take a miracle?"

She shook her head. "That's not the point. I didn't come here to heal my eyesight, Guthrie. I came here to sacrifice it."

"I know that."

"I thought you did."

"It's just that, oh, when we were on the bridge today, crossing the Snake River? I couldn't help wishing you could have seen it."

"Oh, Guthrie," she cried. "Would you like me to tell you what I see when I look at a river?"

Route 52 along the banks of the Payette River to Horseshoe Bend. Then a gravel road running right to a ghost town just below Placerville, and a turn onto another gravel road cutting southeast through New Centerville to Idaho City. Then Route 21 northeast through national forest and into the Sawtooth Range, and cutting southeast again to Stanley, and Route 75 east through Sunbeam and Clayton and north past Bald Mountain and a petrified forest and into US 93, and north along the Salmon River all the way to the town of Salmon, and Idaho 28 switching southeast to Tendoy, and then a road, unnumbered on his map, first gravel and then dirt, heading east over the

Bitterroots and crossing through Lemhi Pass into Montana.

That was the route Guthrie had traced out for them, and it would have been a hard trip in a car. On foot it was harder, the sort of trek where you'd expect a certain amount of attrition, with some people dropping out and deciding to head back.

Nobody dropped out. On the contrary, people kept dropping in. Not all that many, because there was not that large a population base to draw from, but enough so that the group kept growing.

Dingo was an outlaw biker. He had a full beard, a shaved head, one black front tooth, a single gold earring, and a lot of scar tissue on his face and body. He wore jeans and a denim jacket with the sleeves cut off. He had an Iron Cross around his neck and a studded leather wristband on each wrist and heavy ass-kicking boots on his feet. He looked like a middle-class nightmare.

He was one of seven bikers on five Harley-Davidsons who caught up with the group early one afternoon. Dingo would have looked menacing all by himself. With his companions, he looked like Attila on the march.

But the bikers were curious, not hostile. They asked their questions, cracked their jokes, offered various illegal substances around, then gunned their engines and took off.

A few miles away, Dingo accelerated to pull up even with two brothers who were riding double. "Hey, let Weasel ride with me some," he said.

"What, are you two sweethearts?"

"Yeah, I want a cock to play with while I ride and I can't reach my own."

"If it wasn't so fuckin' small you could reach it."

"Yeah, well, your mama never complained. Pull the fuck over, will you?"

175

Riding with Weasel, he said, "How'd you like those people we met just now?"

"The walkers? Assholes."

"Maybe. Got to be some kind of righteous duty, though. Walking across the country."

"Got to be crazy to do it."

"Maybe," he said. Then he said, "Hey, Weeze, you like my hog?"

"This here bike?"

"Yeah. You like it?"

"Shit yes."

"You want it?"

"Huh?"

"I said do you want it?"

"The bike? Do I want it?"

"Do you?"

"Fuck, man. Would a dog lick hisself? Of course I want it."

"It's yours."

"Huh?"

"It's yours, Weasel. All you got to do is run back with me to where the walkers are, and you can keep the bike."

"What are you gonna do?"

"Walk."

"You gotta be crazy, Dingo."

"So?"

When they'd caught up with the group Dingo uncoupled a bag with his gear in it and slung it over his shoulder. He gave the Harley a pat and told Weasel to take over.

"Just treat her good," he said. "You do right by her and she'll always give you her best."

"Like a woman," Weasel said.

"Well, no," Dingo said. "You got to kick the shit out of a woman now and then."

He started walking, picked up his pace, and took a

position around the middle of the group, falling into step with John Powers. "Hey, nice day, huh?" he said.

"Real nice," John said.

"My name's Dingo."

"Mine's John."

"Oh, yeah? My name used to be John. Before it was Dingo."

"Oh."

"Yeah. It sure is a beautiful day."

Later, walking with Gary, he said, "Cowboys and bikers, now there's two kind of people never did get along."

"I know. We always hated you people."

"Yeah, we felt the same about you. Cowboy walks into a biker bar, he's askin' to get stomped. No other way to look at it."

"That's a true statement. Only thing dumber is for a biker to walk into a cowboy bar."

"I saw a cowboy get killed once."

"Yeah?"

"Biker hit on a girl, cowboy and his friends didn't like it, biker took a beating. Biker came back with his brothers, couldn't find but one cowboy, and it was nothing but boots and chains. He wasn't even the one who started the whole thing, I don't know if he was even part of it."

"If you saw it," Gary said slowly, "you must have been one of the bikers."

"Well, fuck, I wasn't the girl. Man, we were fucked up. I mean, crank and reds is a destructive combination."

"I don't know about drugs," Gary said. "Seems to me cowboys get mean enough on beer and whiskey. I never saw nobody killed, but I did see a biker get cut once."

"What, stabbed?"

"Nutted. You know, castrated. His balls cut off."

"Is that true?"

"I'm afraid it is."

177

"What'd he do?"

"Nothin'. He was just there, is all. There was a bunch of hands spent the whole day nuttin' calves."

"What for?"

"Are you shitting me? That's how you get steers, man. You take the calves and cut their balls off. You order a steak, that's what you're eating."

"You're eating the calves' nuts?"

"No, shit, don't you know anything?" He laughed. "You get a bull calf, you nut him, and then he's a steer and that's what your beef is. If you don't cut him he grows up to be a bull and you can't control him on the range and the meat's not right. I thought everybody knew that."

"I grew up in Oakland, man. Meat came in packages wrapped in plastic. Milk came in cartons. Chicken came fried. What happened to this biker? You wouldn't know what bunch he rode with, by any chance? Like Hell's Angels, Rebels, Savage Skulls? One of those?"

"Hell, I don't know. He was a biker is all, and he was there. And these guys been cutting calves all day, and big surprise they're drinking pretty good, and somebody gets the idea of cutting the biker same as they been cutting the calves. And so they do it."

"He lets 'em?"

"They didn't give him much choice. There was six or eight of them, and they just held him down and did it."

"They cut off his whole works?"

"No, just his balls. You cut the cock, a man might bleed to death."

"Cut the balls off and he'll just wish he did. I never heard anything like that. Didn't his brothers come back at you?"

"Never."

"Maybe he never said anything. Maybe he didn't want to spread it around. Fuck. That is some story."

178

"Well, cowboys got a lot of stories," Gary said. "I guess bikers got a few, too."

"I guess," said Dingo.

Gene was a jack-Mormon who lived in a shack on federal land. He trapped, hunted, and made a little beer and whiskey. He had two wives, Essica and Lily, and five children between the ages of eight and eleven. The first chance he got, Thom asked one of the older boys whether there were any Chinese Mormons. The boy said he'd never met any.

"You got a nice little family," Jody told Gene. "I didn't think Mormons could still have more'n one wife."

"You can't," Gene said, "but there's a lot that do. What are they going to do, run around locking people up? Of course you can't be in good standing with the church, but that only matters if you give a shit about it. Which I don't."

"Yeah. How is it having two wives, anyway?"

"Well, I'd say it's good," Gene said judiciously. "They sort of keep each other company. They're in the kitchen together, they care for the children together, they do their chores together. It works real good that way."

"They don't get jealous?"

"Naw."

"You have some kind of schedule?"

"Schedule? Oh, you mean for who to sleep with? No, we just all three sleep together."

"Oh."

"It works real fine that way."

"I guess," Jody said, and clapped him on the shoulder. "Just one more question, hoss. Who do I see if I want to join this church of yours?"

Kate and Jamie were picking raspberries at roadside just east of Lowman. Kate was Boston Irish, and she had gone through a period in her late teens when she had Gaelicized her name to Caitlin. Jamie was a black woman from the South Side of Chicago. Both were nearing thirty, both had short hair, and both were dressed alike in baggy fatigues from Banana Republic and unpatterned flannel shirts from Norm Thompson and duck hunter boots from L. L. Bean.

They lived together at a lesbian commune half a mile up a dirt road, and the group waited while they went back there to fill a pair of backpacks and say their good-byes. They returned with a couple of spare backpacks and some extra canteens, a hamper of food, and two half-gallon jugs of homemade elderflower wine. They also brought Neila, a big-eyed thin-limbed waif of a woman with a skittish manner and a haunted look about her.

"She doesn't say much," Kate told Martha and Sara, "but you should have seen her when she turned up back in November. I don't think she spoke a word the first week she was with us. Somebody must have done a number on her. I thought she probably should have stayed with the other women, but she wanted to come. Something told her to come to the Hen House when she needed us, and the same thing must be telling her to leave."

Sara grasped Neila's hands and saw child abuse that started in the cradle, a tough little brute of a father with a predilection for sexual torture, a slow-witted mother, herself terrified of her husband, who acquiesced in and abetted her daughter's exploitation. She saw more than she wanted to see, and had to fight the impulse to close her inner eyes and draw away. Instead she made herself center her energies in her heart, letting herself feel Neila's pain and revulsion and beaming back love in return.

"It's right for her to be with us," was all she said.

A mile or so on down the road, Sue Anne found herself walking alongside Neila. Neither of them spoke. After they had walked together for a few minutes, Sue Anne opened the clasp of the gold chain and hung it around Neila's neck. The blue crystal lay between Neila's breasts. Neila stiffened at first, but then she took the crystal in her hand and looked at it, and her features relaxed into what was almost a smile.

Later on, Sue Anne caught up with Lissa. She said, "That crystal you gave me? The one you got from Grace?"

"What about it?"

"I gave it to Neila."

"Oh."

"I don't know why I did that. I liked wearing it, you know? But something just told me to give it to her."

"Well, something just told me to give it to you."

"I thought maybe I should keep it because you gave it to me."

"Grace gave it to me, and I had the same kind of thought, but it seemed the right thing to pass it on."

Walking with Jordan, Thom said, "You must be glad to see Jamie."

"Why? We supposed to be old friends or something?"

"Well, she's black. Now you're not the only black person in the group."

"She doesn't like me."

"What are you talking about? She hasn't even met you yet."

"We already know she hates guys," Jordan said. "She's probably got no use for Indians, either."

Jerry Arbison was the man who had abandoned his Ford Taurus as a prelude to discarding his car keys, tie, jacket, his vest and his wristwatch. The last was a Rolex, he confided, but not the expensive Rolex.

He had been born in Ohio in a Cleveland suburb and

181

had majored in English at Western Reserve. After graduation he went west to get a master's in film studies at UCLA.
He wrote two unsuccessful screenplays before landing a job
at the William Morris Agency. After a few years there he
opened his own office as an agent, representing film and
television writers. He closed the agency after a year and a
half and became a stockbroker with Smith Campbell
Hamilton, where his client list consisted largely of screen-
writers and their friends.

He had gone back to Cleveland for his grandmother's
funeral. He'd flown east for the funeral, but he hadn't
wanted to fly back so he'd bought the car in Cleveland. He
planned to drive straight back, but first he drove down to
Dayton to visit an old college buddy. He stayed three days,
and from the buddy's house he called an old girlfriend,
divorced now and living in Fond du Lac, Wisconsin. He
stayed at her apartment and they spent three days drinking
chilled Beaujolais and fucking like weasels, and on the
third night he asked her to marry him.

"Let's not move too fast, Jerry," she said. "You've never
been married. I have. I'm still getting over the divorce.
Let's live together, you can move right in here or I'll come
out to L.A., whichever you'd rather. I don't really care
where I live. And then, you know, we'll take it from there."

The next morning she went to work. As soon as her car
was out of the driveway he threw all his things in his
suitcase, jumped in the Ford, and got the hell out of there.

Jesus, talk about your narrow escapes.

He drove across the country, but he kept getting off the
Interstate and just driving around. When he got back to
L.A. he'd step back into his life, but he didn't seem willing
to do that. In Grand Junction, Colorado, he took a room at
a Ramada Inn and couldn't leave the room. The first day
he went downstairs to the coffee shop for his meals, but
then he stopped being able to do that, and he would call up

Domino's Pizza two or three times a day and have a pizza and a couple of Cokes delivered. There was a Coke machine on his floor, next to the elevator, but he didn't even want to go that far.

After four days of Coke and pizza he got in his car and split. He didn't even stop at the desk to check out. They had run a slip with his credit card, they could take care of it, and he didn't want to talk to anybody. He hadn't eaten since noon the previous day because he hadn't wanted to talk to the girl at Domino's Pizza, not even over the phone.

At Salt Lake City something made him head north. At Baker, Oregon, something made him get off I-84 and take roads without even consulting a map or paying heed to the highway markers. He had known something was coming moments before he saw them walking at the side of the road. He had felt something waiting for him, feared it, and yet was drawn to rush forward to meet it. He had thought it might be a car wreck, an accident waiting for him to happen into it, and so he had failed to recognize them as he sped past them, but something must have registered, because he had almost wrecked the car, braking savagely to a stop, swinging around, and racing back after them.

Now he was quiet most of the time, his silence pierced periodically by manic episodes and furious rambling monologues. Several members of the group had had experiences similar to Martha's, with a siege of physical or mental agitation leading them spontaneously into hyperventilation, at which point someone would get them to lie down and breathe in a fluid rhythm, with no pause between one breath and the next. The breathing seemed to produce a cleansing energy in the body. Already Jerry had gone into hyperventilation three times. The first time he panicked and couldn't breathe, but Martha talked him through it. The other times were easier, and in each instance he maintained the breathing rhythm for about an hour, rested for an hour afterward, and emerged from the experience refreshed and lighter, cleaner, clearer.

Now, after walking in silence for a mile or so alongside Lissa and Georgia Burdine, he looked off to his left and was struck by the way a long cigar-shaped cloud was just floating across the face of a snow-capped mountain.

It was as if he had never seen a cloud before, or a mountain.

"My God!" he cried. "Will you look at that. You don't see a thing when you drive, do you? Even if you're not watching the road, even if somebody else is driving. Even if you look out the window, even if you see all this, you don't really *see* it, you know? You get a movie, you never get a still photo. You just move through it, you say how beautiful it all is and you remember how it looked and you never really saw it."

He walked off the shoulder of the road, clambered up onto a small outcropping of rock. "Just look!" he commanded. "Everything is different. Every step you take you see a different thing. Every cloud is different. You look at a cloud, I mean really look at it, and it floats off and you'll never see a cloud exactly like it again. They say every snowflake's different. Billions and billions of snowflakes and there's never two identical. I always thought how do they know? Who keeps tabs on the snowflakes? How many billion billions of them fall and melt away and no one ever sees them, let alone holds a magnifying glass to them? How could each and every one of them really be different? Because how much variation is possible in a simple fucking thing like a snowflake?

"Except I believe it now. I believe it. Every man's got different fingerprints. All the prints they've taken and recorded and classified, and they never yet found two sets the same. You see ants swarming in an anthill, and they all look the same, but I'll bet you that there's no two ants alike. If you got close enough and if you knew what to look for, you'd see differences. The ants see differences. Maybe they think we all look alike. Or maybe they think we look like boulders, like mountains, like continents. Or maybe they don't think at all, maybe they have other ant things to do that serve them better than thinking.

"There's no two people alike. There's no two cells exactly the same in your body. A man and woman go to make a baby and there's billions of sperm cells come out of the man, and no two of them are alike, and one of them gets to make the baby and it's a baby like no other in the world.

"And there's never two days that are the same, or two hours of a day, or two minutes of an hour. 'As like as two peas in a pod,' my grandmother used to say, but there's no two peas alike no matter how many pods you open. There's always a difference, and do you know why?

"Because God never repeats himself. He never does! He'd be bored to do the same thing over and so he never does. He finds a new way to do it every time!"

He jumped down from the rock. "Man repeats himself," he said. "Or tries to. As much as God tries to do it different, and does, man tries to do it the same. A million Ford Tauruses rolling off the assembly line, and they're all the same.

"Except they're not, not exactly, and they get less and less alike as time gets a chance to go to work on them. This one gets a dented fender, and this one has a lot of wear on the right side of the brake pedal, and this one gets driven in Cleveland where they put salt on the roads to cut the ice and it rusts out in four years, and this one winds up in New Mexico and doesn't show a drop of rust fifteen years later, and this one gets a new muffler, and this one gets a gash in the seat cover, and this one develops an engine knock, and I could go on like this, I could go on forever, I could think

185

of new things to happen to those cars as long as I have breath in my body—"

Lissa said, "Easy, Jerry. Easy."

"I'm all right. I could do that but I don't have to. But it's all different, do you understand that? Do you realize how fantastic that is?" He got down on his hands and knees. "This square foot of earth," he said, framing it with his hands, "and this square foot next to it, and you can walk over them and never even look where you're putting your feet. But they're *different!* And they're always *changing!* And it's . . . it's *wonderful!"*

He stood there, looking at them, and he breathed, in and out. In and out.

Georgia said, "Jerry, honey, do you want to lie down and breathe?"

"I'm not hyperventilating."

"You could do it anyway. Just breathe for an hour. I'll stay by you and breathe you."

"We'd get left behind."

"It's okay. We could catch up."

He thought about it. "No, I'm okay," he decided. "But maybe tonight, after we settle in. If the offer still holds."

"Any time."

Later, watching the sun drop behind the western skyline, Guthrie recalled Jerry's speech, which he'd already privately entitled "The Sermon on the Rock." There were no two sunsets the same, either, and there was no such thing as a bad one.

Douglas said, "Guthrie, you got a minute?"

"Sure."

They walked off a few yards, and Guthrie asked what was up.

"Well, it's no biggie," Douglas said. "It's this knife I've been carrying. You seen it?"

"Not to look at closely."

Douglas wore the knife in a leather sheath on his belt. He unclasped the sheath, withdrew the knife and gripped it by the blade to offer it to Guthrie. It was a handmade hunting knife with a four-and-a-half-inch blade. The grip was of nickel silver, Douglas explained, with inlaid panels of boar's tusk.

"See, it's fancy," he said, "but it's a working knife. The blade's 440 stainless and that boar ivory holds up better than elephant ivory. You can skin game all day with that knife, you can cut bone with it. It's serviceable and it holds an edge."

"You made it yourself?"

"I did. Made quite a few similar to it. If I ever made one I liked better I'd put this one aside to sell and keep the new favorite. But I haven't replaced this one yet and I've had her awhile. I like the balance and I like the markings on the boar-tooth grips. Pretty, aren't they?"

"Very."

"The thing is, should I be carrying it?"

"Why not?"

"Well, it's a weapon," Douglas said, "even if it's not a true fighting knife. It's a tool first, but even as a tool it's an instrument of violence. Hunting's violent, and skinning and dressing game is bloody work. And this walk of ours, hell, Guthrie, I don't know. I wonder what people think about me going around with a knife on my hip."

"I don't know that anybody has any thoughts about it."

"Well, I guess I have thoughts of my own about it, and I'm not sure what they amount to. I got no real use for the knife now. I'm not about to slip off into the woods and hunt something. I can cut a piece of string with it, but I could do that easier with a bitty pocketknife."

"So you don't know whether or not you should be wearing it."

"That's right. I'm proud of the workmanship in it and I think it's a beautiful object and I like it as an object, but all the same it's an object of violence. Like I said, it's no big deal, but—"

"Do you know who William Penn was?"

"Founder of Pennsylvania?"

"That's right," Guthrie said. "But before he left England he was a military man, and then he converted to the Quaker religion and joined the Society of Friends."

"I knew he was a Quaker. Pennsylvania, Quaker State and all."

"Right. Well, one day Penn went to see George Fox, who was the founder of Quakerism. Fox was evidently a great spiritual leader, but he was also pretty eccentric. I don't know a whole lot about him, but I gather he was sort of an inspired flake."

"Uh-huh."

"Penn explained to Fox that he had a problem. As a former military man, it was his custom to wear a dress sword. He didn't think of it as a weapon. For him it was an article of dress and he felt incomplete without it, but he was concerned that other members of the society might not look at it that way. He didn't want to offend his new friends, and at the same time he felt funny giving up his sword, and he didn't know what to do."

"Yeah, that about says it, doesn't it? What did Fox tell him?"

"Fox thought about it for a few minutes, and then he smiled and said, 'Why don't you wear it as long as you can?'"

"Far out."

"So all I can say—"

"I get it. 'Wear it as long as you can.' Hey, thanks, Guthrie."

* * *

A few days after that Guthrie was leaning against a rock eating a cheese sandwich when Dingo hunkered down next to him. "Great day, huh?" he said. "Say, Guthrie, something I wanted to ask you."

"Sure."

"Well, it's this," Dingo said. He held up the Iron Cross that hung from a gold chain around his thick neck. "I been wearing this thing a long time," he said. "The bro who gave it to me was good people, man. His name was Robbo, he was a North Florida boy. He hauled my ass out of the fire a time or two, and I guess I did the same for him. And he gave me this."

"Uh-huh."

"Robbo, he died some years back. We'd gone down separate roads by then, but you hear what happens to people. He wiped out coming around a turn coming down the coast road from Carmel heading into Big Sur. He just lost it and spread hisself and his hog over a mile of rocks and ocean. If there's such a thing as a good place to die, I guess that's it. If there's prettier spots, I haven't seen 'em yet."

"I know the road."

"Then you can dig what I'm saying. Anyway, that's the farm for Robbo. An' I been wearin' this ever since he gave it to me, but since he died it's not just for myself, but it's more or less of a memorial to him." He drew a breath, ran a hand over his shaved head. "An' now I don't know if I should keep on wearin' it."

"Why's that?"

"Well, do you know what it is, man?"

"It's an Iron Cross, isn't it?"

"You got that right. It's a Nazi thing, they gave it out to soldiers for heroism in battle and shit like that. Bikers love Nazi stuff, man. They go nuts for it because it drives the citizens crazy. 'How can you wear a swastika after what those people did?' Plus the Nazis had great fucking designers. I used to have this Luftwaffe dagger and it was beautiful. I wonder whatever happened to it."

He shrugged. "The thing is," he went on, "there's people here I wouldn't want to freak out, you know? And it's a Nazi thing, and the Nazis did a lot of evil shit, man. You wear a Nazi medal around a Jewish person, you're saying, hey, fuck you, and fuck your whole family that went up in smoke in the camps. And a person wouldn't have to be a Jew to pick up negative vibes off Nazi stuff."

"So you don't know how you feel about wearing it."

"Well, I don't know how everybody else feels, Guthrie. I don't know how many years I wore this thing, never taking it off, and then the other day I took it off and put it in my pocket. And that felt funny, so I put it back on, and *that* felt funny, so I took it off again, and it feels funny no matter what I do."

"I know what you mean," Guthrie said. "Let me ask you something, Dingo. Do you know who William Penn was?"

"Shit, yes. I used to smoke his cigars. Cheap little fuckers but they didn't taste too bad."

"He was also the founder of Pennsylvania."

"I been there. Philly, Pittsburgh. McKeesport."

"Before he left England, Penn was a military man. Then he converted to the Quaker religion and joined the Society of Friends."

It was a cinch, he thought, to be a leader of men. All you had to do was find a good story and tell it whenever the occasion arose.

THIRTEEN

Mark stood in the doorway. A chamber-maid, her back to him, was making one of the beds. The skirt of her yellow uniform was tight on her round little ass.

A Day's Inn outside of Ardmore, Oklahoma. Not his room, not even his floor.

He said, "Miss?"

She straightened up and whirled around. "Oooh," she said. "You scared me for a minute."

"Nothing to be afraid of."

"I just din hear you come in. I'll be through in a minute, or did you want me to come back?"

A Mexican girl, Indian planes in her broad face. A fine shape to her. Straight glossy black hair, cut in Egyptian simplicity. A dark red full-lipped mouth.

He said, "I wouldn't want you to take this the wrong way." She looked wary. "I'll give you a hundred dollars just to take off your clothes and let me see you."

"Are you crazy?"

"I mean it," he said. "A hundred dollars. I won't touch you, I won't come near you. I just want to see you."

191

"I never did nothing like that," she said.

"I just want to look at you," he said. "You're beautiful, I want to see you." He took out his wallet, drew out a hundred-dollar bill. "Here," he said. "Take it, it's yours."

She looked at the money, at him, at the money again. She said, "Close the door. Lock it, push the little button." She took the money from him, folded it, tucked it into a pocket of her uniform. "This is crazy," she said. "I don't know why I'm doing this."

Because it beats scrubbing out toilets for four dollars an hour, he thought. He watched, delighted, as she reached behind her to grapple with buttons and snaps, then shrugged the garment off her shoulders and stepped out of it. Her white bra and panties contrasted sharply with her rich copper skin. She hesitated for just a moment before uncoupling and removing the bra, then looked questioning at him.

"Oh, yes," he said. "The panties too."

She grinned. "Why not?" She wriggled out of her panties and tossed them aside, then stood watching him watching her. She said, "You like me, huh?"

"You're beautiful."

"Yeah?" She struck a pose, then another. *"Playboy* magazine," she said. "Too bad you din bring your camera." She posed with her knees together, her hands cupped beneath her breasts as if offering them to him. "Ta-dah," she said, imitating a drum roll, and put one foot up on the bed, turning to display her private parts.

What a little minx she was! Once he'd given her an excuse to get out of her clothes she was as eager for the game as he was. She gave him good long looks at her firm young flesh from every angle, and before it could occur to her that the show had gone on long enough, he got a second bill from his wallet.

"I'll give you another hundred dollars for a kiss."

192

He could have had the kiss for nothing, and more along with it. She was so hot from the posing that he hadn't had to offer her more money. Still, she pretended to consider the offer. "For a kiss?" she said. "You want to kiss me?"

"Just a little kiss. I want to hold you in my arms and give you a little kiss."

"Welllll," she said, and then grinned saucily, snatching the bill from his fingers. She put it on the table, weighted it down with a glass ashtray, and came into his arms.

She kissed with her mouth open, gave him her tongue almost at once. He tasted her mouth, felt her fine warm body against him, and almost reluctantly settled his hands around her throat.

#72.

He retrieved his two hundred dollars, one bill from her pocket, the other from the table, being careful not to touch the tabletop or the glass ashtray as he did so. He put her shoes and clothing in a lower drawer of the dresser, and he left the little sweetheart wedged into the closet, where she'd be a jolly surprise for the first person to open the door. He wiped his prints from the surfaces he might have touched; outside, he rolled her supply cart down the corridor and left it in front of another room.

He had already put his own bag in the Lincoln's trunk. Now he went directly to the car, and in minutes he was cruising at speed on the Interstate, headed for Texas.

He was turning into—perhaps *had* turned into—a machine that killed women. For eight years his pastime was one that occupied him only infrequently. In the first year he had killed only four times, and after that two months was the usual interval between incidents. Gradually the intervals shrank until they ran about a month.

Now the escalation was more than dramatic. He killed

193

just about every day, and sometimes twice a day. The other day he had finished off two women before noon and might easily have gone on killing with no loss of enthusiasm. Instead he had forced himself to make some telephone calls and read a newspaper. Still, he went out hunting that night, and if he'd seen anyone tempting he would very likely have killed again.

Men Who Hate Women. He'd read that book, thinking to find himself in its pages, and instead he read about brutes who beat their wives, psychological sadists who dominated the women who loved them, others with whom he felt not the slightest common bond. He looked within himself, trying to detect hatred, and he couldn't find it there.

He loved women. And loved killing them.

It was a contradiction, and yet it wasn't. Did any hunter hate the animal he pursued? Not according to anything he'd ever heard or read. The man who went after lion in Kenya respected the lion, admired its strength and courage, and made a robe of its hide and a trophy of its head. The deer hunter loved his quarry for its beauty and nobility, and he sought the most dominant male with the most glorious rack of antlers and pledged his love with a bullet. There were some animals that men hated, and killed out of hatred, but no one displayed a stuffed rat in the trophy room. You didn't hunt vermin, you just killed them, and took satisfaction but little pleasure in the killing. When you truly hunted, when you killed for pleasure, you killed something beloved.

He drove to Dallas and spent hours at the Dallas-Ft. Worth Airport watching the stewardesses. You couldn't do anything in an airport, or at least he had never seen an opportunity, but it was relaxing to sit in air-conditioned comfort and view a steady parade of attractive uniformed young women. There seemed to be nothing he could do that was not connected with his obsession. If he wasn't killing he was hunting; if he wasn't hunting he was planning a hunt; if he wasn't doing that, he was looking at inaccessible women and fueling his fantasies, or sitting back and relishing the memories of past hunts, past kills.

He stayed three days in Dallas, then drove to Abilene. He saw a couple of people he knew and went to a movie, forcing himself to see it all the way through. It was a good enough film but he got restless from time to time, impatient for it to be over, impatient to get out of there. But he made himself stay where he was.

He spent four nights in Abilene at the Kiva Inn. The room was comfortable, the service excellent, and none of the maids he saw was attractive enough to tempt him, which was just as well. He could see that he had run more than a slight risk at the Day's Inn in Ardmore. There was now an official record that he had stayed at that motel at the same time that a woman had been strangled to death. It was nothing all by itself, but it was a strand connecting him to his victim, and enough little cords could bind a giant.

When it was time to leave the Kiva it struck him that chambermaids were still safe targets; he only needed to hunt them in motels where he was not himself staying. There were any number of motels where you didn't have to pass the desk to get to the rooms. Most of the chain motels were that way, so that people could park near their rooms and bring their luggage directly there.

Anyone could go there. You couldn't get into a locked room without a key, unless you had special skills in that area, but you could go up and down the stairs and walk the halls as readily as if you were a registered guest. And if you did just that around the middle of the morning, say, when

195

the maids were making up the rooms of the early departures, you wouldn't have any trouble, would you?

The hypothesis seemed worth testing. He checked out of the Kiva and drove half a mile to the Lamplighter, parking in the back lot. He climbed the rear stairs and walked the corridors, and it was no more difficult than he'd thought it might be.

But the maids themselves left something to be desired. They all seemed to be bulky thick-bodied older women whom he found quite lacking in appeal. He was all set to move on when he saw a woman emerge from a room down the hall. She got some fresh towels from her cart and slipped back into the room.

A big strapping girl, fresh off the farm from the look of her. Yellow hair. Turned-up nose. A husky corn-fed girl, big all over.

When he entered the room she told him she thought he'd checked out.

"I did," he said. This was a no-nonsense girl, not the sort to shuck out of her uniform for a hundred-dollar bill, not even the sort to listen to a proposition along those lines. "I left something in the room," he explained. "My briefcase."

"Didn't see a briefcase here, but you can look."

He went through the motions of looking, opening the closet door, going through the dresser drawers. God, she was a big healthy thing, bigger than he was, probably as strong or stronger. How was he going to manage this? He should have brought something from the car. The only objects in the room he could hit her with were the lamps, and they were bolted to the dresser and tables to discourage theft.

"Maybe it's under the bed," he said. He started to bend, then straightened up in apparent pain, his hand in the small of his back. "Could you do me a favor? Could you look for me? My back's acting up, and—"

"Sure," she said, stooping down.
#81.

Driving to Wichita Falls, he worried about the risk he had run. The last thing he wanted the world to know was that a single serial killer was at work, and the quickest way to do that was by repeating himself. In the space of a week he had killed two motel chambermaids in cities just a few hundred miles apart. To make matters worse, he had not taken a weapon to the Lamplighter. It would have been safer to stab the girl. In the end he'd broken her neck, which was different from strangulation, but would it look that different in a police report?

He had tried to vary other circumstances. He'd tucked the other one naked into a closet; he left this one clothed, and on the floor between the two beds. Was that enough of a difference?

He wasn't sure. The two deaths had occurred on opposite sides of a state line, and that might help. Still, some Texan might remember reading a report of the Oklahoma slaying, or some sharp Ardmore cop might spot a story about the murder in Abilene.

But there wouldn't be any more chambermaids killed, not in this part of the country, not for months.

Not until it was safe again.

In Wichita Falls he took a room at the Holiday Inn. He put on a pair of swim trunks and went out to the pool, and on his way he passed a black chambermaid with velvety skin the color of café au lait. She was just wonderful, and she couldn't have been safer; he enjoyed her attractiveness knowing she was completely out-of-bounds for him.

He swam for a while, lay in the sun awhile longer, then went back to his room. He called a man he knew in town, a fellow named George Kingland who ran a one-man mortgage company. "I'm in town for a day or two, I'm over at the Holiday Inn," he said. "How does your schedule look for tomorrow? Can I buy you a lunch?"

"Let's see, what's today? Today's Monday. No, tomorrow's not so good, Mark, not for lunch. And neither's Wednesday. Hey, I want to see you, though. You say you're at the Holiday Inn? The one right downtown here?"

"No, the one east of town. Why?"

"No reason. Look, why don't you come by my office tomorrow around eleven? I got to take an ol' boy across the river to Tinker's around noon and buy him a big plate of catfish, but at least we can swap a few lies before then. That suit you?"

"Why not?"

He drove to Tinker's himself that night and ate catfish and hush puppies and hot apple dumplings. His table was right at the glass wall, and he looked out across the Red River at Texas on the other side. He spent a long time over dinner but it was still light out when he left. He drove straight back to his motel and watched television until he was tired enough to sleep.

There was nothing on the late news about the chambermaid in Abilene. In the morning he checked the Wichita Falls paper and didn't see anything. On the way to George Kingland's office he found a bank of newspaper vending machines and bought an Abilene paper in one of them. There was a short story right on the front page reporting the death of Wanda Rae Johnston of Sagerton, Texas, who had been found in a second-floor unit at the Lamplighter Motor Inn with her neck broken. While there was the suspicion of foul play, police had not yet ruled out the possibility of accidental death.

What did they think, he wondered. That she'd climbed onto the dresser and fallen off?

He chucked the paper in a trash can and went to keep his appointment. Kingland Mortgage Corp. had storefront offices in a small shopping plaza not far from the center of town. He parked right in front, walked through the glass door, and his heart leapt in his breast.

There was a girl at the desk and she looked up at his approach. She had a little fox face with high cheekbones and a straight narrow nose and a pointed chin. Her hair was the color of clover honey and her large well-spaced eyes were a light brown with a lot of yellow in it. Her brows were plucked, her cheeks rouged, her mouth full-lipped and red. She was wearing a sunflower-yellow dress that left her arms bare to the shoulder; its scoop neckline exposed the tops of her breasts.

The description might have fit a thousand girls, but there was more to her than the words could convey. A musky sexuality emanated from her in waves. She gave off heat, and when she looked up at him and smiled, the message that radiated forth was one of infinite desirability and infinite desire.

He had never wanted anyone more.

She asked if she could help him. He gave his name and said he was expected. She went through the frosted-glass door to Kingland's office and he watched her rolling gait as she crossed the room. Either she walked that way on purpose, conscious of its effect, or it was her natural mode. Both possibilities were equally alluring.

She was in there for almost a minute, then emerged to tell him Mr. Kingland would see him. He passed within a foot of her on the way to the office, and he could swear he felt her aura brush him in passing, sending an electric current racing through his body.

George Kingland was in his late forties, tall and well-muscled, a golfer and tennis player. He was mostly bald, and he kept his remaining hair trimmed to short crewcut length. He got up and came around the desk to shake hands with Mark.

"You look good," he said. "Lost a few pounds since last time, didn't you?"

"I may have."

"Well, it looks good on you. Or off you, come to think of it. Sit down, old son. You fixing to buy up some more of Wichita Falls?"

"Just passing through, really."

"And you thought you'd stop for a visit? Well, it's good to see you." He lowered his voice, flashed a shy smile. "Been some changes around here," he said. "You happen to notice Missy?"

"Is that her name?"

"Uh-huh. What do you think of her?"

"Pretty girl."

"You'd say so, would you? Is that door closed? Missy Flanders. Twenty-six years old, married to a shop foreman over at Waco-Eggert, lives in a crackerbox tract house over in Archer County. Mark, move your chair closer, I don't want to shout. Guess who's fucking her?"

"Her husband?"

Kingland chuckled. "He's crazy as a shithouse rat if he isn't, but I guess she needs more than he's giving her. She's my lunch date every Monday, Wednesday and Friday. And that's why *I'm* losing weight, boy, because the only kind of eating we do don't put weight on you. Three days a week we're over at the Holiday Inn. I swear they ought to give me a rate."

"That's why you wanted to know which one I was staying at."

"Yeah, I didn't want to run into you tomorrow. I didn't know I was gonna say anything, but I had to tell somebody. You know how that is?"

"Sure."

"Let's have another look at her." He picked up the phone, pressed the intercom button. "Say, Missy," he said, "could you pull the Greystone Estates file folder and bring it to me, please?"

She came in a few moments later carrying a manila folder. Kingland had her wait while he pretended to check something, and she stood alongside him. Mark saw the man's arm move, and he guessed Kingland was touching Missy's leg, but her expression never changed.

When she had left, closing the door after her, Kingland let out his breath in a sigh. He said, "Something, ain't she?"

Mark nodded.

"You couldn't see from where you're sitting, but I had my hand up her skirt. She don't wear panties. She was dripping wet."

Don't tell me this, he thought.

There was a photo cube on the big desk, and Kingland picked it up and turned it to look at a picture of his wife. He said, "You've met Gwen, haven't you?"

"Yes, the last time I was in town. You had me over to dinner."

"Fine woman, beautiful woman. But I have to tell you, Mark, I never been close to anything like this little one out there. There's nothing she won't try and nothing she don't enjoy. You know what we did yesterday?" He didn't, but he soon learned, and in considerable detail. "I don't know why I'm telling you all this," George said.

Neither do I, thought Mark. Neither do I.

One time about four or five years ago a doctor had given him Dexedrine spansules to curb his appetite. He didn't like them and never had the prescription renewed. But once he had evidently taken one pill before the effects of the last one had entirely worn off, and he'd been speedy and jittery, and he was like that now.

He couldn't get the damn girl out of his mind. He had never reacted so strongly to a woman, and all of that was made a hundred times worse by the conversation he'd had with George. And there was no way he could lay a hand on her. He knew her, he'd met her in George's office, and it was a greater risk than he was prepared to take to kill anyone to whom he could be that readily connected.

Even if he was willing to break his own rule, there was no way he could get to the woman. Her husband dropped her off each morning on the way to work. He picked her up each night and drove her home, and according to George he never let her out of his sight. George had her for lunch three times a week, and the rest of the time she was either working or with her husband.

So he couldn't have her, and he couldn't stop wanting to.

He had never been obsessed like this before, not to anything approaching this extent. Some women had moved him powerfully, so that he could barely resist acting on his urges, but if he did hold himself back, if he did overcome the immediate impulse, then he could remain the master of the desire. That high-yellow chambermaid at the Holiday Inn, for instance; he found her extremely attractive, he would have loved to do her, but once he had placed her firmly out of bounds she remained there, and when he thought of her or even looked at her now, it was with appreciation but with detachment. She was safe, and consequently he was safe.

With Missy Flanders, the hunger wouldn't go away. And he couldn't find a way to assuage it.

When he got out of George's office, when he finally managed to flee from further reports on Missy's physical excellence and sexual virtuosity, he got into the Lincoln and just drove around without paying any attention to where he was going. He wanted to give himself a chance to calm down, but after half an hour it started to become clear that he wasn't getting any calmer, that he wasn't going to get calmer this way.

He hadn't hunted since Wanda Rae Johnston in Abilene, hadn't even gone out looking last night or this morning. That hardly constituted a long dry spell, but maybe a quick kill would take some of the pressure off.

He had bought a hunting knife somewhere in Arkansas or Oklahoma, and he got it out and took it from its sheath, slipping it into the map compartment in the door with its butt protruding. He drove around but couldn't find a suitable hitchhiker anywhere. He parked at a shopping plaza and sat in his car watching women pushing shopping carts out of the Winn-Dixie. Within ten minutes he settled on one. He slipped the knife under his belt, got out of the car and went after her.

She was a little older than he preferred but still attractive, still lively. She was loading bags of groceries into her blue Subaru hatchback when he caught up with her. He said, "Miss? I think you dropped this."

She turned. He had his hand behind his back, his fingers curled around the butt of the knife. Before she knew what was happening the blade was in her chest.

He stuffed her into the back of the Subaru, slammed the hatch shut, rolled the empty cart away. The knife, its blade wiped clean on the hem of her dress, went back in the map compartment, to be discarded at the first convenient opportunity. He drove out of the plaza parking lot and away.

#82.

Except it didn't help at all.

It had thrilled him, of course. Overstimulated as he was, it could hardly have done otherwise. But it was like scratching one leg when the other one itched. It did nothing to relieve the real source of his torment.

He still saw Missy's face every time he closed his eyes. He saw her with George, doing all the things George had insisted upon talking about. He saw her licking her red lips and squirming on a mattress. He saw her tied up, eyes rolling in terror. He saw her with her throat slashed, with her breasts chewed off, with her flesh pierced by a dozen arrows. Christ, he wanted to do everything to her, he wanted to kill her a hundred different ways, he wanted to drink her blood, he wanted to cut off her head and use her bleached skull for a paperweight.

Maybe he had acted too quickly. Maybe he had settled for too ordinary a woman and dispatched her with too little ceremony to satisfy the blood lust Missy Flanders had provoked in him.

He didn't think that was it, but all the same he drove around and found another supermarket, and this time he picked his victim with care. He wandered through the aisles until he found a lovely little thing with a beauty mark on her cheek and a saucy bottom that was wonderfully snug in her straw-colored jeans. He cleared the checkout counter ahead of her, and he was in his car with the motor running as she walked to hers.

He followed her home. He gave her a few minutes to get settled. Then, clipboard in hand, he walked up to her door and rang her bell.

She was all alone in the house, and she agreed with some reluctance to answer a few questions on her views of foreign policy, brightening considerably when he told her she would receive a twenty-dollar honorarium for her trouble. He caught her off-guard, put her to sleep with a choke hold, stripped her naked and immobilized her arms and legs with picture wire, then gagged her with her own panties. He spent a full thirty minutes with her before he finished her off with another length of picture wire.

#83.

He went back to the motel and took a shower. He sat in a chair, got up, threw himself down on the bed, returned to the chair, and realized he was too restless to stay in the room. He went down to the pool and tried swimming laps to work off some of the energy in his body, but it didn't really help. He got dressed and took himself out to dinner but had no appetite. He picked at his salad, drank two cups of coffee even though he was too tightly wired to begin with, and returned to the Holiday Inn.

He still couldn't get that fox-faced little bitch out of his mind.

The second one that day had been wonderful, one of the best he'd had, and it didn't seem to make any difference. He could go out again. He could work his way through the female population of Wichita Falls. It wouldn't change a thing.

He had to have her, and there was no way he could see to get her.

The next morning he drove to her house.

It wasn't easy. He remembered that her name was Flanders, and that George had said she lived in Archer County. There were a couple of possible listings. George had mentioned where her husband worked, but he couldn't remember.

Waco-Eggert. He called their personnel office. He was doing a credit check, he explained; did they employ a man named Alvin Flanders? They did not, but they did have a man in their employ by the name of J. T. Flanders. That was one of the Archer County listings in the phone book, with an address on Caperwood Court.

He didn't want to ask directions, so he bought a map and drove there. The area where she lived was new, and the map was not entirely accurate. On top of that, the subdivision had been laid out by one of those planners who liked to talk about escaping from the tyranny of the grid, and as a result all the streets made strange turns and looped around in unfathomable directions, and it was impossible to keep your bearings.

Eventually, of course, he found her house. There was no one home—no lights on inside, no car in the garage. And you could tell she and her husband had no children. There was no swing set or jungle gym in the backyard, no toys in the garage.

She was at work now. In a couple of hours she would go out for lunch, and George Kingland, the son of a bitch, would do whatever he wanted with her.

God, it was maddening!

He was parked in front of George's office at noon when the two of them left for their tryst. They rode in George's car—evidently she didn't have a car of her own, George had said something about her husband driving her to and from work. He followed them to the downtown Holiday Inn at Eighth and Scott. She stayed in the car while George went to the desk. Then they drove around back and parked.

What was the point of this? What was he going to do, follow them to their room and listen at the keyhole?

He got out of there. Back at the other Holiday Inn he packed quickly and checked out. He had missed the official checkout time but the girl at the desk winked and told him it was okay. He got on the highway, set the cruise control at sixty-five, and drove to Amarillo.

He thought about her all the way.

He checked into a Ramada, took his bag to the room and

unpacked. He fixed himself a weak scotch and water but left half of it unfinished. He picked up the phone. There was no one he knew in Amarillo, and he didn't feel like calling Marilee and the kids.

He called George. "I left there before I got a chance to say good-bye," he said. "Give my love to Gwen, will you?"

"I sure will. We were hoping to have you to dinner, but I just got through talking to the Holiday Inn and they said you'd checked out."

"Well, they wouldn't lie to you. Incidentally, that file you had your girl bring in yesterday—"

"Greystone Estates."

"That's the one. Is that something I should know about?"

"Oh, shit, no, Mark. Fake Tudor semi-detached townhouses for upscale wetbacks. We're just writing short-term paper on 'em because we don't want 'em falling down before they're paid off."

"I just thought I'd check."

"Well, it don't never hurt." His voice dropped and deepened. "Kid, I had some kind of a lunch hour today. You're not gonna believe this."

Then don't tell me, you bastard, he thought. But he listened, knowing that was why he'd made the call in the first place.

He didn't hunt in Amarillo. He didn't have to struggle with temptation. There was no temptation. When his eyes fell on other women, at poolside, on the street, in a restaurant, he barely noticed them.

He spent the night in his room, touching himself, killing Missy in his mind. He would leave in the morning, he told himself, and he would drive a long ways away. He could go into New Mexico, he could set the cruise control and never stop for anything but gas straight through to Los Angeles.

Once he'd put distance between himself and that little bitch, maybe he could get her out of his mind.

But God, it galled him to leave her alive.

That was it, he realized. It wasn't just that he wasn't getting the pleasure of killing her. It was that it actually infuriated him that she went on living, that George went on having her. Deprivation was one thing, he could probably live with that, but this other thing that he felt—was it as simple as jealousy?—was eating him alive.

He didn't just want to kill her. He actively wanted her to be dead. He would even be willing to have someone else kill her, to have her die in a train wreck or a flash flood, just so he could be free of her.

Sometimes, John Randall Spears had written, you had to walk away from a deal. Sometimes, no matter how many incentives you offered, the seller wouldn't go the necessary distance to meet you halfway. Sometimes, as much as you might want to buy a property and as much as the seller might want to do business with you, the numbers couldn't be made to work out. When that happened you shook hands and wished each other well, and you walked off into the sunset with no regrets, because there were always plenty of other properties out there for you to purchase.

But, Spears had said, when you really wanted something, you could usually get it. If you looked at it from enough angles, there was almost always a way for all concerned to win.

In the morning he told them at the desk that he would be keeping the room for at least one more night. He left his clothes in the drawers and closet, his bag on the luggage stand, his razor and toothbrush in the bathroom. He had breakfast, signed for it, and drove back to Wichita Falls.

It wasn't much easier finding the Flanders house the second time, but he managed it, pulling the Lincoln right into the garage. The door leading from the garage to the house was locked, as was the house's front door. He forced a basement window and got in that way.

The door at the top of the cellar stairs was locked, but the lock was like a bathroom door, a button that you pushed, and he was able to open it. He went through the house, committing the floor plan to memory, finding out where everything was. He touched the clothes in her closet, studied what must have been the couple's wedding picture. Her husband looked like the sort of man who got in fights at country-and-western bars.

When he left, the button lock on the basement door was fixed so that it would open at a touch. The window through which he'd made his entrance and exit was unlocked, needing only to be shoved open.

He drove to a shopping mall that housed a triplex cinema. He sat through a movie, ate a burrito, saw a second movie. From there he drove to a budget motel, where he paid cash for one night. On the registration card he gave his name as James Miller of Roswell, New Mexico. He listed his car as a Plymouth sedan and made up a license number. He hung the Do Not Disturb sign on his door and went to bed.

When he woke up it was past midnight. He showered and dressed, wiped away any fingerprints he might have left, and went to his car. He drove directly to the Flanders house. It was hard to see street signs in the dark, but he had learned the route by now.

The lights were off, and Flanders's car was in the garage. He parked the Lincoln on the street around the corner and walked back. He slipped quietly up the driveway, opened the basement window he'd forced earlier, and lowered himself into the basement.

He had picked up a pair of rubber gloves in the shopping mall, and he put them on now. He took his time climbing the cellar stairs—he remembered which steps creaked, and avoided them. At the top of the stairs he manipulated the lock and eased the door open.

And heard something. He stayed perfectly still, listening, and identified the sound as a television set. He checked his watch. It was twenty to one. He eased the door shut and sat down on the steps and waited. A little after one he opened the door again and listened, and the television was off.

He waited another half hour, his whole body tingling with anticipation now. He had reached a point where he didn't mind the wait. It was important, to assure the affair's success, but it was also part of the excitement. The more he drew things out, the more satisfying they were.

At length he opened the door a third time and moved through it, finding his way to the kitchen. His eyes had long since accustomed themselves to the dark, and he moved across the linoleum tile floor and picked the knife he had selected earlier from the chunk of slotted butcher block. He carried it at his side and glided silently through the carpeted hallway to the bedroom.

The bedroom door was open. He stood outside, listening. The closer he got to her, the more intense his excitement became, as if she was at the center of a magnetic field to which he was relentlessly drawn.

He let himself be drawn into the bedroom. He had already determined, from the contents of the bedside tables, which side of the bed was hers, but the room was light enough so that he could see the two of them, lying on their backs, covered only by the top sheet.

He went to her side and stood there. He could hear her breathing, softer than her husband, and he could smell her scent. He thought of all the things he would have gladly done to her, given world enough and time, and he did them quickly in his mind.

He crouched beside the bed. He wanted to draw this out

but he didn't dare, he was already risking too much. At any moment either of them could sense his presence and stir, and he could not allow that. So he readied the knife, and then he settled his left hand palm-down over her mouth.

Before she could react, before she could open her light brown eyes, before she could even stir beneath his hand, he killed her with a single thrust into her heart.

#84.

The orgasm was unprecedented. It was hardly identifiable as having anything to do with sex. It did not seem to be centered in his loins, but involved every cell of his body in equal measure. It shook him, it dizzied him, and he decided afterward that he had probably lost consciousness for an indeterminate period of time, that his spirit had separated from his body for a moment even as hers was taking permanent leave of her body.

Reviewing it later, he couldn't even say to what extent it had been pleasurable. Pleasure in this instance had been somehow beside the point.

When he recovered his senses, he stayed where he was, crouching at her bedside. His hand, encased in the rubber glove, still gripped the knife. Her life had passed through the knife and up his arm, and in so doing had fused his hand and the knife into a single unit. He had to will his fingers to let go.

He leaned over her, pressed his lips to hers. He did not want to leave her, it felt curiously like an act of abandonment, but it was suicidal to stay where he was. She had ceased to breathe, her energy had departed from the room, and at any moment her husband might sense the change and open his eyes.

Slowly, as silently as he came, he stole out of the bedroom and back out of the house the way he'd entered it. He stayed in shadows as he glided down the driveway and around the corner. Every house on the block was still and dark. He got into his car and drove for a few hundred yards before switching on the headlights. Then he drove out of the neighborhood, negotiating the maze of twisting streets like an old hand, and on out of Archer County altogether.

In five or six hours, if nothing woke him before then, J. T. Flanders would wake up next to his dead wife, with one of their knives in her chest and no explanation of how it got there. He might even grab the knife's handle without thinking what he was doing, obligingly getting his prints on it. Even if he didn't, he'd probably get to tell his story over and over, to a lot of people. Whether or not he ever served a day for her murder, or even stood trial, it seemed unlikely in the extreme that the Archer County Sheriff's Office would look elsewhere for her killer.

He liked the thought of Flanders going to jail for Missy's death. The man had kept her on a short leash, probably knowing he couldn't hold her, and now he'd lost her and the leash was fastening itself around his own neck. Mark hated Flanders, he was just beginning to realize that now. He hadn't hated Missy, but he'd hated the men in her life, the men who had her when he didn't.

Like George. In the same five or six hours George would be getting up, singing in the shower; it was Friday, and he'd be looking forward to lunch. Planning the menu, say.

Forget about lunch, George. Pack a sandwich and eat at your desk. Or be a good boy, run on home to Gwen.

A thought came to him. He drove around, exploring it, studying it like the numbers on a real estate deal. The more he looked at it, the more he found himself smiling.

He drove back to the motel where he'd caught a few hours' sleep earlier. He hadn't planned to return but he still had the key and it was safer than registering anew somewhere else. He parked in front of his unit and got out of his clothes and into bed. He didn't sleep, he couldn't possibly have slept, but he rested.

At eight-thirty he was parked three doors down from George Kingland's house. He was gazing steadily at the house ten minutes later when the garage door opened at the touch of a button and George backed his Cadillac out of the driveway. The garage door swung shut after him.

Mark waited five minutes. Then he pulled the Lincoln into George's driveway, checked his tie in the mirror, and went up to the front door to ring the bell.

When she opened the door he said, "Hi, Gwen. Mark Adlon. It's great to see you. Is George ready?"

"Why, Mark," she said. "We thought you'd left town. You just missed him, he left here not five minutes ago."

"I was supposed to meet him here," he said. "He said a quarter to nine." He looked at his watch. "A quarter to nine. Unless this thing's on strike."

"It must have slipped his mind," she said. "Well, come in, Mark. We'll give him a few minutes to get downtown and then call him, that's if he doesn't remember on his own and drive back for you."

She was a fine-looking woman, tall, aristocratic in her bearing. Her hair was dark brown frosted with silver, her skin just a little crepey around the eyes.

"I swear George never said a word," she said. "He said something about having you over for dinner, and then he called to say you'd left town."

"I did but I came back. I called him yesterday and we made a date to meet here. He was going to take me out to look at some new townhouses, but I guess he forgot."

"It's not like him," she said fondly, "but I guess it can happen to anyone. And he's had things on his mind lately. Well, Mark, you're looking well, I must say. Would you like some coffee?"

"Love some."

Sitting across the table from her, sipping at his coffee, he prepared to violate one of his most basic rules. He had always hunted strangers, had always shied away from women he knew, women with whom he had any connection whatsoever. That principle should have kept him from touching Missy Flanders, George's secretary, but that had been a tenuous connection and the desire had anyway been irresistible.

But Gwen Kingland was a woman he knew socially, the wife of a business acquaintance. He was sitting with her, he was making conversation with her, and in a moment he was going to kill her.

But did he have any choice? None, as far as he could see. Now that she had seen him, his alibi depended upon her death. If he left her alive, he would inevitably become a prime suspect in Missy Flanders's murder. He shouldn't have come to Gwen's house, that had probably been a mistake, but it would be a greater mistake to leave without finishing her off.

And she was attractive, no question about it. Older than he usually chose, but not too old. And, looking at her and knowing he was going to do her, he felt his excitement mounting.

"Something I want to show you," he said, getting up from the table. Then, standing alongside her, he swung his forearm like a club against the side of her neck. She reeled and he struck her a second time, and the second blow rendered her unconscious.

She was naked under the robe. He stretched her out on the living room carpet with the robe open and lay on top of her. When she came to he had one hand under her chin and the other gripping her frosted hair.

He talked to her. He told her about George and Missy, and he told her what he had done to Missy. He felt her struggling beneath him, and he listened as she begged, and he let it go on until he couldn't stand it anymore. And then his hands moved and her neck snapped and the life slipped out of her.

When he left she was lying at the bottom of the cellar stairs. One of her slippers was on a top step, as if she'd caught it on something, lost her balance, and fell.

George, he thought, driving out of town, George, you just got nobody left, you poor bastard. You better get used to jerking off.

#85.

FOURTEEN

When they crossed into Montana on July 2, they crossed the Continental Divide as well. A metal sign at the roadside informed them of this fact, and Dingo told Jordan and two of the jack-Mormon kids how he and a buddy had stood back to back at the Continental Divide in Colorado once, the two of them peeing, one into the Pacific, the other into the Atlantic. The two brothers ran off to try it, while Jordan told Dingo that the urine would never reach the ocean, that it would soak into the ground and dry up.

"Well, it's the idea of it," Dingo said.

Jody had been walking with Mame and Bev. Now he moved ahead and caught up with Guthrie. "Hey, hoss," he said. "Halfway there."

"Halfway where?"

"Halfway to wherever we're going. Remember when we first met up and I had the idea you were going to Chicago? Halfway to the end of the line, wherever that turns out to be."

"How do you figure that?"

"The Continental Divide. That *was* the Continental Divide, case you didn't notice."

"I know."

"I never been across it before. Every time I put a foot down I'm further east than I ever been in my whole life."

"Well, you're a long ways short of halfway across the country," Guthrie told him. "The Continental Divide just halves the country in terms of the watershed. It's way over in the west. If you wanted to draw a line down the middle of the country, it would run pretty close to the border of Minneapolis and the Dakotas. If you wanted a natural line, well, the Mississippi comes reasonably close. Where we are now, we've covered maybe a fifth of the distance across the country."

"That's all?"

"Just about."

Jody considered this. "That's in miles," he said at length. "Aside from that, I figure we're halfway. The hell, hoss, from here on it's all downhill."

From Dillon, in the southwest corner of the state, Guthrie plotted their route north on 41, skirting Butte on the east. Then north on 287 to Townsend and all the way across the state on 12. All the way to Miles City, anyway, and from there he would decide whether to hold to 12 and continue due east or follow the Pumpkin River south toward Broadus and pick up US 212 into South Dakota. Both routes stood out equally when he looked at his new map of Montana, but there was no need to hurry his decision. Miles City was a full four hundred miles away.

He wasn't sure when they'd get there. Originally he'd set out to cover twenty miles a day, occasionally pushing a little ways further. In Idaho, over much more difficult terrain than they'd covered previously, they had still managed to log twenty miles each day. Now, with the last few ranges of the Rockies before them, soon to give way to the Great Plains, it seemed likely that they could increase their mileage without spending more hours on the march.

It stood to reason, but he was beginning to realize that reason wasn't operating too effectively on this trek of theirs. Maybe whatever was guiding them had firm ideas about how much ground they should cover. He'd find out soon enough.

The group was growing. That should have slowed things down, it seemed to him, but it didn't work that way. There were forty-two of them the last time he'd counted, and folks were joining up faster than he could learn their names, let alone get much sense of who they were. At night, camped alongside the road, there would always be six or eight people stretched out and breathing, with someone sitting beside each of them and helping them stay with the breath, bringing them out of it if they went unconscious, talking them through it if they ran into fear or pain or an inability to breathe.

And, while this was going on, more often than not there was someone having hysterics in a corner, or off to one side screaming, or forgiving themselves and their parents and God and their obstetricians, or discovering some hitherto unknown talent within themselves, or in a circle around Jody, learning how to heal pain with their hands.

"I put a foot wrong and my ankle went out on me," Jody had explained, "and I could walk on it but it hurt me some, and when Martha did that the day before I put energy on it for her, so I thought to do the same thing for myself."

"Physician, heal thyself," Guthrie had said.

"Yeah, well, the thing is you can't. It doesn't work that way. I didn't think it would, but I tried, and of course it didn't. And I thought somebody else ought to be able to do it for me, because the thought came to me that if I could do this, anybody could do it. I had a feeling Martha could learn, and I taught her, and she fixed my ankle. And that purely amazed me. I was used to the idea of taking away somebody else's pain, but when somebody took away my pain it felt like a total miracle. A small one, anyway."

"Sara says there aren't any little miracles."

"One size fits all, huh? Could be. Anyway, I got to thinking, and the next thing that came to me was if anybody could do it, shit, everybody could do it. So I taught Sue Anne and Thom, and word got around and people started coming up to me and asking me to teach 'em. And you know how that made me feel?"

"Pretty good, I'll bet."

"Hell it did. Made me feel like homemade shit. Because if everybody could pull off this little magic trick, what was so damn special about Joseph David Ledbetter?"

"Oh, right. I see how that could happen. What did you do?"

"What do we all do when we start going nuts? I went to Sara."

"What did she say?"

"She said to get that I could be perfect without being special, and I could be wonderful without being special, and I could even be special without being special."

"Sounds like Sara."

"And she also said to keep on teaching people whether I got all that or not, because all of us were letting go of crap we'd had stored away since birth, and a lot of people were getting headaches during the process of cleaning out all that crud. In other words, we needed a good supply of psychic anesthetists for all the emotional surgery that was going on."

" 'Just because you think you're a chicken doesn't mean you are a chicken, and it's safe to know that you're not really a chicken, and you can love yourself even if you are a

219

chicken, or even if you think you are. But in the meantime we can use the eggs.'"

"Something like that. Thing is, I learned something by teaching people. Sue Anne told me she got a little headache herself every time she healed somebody, and I realized that you have to protect yourself against picking up other people's pain. I was doing that myself, not realizing it because it always stayed at a low level. And somebody said that massage therapists have that problem; some of them get sick all the time because they're releasing shit for other people and getting caught in the backwash."

"So what do you do?"

"A shower's good. Cleans your aura. That's a little tricky to arrange around here, so I came up with this." He demonstrated. "You put your hand at the inside of your elbow and just sweep it down the arm and see yourself brushing the negative energy off and discharging it through your fingertips. And then you do the same with the other arm."

"And it works?"

"Seems to. Hey, what do I know, Guthrie? I'm just a guy who was driving up to Bend and strayed a little ways off the track."

As the group grew, as it covered distance and increased in number, it seemed to be growing as well in its magnetic power. More and more as they crossed Montana they tended to find people waiting at a crossroads, people who had traveled dozens of miles to cut their route. Sometimes these new recruits were already equipped with a backpack and canteen or water jug, as if the same force that drew them let them know what they ought to bring. Others brought only themselves and the clothes they were wearing. Some of the new people were in a sort of fog, falling in with the group without knowing what was going on or why they were becoming a part of it. Others had had inner visions of one sort or another, or had heard voices, and when the group came into view on the western horizon they were either gratified that their vision was being validated or (and this was especially true of those with some sort of drug history) half convinced that the walkers were just another part of an ongoing hallucination.

Two couples got caught in the group's magnetic field while they were in the middle of a scheduled week at Yellowstone, photographing bears and geysers before returning to Silicon Valley. One said it was time to go up into Montana, and the other three dutifully joined him in their camper, and away they went, heading north on 89. They parked and waited eight miles south of White Sulphur Springs, and when the group reached them they joined in, leaving the camper at the side of the road.

One of the women wasn't sure she wanted to be with the group. Her friends jollied her out of it. "Aggie, you never want to be anywhere, and then once you're there it's fine. You probably didn't want to be in the world in the first place."

That night Aggie was one of several people who went into hyperventilation. Kate and Jamie monitored her breathing, and in the course of it she had a vivid memory of herself as a disembodied spirit, hovering on another plane of existence while two people had a loud drunken argument below her. The argument turned violent, and then the two made a sort of peace and began making love, but the love they made was fueled by their anger.

And Aggie recognized them. They were her parents, and they were fighting and fucking at the same time. And their lovemaking, if you could call it that, reached its climax, and the spirit that was Aggie moved to assume her corporeal form within the fertilized egg they had just created.

They were her parents. This was her conception she was

221

witnessing or remembering, and it was frightening, and she didn't want to be there, she didn't want to take this form, to be in this body, to be the child of these crazy people. But she had done it, she had entered into the egg, and she would be born to them.

She went through it all again now, and her dramatics set up sympathetic vibrations in several of the people around her, prompting them to lie down and breathe their way into altered states of their own. When her own process had run its course, she sat up and looked around. All these wonderful people, she thought. Her family.

"I'm glad I'm here," she said to the eleven-year-old girl who was studying her with interest. "I'm glad I decided to show up. To, uh, put in an appearance. Like."

"Do you have a headache?"

Did she? She tuned in, and discovered that she did. "Yes," she said. "I certainly do. How ever did you know?"

"I'll fix it for you," the child said, and closed her eyes and planted her feet and held her hands at her sides. Then the child put a hand on either side of Aggie's head, and imagination was a wonderful thing, she thought, because it was almost as if she felt *rays* coming out of the little girl's hands.

"There," the child announced. "It's better now."

And indeed it was.

Route 12 headed east along the north bank of the Musselshell, through endless prairie that served mostly as range for sheep and cattle. If the ground was flatter now, the sky seemed determined to compensate. The skies were high in this part of the country, and the clouds were forever shifting and re-forming, a painting in a constant state of revision.

222

Just beyond the town of Twodot, the sheriff of Wheatland County showed up to find out who they were and what they were doing in his domain. He was about thirty-five, built like a cowhand, and you could see he was wary of something weird going on in his county. He wanted to know who was in charge and was dismayed to learn that no one was. Were they members of some camping organization? Did they have permits to camp on private land? They weren't and they didn't, they told him, but no one had objected to their presence, and they cleaned up after themselves.

How did they sleep? Just fall down on the ground in their clothes? What did they do when the nights were cold? How did they keep from fainting in the heat of the sun? Their responses were deliberately vague; a sheriff in the middle of Montana seemed an unlikely candidate for a lecture on energy shields and psychic sun-screens.

Were they some kind of a cult? A sect? And where were they from? He was disconcerted to learn that they weren't exactly from any place, that the migration (or whatever it was) had started in Oregon, but that people had been joining all along the route. On the other hand, he was somehow reassured to learn that several of the walkers were native Montanans, and that one man and woman owned business property in Great Falls.

"I guess this is all right," he said. "There's no problem with unhygienic conditions at your camp because you don't have a camp, you just lie down when you're tired. You're trespassing when you go on private land without a permit, but if no one makes a complaint and you don't do any damage, I don't suppose it's any concern of the county's. If you had any dogs that were running people's sheep that'd be one thing, but you don't have any dogs, do you?" They didn't. "Walking across the country," he said.

223

"Well, at least you picked the right season for it. You wouldn't like this country too much in the winter, not to walk through."

He drove back the way he'd come. As they hoisted their packs and set out again, Dingo told Ellie he was glad to see the sheriff drive off. "I get nervous around cops," he confided. "I got a few wants out on me. No real major shit, but I jumped bail once on an assault charge in Bakersfield, and if anybody ever ran my prints I might have to go back and maybe even do a few months."

"He'll be back," Ellie said. On her back, Richard smiled and cooed. Dingo gave the baby a finger to hold onto and asked her what she meant.

"Look at all the time he spent with us, Dingo. While he was asking his ridiculous questions, tentacles of sneaky group energy were wrapping themselves around his astral body with a grip of steel. He was too busy playing Clint Eastwood to realize what was going on, but what do you bet he'll be back with a knapsack and a canteen?"

"You're kidding."

"You want to bet? If he comes back, you carry Richard."

"You want me to carry Richard? I don't mind carrying Richard."

"No, I don't mind either. I'd feel naked without you, wouldn't I, Richard? But that sheriff'll be back. You'll see."

"Not everybody who talks with us joins in."

"They do if they're supposed to."

"How do you know that dude was supposed to?"

"Because he never would have come after us otherwise. Dingo, how long have we been walking? And how many cops have stopped us to ask us what the hell we were doing?"

"In the time I've been part of the group? None. I never

thought about it, but that's true. You hardly ever see a cop, and when they do roll by they don't even slow down. You know, I never thought about it, but that's not natural. Any righteous cop would want to know what we were up to."

"Exactly. Because they don't see us, Dingo. Oh, they *see* us, but it doesn't really register."

"There's Chinese dudes who can make themselves invisible," Dingo said. "It's a part of one of the martial arts. If they don't want you to see them, you don't see 'em. You can be looking right at 'em and it don't matter, you don't see them. Your eye takes it in but your mind erases it before it can get to the brain."

"He'll be back, Dingo."

"Well, if he's supposed to be with us, I guess it'll be all right." He drew a deep breath, let it out between pursed lips. "If I can be best buddies with a cowboy," he said, "I suppose I can hang out with some sheepfucker sheriff. You get him going, he's probably got a few good stories to tell."

The sheriff brought his wife, his two sons, and his widowed father-in-law. Sara managed to get a reading on him and saw a man trapped in judgment, assessing everybody and making them right or wrong. She saw the child he had been, always judged, judging now in return. How brave he was, she marveled, to have met the group, decided they were aimless and crazy, and followed his inner guidance and joined them in spite of his judgment.

He might have a hard time, she sensed, getting far enough past his own judgments to allow the healing to happen to him. But she was confident it would happen sooner or later. He wouldn't have come except in search of something, and he would get what he'd come for. She knew that much.

* * *

225

Al came out of spite. He wheeled himself all the way from his place out in the country to the little town of Cushman, where he sat in a patch of shade alongside the feed store to wait for them. "I understand you're walking," he told the first ones to reach him. "You got something against wheels?"

"Not on a chair," Jerry Arbison said.

"I'd walk if I could," Al said. "I'd walk the asses off of the lot of you. But my damn legs don't work. You got anything against cripples joining up?"

Nobody did.

"Well, what do I have to do? There some kind of fee I'm supposed to pay?"

"There's no charge for people in wheelchairs," Jerry said.

"What's the regular charge? I don't want any special treatment. I'll pay the same as everybody else."

"There's no charge for anybody," Gary said.

"Well, why didn't he say that in the first place? Why say there's no charge for wheelchairs?"

"I was just being a prick," Jerry said disarmingly. "Look, we've been doing about twenty-five miles a day, sometimes a little more than that if we're making good time and everybody feels like moving. I have no idea if that's a lot or a little for a man in a wheelchair. Intuitive being that I am, I somehow sense that you'd rather propel yourself with your arms than have anyone assist you. That's great, but if it turns out to be hard on your arms, just say the word and somebody'll help out."

"I don't need anybody's help," Al said. "My arms can do anything your legs can do."

"That's great," Jerry murmured to Gary. "Let's strike up some music and Mr. Warmth here can show us some of the old soft glove."

* * *

226

He wound up with Mame for a companion. He groused and bitched about one thing after another, and she simply strode along beside him and responded to his words as if they were delivered in perfectly polite fashion.

"You walk like you win medals for it," he snapped at one point. "You don't have the slightest goddam idea what it's like to be crippled, do you?"

"I sure don't," Mame said. "How did you happen to lose your legs?"

"Are you blind or just stupid? I haven't lost my legs. What do you think I've got in my pants, rolled newspaper? I've got my legs. I just can't do anything with them."

"How did it happen?"

"Vietnam," he said. "Maybe you heard of it."

"Oh, yes."

"'Oh, yes.' As far as how it happened, I don't want to talk about it."

"All right."

"We were on patrol, I was right behind the point man, he stepped on a mine, he caught most of it, I got a little. Enough, as it turned out. He went home in a body bag. I went home in a wheelchair. You want to know the worst part?"

"What?"

"Idiots telling me how lucky I was. I can't feel anything in my legs, can't move them. Can't wiggle my toes. Can't remember what it was *like* to wiggle my toes."

"It must be difficult."

"No, it's a bed of roses. I'm continent, in case you were worried about that. I have full control over my bowels and bladder. And I can generally lift myself on and off a toilet if there's space to maneuver the chair. Otherwise I need someone's help."

"How badly do you have to go before you'll ask for it?"

"What's that supposed to mean?"

227

"Nothing," she said sweetly.

"I don't ask for help if I don't have to," he said. "I don't believe in it."

"You know," she told him, "I know you don't want to be told how lucky you are, but there's one respect in which you're very fortunate."

"What's that?"

"A lot of men in your position suffer terribly from self-pity. You're sure lucky that's not a problem for you."

For three days he griped and snapped and snarled and whined and rolled his wheelchair across Montana. A couple of the men would help him on and off the chair when he was ready to go to sleep, or when he wanted to attend to a bodily function. But it was always Mame who walked alongside him and listened to his bitching, and she was generally alone with him, because no one else much wanted his company.

"I know he'll be terrific when he gets off this cripple shit," Lissa said, summing up the majority opinion, "but until then I really don't want to know the man."

"You don't have to put up with him every day," Mame was told. "Get somebody to spell you. You listen to that garbage all day long and it does funny things to your head."

"Oh, it's good for me," Mame said. "Every time he opens his mouth I hear things I never let myself think when I had the arthritis. Let alone say them. I don't mind listening to him. You know, he never does know when a body's teasing him. It just sails right past him."

"That's great," Jerry said. "The best thing you can say about the son of a bitch is he has no sense of humor."

On the fourth day, just after they'd crossed into Rosebud County, immediately putting Guthrie in mind of *Citizen*

Kane, Al felt something in his feet. He stopped propelling the wheelchair forward. "My toes!" he said.

"What about them?"

"I can feel them. Can't be, the nerves are all gone. Must be like an amputee feeling ghost pain in a missing limb. Damn!"

"What's wrong?"

"That *hurts!* My God, I'm in pain. I'm getting shooting pains all through my legs. Christ, I'm on *fire.* The base of my spine feels like it's being stabbed with a flaming sword. God, I can't take it!"

"You have to," Mame said evenly.

He fought the pain in silence, then gave up the battle and screamed. "I can't do it," he cried. "I can't go through this, it's too much. God, I can't stand any more!"

"Yes you can," she told him.

They had been quite a few yards away from the nearest of the others—no one was too anxious to be too close to Al—but now they were drawing a crowd. Jody pushed through the circle, willing power into his hands, but before he could extend them to cover Al's legs, Mame thrust herself into his path.

"No," she said firmly. "Don't you dare take away his pain."

"But he's hurting, Mame."

"I know, and thank God for it. It's all the pain he never had a chance to feel. He's got to feel it now. He came here to feel this pain, Jody. Don't ruin his chance."

Jody considered, then nodded shortly. "I guess Mame knows what's happening," he told the others. "Let's give them some room."

The others drew away, and Mame rested her hands on the back rail of Al's wheelchair and rolled him slowly forward. He was crying out in agony, rocking a little on the base of his spine to fight the pain. "Just let yourself feel it," she crooned to him. "It can't kill you. All the pain in the world can't kill you. It's been in your body all this time, you poor man. You're feeling it now because it's on the way out."

"Oh, Christ, it hurts," he said. "Nothing ever hurt so bad."

"It hurt even worse holding it in. But you just didn't know it, that's all."

"There are these waves of pain, like waves in the ocean, like sheet lightning. Oh, God, I can't stand it."

"Yes you can."

"I can't."

"You *are* standing it."

"Oh, Jesus, I'm afraid."

"Of course you are."

"I'm so *scared!* I don't want to die. I'll be torn apart, I'll disappear. God, dear God, I'm afraid."

"It's all right to be afraid."

"No it's not. It's soft."

"You can be soft."

"I *can't!* I have to hold it together, don't you see that? If I let go for a moment I'll fall apart."

"And what would happen if you fell apart?"

"I'd . . . I'd be nothing."

"You think you're Humpty Dumpty? You think we couldn't put you back together again? You think you couldn't put yourself back together again?"

"I just want it to stop," he moaned.

"No! You can't make it stop. I won't let you. Why do you think I put up with your whining and your nasty mouth and a pool of self-pity deep enough to drown a stork? Because you are going to go through this, mister. You're going to suffer your pain and shiver through your fear, and worst of all you're going to look in the mirror and see a fearful man looking back at you. What's so bad about getting scared?"

"It means I'm a coward!"

She laughed at him. "You think only cowards are fearful? You think a brave man's not afraid? Why, you can't be brave without fear. There'd be nothing for you to be brave about. Brave ain't fearless. Brave is being afraid, and owning your fear, and going ahead anyhow. And you're brave, mister, and you're going through this."

"Why do I have to?"

"Because it's what you have to do to get your legs back," she said. "And we don't allow no cripples in this family."

He could move his legs.

The pain had vanished at last. It had been unbearable but he had borne it and now it was gone. There was a pins-and-needles tingling in his legs, as if they had gone to sleep—as indeed they had, and for years. But he had sensation and movement throughout them, and that was clearly impossible, but it was true.

"The nerves were severed," he told Mame. "There was no sensation there, and no muscular control. It was like a marionette with the strings cut, no more capable of movement than that. What I'm trying to say is I wasn't imagining it. It was organic damage, the doctors could see that it was there. They just couldn't fix it."

"So you had to fix it yourself."

He opened his mouth, then closed it without saying anything, and she could see his belief system struggling to incorporate this new phenomenon. It was impossible, it had happened, impossible things did not happen, and therefore . . . therefore what?

"How do you feel, mister?"

"Confused. Foolish. You mean physically? All right, I guess."

"Good. Because it's time you started learning to walk."

"Learning to walk?"

"Well, you're a big boy, I shouldn't think you'd have to learn how to crawl first. Now that you've got two perfectly good legs, why would you want to spend any more time in that wheelchair?"

"But the muscles have atrophied," he said. "My legs have wasted away, I haven't exercised them since the injury."

"All the more reason to get started. Take my hand, I'll help you up."

"But I'd just fall down again! I'll need to rebuild myself carefully and deliberately. There's probably a physical therapist in Billings I can work with, and a good nutritionist can put me on the right diet for rebuilding muscle tissue. I don't want to risk damaging my legs all over again. Slow and steady wins the race."

"Not this race," Mame said. "You haven't got the time to waste on slow and steady. Mister, are you going to sit there and tell me it's impossible for you to walk on the legs you just got handed back to you? You think that's any more impossible than what you just went through? You just swallowed the camel. Are you really going to strain at the gnat?"

He got up from the chair, hanging onto it and to her for balance, swaying precipitously on unsteady feet. He took a step. He almost fell, but he didn't, and he took another step.

As they walked together, she told him about her arthritis. She said, "See these hands? They looked like witch's hands. They were all knobs and knots. And they are perfect now, the body absorbed the spurs and dissolved the calcium and restored everything. You think your body can't build muscle? You know you could build it in the gymnasium over the months, build it out of sweat and

232

protein. You think it has to take such a long time? I walked out of my arthritis in an afternoon. Why should it take you longer than that to walk back into your muscles?"

"You have to build muscles out of something. You can't make them out of thin air."

"What do you build them out of? Protein? That's all muscles are is protein, and all protein is is nitrogen. Nitrogen! Four-fifths of the air you breathe is nitrogen, so what do you mean you can't build them out of thin air? You can breathe all the nutrition you need, if your mind can just tell your body how to do it."

"But—"

"Just walk," she told him. "If you wait until it makes sense to you you'll be in that wheelchair all your life."

He walked, and there was pain in his legs, but it was the soreness that came with the use of muscles, not the searing pain he'd had earlier. More walking made the soreness recede. He never had the strength to walk a full mile, but he kept having enough strength to walk ten yards and ten yards more, and as the yards passed so did the miles. He started out expecting to grow weaker with each step, and instead he grew stronger, until finally he rounded the last corner in his mind by knowing that each step would strengthen him.

"The pain was so great you didn't dare feel it," Mame told him, "and so you didn't feel it. You blocked it."

"It's funny," he said. "I don't remember any pain when Miguel stepped on the mine. I remember the impact, I remember how it picked me up and threw me, I remember metal fragments going right into me. But I don't remember the pain."

"Because you never felt it. Not then and not afterward."

"Not until today. But—"

"But what?"

"It was real damage."

233

"I know that, Al."

"It wasn't just in my mind. It was organic, it was real."

"Of course it was. You gave yourself real healing today. Don't you think you could have given yourself real damage back then?"

He said nothing for a time. Then, more in wonder than in bitterness, he said, "What a coward I was. What a fool."

"Nonsense."

"I was! Look what I did to myself. I made myself a chairbound cripple for all those years."

"There's another way to look at it."

"Tell me."

"Look how *wise* you were, Al. All that pain and fear, and some part of your wonderful mind saw that it was more than you could handle. And so you blocked it off and stored it up, and you kept it cordoned off where it couldn't do any harm. Then you joined up with us, because you knew we could give you a safe space to deal with it. And look at you. You're walking."

"I am, aren't I?" He looked down at his legs, watched in wonder as he put one foot in front of the other. "All those years," he said.

"Forget them. You had to go through it to get to it. Don't regret what put you where you are now."

"I'll have to remember that." He shook his head. "How could you ever stand to walk with me, Mame?"

"Oh, I made fun of you a lot," she said. "That helped, and I didn't feel too bad about it because you never knew. But mostly I stood it because I saw past all of that stuff. I saw beyond the surface, Al. It's not too hard to put up with a person once you can see who they really are."

FIFTEEN

That night Jody sat down next to Guthrie. "Well, now we're about to abandon a wheelchair," he said. "It was bad enough leaving an aluminum walker by the side of the road, but this'll get us a littering summons for sure."

"They're talking about bringing it along tomorrow, in case Al's legs give out."

"His legs aren't about to give out. We're like broken bones, hoss. Once we mend we're strongest in the broken places. You take Mame, she can walk anybody into the ground. Another day or two and old Al's gonna be leggin' it out to Green Bay, askin' the Packers can he try out for kicking field goals. Speaking of Green Bay, where we headed?"

Guthrie dug out the map, unfolded it. "I was thinking about that myself," he said. "I was thinking originally we'd go clear to Miles City and then either stay on 12 going east into North Dakota or come down 59 and pick up 212 down into a little bit of Wyoming and then into South Dakota. See where we just slice off the northeast corner of Wyoming?"

"Uh-huh."

"But if we do that we've got this whole stretch from Forsyth to Miles City where Route 12 becomes part of the Interstate. Now it looks as though there are stretches of road alongside it, so we wouldn't have to go all that way right on I-94, but maybe we're better off cutting south right after Forsyth on 447 and picking up 212 at either Lame Deer or Ashland. We're a long ways from the mountains, so it doesn't matter how rough the road is. The only thing against it is it means committing to 212 and the southern route, and I was thinking I wouldn't be deciding that until Miles City." He shrugged. "That what you wanted to know?"

"Well, not really, hoss."

"Oh?"

"Thing is, I was thinking in long-range terms. Oh, hell, I'll just come out and ask it. Are we on our way to Washington?"

"Washington? Oh, you mean D.C."

"Of course I mean D.C. If we're bound for Washington State you got a pretty unusual sense of direction."

"Washington, D.C.," Guthrie said. "Why would we be going there?"

"Well, some of the folks were talking, and they seemed to take it for granted that was where we're going. To make some sort of protest."

"A protest? You mean like a peace march?"

"I guess."

"Jesus," Guthrie said.

"Because I didn't think that's what this was, but—"

"Christ, I certainly hope not. You mean assholes making speeches? Guitars, 'We Shall Overcome,' all of that stuff?"

"I don't know."

"I don't get involved in all of that political crap," Guthrie said. "Man, I got up one morning and decided to

236

go for a walk. That's *all* I intended to do. I didn't expect half the population of the Great Northwest would decide to tag along after me, but I'm not complaining, I sort of like the company. But if this is a peace march, somebody else is going to have to lead it, because I'm gonna go catch a train home."

"Back to Roseburg, huh?"

"Bet your ass."

"So we're not going into North Dakota to protest the missile installations?"

"What!"

"Well, I didn't *think* so."

"Who was it said—"

"I don't remember. But somebody was saying how there are these missile silos in North Dakota, in between the wheat fields or some such thing, and we could march around them and chant and send out energy and fuse their fucking nose cones or something. And the troops guarding the silos would desert their posts and march with us."

"Especially if we pelt them with flowers. Jesus Christ."

"So I thought I'd check with you."

"Yeah. Right." He thought for a moment. "You can tell people we're not going to Washington, D.C. or state. And we're not going to North Dakota, either, so that'll make it easy to decide about going to Miles City. We'll cut south at Forsyth to 212. If people are even talking about missiles in North Dakota, we won't go there."

What did you do when you were confused? You went and talked with Sara.

"I never even thought about going to Washington or trying to tell the government what to do," he told her. "The minute Jody said that, I got a sick feeling in the pit of my stomach. That's not just my kind of thing, and it feels dead wrong for this group. For Christ's sake, we've got every kind of person there is, and from every kind of political perspective. Some of our people, if they were going to present a demand to Washington, it would be that they start the Vietnam War all over again and use nukes this time around. It seems to me that people haven't been getting politicized since joining up with us. If anything, they let go of whatever politics they had."

"It usually seems to work that way," she agreed.

"I think it's all right not knowing the destination," he went on. "I don't mind that. It feels fine. We haven't yet come to a fork in the road with no idea where to go next. I always get the route a few days ahead of time, and I have the feeling it may not matter too much where we're going. If we keep going generally east sooner or later we'll get to the ocean, and then we'll either stop or turn around or walk on water. The way things have been going lately, it wouldn't surprise me if we could."

"You're getting hard to surprise, Guthrie."

"Hard to surprise but easy to baffle. I'm glad Jody told me what people were saying. I don't think it's a problem, nothing like that, but it got me thinking. Sara, I wish I knew what this was all about."

"Ah."

"I mean it. I'll tell myself it's not about anything, I just went out for a walk and look what it led to, but what *is* it leading to? Not the destination, it doesn't matter if it's Boston or Miami or Newport News, or if we stop in our tracks somewhere in the middle of Arkansas. But what's the purpose? Are we a sort of traveling medicine show, clearing up people's sinuses and fusing their broken bones? I'm not making light of that. If that's what this is about, that's fine. Every day there are more miracles, more healings, and it's exciting to be part of it."

"But?"

"But I have a feeling there's more, and I'm starting to think I ought to know what it is."

"Have you looked within for the answer?"

"I had to look within to find the question. If there's any answers hiding in the same cupboard, I can't find them."

She took his hand. For several moments neither of them spoke. Then she said, "I've been having some of the same thoughts. That it's time I knew."

"And?"

"Do we still have Al's wheelchair with us?"

"Yes. He's still not sure he won't need it."

"Good. He won't need it. I will."

"What for? You're not, uh, weakening physically, are you, Sara?"

"No, eyesight was the only sacrifice I've had to make. But I'll ride in the wheelchair tomorrow. Someone will have to push me."

"Why?"

She brushed her fingertips across her forehead. "I guess you could say I'll be going on a vision quest. I'd go sit on top of a mountain for a few days but we've left the mountains far behind, and if I sat anywhere the rest of you would leave me as far behind as we've left the mountains."

"Don't be silly. We'd wait for you."

"I don't think there's any need. We've got the wheelchair. I'll sit in it. People can take turns pushing it. I'll be in a sort of a trance, so it would be better if no one tried to talk to me. And don't worry about food. I won't need any food."

"What about water?"

"I won't need that either."

"How long is this going to take?"

"I'm not sure. Two, three days."

"And when it's done we'll know what's happening?"

"Well, we'll know something," she said. "At the very least, we'll know that a wheelchair's the wrong vehicle for a vision quest."

They set out the next morning with Sara in the chair. She was positioned at her request about midway between the front and rear of the procession, with a substantial gap immediately in front of and behind her. While she had said that she would probably be unable to hear anything, Guthrie decided there shouldn't be any conversation carried on too close to her, on the chance that it might distract her.

He took the first turn pushing the chair. He had gone perhaps fifty yards when there was a tug at his sleeve.

He turned. It was Neila, wide-eyed and silent. She was holding a crystal on a gold chain, and when he stepped aside she placed it around Sara's neck and fastened the clasp. She flashed a quick half smile, then hurried on ahead.

Sara took hold of the blue stone with both hands, then let go of it and settled her hands again in her lap. Guthrie resumed pushing the chair, and it rolled easily over the blacktop pavement. The air was warm but not too warm, with a cloud just blocking the sun and the sky a vivid blue. He walked along, pushing the chair, enjoying the sense of Sara's presence.

And then he felt that she was gone. She still sat in the chair, but she had left him.

After an hour or so, her son Thom took over and Guthrie picked up his own pace and joined some of the others further ahead. Someone else spelled Thom after another hour, and so it went, with someone always ready to take over the solitary task of pushing Sara's chair.

At first she was the subject of a good many conversations, the focal point of much of the group's attention. But when nothing happened, when she continued to sit motionless in the chair as the miles rolled away, when not even the person who pushed her had any real sense of her presence, people stopped talking about her and paid less attention to her. When they made camp the first night there was some discussion as to whether she should be left in the chair overnight. Guthrie decided against moving her. Since she could not be described as awake, there was no reason to assume she would need to sleep. They stationed her chair where she was unlikely to be disturbed, and in the morning she was as they had left her, with no visible change in position or attitude.

She was breathing. Her respiration was very shallow, and at one point Guthrie borrowed a pocket mirror from Georgia Burdine to make sure that she was breathing at all. She produced just enough breath to fog the mirror. Afterward, he wondered what he would have done if the mirror hadn't fogged. She had to be sustaining life if she was breathing, but the reverse didn't necessarily follow; for all he knew, she could enter into a state of suspended animation in which breathing was as unnecessary as eating and drinking seemed to be. So, he decided, he probably would have done nothing if she were not breathing—but it was reassuring to know that she was.

Toward the end of the third day, with Douglas pushing the chair, her body trembled profoundly. Then she sighed. While Douglas was trying to decide whether it was appropriate for him to say anything, she spoke his name.

"Yes, it's me, Sara," he said. "But how did you know?"

"I looked down and saw you. On my way back." Her voice was very faint. "Did you push me all the way, Douglas?"

"Oh, gosh, no. I took over for Bud about forty minutes ago. Just about everybody's had a turn."

"How long was I gone?"

"Gone?"

"How long have I been in the chair?"

"This is the third day."

"That long," she said. "Or that short. There was no time where I went."

"Where did you go?"

"Far away," she said. Her voice still sounded slightly disembodied. "I'm thirsty," she said. "Could I have a sip of water? Thank you. Where are we? Are we still in Montana?"

"Oh, very much so. We'll be in Montana for a good long while yet."

"That's nice," she said placidly. "I think I had better rest. Thank you, Douglas."

When they made camp that night she got up from her wheelchair and announced that she wouldn't need it anymore. Al said he certainly didn't have any use for it, and they decided to abandon it at roadside. "You don't see a whole lot of abandoned wheelchairs," Jerry told Sue Anne. "It's not like umbrellas, with people constantly forgetting them in restaurants."

Guthrie had come over to say a few words to her as soon as he learned she was conscious. Then he left her alone until everyone had settled in for the evening. After dinner he watched the smoke from the cookfire for a few minutes. Then he found Sara and took her by the hand. They walked off a little ways, and he studied her face and looked into her sightless gray eyes. She looked different, he thought. There was a weightlessness about her, as if she had not entirely returned to her body, and at the same time he felt an air of preoccupation, of concern with matters of great importance.

"Well," he said. "It's good to have you back."

"It's good to be back."

"Where'd you go? Did you have a vision?"

"Did I? I don't know if it was a vision. It seemed like rather more than that. I got what I set out for." Her smile looked sad to him. "As for where I went, I don't really know. I was gone from my body the whole time."

"I could tell that. I was beginning to wonder if you were planning to come back."

"I went to some . . . other place. I saw things, I was told things. I was given to understand things."

He waited for her to say more. When she didn't, he said, "Well, they didn't stop the carnival just because the fortune-teller was taking a trip. We had a lot of things happen while you were out there. Douglas was pushing you when you woke up. Did you notice anything different about him?"

"I don't think so."

"Well, maybe it's not the sort of thing that shows up in a person's aura."

"Wait a minute," she said. "He was walking normally, wasn't he?"

"Uh-huh. That little limp of his went away. His hip went and healed itself."

"I guess he was ready to let go of whatever he was holding. It doesn't matter what it was. You don't have to sift through the garbage on the way to the dump, you know. Just so you haul it there and get rid of it."

"So you've said."

"Have I?"

"Sara, you sound tired. Want me to let you get some sleep?"

"No, I'm fine. I *am* tired, but I'm not ready to sleep yet. What else did I miss? I might as well have been on the other side of the world, you know, for all the sense I had of

243

being here. What else went on? Are there many new people?"

There were a few, and he told her about them. And there had been some breakdowns and breakthroughs, and a healing or two on the physical level, and he brought her up to date.

"And you remember Bud," he said. "Don't you?"

"Of course I remember Bud. Richard's father, Ellie's husband. How could I not remember Bud?"

"I didn't think you'd forgotten him, Sara. What I was wondering was if you remembered what he looks like. I never know exactly how much visual sense you have of people you've never actually seen, not with your eyes. I know you see them with another kind of vision, but does that show the same things I see? For example, when you looked at Bud did you notice he was missing a front tooth?"

"Yes," she said. "In fact I remember thinking that he ought to replace it. It shows whenever he smiles, and he has a beautiful smile otherwise."

"Well, he's replacing it. Without visiting a dentist."

"He's growing a new tooth?"

"Uh-huh."

"Oh, that's wonderful, Guthrie."

"He had this soreness in his gum, so somebody took the pain away for him, and then it came back as the tooth kept cutting through the gum, and somebody took the pain away again, and then he stuck his tongue in the gap and noticed something poking on through."

"That is just marvelous."

"And you know Jody's tattoo?"

"The spider? It's one of the last things I saw with my eyes. *And* I saw it when I scanned him; I saw him getting it in Seattle. What about it?"

"It's almost gone. Jody is absolutely dumbfounded. He says evidently he doesn't need it anymore, and he's all

244

right about it. But who ever heard of the spontaneous remission of a tattoo?"

"That is so exciting," she said.

"Is it? I mean, I think it's something you could send in to *Believe It or Not,* but how important is it in the overall scheme of things? Jody doesn't mind losing the tattoo, even if he is a little wistful about it, but he didn't mind having it, either, so—"

"No, that's not the point," she cut in. "It's a miracle."

"We've been turning out miracles every day, Sara. What's different about this one?"

"A new tooth, a disappearing tattoo. I know I was the one who said there's no order of difficulty in miracles, and it's true, but every time we produce a new type of miracle it helps make it obvious that all miracles are possible, that we have to change our vision of what's possible and what isn't. And it helps me to know that."

"What did you learn out there, Sara?"

"Quite a bit." Her hand moved to touch the crystal at her throat. "That's why I'm the way I am right now," she said. "It's not tiredness, it's that I feel overwhelmed. I found out what our job is."

"And?"

"We're supposed to cure cancer."

"We've already done that. Didn't you say Sue Anne had cancer and cured it?"

"Not individually. We're supposed to cure the planet's cancer."

"How do we do that? Go around wiping out the disease all over the globe?"

She shook her head. "No, you still don't understand. I'm not talking about the kind of cancer that Sue Anne had, the cancer that human beings get and die of." She took a breath. "The planet itself has cancer," she said. "And we're it. And *that's* what we're supposed to cure."

SIXTEEN

She said, "This may be difficult to explain. Nobody sat down with me and told me things. I was shown, I was given to understand. Do you know what cancer is, Guthrie?"

"More or less. Something starts growing in you, and if they don't cut it out it keeps on growing until it kills you."

"Yes."

"Or unless you cure it yourself. The good cells run around eating up the bad cells, or however Sue Anne did it."

She nodded. "'Something starts growing in you,'" she said. "The something that grows is part of you. Let me tell you what cancer is. Cancer is cellular ego."

"I don't follow you."

"Let me try to explain. Picture a cell in your body. It's a part of one of your organs and it has a job to do and it does it. But one day something upsets that cell and causes it to change its behavior. Maybe it's a cell in your lung, and you've been bombarding it with tobacco smoke for years until the cell's engulfed in tar. And finally the cell says, 'Hey, this isn't working. I'm in real trouble here, and if I

246

just keep on doing my usual job I'm not going to survive, and then where'll we be?' So the cell goes on a crash program for survival. It multiplies like crazy to guarantee it'll be around for a while. It kills any other cells that get in its way. And it does such a good job of survival that it spreads wildly all through the system, and eventually it kills the body it's been a part of, and, because in the long run it's just a cell and not a complete organism and it can't survive alone, finally it dies along with the rest of the body."

"And that's what cancer is?"

"What it is and how it works. Cancer's a cell with a mind of its own. It may be an irritant, like tobacco smoke or asbestos fibers or food additives, that nudges it into a cycle of eccentric behavior. It may be emotional. Look at all the widows who manifest breast cancer. They stuff their grief and their anger at being left, and a cell feels threatened by all that psychic pain, and starts growing in self-defense. One way or another we choose our diseases and find a way to bully our cells into creating them. One way or another we activate the cell's ego and the label we put on what follows is cancer."

"Why cellular ego? How does ego enter into it?"

"Because your ego is the part of you that believes you're separate from the rest of the universe, and that thinks you have to be separate in order to survive. When a cell behaves as if it had an ego, and allows that ego to dictate its behavior, the result is cancer."

"Okay, but how does a planet get cancer? The earth's not a living thing."

"Of course it is. Did you think it was just a chunk of lifeless rock?"

"No, but it's a setting for life rather than a living being. It's a home for all of us, it's a nurturing environment, but it's not a creature itself, is it?"

"Isn't it? Every last bit of the planet's alive, you know. Every molecule, every atom, is buzzing with activity. Nothing stands still. Everything is changing, growing, evolving, going through cycles of birth and death. The rocks are alive. The water is alive."

"And the hills," he said. "With the sound of music."

She leaned forward, touched his arm. "Guthrie," she said, "I saw the earth the way the astronauts have seen it. It looks like a beautiful blue pearl, and it's a living being. The rivers are its bloodstream, the atmosphere is its respiratory system. The rocks and mountains are its bones. Everything that lives, everything that is, is part of a tissue or organ or system of the planet it lives on."

"And what are we?"

"As human beings? You can answer that by looking at what we have that distinguishes us from the other animals. That's what we are to the planet."

"What does that make us, the earth's opposable thumb?"

She laughed. "Oh, that's lovely. No, our wonderful thumbs are just tools we grew to make it easier to be what we are. It's our brains that make us unique, and that's what we are. The human race is the cognitive brain of the planet earth."

"I think the earth must have a headache."

"Yes," she agreed. "It does."

"No, I was just joking, Sara."

"I wasn't. The earth has worse than a headache. It's got brain fever. The human race is cancerous, it's a planetary brain tumor."

"'The goddamned human race.' That's what Mark Twain called it."

"More than that, surely. God damned perhaps, but God blessed as well. Awful and wonderful."

"Those meant the same thing once, you know. Full of

248

awe and full of wonder. Now one's good and the other's bad."

"Yes," she said. "Awful and wonderful. Could you get me some water, Guthrie? This is thirsty work."

"Ego," Sara said. "Cancer. Human beings behave like cancer cells. They think they can survive independently at the expense of the rest of the world. They spoil the planet. They kill the other animals and they kill each other. Every faith tells them that they're all one flesh, that all men are brothers, but none of them act as though they believe it."

"Hasn't it always been that way? Isn't that just part of the human condition?"

"Yes. And for thousands of years it didn't matter. Man, exercising his cognitive brain, indulging his ego, could do whatever he wanted as he grew in mastery over his environment. He could kill his brothers and be killed by them in turn. There's no danger in it. He kills, he's killed, the earth abides and the mountains remain. Souls learn the lesson they came here to learn. Life goes on. The planet goes on.

"Oh, there are some events that look catastrophic. Genocide erases the last passenger pigeon and almost wipes out the bison and the Jew. It is indeed awful and wonderful, the history of mankind. On the bus ride west I would look out at a river or a mountain and see its progress through all of time, and every vista I looked upon that way was awful and wonderful, because that's what man's story has always been.

"And it didn't matter. The earth could allow man to slip his leash and range at the effect of his ego. He wasn't dangerous. The harm he did wasn't lasting." She took a breath. "But it's different now."

"How?"

"His tools and weapons are more powerful. Cain doesn't

just kill Abel now. He blows up the world. You can't do the things you used to do when they have the power to do permanent damage on a global scale. Man is strong enough to destroy the planet now. And he's been doing it."

"You mean nuclear weapons?"

"Of course, if they're used. And if enough countries have them and enough people take them for granted, sooner or later they'll be used. Nuclear power could destroy the world without a war, if there's an accidental meltdown on a large enough scale.

"But that's just one area. A few hundred years ago the Indians in eastern North America used to burn the forest on purpose to flush game. It didn't matter. There weren't that many Indians, they didn't set that many fires, and the forest always grew back. Then the white man came and cleared the land for farming and settlement, and the forest was gone forever.

"In Brazil the rain forest is disappearing. Every single day more acres of it are cleared and burned and more tropical rain forest is gone forever. And, as it goes, the planet's ozone layer is eroding and starting to go, and the temperature of the planet is probably going to increase a degree or two, and there'll be some melting of the polar caps, and the seas will rise and the whole climate of the earth will change. No one knows quite what will happen; predictions range from a new Ice Age to subtropical conditions in northern Europe. No one is certain, but everyone knows the rain forest is too valuable to be lost, and it goes on disappearing every single day. Because the people who are cutting it down think they have to do that to survive."

She took another sip of water. "And that's the problem," she said. "Not what man does but how he thinks, because that's what determines what he does. We don't need more knowledge. We already know that global population has to stabilize, that irreplaceable resources can't be squandered, that war and preparations for war are more than any nation can afford. We know that. Everybody knows it. But the population grows and the world's stores are depleted and nations arm themselves and make war.

"Everybody knows better, but ego makes villains of us all. The Japanese think they have to go on slaughtering whales. The Arabs think God wants them to blow up airplanes. In Ireland the Catholics and Protestants are having a religious war. That may even have made a certain amount of sense in the seventeenth century, but it's completely ridiculous now. And everybody knows that, everybody on both sides knows that, and nobody can stop it."

"You said it's always worked out in the past."

"Yes."

"Maybe it'll work out now. Some people will be killed and some species will die out, but that's been happening since the Flood. Maybe it's still just part of the process, maybe—"

She was shaking her head. "No. We're running out of time."

"How do you know?"

"I was given to know it. But people have always known. So many of the religions talk about the Last Days, and many of them seem to agree on a date somewhere around the year 2000. The Mayan calendar runs out in the year 2011. The predictions of Nostradamus grind to a halt around the end of the century. According to a Brahman story, Brahma began breathing out the universe in a single breath—which, incidentally, fits remarkably well with the Big Bang theory of creation. Around the year 2000, Brahma runs out of breath."

"And the world ends?"

"No—he begins inhaling what he breathed out. You can

interpret that as you please. Maybe it's the end of the world. Maybe it's the beginning of something else."

"Like what?"

"A new age. There's a theory that says Nostradamus and the other prophetic systems end when they do because a new time is going to dawn, and history will cease to be predictable. Everything will be so utterly different that no one with his feet planted in the Old Age can guess what it will look like. Nostradamus can't foresee it and the Mayans can't count the years or predict the eclipses." She held out her hands. "So those are the choices, my friend. Heaven on earth or the end of the world."

"Either way, a whole new ballgame."

"A new game or no game at all."

He scratched his head. "This is hard to take in," he said.

"I tried to explain as well as I could."

"You did fine. The hard part isn't understanding what you're saying, it's getting my mind to wrap itself around the idea of it. Either the world ends or Man behaves in a completely different fashion, is that what it adds up to?"

"Yes."

"But knowing we have to act differently won't cut it, because we've known that all along, and we can't do anything about it."

"Yes, because it's not a logic problem. We know right now how to feed the world. Instead we have farm surpluses and banks foreclosing on farmers and grain rotting in warehouses and famine in Africa, all happening at once. Knowing doesn't help."

"Then what the hell do we do? If we're the cancer, how do we cure the planet without destroying ourselves? What you're talking about is a wholly revolutionary change in human behavior."

"Yes."

"It's human ego that's the planetary cancer, isn't it?

How do you cut the ego out of a human being? What kind of scalpel do you use?"

"That's not it," she said. "You can't remove the ego surgically. You can't kill it or crush it. Human destiny doesn't call for us to wind up as ants in an ant colony, the selfless servants of a despotic planet. The way we have to deal with ego is by transcending it. We have to outgrow the illusion that the ego is right and that anything can be good for one of us if it's not good for all of us. We have to remember who we really are."

"'Things fall apart, the center cannot hold.' You know the Yeats poem?"

"Yes."

"That's what this is beginning to sound like. 'The Second Coming.'"

"Yes, it is, isn't it?"

He looked at her. "Sara," he said, "this isn't some elaborate cosmic joke, is it? Jody wanted to know if we were heading for Washington. Should I have told him that our actual destination is a little north of there, where a Pennsylvania Dutch farmgirl will soon be preparing to give birth to a babe in a stone barn outside of Bethlehem?"

She laughed.

"Well? When we pass Harrisburg, do I start looking for a bright star?"

"No," she said. "That's not how it will happen this time around."

"Then we really are talking about the second coming."

She nodded. "The first time the Christ Consciousness came to earth it was in the form of a single man. It happened more than once, incidentally. There have been Christs besides Jesus. There was Krishna, there was Buddha, there were others. Different civilizations had their individual visitations. The second coming will be for the whole world, and it won't be one man. The second coming

253

will occur when the Christ Consciousness is instilled in the entire human race."

He thought about this. "And that's what this is all about," he said. "What we're walking for."

"Yes."

"High-stakes poker. Either the world comes to an end or it's heaven on earth and two cars in every garage. Two smog-free cars, I suppose. Solar-powered, probably."

"Could be."

"All because an aimless bartender in Roseburg, Oregon, decided it was a nice day for a walk. Shouldn't I have talked to a burning bush first, Sara?"

"I thought you heard a voice."

"Yes, I did. I tend to forget that. Well, what did I do? I went for a walk and ran into a strange sort of St. Paul who fell out of his truck and joined the party. Then we met a lady who phased out her eyes so she could see better, and now we're within a few miles of the spot where the Indians brought Custer an abrupt sense of his own mortality, and I'm having a wonderful time, Sara, I really am, but it's hard to believe we're saving the world."

"What happens to people when they start walking with us, Guthrie?"

"They quit smoking, they hyperventilate, their tattoos fade, their arthritis dissolves, their acne clears up, their warts disappear, and now it looks as though they grow themselves new teeth. Suppose we pick up a guy with an arm missing. Will he grow a new one?"

"Why not? Crabs and lobsters do it all the time. What else happens to people, Guthrie? What happens on the inside?"

"We change."

"Yes."

"We don't turn into clones. If anything, people become more completely themselves."

"That's right."

"We walk out of our old lives. We let go, we open up. We forgive and forget, and one of the things we forget is who we thought we were."

"And we remember who we really are."

"Yes."

"And love our neighbors as ourselves, and act out some of the other radical notions that fellow was talking about on the mountain."

"Uh-huh. But—"

"What, Guthrie?"

"Well, does it amount to anything? It's wonderful for us, I'm not asking for a better way to spend my summer, but I didn't know I was doing this to save the planet. Are we reaching enough people? Shouldn't we, well, find a way to get the word around faster?"

She smiled. "You think we need media attention? We could get one of the networks to send a film crew to follow us around. You could hold press conferences and announce all the latest miracles."

"Jesus, don't even say that."

"You and I could go on Donahue and Oprah Winfrey and spread the word. We could answer provocative questions from the audience. Or maybe it would be better to buy some TV time. Should we start raising money?"

"Stop it, Sara."

"We could get one of the shoe companies to sponsor us. 'When you're walking to Glory, only Reeboks will do.' Or should we offer it to Nike first? After all, this whole thing started in Oregon, so maybe we ought to do business with a local firm."

"I get the point, Sara. I really do."

"Wanting to make it happen faster is just ego, Guthrie. It's thinking, 'Oh boy, God's in deep shit without my help.' It's thinking we have to get people to do what we want

255

them to do for their own good. But we haven't been trying to make anybody do anything, and the only people who join us are people who want to, and that's why it all feels right. We're not going to make this happen by marching on Washington and telling the government what to do. But if we go on walking wherever your intuition happens to lead us, and if people join us because they're led to join us, somebody in Washington's going to get up from his desk one of these days and decide he feels like going for a walk."

"And who runs the store when everybody goes for a walk?"

"It doesn't matter. Who's tending bar in Roseburg? It really doesn't matter. You know that line, 'It's a lousy job but somebody has to do it'? If it's really a lousy job, then *nobody* has to do it."

SEVENTEEN

A Holiday Inn in Pueblo, Colorado. Mark signed in, went to his room. He showered, then put on a pair of bathing trunks.

They were loose in the seat, and the last time he'd worn them they had been tight. There was no question about it—he was losing weight. George Kingland had pointed it out to him before he'd noticed it himself, and the process had gone on uninterrupted since. He'd lost almost two inches in the waistline, he was wearing his belt two notches tighter, and he had slimmed down proportionately all over. When he shaved that morning he'd noticed definition around the jaw that he hadn't had in years. His jowls were disappearing and he was losing that smug plump look.

He rather liked the change. He hadn't minded carrying the extra weight, and now he found that he enjoyed losing it. He especially liked the fact that he never deprived himself at the table; indeed, he'd begun losing weight without any intent, and continued to eat whatever he wanted whenever he wanted it.

Still, he was eating less. Until he'd decided to devote the summer to the pursuit of young women, he had lived with

Marilee and the children and eaten breakfast and dinner at home. When he'd gone away overnight, on a two- or three-day trip to some other city, he had eaten in much the same fashion.

Now there were no points on his compass, no true rhythms to his days. Since his final departure from Wichita Falls, his sleeping habits had been erratic. He might go to sleep or get up at almost any time. Many of the chain restaurants stayed open twenty-four hours and offered their entire menu around the clock, so that you could get up in the late afternoon and go out for breakfast, then have a dinner salad at seven-thirty in the morning. Sometimes he would forget to eat; other times he would consider it and decide he wasn't hungry.

It seemed to be agreeing with him. He felt fine, and his energy level was high. He didn't look drawn or wasted, as people sometimes did after rapid weight loss. At first he had been a little concerned, because weight loss without dieting could be symptomatic of various illnesses, but then he'd realized that he *was* dieting, but that it was unintentional. He was snacking a lot less, and he suspected that had something to do with it. He didn't seem to crave cookies and candy bars as he once had, and if he did have a snack it generally wound up serving as a replacement for a meal.

The Easy Weight-Loss Diet, he thought. When hunger strikes, just go out and kill someone lovely.

He went down to the pool, swam a couple of laps, stretched out on a chaise and let the sun dry him off. It was fairly late in the afternoon but the sun still had plenty of power left in it. He took a moment to look around the pool, noticing who was there, deciding which of the women he found attractive. There was a slender brunette who was sitting with her husband; she was a little thinner than he liked, but she would do. And there was a chubby teenager who kept climbing up the ladder, tugging the top of her one-piece suit up over the tops of her breasts, then mounting the diving board and plunging into the water, only to repeat the entire process moments later. She looked to be a blonde—it was hard to tell, her bathing cap covered everything but the nape of her neck—and she was cute, with a nice little puppy-fat body and shapely young legs. But she was too young, sixteen at the most.

Still, both of them would do for fantasy material, and that was as much as he wanted right now. He had killed a hitchhiker the previous morning, leaving her body in a culvert where it might never be found, and he might not hunt at all today, or tomorrow either, for that matter. Something had crested in Wichita Falls. Missy Flanders had been quite literally irresistible, and he never could have rested until he had taken her. Since then he had been able to resume killing for the pleasure of it. When he was lucky enough to find a woman who really moved him he just had to have her, but not out of the absolute need that had operated in Wichita Falls. Now, if he found some little darling irresistible, it meant that he chose not to resist her. With Missy there had been no choice involved.

Now he closed his eyes and remembered the hitchhiker from yesterday morning. He remembered her eyes, and the way she had nibbled her lower lip when she asked him how far he was going. He thought about what he had done, and for just the shadow of a moment he wondered who might be waiting for her to come home, but those sort of thoughts were rare, and they never occupied him long.

He thought his thoughts, and he opened his eyes from time to time to glance at the teenager (pulling the top of her suit up again; why didn't she give it up, those tits were not going to stay completely covered, not by that suit) and the married woman.

259

He liked the tight feeling in his groin, and the warmth that was centered there. He liked the heat of the sun, too, and the breeze that blew up every now and then.

He dozed off, and when he stirred and opened his eyes the pool area was almost empty. The sun was gone; it wouldn't set for some hours yet, but it had dropped from view behind the wall of the hotel. He was almost alone at the pool. The puppy-fat teenager was still there, lying on a chaise now with her bathing cap off, and yes, she was a blonde, and at last her suit was able to cover her breasts, and would probably continue to do the job until she moved.

The brunette and her husband were gone, and so were almost all of the others. One older man, gray-haired and slack-muscled, splashed himself in the shallow end, and a couple across the pool from him were even now gathering up their towels and returning to their room.

The old man left a few moments later, tucking his feet into a pair of beach slippers and shuffling off. Only the girl was left, and as Mark considered this fact she sat up, exposing the top portion of her breasts, and gave the suit her usual yank. She tucked her blond hair into her bathing cap, doing a careful job of it and fastening the strap under her chin. Then she stood up and walked to the diving board.

He studied the backs of her thighs as she walked. Come back in a couple of years, he told her silently. Come around when you're old enough. You don't even have to lose that puppy fat, it's charming, but get a little older and turn up again in my life, and we'll see what we can do with you.

She did a series of simple dives, each time adjusting the suit as she emerged from the water. Watching her, an audience of one, he began to feel intimately connected to her, as though she were addressing her performance exclusively to him. The pool area became a secluded world, and they its only occupants.

He placed a hand on his groin and felt himself. He was fully erect, urgently so, and he ached, but not unpleasantly.

> *There is nothing you can take*
> *To relieve that pleasant ache . . .*

Not true, he thought. There was something he could take. He could take her.

He sat there, still touching himself, still watching her, and objections occurred to him. She was too young. He was a registered guest of this hotel. And, more to the point, anyone could approach the pool at any moment and see what was going on. Even if no one decided to go for a swim, there was a wall of windows overlooking the pool. Someone could look out at them, someone could see.

She dove again and he waited for her to swim to the ladder. This time, however, she swam the length of the pool, turned, swam back. He watched her swimming laps, her crawl stroke choppy but effective. The quick glimpse of her hairless underarm midway through each stroke was a special intimacy.

He stood up, his legs trembling slightly, and walked over to the shallow end, lowering himself slowly into the water. He glided toward her in an economical breaststroke. She had switched from the crawl to a modified backstroke, using her arms as oars and rowing back and forth across the pool. He stayed with the breaststroke and matched her pace, swimming a few feet away from her.

When she relaxed and floated on her back, he swam over to her. She opened her eyes at his approach and smiled at him. "Hi," she said.

"You shouldn't keep pulling your suit up," he said.

"Huh?"

"Those titties are too nice to hide. You should let people see them."

The shock in her face was something to see. She didn't know how to react, and before she could decide he had her by the shoulders. He flung his body upon hers and extended his arms, pinning her beneath the water's surface. She fought, she struggled, and she was strong and agile from all that swimming, but he was stronger and he had the great advantage of surprise. She put up a good fight, she was game as a trout, but at last she weakened and she was his. His climax came when the fight went out of her and the first bubbles issued from her mouth and nose.

When she was still, her lungs filled with water, her eyes open and staring, he lowered the top of her bathing suit and took her milk-white breasts in his hands. He held her for a moment. Then he released her and she slipped down toward the bottom of the pool.

#94.

In Denver he spent part of an afternoon going over some figures with his property management people. He drove by the house where Mr. and Mrs. Minnick still occupied the top flat, and he remembered how urgently he'd responded to the round-faced round-bodied little creature. Was she home now? Should he knock on her door, tell her how proud he was to be her landlord, and give her a gentle little push into the next world? Two months ago the risk had seemed too great. Now it didn't appear all that dangerous.

Still, he decided against it. Maybe later, maybe on another trip to Denver. That was the nice thing about Mrs. Minnick. He knew where she lived, and she wasn't going anywhere. She could remain indefinitely on his unwritten list, and someday, when the time was right and the need was great, he'd put a little checkmark next to her name.

He drove down into Littleton and managed to find the 7-Eleven store where he'd stunned the cashier with a can of motor oil and finished her off in the lavatory. It seemed ages ago, and he remembered how he'd had to improvise, how driven he'd been and how he'd had to hurry.

Nowadays he was calmer, more confident. He walked through the store's aisles and paused to pick up a can of motor oil and feel its weight. He put it back, picked up a newspaper and took it to the counter.

The attendant was a young woman with a mouthful of chewing gum. Her plastic badge said her name was Tina. She wasn't pretty enough; anyway, the store was crowded. He paid for his paper and left.

After Denver he intended to drive home to Kansas City to see Marilee and the children. He got on the Interstate and drove east through Kansas, but something made him get off halfway across the state to Salina.

In the morning after breakfast he went hunting. He drove to a supermarket and pushed his cart up and down the aisles, looking for women. For almost an hour he cruised the air-conditioned market without finding any-one. The few women who appealed to him had children in tow, either walking at their sides or sharing cart space with heads of lettuce and boxes of Tide.

He left because he was afraid he might be making himself conspicuous. He abandoned his cart rather than go through the charade of buying groceries he didn't need, and it seemed to him that people were regarding him with suspicion as he left the store. He drove right out of Salina and headed towards Kansas City again, but once more he stopped short of his destination, getting off I-70 at Junc-tion City and driving up to Manhattan.

He found a suburban supermarket and began cruising the aisles, and within ten minutes he had spotted someone, a tall brown-haired woman who wore her hair in Indian-style braids. The hairdo plus her bib overalls and sandals made her look younger than she actually was; on closer inspection, he guessed her to be around thirty.

Nice figure. Good long legs. He beat her to the checkout counter, paid for a loaf of bread and a can of ravioli, and went to his car. When she drove out of the lot he was right behind her.

And she led him a merry chase. Instead of going straight home she drove to her bank, to another plaza to pick up her dry cleaning, to a K-Mart, and to an open-air farmers' market just outside of town. Finally he followed her into the subdivision where she lived, but when she pulled into a driveway there was another car already parked there, and he looked at his watch and guessed that her husband was home. He made a face and tried to figure out how to get out of the subdivision.

In the morning he woke up thinking about her. He wasn't obsessed, it wasn't like Wichita Falls. He skipped breakfast and scouted a chain drugstore and a supermarket without finding anyone he liked. Back in his car, he wondered if he could even find her house. He hadn't been paying attention when he drove there, and on the way back he'd just been trying to make his way out of the maze.

He started by finding the farmer's market, and then he was able to retrace his route with surprising ease. He might have had trouble recognizing her house but her car was parked in the driveway and he had spent enough time following it to spot it at once. And this time her husband's car was not present.

He left the Lincoln at the curb, picked up his clipboard, and rang her doorbell. She came to the door wearing a flared denim skirt and a white cotton blouse with a scoop neckline. A golden chain around her neck held a small gold cross set with diamonds. She had gold hoop earrings, and several bracelets on each wrist.

"Water company," he said.

As soon as she turned her back on him he got a forearm around her throat and a hand over her mouth. She squirmed in his embrace, and it felt so good and he had waited so long that he was terribly eager, with the result that he very nearly throttled her on the spot. He wanted to, but at the same time he had invested enough time and effort in this to make him want to get his money's worth out of her. So he eased into a choke hold and put her to sleep.

He had brought nothing with him but the clipboard, so he found her hardware drawer and searched through it. He stripped her naked and bound her hands and feet with picture wire, then looked for some tape for her mouth. He couldn't find any. There was a nice icepick and he took it from the drawer and set it down next to her, but there was no tape.

He was closing the drawer when he saw the tube of Krazy Glue. He looked at it and read the instructions carefully. Then he spread a thin film of the stuff on her upper and lower lip and pressed them together. He capped the tube, waited a minute or two, and tried to spread her lips with his fingers. They seemed to be stuck together firmly.

He ran a hand idly over her body and waited for her to come to. At last her eyes opened, and she looked at him in unbelieving terror and tried to open her mouth to scream, and of course she couldn't. No matter how she fought, her lips refused to open.

He spent half an hour with her. Once the phone rang, and the calling party let it ring a full dozen times before giving up. When it finally stopped he decided he couldn't wait any longer, and he reached for the icepick. Just as he was about to drive it into her ear he had another thought, and he set the icepick aside and retrieved the tube of glue.

He put a small drop in each nostril and gently, gently, pinched them shut.

#95.

He was already out of town, heading north into Nebraska, when he remembered that he'd intended to go home to Kansas City. He thought about turning the car around but instead kept on in the direction he was going and drove into Lincoln. He hung around Lincoln until he got a nurse who'd just finished her shift at St. Elizabeth Hospital. From there he drove to Omaha, where he stayed two nights, then drove over the bridge to Council Bluffs and killed a housewife with the icepick he'd carried off from the house in Manhattan.

He got two women a few hours apart in Des Moines. North of there, in Ames, he scouted a supermarket and liked one of the checkout girls best of all. He was in his car when the market closed, and when she emerged heading for her own car he stalked her and picked a good spot and swooped down on her, striking her over the head with a tire iron. He didn't bother to immobilize her with wire or tape, just bundled her into the trunk of his car and drove off with her, and he didn't stop to open the trunk until he was miles from town on a country lane.

And she was already dead. Evidently he'd hit too hard with the tire iron. She was his hundredth kill, too, and it seemed to him that there should be some significance to the number, yet here she was, pointlessly dead.

She was pretty, too.

He carried her fifteen yards from the roadside and set her down where she wouldn't be quickly found. A wave of nausea struck him, and he was almost sick. He went back to his car and sat behind the wheel for a while, thinking about things. Then he turned the key in the ignition and drove off.

Maybe it was time to stop.

The thought kept coming to him. He drove south from Ames, skirting Des Moines. It was late, he ought to get a hotel room, but he didn't feel like it. He drove west on 80, thinking he could take a left at Council Bluffs and drive right through to Kansas City.

Instead he turned right and drove north on I-29 all the way to Sioux City.

He checked into a Ramada, slept for two hours, and woke up clawing his way out of a nightmare. In it, he kept killing the same woman over and over again and he couldn't make her die. She came back to life again and again. He strangled her, he snapped her neck, he cut her and stabbed her, and she wouldn't stay dead. Finally she was laughing at him, asking him if he knew who she was. Her face began to come more sharply into focus, he was on the point of recognizing her, and he came abruptly awake, breathless and covered with a fine film of perspiration.

Maybe it was time to stop.

He thought of the girl in Ames, the checkout girl, and how her death had been wasted. But weren't they all wasted? He remembered the nausea that had threatened to overwhelm him, and as an experiment he let himself recall one of his other recent kills. The nurse in Lincoln, with her white uniform, wilted after a long day's work, and her big soft pillow tits. He thought of her pain and her absence from the world now, and the nausea welled up in him, if less vivid than in Ames.

But he felt excitement, too. He was sickened and excited at the same time.

267

He couldn't go back to sleep. He found an all-night Denny's and had something to eat, drove around, returned to his room. He watched Australian Rules Football on ESPN, the announcer chattering away excitedly about something that made no sense to Mark. The bodies on the screen were just a blur, the voice just noise.

He couldn't decide what to do.

After two days he checked out of the Ramada. He drove around, unable to decide where to go, and wound up staying in Sioux City, checking in at the Rodeway Inn. The television set at the Rodeway got the same cable stations as the one at the Ramada. The pool was a little smaller, but they had a sauna.

What difference did it make where he stayed? Or which city he stayed in?

Maybe it was time to stop.

The following night he went out for dinner. He wasn't hungry but he made himself order baked chicken with a green salad. His waitress was a striking young woman, with long black hair and strong facial features—a hawk nose, deep-set eyes, a red slash of a mouth. Her uniform was tight over her breasts, and the skirt was short enough to show good legs.

He had brought a newspaper to the table, and he read it while he ate, but from time to time he would set it aside and steal a look at the waitress. She was nice. He wasn't going to do anything about it, hadn't done anything since the episode with the tire iron in Ames, but this didn't mean he could stop looking at her, or thinking about her.

He ordered coffee but no dessert. He had drunk about a third of the coffee when she came unbidden to refill his cup. Quietly, without moving her lips, she said, "I get off at eleven. If you're interested." He was too stunned to reply. "Meet me in the lot outside," she went on, her voice just strong enough to reach his ear. "My car's the white Trans-Am. If you're interested."

"I'll be there," he said.

"I figured you might."

He didn't know that he'd come back for her. All the same, he paid the check in cash instead of with the credit card he'd planned on using. He left a good tip but not an outrageous one. On his way to the Lincoln he saw her white Trans-Am parked all the way at the back of the lot.

He drove around for two hours, trying to decide what to do. At ten minutes of eleven he was back at the restaurant lot, the Lincoln parked alongside the Trans-Am.

He got out of the car, leaned against the fender and waited. At five past the hour she exited the restaurant by the side door. She was still wearing her uniform and carrying her purse. Her face lit up when she saw him, and she hurried across the blacktop to him.

"I didn't know if you'd be here," she said. "I didn't know for sure if I wanted you to. But the minute I saw you I was glad you came back. I don't do this often."

"Neither do I."

"But the way you were looking at me, it really got to me. I mean it got me hot."

"I didn't mean to stare."

"Hey, I'm not complaining." Her eyes were very dark, black in the dim light of the parking lot. "My name's T.J. You don't want to know what it stands for."

"I'm Mark."

"Well, Mark, do you want to go for a drink? Because I don't, particularly."

"What do you want to do?"

For answer, she came into his arms and kissed him. The

move took him a little by surprise, but he put his arms around her and felt her body against him and her mouth on his, and the kiss lasted.

"Wow," she said.

"You're a pretty good kisser, T.J."

"So are you. That was research, I wanted to check the chemistry. While I was at it I seem to have broken the ice. You want to come to my place?"

"Sure."

"This your car? I think we better take two cars. If we got in yours we'd never make it out of the lot. Have you got the leather seats? Maybe we *should* get in your car."

"You like leather, T.J.?"

"I like everything," she said. "God, you got me hot. Feel," she commanded, and pressed his hand between her legs. He had just a moment to feel the damp warmth of her before she danced away, laughing. "Now you follow me, okay?"

Tagging along after her, he realized that he didn't have to hurt her. She wasn't a stranger now. They knew each other's names, they had kissed, she was eager to be his companion for the evening. He could make love to her.

He hadn't done that in a long time.

Her apartment was a one-bedroom unit in a garden apartment complex north of town near the river. She parked in her space and showed him where to leave the Lincoln. Inside, she showed him around, then offered to make coffee. He said he didn't want any.

She lived in comfortable disorder. One wall was given over to bookcases made of boards and concrete blocks. The books, almost all paperbacks, filled the shelves and spilled over onto the floor. There were several unframed posters tacked to the walls, their edges curling around the tacks. Two of them advertised resorts on Mexico's Pacific

Coast. A third was a movie poster, with Jeff Bridges aiming an enormous pistol at the audience.

Her bed was a foam mattress on a plywood platform, and they were stretched out on it not ten minutes after they entered the apartment. "I'd hate for you to think I'm easy," she said, after kissing him, "but why waste time?"

She was beautiful. Her uniform had hinted at the lushness of her figure, but with her clothes off she was better than he had expected, with beautifully shaped full breasts and a very narrow waist. He lay on the bed with her and held her in his arms and kissed her mouth, and he knew that this was going to be all right, that everything would be fine. He didn't even want to harm her, he just wanted to give her pleasure.

"Lie still," he told her after a moment, and he moved lower to pay some attention to her breasts. She responded nicely, she loved what he was doing to her, and he lingered awhile at her breasts, delighting in them.

Then he moved lower, stationing himself between her thighs. She was gratifyingly passionate, very vocal in her enthusiasm. He brought her to a shattering orgasm, then went on licking her until he had coaxed the last sweet tremor out of her body.

When he lay down beside her she said, "Holy shit. I think the phrase we're looking for is 'beyond her wildest dreams.' Where'd you learn to *do* that?"

"There was this special on public television."

"Is that right? I bet you watched it more than once. But now we've got to do something for you."

"No, I'm all right."

"Are you? Oh, my, look what you're trying to hide from me. 'Officer, he had a concealed weapon.' Mark, I have a place for you to conceal it." Her hand fastened on him. "Come on," she said, tugging. "If you think you're going to escape with that beauty you're out of your mind."

271

And after all, why shouldn't he do what she wanted? He didn't have to worry about evidence. If his pubic hair cared to merge with hers, what difference did it make? He wasn't going to hurt her. He could leave behind all the evidence in the world.

He slipped easily, deliciously, inside her. Her arms held him, her breasts cushioned him, her hips rocked him. They found a rhythm together and held it, and he gave himself up to the sensations of her flesh on his.

He brought her twice to climax that way and got no closer to it himself. He considered pretending, but now he wanted the release of orgasm, even needed it. Carefully, deliberately, he allowed himself a fantasy.

And in the fantasy he was with the checkout girl from Ames, but the fantasy took a different turn from the moment he parked the car on the deserted country road and opened the trunk. Instead of a corpse she emerged wild-eyed and furious, brandishing the tire iron with which he'd struck her down. And he took the tire iron away from her, snapping her arm at the elbow as he did so, and she cried out in pain and shock, but they were miles from the nearest house and no one could hear her.

And he stripped her naked, and first he had to punish her for attacking him, and he punished her brutally and with imagination. He used the tire iron. He used his hands and his teeth. He was cruel, very cruel. . . .

And he was careful now, very careful, careful to keep his own hands away from T.J.'s neck, careful to let the fantasy play only in his mind while his body made love. And it worked, he reached his dry climax, and lay spent upon her.

But she wouldn't leave it alone.
"Mark? How come you didn't finish?"
"I did."

"Then why aren't I all wet and sticky?" She got up on an elbow. "Listen," she said, "I feel like a violin that somebody just played the living shit out of. I never had loving this good. I mean it."

He didn't know what to say.

"If there's something special you like—"

"There's nothing."

"I don't believe you. Look, you don't have to be embarrassed with me. I'm as kinky as you are, I like everything. You know what I am? I'm tri-sexual. If it's sexual, I wanna try it."

T.J., T.J., leave it the hell alone.

"Tell me what you like," she said, "and we'll do it."

"How would you feel," he said slowly, "about being tied up?"

She found a ball of binder's twine and he tied her spreadeagled on her back on the bed, a pillow underneath her bottom. There were storage drawers in the platform the mattress rested on, and he anchored the twine to the drawer handles. When he was satisfied with her bondage he told her to try to move.

"I can't," she said, grinning.

"Do you feel helpless?"

"Sort of."

"I may do things that frighten you a little," he told her. "That's part of the excitement. Let yourself be frightened, but at the same time remember that it's safe."

"Like a horror movie," she said. "It's a way you can be comfortable with your fear."

He ran a hand lightly over her body. She moaned softly, appreciatively. "I think I could learn to like this," she said.

"I'll be right back," he told her.

In the bathroom medicine cabinet he found a roll of

white adhesive tape. He tore off strips and made a patch three inches square. He returned to the bedroom and sat down on the bed beside her.

"Now I'd like to tape your mouth," he said, "but first I want to make sure it's all right with you."

"Well—"

"Because obviously you're more helpless when you can't make a sound."

"You're really an expert on this, aren't you?"

"Well—"

"And you weren't going to say a word about it, were you? I had to coax it out of you. How can you get what you want in this world if you don't ask for it?"

He shrugged.

"Go ahead," she said. "Tape my mouth. It's the only way you'll ever get me to shut up."

He fastened the patch over her mouth, but first he gave her a kiss. Then, when she could not make a sound, he put his hands between her parted thighs and began playing with her. Her eyes were locked with his at first, but after a few moments she was sopping wet and she had to close her eyes. He made her come with his fingers, and when she opened her eyes at last she looked awestruck and overwhelmed. He knew that she wanted to say something, but of course her mouth was taped and she couldn't.

He went to the kitchen. Sabatier carbon-steel knives hung on a magnetized board next to the sink. He took down the largest one and tested its blade for sharpness with his thumb. In old Japan they had tested samurai swords by lining up peasants and seeing how many the blade would slice through in a single pass. *"Ah, very good, a six-peasant sword."* And what would be a fitting test for this knife?

He saw himself sitting on the bed beside her, showing her the knife, then laying the flat of it upon her stomach.

"Now here's the part you might not like, angel. Here's where I cut your tits off."

She would think it was part of the game. She would be frightened, but not really frightened, not really thinking she was in danger, and she wouldn't really believe it until she felt the knife.

He swayed, leaned against the sink for support. Ignorant armies clashed on a battlefield within him. At length he opened his eyes and put the knife down on the sinkboard.

His clothes were piled on a rush-seated chair in the bedroom. He scooped them up, bent to retrieve his shoes. From the bedroom doorway he told her he'd be back in a minute. "You stay right where you are," he said.

He dressed in the kitchen. Making as little noise as possible, he let himself out of the house and got behind the wheel of his car. The motor was running before he realized he had brought the kitchen knife with him. There it was, gleaming on the seat beside him.

He didn't dare try to return it.

A mile down the road he thought he ought to call someone. An anonymous phone call to the police, saying merely that a woman needed assistance at such-and-such an address. She'd be embarrassed when they showed up and found her like that, but at least she'd be cut loose.

But how could he make the call? He didn't know the name or address of the apartment complex, or the number of her unit. He didn't know her name, either, not her last name or her first name, just a pair of initials.

So let her work it out herself. She wasn't tied all that tightly, or that securely. Sooner or later she'd work a hand loose.

In any case, he couldn't go back. If he went back, if he set foot again in that apartment, he'd kill her.

* * *

275

There was no way out.

Driving, driving aimlessly, he began to see the hopelessness of his situation. He had almost killed T.J. Never mind that the knife was never in the same room with her; in point of fact, she had been within inches of death. He hadn't wanted to kill her, he had made a firm conscious decision that he was not going to kill her. It wasn't just the risk he'd have been running—his pubic hairs shed in her bed, his fingerprints idly impressed on more surfaces in her apartment than he could ever remember to wipe. More to the point, he had wanted the night to end with the woman alive and well. He had made love to her, he had felt something for her, and the last thing he'd wanted to do was kill her.

Yet he'd very nearly done it anyway. He'd had to fight with himself, and he'd come very close to losing.

He wasn't going to be able to stop killing. If it had ever been a matter of choice, it had long since become something else. He would go on killing, and he would never entirely enjoy it again.

It would still thrill him. It would have thrilled him just now, with T.J., although it would have sickened and revolted him in the bargain. It would even continue to provide a measure of satisfaction. But he had reached that point in the cycle of addiction where he could no longer genuinely enjoy what he now more than ever required.

And what would happen to him?

Well, sooner or later they would catch him. They might already have realized that a serial killer was circling the region. As much as he'd varied his victims and his methods, the sheer quantity of his work would establish some sort of pattern. There was probably something about the way he tied a woman's hands behind her back, for instance, that would mark several of his killings as the work of a single killer.

And he'd take more chances, not to test limits or raise the stakes, but because there seemed less reason for caution. Sooner or later they'd catch up with him, and when that happened he suspected he would most likely confess. Once it was over, why draw it out?

And then? A death sentence, a life sentence, or a state hospital for the criminally insane. All three prospects seemed about as attractive. Until then he would do what he had no choice but to do. He would keep traveling, and he would continue killing, and he would play the string out to the end. He would not make it easy for them.

He stopped for gas at an all-night station on the highway. He filled the tank, went to pay. The clerk was a woman, not pretty, but there was something about her. He put his credit card away and paid cash and went back to the car for the kitchen knife.

#101.

Driving again, he thought of T.J. By now she had surely realized that he wasn't coming back. She'd think it was the kinkiest thing ever. She might even like it.

But she'd never guess how close she had come to dying. And, thinking of that, he realized why he had been unable to allow himself to return to Kansas City. Somehow he had known that he could no longer trust himself around his wife. Or his daughter.

He drove into South Dakota. He didn't pay any real attention to the route. The car seemed to know where it wanted to take him.

EIGHTEEN

Belle Fourche, the first place they reached after cutting across the northeast corner of Wyoming, was a dusty cowtown with wide streets and a population of around five thousand. There were still some banners to be seen proclaiming the annual rodeo, which had taken place the first week of July.

They spent a whole day in Belle Fourche, splitting up into twos and threes and exploring the town. The laundromat got a steady stream of business, and at the Lariat Motel on Elkhorn Street Guthrie made arrangements with the owner for them to take over three of the units for showers. All day long they were drifting over to the Lariat, stripping and bathing and dressing and moving on. The owner, a stolid widow with arms like hams, sat in the office throughout the day and tried not to think what her water bill would come to. She kept reminding herself that she was getting paid six times the day rate for the rooms, and that they'd be vacant and cleaned up in time for her to rent them out that night, and that would pay for a lot of water. Her good feelings were qualified somewhat later on, however, when she had to make up the three rooms herself; the Indian girl who normally took care of those things had walked off with the rest of them, and it didn't look as though she'd be coming back.

There were half a dozen new walkers, in addition to the Lariat's chambermaid, when they walked out of town late in the afternoon. It was on their account that Guthrie marched eastward for two and a half hours before making camp. He wanted the new people to walk far enough to get caught up in the group's energy before settling in for the night. It wasn't that he was afraid they'd drift away if they made camp closer to Belle Fourche—anyone who was supposed to be part of the group would stay part of the group, no matter where they spent the night. But it seemed to be easier for people to get into the rhythm of things when they started out putting one foot in front of the other.

"Just remember to alternate feet," he had told Jody their first day together. And that was really all there was to it. The preparations, the supplies, became less important with the miles. Most of the people who'd been walking for more than a couple of weeks carried less than they'd set out with. Extra clothing tended to be passed out to those who'd come with only what they were wearing. If no one had a use for it, it would be abandoned at roadside, along with other items that turned out to be not worth their weight. Not everyone bothered to carry a canteen; some who had had them had lost theirs, and the newer people rarely troubled to obtain one. Someone else always had water to share, and there was often a stream you could drink from.

They were still on US 212, heading more or less due east across the state. At first, studying a state map while people showered at the Lariat, Guthrie had wanted to go down into the Black Hills and then on through the Badlands. He

wanted to see Mt. Rushmore and the Crazy Horse monument, he wanted to walk through the surreal lunar landscape of the Badlands that he'd seen only in pictures. He
traced a route through the old gold towns of Deadwood
and Lead, down through Rapid City.

But it just didn't feel right, and now he could see reasons
to prefer the route they'd actually taken. At this time of
year the Black Hills would be alive with the sound of
tourists, and people by the hundreds would be camping in
the Badlands, and you'd have to get in line and take a
number to sneak a peek at Mt. Rushmore.

He still wanted to go there sometime. But it was important to keep one's priorities in order. First you saved the
planet. Then you saw the sights.

The healings went on. Scar tissue disappeared, replaced
by new skin. Liver spots faded from the backs of hands.
Gray hair grew in dark, and new hair sprouted in bald
spots. Eyesight improved for almost everyone; eyeglasses
and contact lenses became part of the roadside litter, and a
rancher who'd joined the walk just before they crossed
from Montana into Wyoming had his cataracts dissolve
two nights out of Belle Fourche.

Inspired by Bud's example, any number of people began
growing new teeth. Mame Odegaard was cutting a whole
third set, while others merely replaced missing teeth. One
woman reported that a filling had fallen out, and wondered
when they would come to a town large enough to support a
dentist; she wanted to replace the filling before the tooth
sustained further damage. The next morning she announced that she wouldn't need a dentist; the hole was
gone, the tooth having filled itself with new growth.

"Skin does that all the time," Sara said. "Why should
teeth be different?" And from that point on, fillings began

loosening and falling out left and right, with the resulting cavities rarely remaining unfilled for more than a day.

Just past Mud Butte, where the highway doglegged to the right and began running due east, a crew from the workhouse labored to spruce up a roadside picnic area. Men in county-issue gray clothing painted tables and outhouses and stacked firewood, all under the supervision of a uniformed deputy with a shotgun. When the first of the walkers passed them, one of the prisoners put down his paintbrush and stared at the procession. After a few minutes he walked to the road and fell in step with a pair of walkers.

No one seemed to notice his absence. A few minutes later, two more men deserted and joined the parade. Soon there was only one left of the original eight prisoners, and as the tail end of the group drew even with him, he tossed a length of firewood onto the pile and trotted after them.

The deputy watched him go. He seemed unable to act, and stood motionless until the band of walkers was almost out of sight. Then he put his shotgun on a freshly-painted table, unpinned the star from his breast and set it down beside the gun, and took off after them. He walked at a brisk pace, and it didn't take him long to catch up.

The next day, halfway between Maurine and Faith, a band of two dozen men, women and children waited patiently at an intersection. They were from Minot, North Dakota, they explained, all of them except a hitchhiker they'd picked up along the way who had decided to stay with them. They had heard the call and wanted to join. They had come down from Minot in three cars and a pickup truck, and they left the four vehicles at the side of the road, the doors unlocked, the keys in the ignition, in case somebody happened along with a use for them.

"Because we're walkers now," said the apparent leader, a wheat grower named Arne. "We would have walked down from Minot, but we got the call too late for that. We never would have made it in time."

There were well over a hundred of them now, and Guthrie was both elated and alarmed at the rate of growth. It was obviously their mission to bring in more and more new people. Whatever it was exactly that they were supposed to accomplish, and his mind kept having trouble coping with what Sara had told him, they could do it more effectively if there were more of them.

"But we don't get a chance to know people," he complained to Jody. "A batch of folks turn up, and before you can get their names straight another slew of people join in, and the ones from yesterday are old hands already."

"Things are happening faster now, hoss. When you and I started walking together it took us three or four days just to get used to each other. The way things are going now, in three or four days a person's hyperventilated twice, thrown away a cane and a pair of glasses, and grown a new tooth. I liked it better when I knew everybody, sure, but I have to say I like being in the middle of all this growing and healing and love. It just feels good, Guthrie. I used to put away a lot of cold beer trying to feel this good, and I like it a whole lot better without all that swallowing and belching and little cuts on my finger from those ring-top cans."

Even so, Guthrie wondered, could the group absorb so many people so quickly without losing its own identity? Would the magic continue to work if people walked together without really getting a chance to know each other? And was something lost when people joined in a body? Suppose the Minot people kept to themselves, suppose they constituted a group within a group. Wouldn't that make for trouble?

After the North Dakotans joined the walk, the first town they came to (pop. 576, according to the sign) was Faith. That's what this took, he thought. Faith. And a leap of faith, as Sara had once assured him, was never from Point A to Point B. A leap of faith was from Point A.

Just beyond Faith they entered the Cheyenne River Indian Reservation; according to the map, they'd be walking through it for the next hundred miles. Guthrie wasn't sure what rules they would be violating by pitching camp on Indian ground, but he had come to believe that it didn't matter. No one seemed to care where they slept.

That first night Sara had everyone lie down in rows just a few feet apart, all of them on their backs with their heads facing north. At her direction, they began doing their rhythmic breathing in unison, drawing the breath into the upper part of the lungs, beginning each inhalation upon the completion of the exhale, making of the breath one unending flow.

As always happened when any of them breathed in this fashion, a strong current of energy was generated in their bodies. But this time, breathing together as one, there was a powerful group energy in evidence as well. Their bodies remained a few feet apart, but whatever had previously separated their spirits dissolved in the white light of their shared breath.

They breathed together for between thirty and forty minutes, by which time everyone had gone unconscious. By the time another hour had passed, they were all awake again, and an easy calm lay upon the group like morning mist in a valley.

They spent three more nights on Indian land, and on each of those nights Sara led them through a similar session of breathing in unison. By the time they left Indian territory and crossed the long bridge over the Missouri

River, they knew each other as intimately as if they had shared a womb.

And they all knew what they were there for. One way or another, each of them had been given a taste of Sara's vision.

East of the Missouri, Route 212 continued across the state, but Guthrie took them south on 83, heading toward Pierre. A number of Indians had walked off the reservation with them, and more people joined as they paraded south through Agar and Onida. They left the highway before it reached Pierre, turning east on 14. They passed through Blunt and Harrold, Holabird and Highmore and Ree Heights, Miller and St. Lawrence.

There was more wheat being grown on this side of the Missouri, and less open range for cattle, but the terrain was otherwise much the same, perfectly flat, and sectioned off by roads that were perfectly straight. A wind from the west had been at their backs all the while they crossed the Indian land, and it was blowing with more force now, never letting up, never changing direction. There was nothing to stop it in this flat treeless land, nothing to slow it down.

Every ten miles or so a road intersected theirs, and at virtually all of those intersections there was a village of a hundred or four hundred or eight hundred people. At each intersection, in each village, people were waiting to join them. Most of them lived within a few miles of the town, but some had traveled long distances, although none yet had come from as far as Minot. There were a few from Nebraska, however, and several from farms close to the North Dakota border.

Some arrived at the roadside just as the procession was reaching it. Others stood for days, scanning the horizon like nineteenth-century Millerites waiting for the world to end. Something kept them from wandering off, and finally the group came into view, and when it reached them they gave themselves up to its embrace.

People reacted to them now in one of three ways. Some, of course, dropped what they were doing and joined in. A farm wife weeding the kitchen garden called her husband from the fields and her children from their play, and before the procession had passed it would be larger by one family. Others waved or spoke to them and wished them well, but either never considered joining in or dismissed the notion easily.

And, finally, there were those people who did not see them at all. Sheriffs and state troopers were generally in this category, but they were not alone; any number of motorists passed them on the highway without taking their eyes for a moment from the road. They were, to be sure, an increasingly visible phenomenon, two hundred of them or close to it, strung out along the highway and edging onto the shoulder when a car neared them. It took a sort of willful blindness to overlook them, but an increasing number of people managed to do just that.

It was, Guthrie decided, much of a piece with the protective shield they seemed to have against harsh weather and extremes of temperature. The same force field screened them from eyes that would not like what they saw.

Kate, the Boston Irish woman who had reached them by way of the Hen House commune in Idaho, had an alternate explanation. They were, she pointed out, an extraordinary lot, workers of miracles, altogether miraculous in their own right. As such they existed somewhere outside the boundaries of the belief systems of some people, and so they became like leprechauns in Ireland, quite invisible to those who did not believe in them.

It was hard to think of people like Dingo and Jody and

Les Burdine as leprechauns, but Guthrie could see her point. At the beginning, when he had set out across Oregon on his own, he had never run into anyone who had failed to notice him. Every person he talked to answered him, every driver he waved at raised a hand or an index finger in response. But then he had not yet constituted any great threat to anyone's belief system. McLemore, the motel owner, had been outraged at the idea of his sleeping out in his clothes, and had maintained the integrity of his understanding of how the world worked by dismissing Guthrie as a liar. Transport McLemore across half a continent, confront him with people who were growing new teeth and walking away from their wheelchairs, and their mere existence would be a serious threat to his sanity. If he couldn't stretch his mind, he could at least protect himself by closing his eyes.

On a Tuesday morning, midway between the little towns of Cavour and Iroquois, Ellie woke up, fed and changed Richard, and went down to the stream to fill her canteen. She got a sudden painful tingling sensation in her left thumb, and responded to it by putting it in her mouth. Georgia Burdine, who was washing her hands and face in the stream, accused her of having learned the trick from Richard.

"Richard doesn't suck his thumb," Ellie said. Then, without thinking, she added, " 'By the pricking of my thumb, something wicked this way comes.' "

"Gosh, I hope not," Georgia said. "Is that from something?"

"*Macbeth.* The witches say it. Well, one of the witches says it. Ouch!"

"It hurts, huh? Let me see it, Ellie. I don't see anything wrong with it. It's not swollen or infected."

"I'm sure it's nothing."

"There were bees around yesterday. Did you get stung?"

"I don't think so. It's the sort of thing you tend to notice when it happens, isn't it?"

"Maybe you stuck yourself on a thorn then. Well, what the hell, let's deal with it." She closed her eyes, rubbed her hands together briskly, held them down at her sides, and breathed deeply three times, willing energy into her hands with each exhalation. When her own hands were tingling she held them on either side of Ellie's thumb. She kept up the treatment for about a minute, then withdrew her hands.

"How's that? Better?"

"All better. Thanks."

"'Snothing. Hey, say that again, will you? From *Macbeth?*"

"'By the pricking of my thumb, something wicked this way comes.' Except I think it's thumbs, plural, which would rhyme better, wouldn't it? 'By the pricking of my thumbs, something wicked this way comes.' Yeah, I'm sure that's it. I got it wrong because I only had a pricking in one of my thumbs."

"Well, that's a relief."

"Why?"

"It means we don't have to worry," Georgia said. "About something wicked this way coming."

They were just a mile or two past the town of Manchester that afternoon when a car passed. Many of them waved but the driver didn't wave back. He had looked at them, though. Usually the drivers who looked right at them responded in some way or other. But not always.

A few minutes later the same car passed them going the other way. At least it looked like the same car. And a few minutes after that it appeared a third time, and this time the driver pulled off onto the shoulder and asked directions to the Laura Ingalls Wilder memorial.

"That's in De Smet," a young woman named Kimberley said. She was a native South Dakotan and had just joined them three days ago in Wessington. "We haven't come to it yet. You must have passed it, it's eight or ten miles back the way you came."

"I saw signs," he said, "and then I must have missed it because the signs stopped. My kids read all her books, and of course there was the television show. I figure if I'm this close, I ought to be able to tell my daughter I saw the original little house on the prairie."

"There are a couple of houses that she lived in," Kimberley told him, "and pots and pans from their kitchen, and lots of great stuff. I went when I was a kid and I loved it."

"Maybe I'll walk with you," he said. "Is that where you're all headed?"

"Well, we'll be passing through De Smet. I don't think we'll stop. We stopped in Huron yesterday to look at the world's largest pheasant, but that only took a few minutes. You just stood there and looked at it."

"How large could the world's largest pheasant be?"

"Pretty large. I'd seen it before, of course, because we lived around here and we used to go into Huron all the time. The world's largest pheasant is forty feet high and weighs twenty-two tons."

"That's a pretty big pheasant."

"I told you. Or wait a minute, did I get that right? Maybe it's twenty-two feet high and weighs forty tons. No, I think I had it right the first time. It's made of steel and fiberglass."

"No feathers?"

"No feathers. We'll pass close to the Ingalls memorial, but I don't think we'll actually go in. I mean, look how many there are of us. And it's just a little house."

"On a prairie."

"In town, actually. They don't have the prairie house, but there are pictures of it. You're welcome to walk with us, and that way you won't miss it this time."

They had been walking as they talked, and his car was by now quite a ways behind. But this was not unusual; every day someone walked away from a car to join them.

"Eight or ten miles," he said. "I guess I can walk that far. And you're going on from there? That's a lot of walking."

She laughed. "Some of these people have been walking all the way from Oregon."

"You're kidding."

"Nope. I wish I could have been with them all the way, but here I was in South Dakota, so I let the parade come to me. I'm Kimberley, by the way."

"I'm Mark."

NINETEEN

He was surprised how much he enjoyed walking.

Of course it didn't hurt that it was a glorious day. The sun was high and bright, but it never shined for long without interruption; just as the heat was on the verge of becoming oppressive, a cloud would interpose itself. And the wind, a steady force at his back, kept the heat from building up.

Amazing how much color the prairie had. He'd been driving through similar country for months, but when you slowed to a walk you saw the different patches of wildflowers. At highway speed the colors blurred.

Lunatics. Walking across the country, talking about miracles. This one had thrown away a pair of glasses, that one had discarded a hearing aid. Like the dimwits who made a pilgrimage to Lourdes, hobbled into the cathedral, walked out beaming, pronounced themselves cured, cast aside their crutches, and fell down a flight of stone steps. Still, they were a happy bunch, physically attractive, glowing from within. Pleasant enough to be around.

And wonderfully accepting, perfectly delighted to have

him in their midst. If he was harebrained enough to walk away from his car and tag along with them to De Smet, he was obviously their kind of people.

A pretty girl, Kimberley. Young, certainly, but older than the swimmer in Pueblo, the pudgy little darling whose swimsuit wouldn't stay up. Kimberley was a different physical type entirely, tall and slender, one of those clear-eyed Scandinavian country girls you found all over these parts.

He reached into his pocket even as he gazed at the back of her neck. A gold chain circled her throat, but it would snap like a twig if he tried to strangle her with it. But the picture wire in his pocket, that would do the job nicely enough. He'd just have to find some way to cut her out of the herd. Then a quick silent kill and the parade could go on without her.

The tricky part would be rejoining the line of march himself, so that he could select his next target.

Within the hour he got her off by herself.

She had been sharing her water with him, and it was almost gone. She spotted a farmhouse and said she wanted to refill her container from their pump. He said he'd go with her. She offered no objection, and no one volunteered to join them.

Up a straight gravel road to the white clapboard farmhouse. She rang the bell and no one responded to it. "Let's see," she said. "They won't miss the water, but where do you suppose the pump is?"

She looked for it and he stayed at her side, his hand in his pocket, fingering the length of picture wire. Or should he use his hands? God, she was nice. He'd get her from behind, press up against her, let her bottom rub against him as she fought. . . .

She had found the pump and was working its handle.

Water spurted forth. She caught some in one cupped hand, lapped it up. "It's good," she announced. "Not sulphury. Drink, I'll pump."

She worked the pump handle. Now, he thought, willing his hands to reach for her.

But first he'd have a drink. He bent over, put his mouth to the faucet, let her pump the cold well water for him. He drank deeply, water splashing all over his face and onto his shirt. Then he stood up, and it was his turn to pump for her. She held her hair out of the way but made no effort to keep the water from soaking her face and chest as she drank. She stood up at last, laughing, her T-shirt clinging to her body, her nipples clearly visible through the wet cotton.

"Gosh, look at me," she said. Then her eyes caught his. "Uh, I guess you *are* looking at me, aren't you?"

"I was just noticing that," he said, pointing to the crystal suspended from the gold chain.

"It's pretty, isn't it?" She held it out, displaying it to him. "Gary gave it to me last night."

"Is he your boyfriend?"

She laughed. "No, it was just, well, a gift. Somebody gave it to him and he gave it to me and I guess in a couple of days it'll be time for me to give it to somebody else. He said it gets stronger every time you pass it on."

"It gets stronger?"

"I'm not sure what that means. I asked him if he was sure he didn't want to keep it, and he said you had to give it away in order to keep it, and I don't know what that means, either."

Kimberley is your sister.

He thought for a moment that the words had been spoken aloud. But only he had heard them. A voice in his head, then. And a meaningless one at that. He had no brothers or sisters. Anyway, Kimberley was young enough to be his daughter.

She said, "Mark? You want to pump some more and I'll hold the bottle?"

He worked the handle. She held the container, an empty plastic bottle that had originally held a diet soft drink, and capped it when it was full.

The pump handle was a bar of white metal a foot and a half long. It was removable, and it would do if he wanted to knock her out. But he didn't have to knock her out.

"Kimberley? Hold still a minute."

She did just that while he moved to stand behind her. His hands settled themselves on either side of her neck.

"Oh, great," she said. "How did you know I needed a neck rub?"

And his hands, as if with a will of their own, began to knead her trapezius muscles, his fingers going right to the tight spots and working at them. She made appreciative noises while he massaged her gently but firmly for several minutes. Then, with a sigh, she straightened up. "We'd better get going," she said, "if we want to catch up with the others."

It didn't take them long to overtake the rest of the group. Kimberley fell into conversation with a young woman who was carrying an infant in a sling on her back, and Mark found himself drawn forward in the procession until he was walking with a woman named Sue Anne and a very soft-spoken Indian named George. Sue Anne did most of the talking. She was telling him and George about some woman named Sara, and was clearly in awe of the woman. He found himself picturing Sara in his mind. He visualized a tall fiery-eyed woman with a tawny mane of hair, a sort of combination of Amazon and Valkyrie, and he was taken aback to learn that Sara was actually a short slender gray-haired woman who happened to be blind.

"Wait a minute," he said. "I thought people get healed right and left on this hike. I keep hearing about the deaf hearing and the lame walking."

"That's what usually happens," Sue Anne said.

"Sara chose to be blind," George put in. "So she can see better."

He didn't stop in De Smet. He'd had no interest in the little house on the prairie, that had just been a way to start a conversation with Kimberley. Bunches of them stopped at various stores and eating places in De Smet to buy food, and then they all moved on, and he moved along with them.

He wasn't sure why. There were any number of good-looking women in the group, but he was beginning to realize that he was not going to be able to do anything about it. He had had his hands on Kimberley's throat, for heaven's sake, and had wound up giving her a massage. And now whenever he began to make one of his companions the object of a fantasy, that voice sounded in his head, insisting that the woman in question was his sister.

Whatever that was supposed to mean.

As De Smet disappeared behind them, he felt as though he had let go of the steering wheel of his life. He'd certainly let go of the Lincoln; it was close to three hours west of him by now, and every step was taking him farther away from it. He could still turn around and walk back to his car, but would it even be there if he did? He seemed to remember having left the key in the ignition, and he knew he'd left the doors unlocked. The crime rate was undeniably low in rural South Dakota, but a Lincoln with the keys in it, parked at the side of the road, might still prove an irresistible temptation to some local teenager. It wouldn't

294

have lasted fifteen minutes in downtown Kansas City. How long would it last out here?

It struck him that he would probably never know. Because he wouldn't go back for the car. He couldn't go back. He could only go forward. Whatever that meant, and wherever that led.

He was walking now with a man named Douglas and a woman named Lissa. He tried to have a fantasy about Lissa—she was quite attractive—but it wouldn't work. He felt somehow connected to Lissa. She had just been talking of astral bodies, a concept he had never understood but seemed almost able to grasp now, and when he tried to fantasize about her all he could think of was that they were Siamese twins on the astral plane, their spirit bodies joined at the nape of the neck. When his hands reached for her throat they fastened at the same time upon his own. He could not strangle her without cutting off his own air line.

He stopped trying, but then it came to him that Lissa was very like a woman named Marguerite whom he had killed in her own home six years ago in Kansas City. He had strangled her with her own pajama cord, winding it twice around her throat and drawing it tight, watching her pale eyes as the life drained out of them. When had he last thought of Marguerite? Not in months, maybe years, but he remembered her now—

And felt her pain. And felt her terror. Before he had witnessed it but now he felt it, and he and Marguerite shared a throat and the cord was choking both of them at once. *Marguerite was your sister,* said the damned voice in his head, and suddenly they were all his sisters, they were all linked to him, they were all part of him, and he felt his own being rent by a hundred and one mortal wounds.

"Mark? Are you all right?"

Yes, he told Douglas. He was okay.

295

"You look like you're hurting, man."

He had a headache, a brutal one, a line of fire bisecting his skull. He said as much to Douglas, and asked who was likely to have an aspirin.

"Hold still," Douglas said. And he thrust his hands down at his sides, huffed and puffed like a weightlifter about to attempt a new personal best, and then placed his hands on either side of Mark's head. Something buzzed —around Mark's head at first, then within it. After a moment Douglas dropped his hands. "There," he said. "That any better?"

"The headache's gone," Mark said.

Douglas was wiping his forearms with his hands, as if flinging some invisible unpleasantness from them. "If it comes back," he said, "just tell somebody. Most everybody who's been here a few days knows how to do that."

"You'll learn," Lissa assured him. "I'll show you tonight, if I'm not busy. Or somebody else will. And in a week you'll be teaching people yourself."

But they were wrong, he thought. His hands didn't take pain away. They inflicted it.

His headache was gone. He wanted not to believe that so much pain could be lifted with so little effort, but he did believe it almost in spite of himself. Maybe they weren't completely crazy. Maybe they truly were capable of miracles.

No matter. They could heal headaches, but he had an ache in his heart now where nobody's hands could possibly reach. Something was happening to him.

And there didn't seem to be anything he could do to halt the process. He wanted to leave, to turn his back on these people, but he knew that was impossible. He had the strongest feeling that he would die if he separated himself from the others. It was ridiculous, it didn't make any sense, and yet he was certain of its essential truth.

He thought of leaving even if it meant death, of seeking death, of welcoming it. He saw now that he had been killing pieces of himself for eight years. Every time he killed a woman he had killed something within himself. They were all his sisters, they were all parts of what he was a part of, some interconnectedness of all things, something he had heard of and read about and never ever felt.

He felt it now.

The pain stayed with him, a deep soreness at the base of his throat, a dull ache in his heart, dancing pinpoints of pain in his shoulder blades and the middle of his back. It never went away, and it always seemed to be just a bit more than he could bear, but it never truly got so bad that he could not in fact endure it. And the desire to leave stayed with him, but it too never reached the point where he was able to act on it.

Something carried him along. He could not stand it, but he stood it. He could not bear it, but he bore it. He could not go on, but he went on.

There was a wooded area east of De Smet and they made camp there, along the shores of Lake Preston. By the time they were settled in Mark was in a sort of a daze. Years ago as a child at summer camp he'd been hit in the forehead by a thrown baseball, and he'd suffered what was later diagnosed as a concussion. But at the time no one had made him go to the infirmary, and he'd wandered around for hours seeing through a fog and hearing through a filter, his senses muffled, the world at a distance.

He was like that now. He could walk around without bumping into people, he could carry on a conversation when spoken to, but everything was dimly perceived and imperfectly defined. Someone shared food with him and he ate. Someone made a place for him and he sat down. Several people asked him if he was all right. He said that he was.

When a young teenage boy asked him, he found himself at a loss for an answer. "I'm mixed up," he said finally.

"Yeah, I thought so," the boy said. "When we're really confused, what we generally do is we go talk to Sara."

"I've heard about her," he said. "Everybody mentions her. Do you know her?"

"Well, kind of," the boy said. "She's my mom. Come on, I'll introduce you."

She was just as she'd been described, and he wondered why he hadn't encountered her earlier. At one time or other he'd been at the front and middle and rear of the procession, but his eyes had never taken note of this gray-haired gray-eyed woman. It was hard to believe he could have missed her. She was quite striking in appearance, and, more than that, she had a remarkable presence. You could not be near her and remain unaware of her, or unconscious of her power.

The boy introduced them and she extended her hand. He wouldn't have known she was blind, and even now he found it hard to credit. She looked straight at him, and her eyes seemed to be focused on his. He took her hand, and the current that ran through their bodies almost brought him to his knees.

"Oh," she said.

And he felt her mind touch his, maneuvering to get a grip, extending fingers of thought that probed his mind and soul. He resisted for an instant, then relaxed some mental sphincter and let her in.

He felt all his emotions at once, fear and relief and

shame and anger and dread, so many conflicting emotions with the gain turned so high on all of them that he quite literally did not know what he was feeling. It was like listening to a radio that got every station at the same time, and played all of them at ear-splitting volume. Hearing everything, you could make out nothing.

She was holding his right hand in hers. Without letting go she turned him so that they were facing in the same direction, and she slipped her left arm around his waist. She led him through the trees and across a clearing, told him to sit down, and sat down facing him, her legs folded. She extended both hands so that they rested palms-up on her knees, and, in obedience to an unvoiced command, he put his hands in hers. Again a current ran through him, and again he felt her mind grapple with his. She was in there with him, she was accessing his memory, she was looking at his life.

She said, "You've never told anyone."

"No."

"How could you stand it?"

"You don't understand. I enjoyed it. I loved it."

"And you never made contact with the part of you that didn't love it. Not until today." Her eyes regarded him, and he had to remind himself they were sightless. "Everything you've felt today has been in you since the first woman you killed. You just didn't know it until now."

"I want to die," he said.

"No you don't."

"I do!"

"If you really did you'd be dead. Oh, a part of you wishes you were dead, but a bigger part wants to live. Everybody has a death wish and everybody has a life urge. As long as the life urge is stronger, you stay alive. When the

299

death wish is stronger, you die. Why do you think you came here? Not to die. People don't walk with us because they want to die. They walk into life, not into death. They come here to save themselves, to heal themselves."

"And that's what I did?"

"Of course."

He shook his head, then remembered she couldn't see the gesture. He said, "No, that's not true. I came here—"

"To kill someone."

"Yes."

"To kill all the women you could. All the pretty ones."

"Yes!"

"Well, who's missing? Where should we look for the corpses?"

"I—"

"You're an accomplished killer and we have plenty of pretty women with us. And you've been walking for how many hours? Eight or nine? How many did you kill?"

"None."

"And you still think that's what you came for?"

He remembered what the boy had said. When you were confused, you talked to Sara. He wondered why. The more he talked with her, the greater his confusion became.

He said, "I almost killed Kimberley."

"I don't know her. She must be fairly new. Tell me about it." He did, and she said, "Yes, I'm sure she's new. If she'd been here awhile you wouldn't even have come that close to harming her. And you didn't really come very close, you know. In your mind, your conscious mind, you were about to strangle her. In reality you were going to give her a massage. Kimberley picked up on the reality, not your perception of it, and she welcomed the massage, and that's what you gave her."

"But in another minute I would have—"

"Would have what? Would have killed her? No, Mark.

300

You did what you would have done, in a minute or in all eternity. And you couldn't have harmed Kimberley. Not many things can harm us on this walk, you see. The cold doesn't freeze us and the sun doesn't burn us, and with a few rare and not unpleasant exceptions, the rain doesn't fall on us. Something protects us. And even if it didn't, you can't kill someone who isn't ready to be killed. And we're none of us ready to die because that's not why we came here."

"Something you just said."

"That you can't kill someone who isn't ready to be killed."

"Yes."

"Did you think you were the Angel of Death? A terrible swift sword, a divine scythe harvesting women in their prime? How did you choose your victims? Did they run to type? Were they all classically beautiful?"

"No." He thought. "They were women who attracted me."

"And?"

"There was something about them," he said. And then he remembered Missy Flanders in Wichita Falls, something in her that had cried out to him, that wouldn't leave him alone until he had stabbed her in her bed. He reeled a little at the memory, and when he looked up Sara was nodding at him.

He said, "Are you telling me it was their fault?"

"It was their *choice,*" she said. "Is it your fault they're dead? No. Every death is a kind of suicide; the one who dies chooses it. You were the rope they used to hang themselves."

"But—"

"So does that mean you're blameless? Of course not! It was *your* choice, time and time again, to play that role in their lives, in their deaths."

301

After a long moment he said, "What's going to happen to me?"

"What do you think should happen?"

"I suppose you'll have to turn me over to the police."

"And then you'll confess, and there will be headlines in the newspapers, and a trial, and you'll go to prison or to a hospital. Perhaps you'll even be executed. Is that what you want?"

"Isn't it what I deserve?"

"I don't know what anyone deserves. The only way to find out what you deserve is to wait and see what you get. Is that why you came here, Mark?"

"Here?"

"Here. On this walk. You didn't come here to kill anyone, whether you thought so at the time or not. You came here because you were done with killing."

"But I couldn't stop. Even after I let that woman go in Sioux Falls, even after I knew I was sick of it, I killed another woman. I couldn't stop myself."

"Maybe you came here to stop."

"Maybe I came here to be punished."

She laughed. "Punished? You're already being punished. The crime was the punishment. Your punishment started eight years ago when you committed your first murder. It's been going on all along, distancing you, isolating you from the people you love, cutting you off from all the best portions of yourself. You've been punishing yourself all that time and today's the first day you've been able to feel it."

"I don't like the way it feels."

"No," she said. "I don't imagine you do."

"What do I do now?"

"Let me think." She closed her eyes. After a moment she opened them and said, "I think you're going to have to tell us what you've done."

"You already know."

"You're going to have to tell everyone. You'll tell us about all the women you've killed, from the one eight years ago to the one last night."

"Do I have to?"

"Yes. You have to."

"And then what? You'll decide how to punish me?"

"No, Mark. I told you you didn't come here to be punished."

"Then what? Why did I come here?"

"For the same reason everybody else did," she said. "Did you think you were so special?" She got to her feet. "Give me your hand," she said, "and we'll rejoin the others. You've got a long story to tell."

T W E N T Y

At Sara's instruction, they formed a great semicircle in front of him, sitting with their legs folded or stretched out full-length. He sat by the side of the fire, waiting. At a nod from Sara he got to his feet and faced them.

He said, "My name is Mark. Sara says I'm supposed to tell you my story. I'm a killer. In the past eight years I've murdered a hundred women." There was a collective intake of breath. "A hundred and one women," he said, and turned toward Sara. "I don't know where to start."

"With the first woman."

"She was a prostitute in Kansas City. I went with her to a motel. I hadn't intended to kill her. She said something that made me angry and I hit her and knocked her out. Then I thought of killing her to protect myself, and I did, and it was very exciting. I enjoyed it, I loved it."

"Tell us how you did it, Mark."

"I strangled her. With her blouse." His eyes were closed. He couldn't meet their gaze. "Now what?" he asked.

"Tell us about each of them, Mark."

"I can't remember everything."

"Yes you can. No one ever forgets a thing. It's all in there somewhere, every book you ever read, every person you ever met. I'll help you remember."

He took a breath. "The second woman," he said, and he felt Sara walking around in his mind, opening cupboards in his memory. "The second woman," he said, and her image came into his mind, "was a student at KU. That's the University of Kansas, that's in Lawrence. She was hitchhiking. I asked her to get something from the glove compartment, and when she leaned forward I grabbed her head and slammed it against the dashboard until she was unconscious. I took her into an unplowed field and killed her the minute she regained consciousness." He could smell the tall grass and hear the chirping of crickets. He could feel her fear and resignation as she saw death coming. "I strangled her. I used my hands. At first I couldn't kill her, but then I got the right grip and, and I killed her."

"And the third woman?"

"I don't remember." A nudge within his mind, a shift, a clearing. "She was working late in an office. I was in the building to see somebody and he had forgotten the appointment, his office was closed. I was on my way out and I saw her at her desk. She looked very scholarly, she had aviator glasses and a short haircut, and she was bent over a deskful of papers. I went in and asked her if she had a key to the men's washroom, and when she turned to get it I picked up a letter opener from the desk. . . ."

And the fourth, and the fifth, and the sixth. And the twenty-sixth. And the fortieth.

And on and on and on.

Early in his recitation, a woman named Ardith sprang to her feet and cried out that she could not listen to this. She made her way out of the semicircle and headed off through

305

the trees. Bud and Martha caught up with her and got her to lie down and breathe.

As Mark continued telling his story, more people went into hyperventilation. Sometimes this was preceded by an emotional outburst. One woman said she had been a rapist's victim, another that her father had abused her sexually. In each case, the person wound up on the edge of the semicircle, lying down, breathing, with someone on hand to monitor the process.

Women were not alone in reacting in this fashion. Men, too, found themselves launched into emotional upset by Mark's story, and it didn't much matter whether they were newcomers or veteran walkers. Dingo, the outlaw biker, stalked from the circle while Mark was telling about a schoolteacher he had killed with a hammer; moments later he was lying on the ground at the foot of a tall tree, his whole body rigid, his breath locked in his throat, while Kimberley sat on her haunches beside him and stroked his forehead and soothed him and made sure he continued to breathe without interruption.

Sometimes, when something dramatic occurred in his audience, Mark would stop talking. But when the drama subsided and the person involved was off to one side breathing, he would pick up his narrative precisely where he had left off. The memory he needed was always available to him. As he finished reporting each act of murder, the memory of the next was immediately at hand, sometimes with a little mental nudge from Sara. He described some women at length and others not at all, told the manner of killing in a few words or a paragraph. Often he found himself recalling things of which he'd had no conscious awareness at the time, and once in a while he would fall silent, struck by something he'd just heard himself say. No one interrupted those silences, and after a time he would resume speaking.

It was fully dark by the time he finished. He told of how he'd decided not to kill T.J. and had had to struggle with himself to keep from murdering her anyway. And he told about the woman at the gas station, and how he'd driven the kitchen knife clear through her body. And then he was done.

The fire was a heap of glowing coals. Guthrie approached, put some more wood on it. Flames sprang up. Guthrie went back and sat down again. Mark was still standing, facing them.

Sara said, "Well, what are we going to do with Mark? Shall we turn him in to the police?"

"No," someone said.

"Why not? Look at all the crimes he committed."

"What can the police do with him? Lock him up?"

"If he's locked up he can't commit any more crimes," Sara said. "Mark, are you dangerous? Will you kill again?"

"I don't know."

"Could you kill now? Look around you. Is there anyone here you could stab or strangle?"

He shuddered. "It makes me sick to think of it," he said. "But I did it before. I did it over a hundred times."

"You're not that person now."

"But where did that person go? Isn't he still inside me?"

"Yes, indeed he is. Well, what could we do with you if we don't turn you in to the police? Earlier you said you wanted to die. What does everyone think? Should we kill Mark?"

"No."

"No, we don't kill people."

"No, Mark is our brother."

His throat knotted at that last remark. He felt an ache at the back of his throat, fierce pressure behind his eyes.

"Should Mark kill himself?"

"No."

"Mark is done with killing. He's killed himself a hundred and one times, isn't that enough?"

Sara sighed. "They won't let you die," she said. "And it's just as well. You didn't come here to die. You came here to be healed, the same as everybody else."

"To be healed from killing?"

"To be healed of all that's ill within you. That's the real reason everybody does everything. Why do you think you killed those women?"

"Because I enjoyed it. Because it thrilled me, because it brought me pleasure."

"And why do you think that was so?"

"Because—" He looked at her. "I don't know," he said. "Maybe because I'm a monster."

"You're not a monster. You've done monstrous things, but that doesn't make you a monster. You killed to heal your hurt and anger, you killed to mend the tears in your spirit. And it felt good. But it didn't really work, and when the good feeling wore off you hurt more than ever, and so you had to kill more and more. And finally it didn't work at all and it didn't even feel good, and you couldn't stop. And you had to stop, and you knew that, and you came here. Because you knew you would find the space here to heal yourself."

"How?"

"By doing what you've already done, coming in touch with the parts of you that were always sickened by what you've done. And by standing in front of us and telling us who you are and what acts you've performed. You've already had a powerful healing experience tonight, Mark, and we've all been healed for sharing in it. Look at all the people who had to lie down and breathe. You touched something in each of them, something they needed to process in order to be whole themselves. Their own bottled-up pain, their hurt and fear and anger. Their death

308

urges. And the killer inside them, the killer they couldn't know about until you revealed your own killer self. You've played a great part in helping all of us grow, Mark. That's why we're so grateful to you."

"Grateful," he said.

"Oh, yes. You've given us a great gift. You'll give us another when we manage to forgive you."

"How can anyone forgive me?"

"How can we dare to do otherwise? We don't do anything for you by forgiving you. And we don't hurt you by withholding our forgiveness. We only hurt ourselves. There's a woman here who lost most of her family in Nazi concentration camps. She spent two days last week forgiving Hitler. Do you think it had any effect on Hitler? The son of a bitch has been dead for over forty years, and I don't suppose it makes much difference to him whether or not Ida Marcum forgives him. But she had angina so bad they wanted to do bypass surgery, except they didn't think she'd survive it. And now she's fine."

He closed his eyes, trying to concentrate. It seemed very simple to him. He had done bad things. Now he should be punished. Instead she talked about healing, and he didn't know what he had that had to be healed.

As if reading his mind, she said, "Of course you'd rather be punished. That would be much easier than going through what you haven't gone through in forty years. Who do you think you've been trying to kill all your life, Mark?"

"I don't know."

"Yes you do."

"When I was with Kimberley," he said, "a voice told me she was my sister. And ever since then, whenever I've looked at one of the women here, I had the same thought. That she was my sister."

"So?"

"Maybe all along I've been trying to kill my sister." He

309

considered it, then shook his head decisively. "But that doesn't make sense. I was an only child, I never had a sister."

"You wanted to kill all kinds of women, didn't you, Mark?"

"Yes."

"They weren't all of a physical type."

"No. I once had the thought—"

"Yes?"

"I hate to say it. *All right.* I had the thought that I wished all the women in the world had a single throat, and I had my hands around it."

Three women who had sat through everything up to this point rose as one, made their way through the crowd, and stretched out and began breathing. Sara didn't pay any attention to them. She said, "When someone's angry at all the women in the world, it usually means there's one woman he's really angry at."

"Who?"

"Can't you guess?"

"Not my mother."

"Are you sure?"

"Oh, Christ," he said. "It's always your parents, isn't that the message of psychology? But it can't be true this time. I never knew my mother. She died when I was born."

"So you couldn't possibly have any feelings about her."

"How could I? I never laid eyes on her. I have no memory of her. And how could I be trying to kill somebody who's been dead as long as I've been alive?"

"Do you remember your birth, Mark?"

"Of course not. Nobody does."

"Everybody does, but not everybody allows the memory to surface. Do you know anything at all about your birth?"

"Just that I lived and she died."

"Nothing else?"

"No."

"I'm not surprised. I could tell you things, but you have
to look at them yourself. You're going to have to lie down
and breathe, Mark. Everybody here will be supporting you
with their breath. You're going to have to go to a very
frightening place, but you were there once before and you
survived it the last time. You'll survive it now."

"I'm—"

"Yes, Mark?"

"I'm afraid."

"Good," she said.

The semicircle was a full circle now, and he was in the
middle of it. He was lying on his back with his arms at his
sides and his eyes closed. Someone's long-sleeved shirt,
rolled into a ball, was under his neck for a pillow. Sara sat
on one side of him, Richard's mother Ellie on the other.

He did as he was told, drawing full breaths into his upper
chest, beginning to exhale as soon as he had completed
inhaling, then letting the next breath flow out of the first
one. Sara held his hand and Ellie guided his breathing,
telling him when to breathe faster or slower, more shallow-
ly or more deeply, to see his chest filling with light when he
inhaled, to let the exhale flow effortlessly out of him.

Almost immediately something started to happen. He
felt a light tingling, first in his hands and feet, then
deepening there and spreading gradually throughout his
body. His arms were rigid at his sides, and the volume of
energy flowing through his hands was so great that he could
not flex his fingers. He no longer knew if Sara was still
holding his hand. He couldn't even feel the ground beneath
his palms.

Thoughts tumbled through his mind, vanishing from
view before he could identify them. He was bathed in
feelings, one after another. He would snatch at an idea and

311

try to follow along after it, and evidently it led him away from consciousness, because Ellie would be shaking him, urging him to breathe, and it would seem to him that he had never stopped breathing, but at her command he would rouse himself from his reverie and fill his lungs with air.

And then there was a point where he felt cramped, confined. He was warm, too, impossibly warm, roasting, and furious with whoever had decided to build up the fire. He was going to suffocate or die of the heat, and he couldn't understand why nobody would do anything, and his fury mounted and he pounded at the earth with his rigid hands and vented his anger in a wordless roar.

Then more things happened, and it seemed they happened very quickly. His breathing accelerated, so that he was gulping air as quickly as he could. But he could not get enough air, and his throat locked and he couldn't breathe. Sara was bending over him and Ellie was cradling his head in her arms, shouting at him to breathe, telling him he could do it, but he couldn't do it, his throat was locked shut, he couldn't get any air in or out, he was going to die like this, he was going to suffocate, the light within him would go out, and all these fucking women could think to do was tell him to breathe breathe breathe, what was the matter with the bitches, why didn't she do something, why couldn't she help him, what fucking good was she, she might as well be a corpse for all the goddamned good she was doing him—

And then he got the breath release. Whatever had been holding on let go, and he drew air into his lungs, and the breath flowed in and out of him now as if it were breathing him. His lungs filled and emptied, filled and emptied, keeping time to some unheard metronome. He had never breathed so deeply before, his lungs had never filled themselves so completely, and air had never had such a sweet richness to it. You could live on air like this, you could nourish yourself with it, and it was so good, everything was so good, the world was so good and all the people in it. And he felt their presence now, all of them, circling him, breathing with him, supporting his breathing with theirs, and his heart filled up and overflowed, it felt too big for his chest, and he wept, God, how he wept, he couldn't help it, he couldn't stop crying.

"Mark? How do you feel?"

How did he feel? "Strange. Different. Wonderful."

"Do you know what happened?"

"I breathed and I couldn't breathe and then I could."

"Yes."

"It was very hot and I felt . . . trapped. I couldn't get out. Oh!"

"You know what was happening?"

"It didn't feel like a memory. It felt as though I was reliving it. I was there, I was going through it."

"You were in the birth canal."

"Nobody would help me. She wouldn't help me. She just quit." His eyes widened. "Is that when she died?"

"Yes."

"I was so angry. I wanted to kill her. And she died."

"Yes."

"And then I couldn't get out. And I couldn't breathe! My neck, I was strangling, I couldn't get any air."

Her hand settled onto his. She said, "Mark, your mother died giving birth to you. I get that her heart gave out, but it's not too important exactly what happened."

"That's what it was, she had a weak heart. Someone told me that. How did you know?"

"I picked it up, but it's not too important exactly what

313

happened to her. What happened to you is that she stopped helping you, and you had a tough time being born. And you came out with the cord wrapped twice around your neck. You couldn't breathe. You came fairly close to dying."

"But she was the one who died."

"Yes, she was the one who died and you were the one who lived. And you had been angry at her, you wanted her to die, you were mad enough to kill her. So you grew up thinking you had killed her."

"That's crazy. I didn't know her, I didn't remember her. I didn't remember any of this."

"If you didn't remember it, what was it doing in your memory just now? How could you relive it if you didn't have the memory tucked away in there?"

"But I never *knew* I remembered it."

"You knew enough to suppress the memory. If you didn't know that much you couldn't have forgotten what happened. Because you picked up some powerful false information about yourself on the way through the birth canal. You were a killer. Your aliveness killed the woman you cared most about. In order for you to be fully alive, a woman had to die."

"God."

"You kept all of this hidden from yourself, but it was always there. For years you killed women in your fantasies. They died and you were alive. Then, when you began to succeed in the business world, you expressed more of your aliveness in the real world. And, if you were going to be alive, women were going to have to die."

"It's so crazy."

"But so logical. They died and you drew life from them. The light went out of their eyes and came into yours. Some of them you stabbed in the heart and they died as she did.

314

But more often they died the way you almost died, gasping for air with the cord around your neck. A cord, a piece of clothing, a length of wire, they were all stand-ins for the umbilical cord. For nine months you drew life through it, and at the end it almost took your life back."

"I didn't strangle all of them."

"No. But you just went through the list for us, Mark, and most of the deaths were of that type. Some died of broken necks, and that's pretty close. And there were the ones you drowned and smothered, the one with her lips and nostrils glued shut. They all died for lack of air. And you liked to look at their eyes when they were dying. You wanted to see what had almost happened to you."

"I killed in other ways."

"Because you became addicted to it. Once an addiction is established it doesn't matter what initiated the behavior. By the time a person has become an alcoholic, it's immaterial what led him to drink. From that point on, the habit causes itself. It works the same way with killing."

He thought about it, then nodded. She couldn't see him nod, but it didn't seem to matter what she could or couldn't see.

He said, "What happens now?"

"Everybody goes to sleep. It's pretty late, and we get up when the sun gets us up."

"After that. What happens to me?"

"What do you want to happen?"

"I don't know."

"Yes, you do."

"You won't let me get away with a thing, will you?"

"Only murder. What do you want to happen?"

"It's crazy. I'm afraid to say it."

"Say it anyway."

"I want to stay here."

315

"Here? Here in De Smet Forest? Here in South Dakota?"

"I want to stay with all of you."

"We're not staying here, you know. We're walking across the country."

"I know that. I want to walk with you."

"Why were you afraid to say that?"

"I'm still afraid."

"Of what?"

"That you won't want me to come."

She nodded slowly. "Well, that's understandable," she said. "And I can't really answer for the group." She extended a hand to them. "What do you all say? What should Mark do?"

And they answered her:

"Come with us, Mark."

"You have to come."

"He's part of it now. He can't quit."

"Mark is our brother."

"Mark, you couldn't leave us even if you wanted to."

"Mark, we love you."

"You belong with us, Mark. You're one of us."

He was crying again. He couldn't help it.

Through his tears he said, "How . . . how can you all want me?"

"Look at the show you put on for us," Sara said. "We don't have television out here, you know. We're starved for entertainment."

"But I'm a murderer."

"A murderer kills people. You used to kill people. You used to be a murderer. But you don't do that anymore."

"But—"

"That was then and this is now."

"Is it that easy?"

"Do you want it to be harder?"

316

"I don't understand," he said. "How can you forgive me after what I've done?"

"That's the easy part. How can you forgive yourself?"

"I can't."

"You will, if you stay with us. It won't be easy, but you'll find out how. Can you forgive your mother?"

He stared at her. "Forgive her? There's nothing to forgive!"

"There must be. You've been trying to kill her for the past eight years. And what do you mean there's nothing to forgive? That bitch quit on you. She almost smothered you and then she almost strangled you. Can you forgive her?"

"Of course."

"It's not that easy. You have to find the part of you that hasn't forgiven her and let go of it. You've got a lot of work to do."

"What kind of work?"

"The kind you did tonight. Breathing. Sharing yourself. Opening the doors to all the sealed-off chambers. Seeing everything you don't want to see. Facing everything you're afraid of. But all you really have to do is walk. If you do that, everything else you have to do will reveal itself to you."

He thought about what she'd said. "I don't have much choice," he said. "Do I?"

"Not a whole lot."

"I can't go back to Kansas, can I?"

"Not without a pair of silver shoes."

"I mean—"

"To your family. No, I'm afraid you can't, Mark. Maybe someday you'll run into them on the road somewhere. But you can't ever go back."

"And the police—"

"Won't bother you while you're walking. You're safe as long as you're with us."

317

"It makes the choice easy, doesn't it?" He drew a breath. "The only thing is it seems as though I'm getting off too easy."

"Too easy?"

"Yes. I killed over a hundred women, and all I have to do—"

"Is spend the rest of your life healing yourself and the planet. You're right, Mark. You're getting off much too easy. It would be ever so much harder for you to have to spend three minutes in an electric chair. And it would do so much more for you and the world." She touched his hand. "Go to sleep now," she said. "Things will make more sense in the morning."

TWENTY-ONE

In the morning they walked east on 14, into the rising sun. At Arlington the road turned south, joining with US 81. After two miles 14 ran east again, toward the small city of Brookings, but Guthrie chose to stay with 81 south to Madison. The wind which had been behind them for days was at their right now, blowing with the same unremitting vigor.

Several new walkers joined them that day, including the group's second babe in arms, an angelic little girl named Jane. She was just weeks older than Bud and Ellie's Richard, and people kept teasing Richard about his new girlfriend. Richard giggled as if he knew precisely what they were talking about.

Jane's single mother was a delicately beautiful woman named Amanita; she had worked as a teacher of deaf children until days before Jane's birth, and when she spoke her fingers often echoed her words, flashing unconsciously in sign language. When anyone commented on her name, she would explain that it was the Latin name of a genus of poisonous mushrooms. She said, "What can I tell you? I'm a child of the sixties and my parents were crazy. They did so much acid I'm lucky I've only got one head. I've got a brother named Bozo and a sister named Cloud Nine, so I figure I got off easy."

Just before they turned south on 81, a convoy of three army troop carriers passed them. Members of the group waved at them, but no one waved back. The third vehicle slowed, however, for no apparent reason, and before it resumed speed a pair of young soldiers vaulted the tailgate and dropped to the road below. The carrier drove off after its fellows, and no one appeared to notice the two deserters.

Their names were Jeff and Ken. One was from Lansing, Michigan, the other from southern Indiana. They were dressed in fatigues and sported quarter-inch crewcuts, and they had just recently finished basic training and were en route to a base in eastern Wyoming. They had enlisted and they liked the Army.

Then why had they joined the walk?

"Gosh, I don't know," Ken said. "I just saw you all walking, and something said go, and I went. I looked over my shoulder and here's Jeff standing next to me and dusting himself off. What's funny is the other night I had a dream I was marching with a whole regiment of troops, and everybody quit marching in step, they were just sort of walking along, and falling out of ranks, doing all the things you don't do when you're marching. What they were doing was they were turning into civilians. And that's what they did, see. They weren't all guys my age. In fact they weren't all guys. They were men and women all ages, and they weren't carrying rifles anymore, and they were, well, like this."

Jeff said matter-of-factly that he'd had essentially the same dream. "We're AWOL now," he said. "Are we going to get in trouble for this?" No, he was assured. They were not going to get in trouble.

Ken had only one regret. "My teeth are in bad shape," he said, "and I was going to get all this dental work done for free, and army dentists are supposed to be pretty good."

He was baffled when everybody started laughing at him. Then Jody clapped him on the shoulder. "Little brother," he said, "you got here in the nick of time."

Throughout the day, Guthrie found himself avoiding Mark Adlon.

This wasn't all that hard to do, and he wasn't obvious about it; at first, in fact, his efforts to steer clear of the serial killer weren't even obvious to Guthrie himself. With over two hundred of them, the line of march typically stretched for more than a quarter of a mile, and you could walk all day without getting a close look at some of your fellows. On several occasions, though, Guthrie was aware of Mark's presence nearby, and purposely drew away from him.

He wondered why. He had run a gamut of emotions the night before, shocked and sickened by the horrible story Mark told but struck nevertheless by whatever gave him the strength to tell it. He knew what it cost the man to go through the whole long list of killings, seeing them differently now. And when Mark lay down and breathed his way back into the terror of his birth, Guthrie had been right there with him, knowing exactly what Mark was going through and, to a great degree, going through it with him.

When Sara had asked the group whether Mark should stay or go, Guthrie had not raised his voice with the others. But if he had he would have said what they said, urging

Mark to stay. It was clear to him that Mark was supposed to be with them. So far no one had found his way to the group by accident, and no one had walked along with them without adding to the group's strength and enriching his own life in the process.

Certainly Mark needed the group. He had done awful things, with an awful effect upon his spirit, and it would take everything the group had to offer for him to recover. At the same time, Guthrie was willing to believe that the group needed Mark. He had already had a powerful impact upon them, and his was the sort of dramatic healing—like Mame's, like Al's, like Bud's new incisor—that touched off new miracles of healing in others.

Still, something bothered Guthrie.

What it came down to, he realized, was that it rankled that Mark was getting off scot-free. It was one thing for Ida Marcum to forgive a Hitler who'd killed himself in the bunker back in 1945. It was another matter to forgive a living mass murderer and welcome him with open arms. *"We forgive you! Now all you have to do is forgive yourself!"* Well, nifty. That was fine when the offense was spitting on the sidewalk or cheating on your taxes or aborting a child or slapping a woman around. But this son of a bitch had killed a hundred and one women and loved every minute of it. He killed them, he got off on killing them, and they were dead, and now it was *Mark, you are our brother*, and they were doing everything but pelting him with flowers and kissing his ring.

As the afternoon wore on he couldn't avoid recognizing three things. He was standing in judgment of Mark. He wanted to see him punished. And, finally, he was afraid of him, afraid that he was a very real threat to the women in the group.

He considered discussing this with Sara but didn't, not wanting to hear what she might tell him. But this was no help; his own mind obligingly supplied the words she might have said.

"When you judge anyone you judge yourself. When you seek to punish anyone you are seeking to punish yourself. What you fear in others you fear in yourself."

That evening, as soon as they had made camp just north of Madison, he sought out Georgia and asked her if she would supervise his breathing. Off to one side, he lay on his back and looked up at the gathering clouds. He closed his eyes and began the rhythmic connected breathing.

He went far away. He met a boy who never quite believed that his mother approved of him, no matter what he did. He met a man who longed to feel powerful and in control, and whose heart sang at the thought of having his hands around a woman's throat. He met facets of himself whose existence he hadn't expected, saw the scraps of fear and anger and hatred tucked away in sealed drawers of the self. Confronted, at last, the killer he might have been, the self within the self that thrilled at the thought of murder.

Georgia must have sensed the play of emotions within him, however much she knew exactly what he was going through. From time to time she would supply a thought. "It's safe to feel your anger," she told him several times. "It's safe for you to see exactly who you are," was another sentence she uttered just when he most needed to hear it.

When he was finished he rolled onto his side and opened his eyes. "Thanks," he said.

"You were really out there, Guthrie."

"Well, I'm back now."

He walked over to where Mark was sitting. He looked within himself for the fear, the judgment, the desire to punish. All were present, but not nearly as strong as before.

I forgive you, he said silently, *for making me look in the mirror.*

* * *

323

"Mark is amazing," Lissa told a couple of people. "He gives the best massage I ever had in my life."

"You let him massage you?"

"I asked him to. You know, I walked with him yesterday, before we knew anything about him. And I didn't pick up any killer vibes or anything, so I sort of got to know him before I got to know him, if you follow me. And this morning I was talking to Kimberley and I asked her if she'd picked up anything that I didn't, because she was the one he almost killed. I mean, he went to that farmhouse with her and he was all set to kill her, except he didn't."

"He couldn't," Dingo said. "It's like when you're an absolute master at Tai Chi, you never have to defend yourself. Say somebody wants to attack you. You don't do anything, you may not even notice them, but as they're getting ready to attack you, they forget. The idea of killing you slips their mind."

"Maybe that's what happened, I don't know. Anyway, she said she never picked up any hostility, but that he gave her the best neck rub ever, that his fingers knew just how to get the kinks out." She shrugged. "So I figured what the hell. He thought I was joking, and then he said he didn't know anything about massage, that he'd never given a massage, that he'd hardly ever even had one. But then I guess *he* figured what the hell, and he started on my neck and shoulders and worked on my whole upper back, and it was amazing. I didn't even feel tight to begin with, but his fingers went where the tension was and knew just what to do. He may not know anything about massage, but his hands know, and they're wonderful. You know the feeling I had afterward? I felt as though he took bad stuff out of my body."

"Bad stuff?"

"Yeah. I don't know how else to put it."

"He probably did exactly that," Martha Detweiller said.

"He had all that killer energy. When it turns around, it gets transformed into an incredible amount of healing energy. It sounds to me as though he's gifted."

"Well, it certainly felt that way."

"I'd better talk to him," Martha said, rising. "If he's taking negativity out of people, he's got to learn to discharge it or it'll build up in him. There's the way Jody taught everybody of wiping your hands when you're done getting rid of pain, and there are some other things I can teach him. If he'll visualize white light around himself before and after he works on somebody, that'll help. Or he can discharge the bad stuff by willing it to flow out of his hands and into the ground, or into moving water."

"Poor Mark," Lissa said after she'd left. "To think that all along he had this great gift for rubbing necks, and he wasted all those years wringing them."

In the morning, Guthrie woke up knowing he had had further healing in his sleep. He had forgiven Mark some more, and he had begun forgiving himself. He was looking for Mark, not sure what it was that he wanted to tell him, when Jody drew him aside.

"Wanted to talk to you for a minute," he said. "About our route."

"We're still not going to Washington."

"God, do you remember that, hoss? No, I know that, now that Sara let us see how all we have to do is save the world. No, it's something else. You know where you're fixing to head from here?"

"Well, I know where we're going today," he said. He got out the map, unfolded it to the right section. "We're right here, a couple of miles north of Madison. We'll take 34 east from there, and then it becomes Route 30 in Minnesota, and we'll take it right into Pipestone. There's a national monument north of there; it's supposed to be beautiful, where the Indians used to get the red stone for their peace pipes. I don't know if we'll get close enough to look at it, but we'll pass through there."

"And then?"

"Oh, I don't know, Jody. I haven't been looking too far ahead. Once we cross into Minnesota I'll pick up a state map and see what feels right."

"I've already got one," Jody said. "Picked it up yesterday."

"Oh?"

"I got one for the whole country, too, and one for the region."

"I see," he said. He took a breath, let it out. "Actually," he said, "I never formally applied for the job of pathfinder. I just went out for a walk and people kept joining in. If I'm not doing it right, I suppose—"

"Oh, come on, hoss. That's not what this is about."

"It's not?"

"Hell, no."

"It does sound like it."

"Well, it's not. Here's the U.S. map. Now I know you like to make it up as you go along, but if you had to pick a destination, where would you say you were fixing to take us?"

Guthrie considered. "I've thought about it," he admitted.

"Figured you must have."

"I don't let myself dwell on it, but I've thought about it. Charlotte and Charleston kept coming to mind."

"Charlotte's where, North Carolina? Here it is. And here's Charleston. Wait a minute, *here's* Charleston. There're two of them."

"One in West Virginia and one in South Carolina. I know. That confuses the issue, doesn't it? You know what sounds a little like both of those cities, and that I think might be a good place to go?" He pointed. "Charlottesville. Thomas Jefferson lived there, his home's open to the public. Monticello. Might be nice taking a look at it."

"You want to look at it, all you gotta do is take a nickel and turn it over. But I guess you're talking about a closer look."

"Well, it might be fun."

"And anyway, it'll do for a place to be walking towards."

"That's what it really amounts to," Guthrie said. "It's the walking there that seems to be important, not the arriving."

"You bet," Jody said. "So let's say you're going to go in that general direction, which'd be pretty much the same whether you're going to Charlottesville or Charlotte or either of the Charlestons."

"Right."

"So what does that look like on the map? Here we are, here's Minnesota, and you'd probably want to go on east some through Minnesota, maybe into Wisconsin, maybe coming on down into Iowa. Either way you'd most likely go through Illinois, then Indiana—"

"Or right down into Kentucky. We might be ready for some hill country by then."

"And then east and maybe south. Uh-huh. Now let's look at Minnesota, all right?"

"Whatever you say."

"Where's Pipestone? Here's Pipestone. Now there's a couple of roads out of Pipestone. If you want to go east you could stay right on 30, or you could come over here and pick up 62. Or you could go north on 75, or south on 75, or there's Route 23 here slanting off to the northeast. Or you could take 23 south, as far as that goes, and it runs into Iowa 182."

"What are you getting at, Jody?"

"Shit, hoss, I really hate this. I wish I could see a way

around this, but I think Pipestone's a perfect place for us to go separate ways."

"Why's that, Jody?"

"Well, you know, I was thinking I might head on down to Pass Christian."

"Where's that?"

"Mississippi, right on the Gulf. Lemme find it. There it is, right in there between Biloxi and New Orleans. Right there on the Gulf of Mexico."

"What's the big attraction in Pass Christian?"

"Well, I got an aunt down there. I was thinking I might go say hello to her."

"When's the last time you saw this aunt?"

He scratched his head. "I'm not too clear on that," he said. "There's a pretty good possibility I never did see her, but she might have been visiting us when I was born. She's a great-aunt, actually. My grandma's younger sister."

"So she's probably along in years."

"Either that or she's dead, which is a possibility. I'd have to say we're not too close to that side of the family."

"But you thought you might want to go down and check on her."

"Sure, why not? If she's alive I could pass the time of day with her, and if she's not I could go put flowers on her grave, something respectful like that."

"Either way, you'd be heading south at Pipestone."

"That's the idea. Cut down through Missouri and Arkansas and Mississippi. Might be nice, seeing that part of the country."

"Why do you want to leave the group, Jody?"

"I won't exactly be doing that, hoss. I'll be taking part of the group with me."

"Oh?"

"Guthrie, we're gettin' too damn big! Remember when there wasn't but four of us, and you didn't like the idea of the group getting any bigger than that? Now we're getting new people faster'n I can count 'em, and that's a good thing, but the logistics of it are gettin' tricky. You can't send two hundred people into a restaurant. You can't even shop for 'em at a food store without emptying the shelves.

"And, at the same time that we're growing too fast, we're growing too slow. We're not getting to enough people. If we were two groups we'd be passing through two parts of the country at once and we'd be growing twice as fast."

"And in a week or two we'd have the same problems of growth," Guthrie said. "Because we'd have two groups of two hundred people each."

"That's if we only had two groups, hoss." He pointed to the map. "There's a lot of roads out of Pipestone. Martha and I'll be taking some people south on 75. You'll be staying with 30. Dingo and Gary were thinking about cutting northeast on 23 and taking that right on through St. Cloud and across northern Wisconsin and the Upper Peninsula of Michigan, and then on across Canada." He shook his head. "Be damned cold in a few months, but cold doesn't seem to hurt us a whole lot. Let's see now. Les and Georgia and Sue Anne said they might head south a ways with me, but they'll cut west down through Nebraska and then on into the southwestern desert. New Mexico, Arizona. Bud and Ellie want to go through Texas and into Mexico. That'll probably mean splitting up little Richard and his new girlfriend, unless Amanita tags along with them. And I think it was Douglas and Beverly who wanted to swing wide around Chicago and then skirt the Great Lakes and wind up in New England. I don't guess they'll get there in time for the fall foliage. More likely they'll make it there about the same time the snow does, but he used to be a survivalist, so his training'll come in handy there. You all right, Guthrie?"

"I don't know. I guess the whole group is splitting up."

"It's dividing into a lot of little groups. It's not like everybody's packing up and going home."

"No, I understand that." He heaved a sigh. "You want to know something? I feel threatened."

"Yeah, I can see where you would."

"Where was I when everybody was planning all of this?"

"There wasn't a whole lot of planning that went on, Guthrie. The same kind of idea seemed to come on a bunch of people at the same time, mostly the ones who've been walking since early on. The idea was just sort of there. Maybe the day before yesterday I thought to myself, I wonder how old Aunt Mae is. Now years go by and I don't think of the woman, and I wasn't kidding when I said I don't know for sure if she's alive or dead. But the thought came and I shrugged it off and it came again, and I thought I ought to go down to wherever it is, Pass fucking Christian, and say hello to her. And meanwhile Dingo's having these thoughts about Canada and he hasn't even got an aunt there, and Douglas is telling Bev how the real roots of America are all in New England and he really wants to go there. It just came to everybody. You know how that happens."

"It sounds like what we're supposed to do."

"Well, it seems that way to me, Guthrie. It really does. But I'll tell you something. If you say you don't like it, I for one'll say the hell with it. The others can do what they want, but I'll forget about Aunt Mae and Pass Christian and we'll go to Charlotte or Charleston or Charlie's Left Nut, wherever you say. I mean, shit, hoss, you're the man got me out of Klamath Falls, so you just say the word."

"You had a tattoo then."

"You had a whole carton of Camels and couldn't think what to do with them."

He looked at the map, and now he seemed to see a web of lines radiating out of Pipestone, branching out again and again as they spread across the country. A wave of mixed emotions washed over him, and his first impulse was to shed them like a duck's back, but he had learned better. He let himself feel what he was feeling.

"It's funny," he said. "I know you're all right about this. For all the reasons you said. And just because it feels right. We're growing too fast and too slow, both at once, and this solves both problems."

"It sure looks like it does."

"But my ego hates this. It fucking hates it. I always said we were just people walking together, we didn't have a leader, but I never believed that all the way. I kept being the one who decided where we would go next, I was Fearless Leader all down the line. Now I'm going to be just one of the leaders and I'm going to be leading just one of the groups." He shook his head. "I guess I was more attached to being a big shot than I thought."

"Once again, welcome to the human race."

"That's about the size of it." He folded the map. "It's not just ego," he said. "I'm going to miss everybody."

"We're all feeling that. If there was another way that worked—"

"There isn't. What does Sara say?"

"That she knew this would happen but she didn't know when."

"And how does she feel about it?"

"The same as you. The same as everybody else."

"Who's she going with?"

"Now that's funny," Jody said. "I didn't even ask her."

He was afraid to find out. When they started out toward Madison he managed to be at the front of the group, and he held that post because it served two purposes—it let him tell himself he was indeed the leader, fearless or otherwise, and it kept him from having to look at all the people he was leading and wondering which ones would be leaving him in Pipestone.

Maybe he should just stay in Pipestone. He could sneak into the place where the red stone itself was preserved from rockhounds and set aside for the ceremonial use of the Indians, and he could break off a hunk of it and spend a couple of months carving it to make a pipe bowl. Then he could fit it with a wooden stem and wrap himself up in a blanket and smoke all day. For ceremonial purposes only, of course. Just to put himself in touch with the spirits.

He stayed at the lead until they had swung east again on 34. Then he waited to one side while they went on past him, scanning the ranks for Sara. She was walking along hand in hand with her son Thom; watching them, Guthrie wondered if anyone who didn't know would suspect that the woman was blind.

He fell into step beside her, took her free hand in his. "Guthrie," she said, and squeezed his hand.

"Beautiful morning."

"Yes, isn't it?"

"I figure we'll make it an easy day's walking today. Pipestone's too far to do in a day, so we'll just walk to the Interstate or a little bit beyond it today, and go the rest of the way tomorrow."

"That sounds good."

"That'll give us all two more nights together, and then the next morning in Pipestone we can set out on separate paths."

"It's all one path, Guthrie."

"I guess. I had a talk with Jody."

"He told me."

"I'm not against it. When I think about it I even have the sense that it was there all the time waiting for me to hit on it myself. But it tears me up all the same."

"Of course it does."

"It's the right thing. I remember way back at the beginning when you said you didn't come all this way to play four-handed group therapy. Well, I didn't walk this far just to play Follow the Leader. But with six or eight groups of us, all of them branching out whenever they start to get too large, why, we'll fill the country."

"We'll be the country."

"But I hate losing everybody in the meantime. Jody especially. I'm going to miss him."

"So will I."

"And everybody else, of course. Dingo and Gary and Doug and Bev and Les and Georgia and Martha and—oh, everybody. Even the ones I haven't had a chance to get to know yet, even the ones who'll be joining up today and tomorrow. I feel as though everyone who leaves will be taking something away from me."

"They will, Guthrie. They'll be taking what you've given them."

"That's not what I mean."

"I know it's not. You mean you'll be diminished by their departure, that there'll be less of you for their leaving. But that's not true. Nobody's really leaving, Guthrie. We're just extending the line of march, spreading ourselves out a little farther."

"Maybe."

"If the others always have you for a leader, they'll miss finding leadership within themselves. And we need plenty of leaders."

"I suppose so." After a moment he said, "It's going to be hard for anyone to be a leader without you along to tell him what he's doing."

"I'm not sure about that. I think we may retain some kind of access to each other's minds, no matter how far apart we may be physically. I don't know that distance exists on the plane where our minds are linked up. We've come a long way, you know."

"All the way from Oregon."

"Don't be intentionally obtuse. You know that's not what I mean. The other night, when Mark went back to his birth and went through it again, everybody was linked to him telepathically. We weren't just picking up vibes. We were hooked up with him. That's the kind of connection the whole human race has to make in order for things to work out. When we're all linked up and functioning together as the cognitive brain of the planet, it will be perfectly natural for everyone to act for the good of all. And we forged a link in the chain, Guthrie. There are only two hundred of us and there are five billion people on the planet, but we're growing, and it may not take many to start a reaction. You only need a couple of pebbles to start an avalanche, if they fall right."

He thought about it. "So you'll still be available? People can pick up a phone and call you on the astral plane?"

"I'm not sure how it will work. I think that if they need to know something and I know it, they'll just get it. They'll reach back onto that shelf in their mind, and what they need will be there."

"Could be."

"And they'll know how to make certain leadership decisions because they'll be connected to your mind."

"Lucky for them," he said. "But it won't be the same as having you to talk to."

"You'll still have me to talk to."

"I mean face to face."

"So do I. I wouldn't want to miss the Kentucky hills. They're supposed to be beautiful in the fall." She smiled. "Just wait until I describe them to you."

TWENTY-TWO

They reached Pipestone on the second day, as planned. The famous quarries were on federally-protected land, almost three hundred acres a few miles north of town on Route 75. They walked there, picked a campsite for the night, and then split up into small groups to explore the quarries and look at the rock formations.

The place felt holy to Guthrie. The tribes had held the land sacred, and hostilities had always been suspended here; whoever came to quarry the precious stone did so in peace. He wondered whether this practice had endowed the land with its power, or whether the Indians had merely been responding appropriately to a power the quartzite outcroppings and deposits of catlinite pipestone already possessed.

Whatever the case, it struck him as a good place for their last night together.

There was a cookfire, and a meal. Afterward Guthrie stood up in front of them and told them that this was their last night as a single group. "We'll still be together in spirit," he said, "but we'll be spreading out to cover the country. Some of us will be going north into Canada, others will wind up in Mexico, maybe even farther south." He called on each of the new leaders, and they gave a quick rundown of the route they intended to follow.

"But it's all tentative," Jody said when it was his turn. "You can make your plans, but they're always subject to change. It looks as though the leader picks the route. That's not really how it works. What happens is the route picks the leader."

"The route may not even matter," Guthrie said. "It's the walking that matters. If you do that, you'll get where you're supposed to."

When they'd finished, Sara announced they would end the evening by breathing in unison. In the past she'd had them arrange themselves in neat rows, all of them lying with their heads toward the north. This time she had them form a different arrangement. They placed themselves like the spokes of a wheel or the rays of a sun, with their heads toward the campfire at the wheel's hub and their feet extended outward toward its rim.

"Go where the breath takes you," she urged them. "Some of you already know which group you'll be a part of tomorrow. Some of you haven't decided yet. You'll either find the answer tonight or wake up with it in the morning. Remember, whichever choice you make will be the right one.

"That's one purpose for our breathing together tonight. There are other purposes, more of them than I know. Whenever we breathe like this our spirits touch, and they form bonds that can never be severed. I won't be with all of you after tonight, and yet I will be, however far apart our bodies may be. I love you and I'll never leave you.

"Let's breathe."

They breathed in unison for over an hour. Usually the connected breathing led to spells of unconsciousness, where the breathing was suspended intermittently and the breather sometimes left his body altogether, not responding to the words of the person monitoring him, sometimes insensitive to touch as well. But this time there was no unconsciousness, no interruptions of the breathing rhythm. Everybody managed to stay with the breath.

And, when it was over, Guthrie realized how unnecessary it had been to worry about losing any of them. They were all one being, one flesh, one spirit. They couldn't lose each other even if they tried.

In the morning people got up, packed up their gear, and joined up with the leader they had decided to follow. The mood was low-key, and there was almost a sense of emotional anticlimax to it all. People about to part exchanged long hugs, but there was not a great deal of sorrow in the air.

Guthrie said his good-byes. When he and Jody embraced, he had a flash flood of memories of those first days back in June. Jody incredulous that he didn't want a ride, Jody bringing back a six-pack of Coors, Jody quite incapable of driving off without coming back. Guthrie had been like Robinson Crusoe before he found the footprint, not even knowing how lonely he was. Ever since Jody had abandoned the Datsun pickup and started walking with him, Guthrie hadn't been lonely once.

He felt love for this man, this curious saint who had traded his tattoo for the gift of healing pain. Warmth flowed from his heart as the two of them hugged, but when he let go he did so with no sense of loss. God only knew when he'd see Jody again, but God knew they'd never really leave each other.

"Well," Jody said, holding him by the shoulders. "You go get 'em, hoss."

"You too."

337

"Tell me one thing. What do I do if I get lost?"

"Just don't let on."

One by one, the groups formed and left. Guthrie waited, determined to be the last to leave. When Dingo and Gary moved off with their crew, a large batch headed for Canada, he counted those who remained and came up with twenty-one. Sara was there, of course, as she'd said she would be. So were Herb and Aggie Curzon, one of the couples who'd driven up from Yellowstone in their camper. And Mark Adlon, who evidently had more to teach him. And Neila, the near-silent waif who'd walked out of the Hen House with Kate and Jamie, and who'd lost her silence altogether somewhere in the vastness of Montana. She was getting a massage from Mark Adlon, she the victim of child abuse and sexual torture, he the mass murderer of women; it wasn't hard to imagine that those two had things to learn from each other.

And Jerry Arbison was there, and Amanita and her baby Jane. And two of the jack-Mormon kids; both of Gene's wives were still with him, but two of the older children had decided to strike out on their own. And ten other people who had joined fairly recently, and whom he didn't yet know very well. He'd know them soon enough, he thought. He'd have a chance now, the group was small enough once again so that everyone would know everyone else.

Wait a minute. Where was Thom Duskin?

"He went with Les and Georgia," Sara said. "He wanted a look at the Southwest. And he and Jordan wanted to stick together, and Jordan had a strong vision of the desert during the breathing last night."

"It must have been hard to let him go."

"It was, but it was time, Guthrie. He's a child, he's thirteen, but I think they grow up fast on this walk. He's going to be coming into his powers soon, and he can't do that with his mother around, especially when she can see things that other people can't. Besides," she added, "Les and Georgia can use a little help."

"You don't think they're good candidates for leaders?"

"I think they're excellent, but I think they're going to have their hands full, and not just after the baby comes."

"The baby?"

"In about eight months. Maybe a little less than that."

"They didn't say a word."

She smiled. "I don't think they know yet. I didn't feel it was my place to tell them."

"I suppose they'll find out soon enough. She'll make a good mother. As far as that goes, he'll make a good father. Remember when he couldn't get that tire changed because the spare was flat? What an unlikely prospect he looked to be."

"And he couldn't get away from us. He was just going to walk to the nearest phone."

"And you remember how he was with Mame? He didn't care how slowly she walked, or if he had to carry her back when she couldn't walk anymore. What a sweet man he turned out to be." He frowned. "But how'll they manage when her time comes? Will they be able to get to a hospital?"

"Gee, I hope so," she said, very seriously. "Maybe they can find a hospital for her and a dentist for that kid who jumped down from the troop carrier."

"You mean Ken. Did he go with them? I thought—oh, all right. They won't need a hospital any more than he'll need a dentist. I suppose if we can heal terminal illnesses we can handle a simple birth, can't we? And people will stand in line for the honor of taking away her labor pains. God, imagine being born in a circle of breathers, with everybody tuned in and linked with you. Do you happen to know what she's going to have?"

"A baby."

"Really? I figured an otter. I mean is it going to be a boy or a girl?"

"I didn't notice."

"Would you tell me if you had?"

She grinned. "Nope," she said. "There are some things, my dear, that we are not meant to know ahead of time."

They walked back to Pipestone and headed east on Route 30. The sky was overcast, the day cooler than usual. He walked with Neila, then with one of the jack-Mormon kids. They all stopped for lunch at a Dairy Queen. He ate french fries from a paper cone and thought about Les and Georgia's baby. *"Do you happen to know what she's going to have?" "A baby." "Really? I figured an otter."*

Why an otter? Something somebody had said, but what and when?

Oh, right. *"Then I started hearing all this crap on the news about women dying because of IUDs, or giving birth to otters, or whatever was happening to them—"*

Kit, the day it all started, or got ready to start. Kit, fresh out of the abortion clinic, wearing an Oregon State sweatshirt and an ironic smile.

There was a pay phone down at the end of the counter. And the cashier, breaking a fresh roll of quarters, seemed perfectly willing to sell him as many as he wanted.

He studied the map for a few minutes, then went over to the phone. He could call Information, he thought, without necessarily calling her. It wouldn't even cost him anything.

But when he lifted the receiver her number was just there, obligingly furnished by his memory. He couldn't remember when he'd called her last, but there was her number. At least he thought it was her number.

So he more or less had to call, didn't he? If only to see if it was really her number.

Dialing, he told himself she probably wouldn't be home;

he was still thinking that when she picked up midway through the second ring.

He said, "Kit, it's Guthrie."

"Woody or Arlo?"

"It's hard to remember."

"Where *are* you? Are you in town? What happened to you, where did you go to? When did you get back?"

"I'm not in town."

"So where are you?"

"I'm a few miles east of Pipestone, Minnesota."

"Now that's funny," she said. "I was just thinking to myself, I'll bet the man is a few miles east of Pipestone, Minnesota. Where in the hell is Pipestone, Minnesota?"

"In the southwest corner of the state."

"The state in question being Minnesota?"

"Very good."

"What are you doing there?"

"Eating some french fries," he said.

"They any good?"

"Your basic Dairy Queen fries."

"A little too salty, as I remember."

"A little too soggy, too."

"Besides researching *The Gourmet's Guide to Fast Food*—"

"I'm on my way east."

"And you had a couple minutes between planes and thought you'd call an old friend?"

"No planes."

"How'd you get there? You didn't drive, you sold your car to Harry. Who turned a nice profit on it, according to rumor."

"I'm glad for him. I walked here, Kit."

A short silence. "I could have sworn you said—"

"I did."

"Walked from Oregon?"

341

"That's right."

"This isn't a joke. You walked from Oregon to Soapstone, Minnesota."

"Pipestone."

"'Iceberg, Goldberg, what's the difference?' You remember that joke?"

"Of course I remember."

"Good joke."

"Uh-huh. Kit, there's sort of a reason why I called."

"I was thinking there might be."

"Yeah. Uh, I thought you might like to come east."

"To Grindstone?"

"No, because I'm not staying here. There's a city called Albert Lea due east of here and I'll be getting there in about six days, maybe seven if we take it slow."

"Who's 'we'?"

"There are twenty-one of us."

"All walking."

"That's right."

"And you thought—"

The operator called in, telling him to signal when through. Kit offered to reverse the charges, but he didn't want to prolong the conversation. "Albert Lea is a city of about twenty thousand people, according to the map index. There's an airport. If you decide you want to, you could get a couple of flights and wind up there. There's almost sure to be a Holiday Inn. Get a room there, and I'll check for you when I get to town."

"In about six days."

"Seven at the outside. It's only about a hundred and seventy miles."

"Oh, hey, that's nothing. And then what happens?"

"We'll go for a walk."

"To East Jesus, Kansas?"

"Probably to Charlottesville, Virginia."

"My very next guess, I swear it. As a matter of fact, I was sitting next to the phone when it rang, and I said to myself, 'I'll bet it's old Guthrie, ready to invite me to walk from Staggerlee, Minnesota—'"

"Albert Lea."

"'—to Charlottesville, Virginia.' But the thing is you're serious, aren't you? And you sound sober, that's the funny part of it."

He said, "Kit? Don't try to figure it out. Okay?"

"Okay."

"Just see how it feels. If it feels right you'll know, and you'll handle the plane tickets and show up at the Holiday Inn. If there's no Holiday Inn, hang around the post office or leave a note for me at the General Delivery window saying where you're staying. If it doesn't feel right, well, that's cool."

"What would I have to bring?"

"Comfortable shoes. We'll buy anything you need. And don't worry about money."

"Albert Lea, Minnesota. Is it nice there? Oh, how would you know, you're not there yet. Guthrie, if I actually go and you stand me up, I'll kill you. I'll find you, I'll hunt you down, and I'll kill you."

"I'll be there."

"Just so you know what happens if you don't. Then you can make an informed choice. Albert Lea, it sounds like a fucking good old boy. Joe Bob, Billie Clyde, Albert Lea. I'd have to be crazy to show up there."

"In a manner of speaking."

"But if I do," she said, "you'd fucking well better be there."

There were no new recruits that first day out of Pipestone. It was just as well, Guthrie thought; a day or two on their own would give them a chance to bond as a group

343

before they had to deal with new people. That night they sat around the campfire and went around the circle, taking turns sharing how they felt being separated from the others. For some of them it brought up buried feelings about earlier periods of separation, but nothing came up that anybody had trouble handling.

The next day Sara said, "You know, I saw something when we were all breathing together at Pipestone. I saw other people walking. It's hard to tell the past and present and future apart in the kind of vision I had, but I saw people walking all over the world. I saw walkers in Russia, heading south and west from Siberia. I saw people in South America walking down out of the Andes. I think they've already started out. I think there are walkers in England now, and in Norway and Sweden. I had a very strong sense of people walking in South Africa, and they were black and white all in one group, and they were walking down a highway and no one was bothering them."

"And you think it's already started."

"I'm almost sure it has. We're part of something enormous, Guthrie. And I think it's going to work."

"What has to happen? Does everyone have to walk?"

"I don't know. I don't think so. I think when enough people are walking, the planetary consciousness will reach critical mass, and then everybody will just plain get it without walking. I think that's what happens, but I don't know for certain. And I don't have a clue what the world will be like after everybody has what the walkers have. It'll be whatever we make it, I suppose, and we'll make it whatever we want it to be."

"Whatever that is."

"Yes."

That afternoon a young man named Gregory abandoned a Honda scooter at the side of the road to walk with them.

And the following morning a black couple named Alvin and Lily were waiting with their two daughters at an intersection less than a mile from where they'd made their camp. "This is crazy." Alvin said, "but the last time I heard a voice loud and clear like this it told me the name of a horse, and I didn't go and bet on him, and I been regretting that for the past seven years."

That summed it up, Guthrie thought. You couldn't take credit for much, because once your feet were on the path it was no great trick to keep them moving. And you couldn't pride yourself on thinking up the idea, because something outside yourself put the thought in your mind.

But, if there was anything you could say for yourself, it might simply be that you had listened to the voice once it had spoken to you. Because that was the point where you were at choice. You could follow the lead or not. You could bet on the horse, or you could spend the next seven years regretting it.

He had been the instrument to deliver the message to Kit, but from here on it was her choice. She might be in Albert Lea. She might not.

Either way, he knew what to do. Just take it a step at a time, and remember to alternate feet.